T0367380

POWERLESS

POWERLESS

RICHARD L. SMITH

iUniverse, Inc.
Bloomington

Powerless

Copyright © 2011 by Richard L. Smith.

All rights reserved. No part of this book may be used or reproduced by any means, graphic, electronic, or mechanical, including photocopying, recording, taping or by any information storage retrieval system without the written permission of the publisher except in the case of brief quotations embodied in critical articles and reviews.

This is a work of fiction. All of the characters, names, incidents, organizations, and dialogue in this novel are either the products of the author's imagination or are used fictitiously.

Other Books by Richard L. Smith

Time Lacuna	*2003 Authorhouse*	*ISBN 1-4107-8383-0*
Out of China:	*2005 Xulon*	*ISBN 1-59781-502-0*
New Eden:	*2009 IUniverse*	*ISBN978-1-4401-0781-8*

iUniverse books may be ordered through booksellers or by contacting:

iUniverse
1663 Liberty Drive
Bloomington, IN 47403
www.iuniverse.com
1-800-Authors (1-800-288-4677)

Because of the dynamic nature of the Internet, any web addresses or links contained in this book may have changed since publication and may no longer be valid. The views expressed in this work are solely those of the author and do not necessarily reflect the views of the publisher, and the publisher hereby disclaims any responsibility for them.

Any people depicted in stock imagery provided by Thinkstock are models, and such images are being used for illustrative purposes only.
Certain stock imagery © Thinkstock.

ISBN: 978-1-4620-5365-0 (sc)
ISBN: 978-1-4620-5367-4 (hc)
ISBN: 978-1-4620-5366-7 (ebk)

Printed in the United States of America

iUniverse rev. date: 09/15/2011

Table of Contents

<u>Acknowledgements</u>

Special thanks to my volunteer copy editors:

Ron and Ruth Richter
Anjali S. Angel
Jan Nettleton
Natalia Mead

And special thanks to my sister, Laurie Holmes

Front Cover: Ketchum, Idaho Power Station.
Photograph by Pat Smith

PREFACE

Citizens of the USA are a resilient people, yet we live on a knife-edge, one disaster away from a major change to our lifestyle. We have survived local catastrophes fashioned by fires, floods, earthquakes, hurricanes, and tornadoes, yet none of these natural tragedies affected the entire country. Consider a calamity that would cause nationwide devastation. If a small asteroid struck the country, or the Yellowstone super volcano erupted, or a gigantic tsunami caused by a landslide in the Canary Islands smacked the east coast, we would suffer a national disaster. Fortunately, such events are unlikely to occur in our lifetime, yet there is an event that might take place within the next decade. Scientists predict our Sun could produce such a calamity and there is nothing we can do to prevent it.

The Sun is the source of all life on Earth and we assume that it will continue to warm us, grow our crops and light our day, as it always has. Some ancients worshipped the Sun as a benevolent god, because for them it was an all-powerful, reliable, and unvarying ally of life. However, the ancients were unaware that the sun has a dark side. Scientists now know that our Sun is not only the giver of life, but also a potential slayer. The Sun's nuclear furnace not only provides us with warmth and light, but each minute it spews out tons of elementary particles that can devastate our technology and wipe out life. Fortunately, the Earth evolved a protective magnetic shield that directs these deadly rays away from our planet and for the most part prevents them from reaching the surface. The Sun is not the consistent and reliable partner many assume. Like a spoiled child, it experiences periods of fits and tantrums, solar storms that erupt from its surface in massive explosions. Astronomers observe these outbursts as sunspots and flares, solar storms that discharge vast amounts of matter into the solar system. We call the worst of these tantrums Coronal Mass Ejections (CME), and if one of these was aimed at Earth, it could overcome our protective magnetic shield and cause nationwide destruction to our technologically dependent infrastructure. Electric power systems and orbiting satellites are especially susceptible to CMEs. Should one strike

Earth, our power grid could be destroyed and our satellites disabled. We would be *powerless* for months.

A hundred years ago, we were not as dependent on technology as we are today. A CME back then would have had little effect on civilization, but today we are dependent on a continuous supply of reliable electric power to provide the necessities of life. Our entire infrastructure of drinking water, sanitation, emergency services, police protection, and transportation depends on the electric grid. Orbiting satellites provide weather information, TV broadcasts, communications, and global positioning data, and a CME could either disrupt or destroy them. Occasional power interruptions are inconvenient but seldom life threatening. Eventually, the lights come back on, motors again hum, computers calculate, and satellite TV broadcasts resume. Consider what would happen if we were without power for several months, disrupting water delivery, communications, emergency services, food availability, and even sanitation. Police, fire suppression, healthcare, and emergency services would be unavailable. The government itself might be threatened. Terrorists could take advantage of such national chaos and instigate their plan to establish a worldwide caliphate.

This is the premise of *Powerless*, the story of two families surviving in such circumstances and a group of radical Islamists bent on using the chaos to advance their worldwide caliphate.

Richard L. Smith, June, 2011

PART ONE: DISRUPTION

CHAPTER ONE:
SANTA CRUZ

Dan Justin seethed with anger and frustration as he drove across the small town of Santa Cruz, California. Minutes before, a telephone call from the Santa Cruz police department had dragged him out of an important business meeting. The police informed him that they were holding his youngest son at the city police station. Now he had to leave the meeting and rescue his 14 year-old son, Scott, from the police station. As Dan sat waiting at a red light, his anger turned to bewilderment. Dan and his wife, Nora, had raised three children and not one of them had ever gotten into serious trouble, at least not until now. Scott, the younger of his two boys, was the clown of the family, yet obedient, respectful, and never before in serious trouble. Bright, wiry, and small for his age, he loved the outdoors and sports. A crop of blond, wavy hair, deep blue eyes, and a broad smile made him a favorite with the girls in his class. Dan remembered that once before, the school counselor called him about Scott's behavior, but it was a minor offense and soon forgotten. Although adventurous and prone to push family rules to the edge, Scott was dutiful and had a good head on his shoulders. Dan's apprehension increased as he parked at the police station. What possible trouble could Scott be in? On the telephone, the police had not been specific, only saying that they were holding Scott. It must be something serious. Lately, Dan was concerned about Scott's choice of friends. *Whatever trouble he has gotten himself into must be because of the influence of those bums he has been hanging out with lately,* or so he thought.

Tall, with a crop of black hair, radiant eyes, a square jaw, and lumberjack build, Dan had always easily made friends. An attentive father to his three children, and loving husband to Nora, at 49 years and hair tinged with gray, his responsibilities weighed heavily on his mind. Dan resented this intrusion into his busy life. After settling down in Santa Cruz, he returned to school to work toward a law degree. Now only a few units short of earning his pre-law Bachelor of Science degree at UCSC, next year he planned to apply to the University of San Francisco law school. As he made his way through the Santa Cruz traffic, Dan blamed himself for not paying more attention to his family. His desire to become a lawyer had placed his ambition above the well-being of his family, and now his aspiration had led to this problem with his youngest son. Scott did not seem like a teenager looking for trouble, yet without adequate supervision, he had found it.

Trying to fit school, work, and family into his day was almost more than Dan could handle. He fumed as he worked his way through traffic. His children needed to cooperate with his juggling act and not add to his problems. In his younger days, he had aspired to be a lawyer, and had enrolled in pre-law at the University of Santa Clara. By his junior year, he became financially unable to continue his law studies, and a campus recruiter suggested he write to his Representative for an appointment to the Air Force Academy in Colorado. The appointment came through and while at the Academy, he met fellow student and roommate Peter Dexter. They became lifelong friends. Shortly after graduation, he was assigned to Hamilton Air Force base near San Francisco, where met Nora Ingram. Dan attended a dance sponsored by a sorority at Cal State University and spied Nora sitting across the room chatting with her friends. He asked her for a dance and learned she was completing a business degree. They danced and talked the entire evening, and when the dance ended, Dan asked her for a date and she accepted.

Enchanting, smart, and beautiful, Nora soon captured Dan's heart. Her olive skin and dark hair, warm smile and thoughtful personality attracted many other suitors, but soon she had no time for anyone but Dan. Initially attracted to Dan's handsome face and uniform, she soon discovered the depth and warmth of his personality. She fell in love with him and after dating for a year, she accepted his marriage proposal. They wed in Santa Cruz, the home of Nora's mother and father, Dee and Jim Ingram. Dan spent the next sixteen years as an Air Force flight controller and Nora followed him around the world, from station to station. Two years after they wed, Keith was born in the Azores, and then Scott, in the Philippines, and finally a daughter, Penny, in North Dakota. After sixteen years in the Air Force, a promotion to Captain, and assignments in the Azores,

Philippines, Alaska, Germany, and North Dakota, Dan was encouraged by Nora's father to resign his commission and take a job with a firm in San Jose. Tired of moving their family from station to station, Nora and Dan wanted to put some roots down. Dan resigned his commission and moved his family from his last assignment at the Minot Air force Base in North Dakota, to Santa Cruz. It was a good move for the family.

Nestled between Monterey Bay and the redwood forested hills of the Santa Cruz Mountains, the town of Santa Cruz provided an ideal location for Dan and Nora to raise their family. Situated on California's Central Coast, 65 miles south of San Francisco and 35 miles north of Monterey, Santa Cruz County is ringed by miles of isolated beaches and several nearby parks. The area provided Dan and his family with all the outdoor life they desired. Santa Cruz schools were top-notch, jobs plentiful, and the area provided countless recreational opportunities from surfing to exploring the redwood forests.

With the help of Nora's mother and father, the Justins bought a small three-bedroom house just three blocks from the beach and next to the San Lorenzo River. Dan never ceased thinking about his desire to become a lawyer, and a year after they moved to Santa Cruz he enrolled at the University of California. To allow time for his education, he quit his full-time corporate job in San Jose and took a part-time accounting job at a small business in Watsonville, south of Santa Cruz. Unfortunately, income from this job couldn't pay all the bills and put food into the mouths of his growing family. Although she preferred the role of a stay-at-home mom, to supplement their meager income Nora took a paralegal job with a local firm. Even-tempered, strong, and independent, Nora was the glue that held the family together. She enjoyed her paralegal job, yet her duties did not allow her to supervise the children after school let out. Dan and Nora trusted their oldest son, Keith, now almost sixteen, to look after his younger brother and sister. Athletic, handsome, and a straight "A" student, Keith was a serious and sensitive young man, with ambitions to become a geologist.

His brother, Scott, on the other hand, was the opposite of Keith, always making jokes and avoiding hard work. Gregarious, playful, and imbued with a good sense of humor, Scott pushed life's boundaries, exploring just how much he could get away at home and at school, before the ax would fall. He took pleasure in teasing his eleven year-old younger sister, Penny, and challenging his older brother.

Dan checked in with the police station desk sergeant, who explained that they caught Scott smoking pot under the boardwalk with several of his friends. Scott had less than an ounce of Marijuana in his pocket, so the officer said they were willing to release him to his parents. Dan thanked the officer and herded Scott into the family truck. On the short ride home, Dan said nothing. Scott's stomach churned, as the silence only served to increase his apprehension. He knew his punishment was going to be severe and he imagined all sorts of sentences that ranged from extended grounding to extra household tasks.

They arrived home to find Nora, Keith, and Penny waiting for them in the front room. Dan sent Keith and Penny to their rooms, before explaining Scott's visit to the police station to Nora. The Justin rules were clear. Keith, Scott, and Penny were to come directly home from school and do their homework, until Nora arrived home at 5 p.m. Rather than going directly home, Scott had begun hanging out with his friends and smoking pot. This behavior was a sure prescription for trouble, and as whiffs of marijuana smoke drifted from under the boardwalk, it wasn't long before the police caught him and his friends enjoying weed.

"Scott, what do you think your punishment should be?" Nora asked.

They want me to punish myself? "How about grounding me for two weeks," Scott offered.

"Let's make it a whole month," Dan added.

"But DAD . . . there is a sophomore dance in three weeks, and I have a date," Scott whined.

"A full month," Dan insisted. "Call your date and explain why you cannot take her."

Scott stormed off to his room.

Dan turned to Nora and asked, "Do you think I was too harsh on him?"

"Absolutely not," Nora intoned. "I would have grounded him for two months."

Nora asked Penny and Keith to return to the front room. "Keith, your brother has been grounded for a month. You kids are to come home directly from school, and Dad and I will depend on you to make sure that Scott and Penny stay home and do their homework, until I arrive from work. No one can leave the property without prior permission. Do you understand?"

Keith assured them that he understood and would do as his parents asked. They sat and talked together for almost an hour. Keith told them about his intramural sports that he so enjoyed and Penny explained about a project she was working on, in her arts and crafts class. It was getting late, so they all said goodnight and turned in.

"Nora, tomorrow will be a busy day for me," Dan shared. "I have an Astronomy class at the University in the morning and then have to put in eight hours to prepare a client's taxes. I probably will not be home until after 9 p.m. Don't hold dinner for me, I'll get some fast-food on the way home." As he rushed off to class, Dan had no idea that in the following weeks, circumstances beyond his control would soon conspire to end their comfortable life in Santa Cruz and threaten their very survival.

CHAPTER TWO:
SOLAR MAX

Dr. Jason Rawlins, a prominent Astronomy professor at UC Berkeley, drove as fast as caution allowed through the fog-enshrouded town of Santa Cruz, and made his way along the coast highway toward the University of California at Santa Cruz. The dean of the Santa Cruz Astronomy Department had invited Dr. Rawlins to lecture on his field of solar eruptions, and a late arrival would be embarrassing. He looked at his watch and sighed. It was 9:30. It seemed everything on this dreary morning had conspired to make him late for his 10 a.m. lecture. First, an accident in the Santa Cruz Mountains had delayed him for almost an hour; now this blanket of fog forced him to slow down. A few miles outside town, the fog bank lifted, allowing him to accelerate his 1991 Buick to the posted highway speed. He looked for a sign that would point the way to the University Campus and after a few miles a sign appeared out of the haze, announcing the turnoff to a winding road that led into the hills.

Nestled in the undulating golden foothills of the Santa Cruz Mountains, was the scenic jewel of the University of California system. Jason drove past the unguarded sentry post and granite rock monuments that watched over the campus entrance. Fingers of fog from nearby Monterey Bay crept along the foothill ravines and coated the campus in a blanket of damp, gray mist. He moved slowly up the road until the ghostly sentinels of buildings, perched on knolls and nuzzled in forested valleys, gradually emerged from the mist. Dr. Rawlins had never visited the campus and was uncertain which building could be the science building he sought. He drove along the meandering road that plunged in and out of pockets of fog, which made it difficult to find a sign pointing the way to his destination. Water droplets dripping from roadside trees splattered on his windshield and coated the cars parked along the access road. He clicked on his windshield wipers and was about to ask directions from a group of students, when a sign pointing the way to the College of Science emerged out of the gloom.

He found a visitor parking space in front of the architecturally spartan cement and glass science building, parked his car, and stepped out onto the damp pavement. The caw-caw of a noisy blue jay triggered a chill that crept in waves down his spine. With a shudder, he reached into the Buick and grabbed his sweater that rested in a heap on the backseat. As he slipped into the cardigan, he became aware of the silence that permeated the campus. The fog dampened the din of this busy campus, an eerie contrast to the cacophony of the Berkeley campus. He glanced at his watch a second time. It read 10:05. Surveying the front of the building, he hastened across the parking lot toward the arched entrance. A petite young woman with a blond ponytail, and dressed in shorts and a halter, hurried along the path that led to the front steps of the science building. Already five minutes late for his lecture, he didn't want to stumble about looking for the auditorium, so he called after her and asked for directions to the Astronomy lecture hall. She turned and gave him a warm smile, a smile that chased away the melancholy that had enveloped him.

"Oh, you must be Dr. Rawlins," she beamed. "We're both late to class."

"Yes . . . we are," he responded.

"My last class ended late and I am on my way to hear your lecture. Please . . . follow me."

Jason followed her into the building and down a wide hall lined with pictures, taken by the Hubble Telescope, to the double wide doors of the lecture hall. The auditorium buzzed with chatty students impatiently waiting for the scheduled 10 a.m. lecture to begin.

Dan Justin impatiently sat in a third row seat and stared at the empty podium. Still upset about his son's brush with the law, he opened his notebook and nervously tapped his pencil. Older than the typical UCSC student, and with a family and job to juggle, Dan registered for this Astronomy class to fulfill his science requirement. He resented this late start to the lecture and looked at his watch and whispered, "Five minutes late." The student sitting next to him heard his complaint, formed an empathetic grin and commented, "Well, if the professor doesn't show in another five minutes, we can leave and still get credit for the class." Dan's many years in the Air Force had taught him that time was valuable, and now it was being wasted. As he debated leaving, Dr. Jason Rollins entered the classroom, climbed onto the stage, handed his slide cartridge to the audiovisual technician, and then stepped to the podium.

After taking a few seconds to arrange his notes, Dr. Rawlins grasped the podium with both hands and slowly surveyed his noisy audience. Despite the cold damp weather, he noted the male students mostly wore the standard campus uniform: Jeans, t-shirts, and backwards-facing baseball caps. The women students were dressed in shorts and loose-fitting shirts. Casual dress was typical for UCSC students, except for the older students such as Dan, who dressed conservatively. At first, the class ignored the professor's presence and continued their noisy chatter, but then little by little, the auditorium began to quiet down. To capture his audience's full attention, he used a time-honored speakers' trick and without speaking, continued to survey his audience. After a few seconds, the students stopped chattering, arranged their pens and note books, and focused on the man at the lectern. Convinced he had gained the class's interest, he took a deep breath and began his carefully prepared talk.

"Good morning. I am Dr. Jason Rawlings, from the Astronomy Department at UC Berkeley. I am sorry about my tardiness, but the traffic on Highway 17 was terrible this morning. I am here today to talk about the sun, ironically on a day that it remains hidden behind a blanket of fog. I assume conditions such as this are normal for this campus."

A murmur of agreement swept through the auditorium. Jason gave a nod to the AV technician, and the room darkened as a picture of the sun filled the large overhead screen.

"Our sun, a massive 900,000 mile-wide searing ball of hydrogen and helium, 93 million miles away, makes life on earth possible. The tremendous pressure and temperature deep inside that orb fuses hydrogen into helium, and the resulting nuclear fusion generates light, heat, and a flood of subatomic particles. Nuclear fusion and thermal convection within the sun are so complex that it has taken my entire career to understand this process. My focus has been the study of thermonuclear fusion at the sun's core and convective heat transfer within the sun. Of special interest are the solar storms and Coronal Mass Ejections, or CMEs that result. This is the subject of today's lecture."

Dr. Rawlins paused for a moment to make sure he had the full attention of his audience. Notebooks were open, pens in hand, and students seemed ready to hear his lecture. He continued.

"Scientists in the nineteenth century couldn't explain how the sun continuously produced such a prodigious amount of energy for billions of years. Neither chemical reactions nor gravitational collapse could explain this process. At the turn of the twentieth century, Albert Einstein solved this mystery when he devised his famous equation e=mc^2. Physicists for the first time recognized the sun was converting mass directly into energy. According to the Einstein formula, tiny amounts of matter can produce huge amounts of energy. The sun's core is an immense fusion reactor. When hydrogen atoms fuse into helium, the resulting mass is slightly less than the original amount and the missing mass has been converted into energy."

Dr. Rawlins paused to take a sip of water before continuing.

"Fortunately for you and me, our sun is an average, medium-sized orb, with a moderate appetite for hydrogen. As a middle-aged star, it will continue to shine for billions of years to come. Well-behaved and stable, it favors life with a constant and dependable amount of energy that outflows from its 7,000-degree centigrade surface. Yet, this apparent consistency is misleading. The sun's energy varies over time and sometimes has minor fits and starts and hurls tons of particles out into space."

He pushed a button on the lectern, and a slide showing a picture of the sun's corona, during a full eclipse, filled the overhead screen.

"I am especially interested in tracking total solar energy productivity, which waxes and wanes over thousands of years and sometimes even changes over a few decades. Variations in the solar magnetic field result in CMEs—as these high-energy flares and rarely, huge plasma eruptions. A CME aimed at Earth poses a danger to our technological infrastructure. Increases in the number and size of sunspots predict these infrequent solar outbursts. Sunspots are magnetic storms on the sun's surface. Because they are a few hundred degrees cooler than their surroundings, they appear black against the sun's radiant surface. Scientists have been recording the number and frequency of sunspots since the seventeenth century.

Our sun is not unchanging; it has continued to evolve throughout its entire 4.7 billion years of life. The sun that gently warms us today is not the same as the sun of the past or the sun of the future. Billions of years ago, our sun condensed from a huge cloud of hydrogen. Throughout a sun's entire life, a constant struggle exists between gravity that wants to collapse it and heat that wants to expand it. Today, these opposing forces are in equilibrium and consequently, our sun has settled into a midlife phase, with a stable radius and relatively constant energy output. Such stability is ephemeral. Billions of years from now, when the sun has consumed its supply of fusionable fuel, it will expand into a red giant and engulf Earth in its fiery breath. Today the sun remains as we see it, seemingly stable yet experiencing minor fits and burps in the constant struggle between forces. It is these fits and burps that concern scientists."

A graph of sunspot events over the past 150 years replaced the eclipse picture.

"Sunspots are evidence of solar activity occurring on the sun's surface. This graph is a good example of those storms. By examining this 250-year history of sunspot activity, scientists have found two repetitive cycles of solar turmoil: An eleven year cycle depicted by the blue line and a twenty-two year cycle depicted in red. The activity depicted by the blue line rises to a maximum and then falls to a minimum, every eleven years, while the cycle in red peaks every twenty-two years. The two cycles occasionally coincide, producing an event called a Super Solar Maximum." Dr. Rawlins used his laser pointer to call attention to the peaks and valleys, where the two data streams coincided.

"According to the latest prediction, the solar maximum, or coincidence of solar curves, began in 2008 and will peak by the year 2012. Given the coincidence of the eleven and twenty-two year cycle maximums, we could experience a Super Solar maximum event, in the period between 2008 to

2014. The dramatic increase in sunspots and flares will cause an increase in polar aurora, interference with our communications satellites, and even possible disruptions of our power grid."

"In 1859, a solar maximum storm erupted that, had it occurred today, would take out much of our electric and electronic systems. This storm, named the Perfect Solar Storm, produced spectacular aurora as far south as Rome and St. Louis. The storm did not adversely affect those living in the technologically emerging nineteenth century. People only marveled at the beautiful, heavenly display. If today's technologies, such as electrical grids and artificial satellites, existed back then, they would have been severely damaged, perhaps even destroyed by that 1859 event."

The next slide was a picture of the sun taken from the SOHO solar observatory spacecraft. A group of sunspots was visible near one edge of the sun. Protruding from the center of each was a sprite of plasma, extending thousands of miles from the sun's limb.

"As shown in this slide, explosions and internal magnetic flux events deep inside the sun cause individual flares to erupt from sunspots. The surface broils at thousands of degrees, yet local eruptions are cooler than the surrounding surface and therefore, look dark when viewed against the brilliant background. Should a CME flare point at Earth, huge quantities of elementary particles will stream toward our planet at speeds approaching a few percent of the speed of light. Fortunately, Earth's magnetic core provides an electric shield that deflects most of these charged particles into space. A small portion of the particles are funneled into the North and South poles, where they create the polar aurora, the Northern and Southern Lights. If the flare is unusually powerful and pointed directly at Earth, it can overwhelm this magnetic shield and power into our upper atmosphere. Recent CMEs, much smaller than the 1859 event, disrupted and damaged our national power grid and earth orbiting satellites.

"The National Oceanographic and Atmosphere Agency (NOAA) manage the Space Environmental Center (SEC). Their task is to keep track of these potentially destructive solar storms and issue daily space weather reports. Our UC Berkeley solar weather office cooperates with the SEC, to issue warnings of unusual solar activity to communications and power companies, who take preventive action to protect their more sensitive equipment during these events."

Dr. Rawlins spoke for another twenty minutes, explaining in detail the sun's process of fusing hydrogen into helium, the thermal mixing that takes place within the sun, and the magnetically induced solar flares and CMEs.

"I will now take questions," he offered.

Dan Justin flipped through several pages in his notebook, filled with notes and sketches from the lecture. These would come in handy when he prepared for semester finals. Troubled about the destructive effects CMEs might have on the U.S. infrastructure, he raised his hand and Dr. Rawlins immediately called on him.

"Dr. Rawlins, I'm curious about how likely it is that a major flare or plasma eruption would hit the earth and if it did so, what damage would it cause?"

Jason cleared his throat and answered Dan's question.

"Fortunately, it is unlikely that a major eruption will hit us anytime soon. Strong magnetic fields in the sun concentrate plasma ejections into very narrow beams. One such beam would have to point directly toward Earth when it erupted. Should we be so unlucky, a powerful CME could penetrate our Earth's magnetic shield and wreck havoc with the electric grid, communications and electronic equipment.

"One such flare pointed directly at earth and hit us in 1998. It caused power brownouts in Canada and temporarily shut down the entire East Coast power grid. It also disrupted satellite and land-based communications throughout North America. Fortunately, this particular flare was a moderate eruption."

Dr. Rawlins concluded his lecture with some spectacular three-dimensional pictures of the sun, taken by the SOHO space observatory. As the overhead lights brightened, Dan folded his notebook, placed it into his backpack, and hurried off to his next class across campus.

*　　*　　*

A week later, Dan had nearly forgotten about Dr. Rawlins' lecture. He wouldn't visit these lecture notes again until it was time to prepare for his final astronomy exam in May. Meanwhile, he had other distractions that focused his attention away from school.

As Dan sat in traffic, he tuned into a San Francisco news station. The local talk radio host was interviewing Dr. Jason Rawlins, about his prediction of an impending solar storm. Dr. Rawlins reported the SOHO observatory had recorded a major solar eruption, expected to arrive in two days, specifically on September 6. He warned that this unusually strong CME eruption pointed directly at Earth and could power through earth's magnetic shield. If that happened, it would damage electrical and power equipment throughout North America and disrupt communications, including TV and GMS operations.

Dr. Rawlins went on to say that this could be the largest CME to hit Earth since the Perfect Storm in 1859, and this one had the earth and North America directly in its sights. He railed against the power and communication companies that had ignored his prediction and neglected to take the steps necessary to protect their sensitive equipment from this storm. It was understandable that companies would be reluctant to take action to shut down their equipment, if even for a few hours. A complete power shutdown would disrupt power distribution and communications networks and cost those companies millions in lost revenue. Jason argued that if they did not turn their equipment off for a few hours on the evening of September 6, the CME radiation could damage communications satellites and blow out transformers throughout the power grid. NASA should have the astronauts aboard the International Space Station take precautions. NASA was aware of the impending solar storm and was already acting to protect the ISS and the on-board astronauts. Jason expressed frustration that only one of the dozen electric companies he contacted, Bonneville Power, took his warnings seriously. The local utility, Pacific Gas and Electric Company, warned their customers about possible brownouts on the evening of September 6, yet refused to do anything proactive, like shutting the system down for a few hours. It was just too much to ask them to do.

Dan recalled Dr. Rawlins' lecture and understood the astronomer's frustration with the media. He thought it ironic that just a week after Dr. Rawlins said that such a CME event pointed at Earth was unlikely; he was now issuing a warning about this impending event. He turned the radio off and focused on navigating through downtown traffic. When he arrived at the police station, he paid his son's pot possession fine and drove home. The boy listened to a long lecture entitled "there is going to be a new regime around our house," which would start with Scott's long-term grounding.

CHAPTER THREE:
THE SKY IS ON FIRE

In the week following his lecture at UCSC, data collected from the SOHO satellite began to worry Dr. Rawlins. On September 4, the sun was unusually active for this phase of its eleven-year sunspot cycle. The number of sunspots exceeded even those born during the last solar maximum, eight years ago. After a few days, several sunspots merged to form an unusually large sunspot, and prominences erupted from the limb of the solar disk. Solar storms normally erupt in three stages. The first stage begins with an increase in sunspots and solar flares, followed by an eruption of high-energy protons and finally, a Coronal Mass Ejection. A CME pointed at the Earth with enough flux and polarity can punch through the magnetosphere and affect satellites, ground-based communication systems, and power grids. Stage one and two eruptions can cause the Earth's atmosphere to expand and increase drag on satellites, occasionally causing one to fall from orbit. Stage three eruptions produce intense aurora and disruption of communications and our power grid.

A few monitoring stations on earth and the SOHO spacecraft detected stage one of the eruption, in the last week of August. Scientists now waited to learn the magnitude of stages two and three as measured by the ACE satellite positioned in a synchronous orbit between the sun and Earth. When the ACE data finally came in, it signaled an eruption 50% larger than the so-called Perfect Solar Storm, estimated at 200 Tesla, a measure of magnetic flux. Worse yet, this CME's magnetic pole orientation was south, the worst possible condition, and pointed directly at North America.

Dr. Rawlins had never before witnessed such intense solar activity, not even during the solar maximum in 1981, considered the worst of the 20th century. He telephoned a close friend, Dr. Ernesto Constanez, at the University of Colorado. Dr. Constanez managed the world's largest solar telescope, and Jason was eager to hear his opinion. Ernesto's concern was palpable.

"This is the largest solar storm I've ever measured. For now, it is on the backside of the sun, but in two days, the sun's rotation will point it directly at Earth. This will not be a glancing blow like all the other major solar storms we have recorded. It will be a direct CME hit and could be as much as 300 Tesla," he advised.

Dr Constanez's voice betrayed his frustration. "The Space Weather web site sent solar storm warning alerts out eleven days ago, but it has been hard to get anyone's attention."

Jason knew that few authorities took space weather warnings seriously.

"Dr. Rawlins, you have to warn everyone. Perhaps they will listen to you. In four days, North America will experience the strongest electromagnetic storm in modern times. It will affect all electronic equipment. We should expect damage to unprotected and sensitive electronics and power transformers. It could overpower the electric grid, disrupt satellite communications, and endanger astronauts on the International Space Station. You have to get the word out."

Jason did not consider two days enough time "to get the word out", but it was all the time he had. He promised Dr. Constanez he would do everything possible to pass his warnings along. He called reporters at the Oakland Tribune, San Jose Mercury, San Francisco Chronicle, New York Times and USA Today. The Chronicle transferred him from one disinterested reporter to another, until he ended at the desk of the Chronicle science editor. The editor was polite but only mildly interested in Jason's information. He said he had already read a similar story on the Reuters Newswire, but details were sketchy and the Montreal scientist he spoke with did not seem at all concerned. "A few astronomers have exaggerated this event," the editor asserted. The Oakland Tribune and San Jose Mercury reporters were even less interested, and the New York Times and USA Today never returned his call.

Jason called NASA and spoke to their science adviser about the possibility of a major solar storm. The NASA scientist was aware of the impending solar flare, but his information assumed it wouldn't overpower the earth's protective magnetic shield, which would shunt it harmlessly around Earth and into the Van Allen belts and outer space. He thought there might be some residual effects, such as unusually intense aurora and temporary communications disruptions and perhaps a power surge or two, but nothing his systems couldn't handle. NASA intended to take precautionary steps and on September 6, ordered the astronauts into the interior section of the International Space Station, the safest place to weather a solar storm. However, they did not intend to postpone the next launch of Endeavor, scheduled for September 14.

In the September 4 evening edition, The San Francisco Chronicle printed a one-column news item about a potential solar storm on page 26. Poorly researched, the story contained mostly archival information, and the reporter contacted only one other astronomer: a scientist on Palomar Mountain, whose job it was to capture Type II Nova in distant galaxies. That astronomer had only second hand information about the solar flare, and the article did not report the data that Jason gave to the science editor, nor did the reporter even bother to visit the Space Weather website and look at the SOHO and ACE data. The other papers printed nothing at all about the impending danger of a solar flare.

Jason's greatest frustration came with his calls to the Pacific Gas and Electric Company. The top level manager claimed the NOAA Space Weather people already advised him of the solar storm and he claimed the expected magnitude did not warrant a proactive response. Jason argued that he was misreading the warning which shouted for extraordinary protective measures. He suggested that they shut down the entire Northern California power grid from 7 p.m. until midnight, on September 6. The area manager scoffed at this suggestion.

"You want me to do what?" he asked incredulously. "Do you realize what effect such a massive disruption of service would have on our customers, not to mention on the rest of the national grid? We have had similar warnings from NOAA in the past, and no harm other than a momentary surge and brownout occurred. I don't expect this storm to be any more destructive than previous ones."

Jason snapped, "Do you realize what will happen to your distribution equipment if it is on line when this solar storm breaks through the earth's protective magnetic shield?" The PG&E manager said he was in full control of the situation and accused Jason of overreacting.

There was no reasoning with the fellow. He remained firmly against any shut down of the PG&E power generation system, no matter how temporary.

The sun had set on September 6 when Jason went outside his Oakland foothills home to sit in his favorite backyard chair and watch the stars emerge from the fading light. As usual, smog and light pollution obscured all but the brightest stars to the west, and only Venus managed to cut through the pall of haze and glare. Jason noticed something unusual: a sight seldom seen at this latitude. The entire northern sky blushed with a pink glow. Beginning in the north, curtains of blue, green and orange light rippled their way across the sky, finally dissipating in the city's glare and then reappeared in another series of waves. Jason witnessed similar aurora years ago, but that was when he was stationed at the Erickson Air Station in Alaska. Never had he seen an aurora in California; for such vivid displays were exceptionally rare this far south. He poked his head inside the back door and called to his wife Betty and son Nathan to come outside and see the light show. Betty said she was busy with dinner. Nathan reluctantly interrupted his MTV show and followed his father outside.

When he raised his eyes to the sky, his jaw dropped. "Dad, the entire sky is on fire!"

CHAPTER FOUR:
BLACKOUT

Mild-mannered, six-footer Peter Dexter looked younger than his fifty-eight years. Except for a weathered face and a stock of thinning blond hair, strangers might take him to be in his early forties. In his younger years his ambition had been to fly, and he applied for and received an appointment to the Air Force Academy. While in flight school, he discovered that his inability to withstand high "G" forces cut short his desire to be an Air Force pilot. However, the Air Force had other career plans for him. An exceptional student, Peter graduated in the top 20 of his Academy class. He first served as an air tanker refueling officer in Greece, and then as an Air Traffic Controller, where he worked on U.S. bases from Spain to the Philippines. Before returning to the States, the Air Force promoted him to captain. While on assignment at Fairchild AFB in Spokane, Washington, he met and married Judy Jenkins: a striking brunette, vivacious, smart as a whip, and a recent graduate from Lewiston State College with an elementary schoolteacher's certificate. Peter fell in love with her on their first date, but the feeling was far from mutual. Peter's mild manner and Air Traffic controller job did not impress Judy. His career didn't fit her vision of an Air Force Captain: the square-jawed, fearless squadron leader, who each day flew his Spitfire into enemy territory to shoot down dozens of enemy aircraft. Judy was a homebody, born and raised in the small farming town of Colfax, south of Spokane. She had no intention of getting involved with a lowly Air Force Air Traffic Controller; yet something vaguely compelling attracted her to Peter, and she continued to date him. Three months after they started dating Judy rejected his first marriage proposal. She had other plans, and traipsing around the world as a dutiful wife of an Air Force Captain didn't fit those plans. When she introduced him to her parents at their Colfax farm, her dad immediately saw the potential in Peter and told Judy that he admired the young man. After dating for six months, she fell in love with him and they married in Colfax a year later. Their first child, Pam, was born in the Philippines. Two years later, they had a second child, Trevor, born in the Azores.

After a distinguished career, Peter retired while on assignment at the Minot Air Base in North Dakota. A few months before, and with an eye toward retirement, Judy and Peter bought a 420-acre farm outside the town of Willow Creek, a few miles northwest of Minot. After his discharge, Peter and his family moved to the farm and quickly integrated into the Willow Creek community. Judy, a farm girl at heart and accustomed to farm life, quickly fell in love with the farm and Willow Creek. Peter had never before farmed and knew little about successful farming. With Judy's guidance and some helpful neighbors, Peter quickly learned how to grow and market corn, alfalfa, and barley. Now, five years later, the Dexter family grew and thrived on their farm.

*   *   *

Rain fell from an overcast sky, as Peter began the thirty-mile drive on Highway 83, from Minot to his farm near Willow Creek. Eager to get home in time for dinner, he headed north out of the city and decided not to make his usual stop at the Minot Air Force Base to fill the truck with gasoline. He glanced at his watch. The digits read 8:04 p.m., and he realized his family would worry about his tardiness. His shopping day had taken longer than planned and now, as the sun dipped below the western horizon, he realized that even without a stop at the AFB he was going to be late. As he reached the outskirts of the AFB, the clouds parted and the rain stopped. Waiting at an overhead traffic light to change at the AFB gate entrance, he noticed something odd in the northern sky.

Between parting clouds, the sky glowed a vivid pink. Initially, he thought it was an unusually brilliant sunset, but then he realized he was looking north not west. The sky turned from pink to a pale green, then indigo blue. The power transmission lines alongside the road outside the base caught Peter's attention as a pair of transmission wires glowed with an iridescent blue light. He drove away from the traffic light, pulled over to the side of the highway and stopped as a basketball-sized sphere pf blue light jumped from a nearby transmission tower, ran down a wire to the next transmission tower, and then returned to the first tower, where it rebounded and rolled back to the second tower. The display continued in ping-pong fashion for a few seconds, and then a second blue ball began to dance on a lower pair of wires. The balls of blue light danced back and forth from one tower to the next for several seconds. Peter recalled seeing this strange blue ball of light before when he witnessed it on a flight in the Philippines. A lightning bolt struck the DC-3 cargo airplane he had hitched a ride on and sitting as a guest in the cockpit jump seat, he watched as first, the wingtips and then the instrument panel glowed iridescent blue. Then a blue sphere rolled down the aisle from the cockpit to the back and exited the tail section of the airplane. After they landed, he and the copilot examined the trailing edge of the elevator flap. A blackened wedged-shape chunk of flap was missing. He had witnessed a rare phenomenon called ball lightning and remembered that scientists cannot explain such odd electrical behavior, except to theorize it is some form of inexplicable electric plasma.

The dance of ball lightning ceased, but as the night sky drew darker, the light-show in the sky intensified. Peter climbed out of the car and through a break in the overcast he witnessed the most intense and beautiful northern lights ever seen in the lower 48 states. Red and green curtains of light danced across the sky. To the north, the entire sky blushed orange, then red and finally green. Several other cars pulled over in the turnout to watch the unusual light show. Peter glanced back toward town and watched as a brilliant fireball of blue light lit the horizon then faded to an orange afterglow. It seemed to originate from the power distribution yard, outside Minot. Everything in the yard appeared normal when he passed it a few minutes ago. Crowded with towering transformers, power poles, and overhead cables hanging from huge insulators, the two-acre Ottertail Electric Company substation serviced the city of Minot and surrounding towns. A second, smaller power distribution substation located a mile north of the air base serviced the base and surrounding towns, including Willow Creek.

As the light from the explosion faded, the twinkling lights of Minot wink out section by section. Within seconds, darkness enveloped the entire town. "A major blackout," Peter thought out loud. All the lights along the highway, the lights in the base, and the few homes that bordered it also went dark. He climbed back into his car and cautiously drove along the dark, wet, highway toward the air base substation. Flames and sparks from the substation leaped high into the sky. The entire yard was on fire.

"This cannot be good", he muttered.

He turned off on the county road leading to Willow Creek and his farm east of town, and turned on the car radio to catch the news of the extent and cause of the blackout. As he scanned across the AM band, all he heard was static. Finally, he found a Bismarck station still on the air. The announcer said the radio station was using an emergency backup generator, yet he offered no speculation about the extent or cause of the blackout. After a few minutes, a commentator reported that stations in Fargo, Minneapolis, and Winnipeg were also without power and only those "clear channel" stations with emergency generators remained on the air.

"Oh my God," Peter whispered. "If this blackout extends all the way across the state to Fargo and as far as Minneapolis and Winnipeg, it must be because of a major problem, perhaps similar to the power blackout along the East Coast some years ago."

Twenty minutes later, he drove down the drive leading to his darkened farmhouse. The welcoming overhead lights that surrounded his house and barn were out, and the farmhouse was dark except for an orange glow that radiated from a front room window and the kitchen. He thought that Judy must have lit a few candles. His wife, and children, Trevor and Pam, ran out to greet him as he opened the car door.

"We're sure glad you're home," Judy said breathlessly, "I called our friends in town and they said the whole city is without power, but at least the telephones still work."

"All of Minot and perhaps most of the state is blacked out," Peter admitted. "The power substation north of the AFB was on fire as I drove past. Look at the northern lights."

Judy, Pam, and Trevor gasped in awe at the polar light show. The aurora was more intensive and vivid than any Peter or Judy had viewed while stationed in Alaska. The curtains of light outshone the crescent moon, as it ducked in and out of the retreating storm clouds.

"I wonder if the blackout has something to do with the light show," Judy mused.

Peter smiled. "I watched ball lightning dance on the power lines outside Minot just before the blackout. I am sure there is a connection."

Peter went inside and tuned his battery powered AM-FM radio to the Bismarck station. The announcer said that this blackout included major cities from Chicago to Los Angeles, and later corrected his report to say the blackout included the entire North American continent. Worse yet, the GPS navigation system that airline pilots rely on to fly across the nation also shut down. The FAA ordered all airliners to use VOR and ground-based navigation stations to land at the nearest airport. Fortunately, most airports including the Minot AFB had emergency generators to power landing lights and communication and navigation equipment. The radio announcer claimed this was the most extensive blackout in history.

Fortunately this was not the first time the Dexters had to deal with power outages. As a result, they were prepared for such disasters. Given the substation fire near the Minot AFB, Peter knew it would be some time before Otter Tail Power could restore service. Yet, never in his worst thinking did he assume it would be almost a year before Willow Creek would again have electricity.

CHAPTER FIVE:
THE POWER GRID

The power generation and distribution grid in the United States is a marvel of modern engineering. The power that lights your home, business and shopping mall is produced by hundreds of electric generation plants located throughout the United States and Canada. Generators convert mechanical energy into electricity and feed it to an interconnected distribution grid. Large oil-cooled transformers boost the alternating current (ac), produced by rotating generators to hundreds of thousands of volts, and deliver it through long transmission lines to local distribution stations. Large transformers then reduce the voltage and feed it over transmission lines to smaller substations that further reduce the voltage. Finally, it arrives at a power pole outside your home or business, where garbage-can-sized transformers reduce the voltage to 440, 220, or 110 volts.

Your electric power does not come from any specific generation plant, but from various facilities located across the nation. For example, electrical power produced by the Grand Coolie hydroelectric plant, in northeastern Washington, delivers power to the grid as does a nuclear plant in California, a coal fired plant in Wyoming, and a wind generator in Montana. The main transmission grid is divided into three independent systems: East Coast, West Coast and Texas, and this isolation is the Achilles heel of the power grid. A major disruption in one of the three independent grids cannot call on the other grids to compensate for their loss, and to avoid overloading, that entire grid will shut down. An automatic shutdown of even one distribution station can ripple throughout the grid in what is called a rolling blackout. Some years ago, the East Coast grid experienced a blackout caused by the failure of a single substation. Unable to compensate for the sudden loss, various generating plants went off-line one-by-one, aggravating the strain on the remaining grid. Finally, in spectacular fashion, the entire grid failed, blacking out a major part of the country and Canada. It took a couple of days to correct the problem and gradually restore power.

In another case, a CME from the sun caused an electrical surge that had forced one Canadian distribution station to shut down. Unable to compensate for the sudden loss, and in an act of self-preservation, the entire grid began to shut down, causing a cascading power outage throughout eastern Canada and parts of northeast USA. No one envisioned a rolling blackout of such magnitude; yet, that is exactly what happened.

Once engineers find and repair the source of the problem, restarting and rebalancing the entire network is not as straightforward as it might seem. When electrical equipment such as motors start, for a few seconds they need three to five times their normal running current. The resulting surge forces engineers to reconnect the grid, section by section. After a widespread outage, it can take several hours or days to reconnect and load balance the entire grid. Since a more robust grid would cost billions, the present grid remains susceptible to disruptions.

*   *   *

On September 6, Jim Perkins, the night supervisor at the main power substation outside Salt Lake City, went outside to marvel at the unusual aurora in the northern sky. When a warning alarm sounded in the control room, he ran back inside to answer the jangling red telephone.

"Shut the local grid down, immediately," the area supervisor ordered.

Jim had never before received a general shutdown order but he knew exactly what to do. He ran over to the main control panel and began throwing master power control switches. Unfortunately, he was too late. Before he could shut the power off, the control room lights flickered and a blue flash, followed by a loud explosion, shook the entire substation. He looked out the window in time to see flames envelop one of the main power transformers.

Bolted to a thick cement pad, a ten-foot-high substation transformers, filled with hundreds of gallons of PCB oil, overheated and exploded, sending showers of flaming oil throughout the yard. Despite built-in safety features, a second transformer exploded and launched its two-ton steel lid high into the sky. Hundreds of gallons of flaming oil poured into the yard, starting dozens of secondary fires. Within a minute, a third and fourth transformer exploded and engulfed the entire yard in a wall of flame.

The local fire department arrived at the substation a few minutes after the first explosion and put out the yard fire, however the shutdown order had come too late to save several transformers from total destruction. Until the power company could replace the damaged transformers, a repair that could take months, Salt Lake City and surrounding towns would be without power. The Salt Lake City power station was only one of hundreds of North America substations damaged by the power surge. The entire Western, Eastern and Texas grids shut down in an unprecedented series of transformer failures and substation shutdowns. Power company managers realized that replacement transformers were not readily available and knew it would take months to manufacture new ones and get their stations back on line.

*   *   *

Joe Jefferson, the night manager for Pacific Gas and Electric's power distribution center, gazed out the seventh story window of the PG&E San Francisco skyscraper and marveled at the unusual aurora in the sky. Joe watched in horror as the city lights shut off, section by section, until the entire San Francisco skyline, outlined by the pink sky, became dark. The Control Center in the City managed the entire electrical grid throughout Northern California and Joe shuddered as the office lights flickered and then shut off. Emergency battery powered lights bathed the mostly deserted office in areas of bright light, contrasted by dark shadows that spread across the office. His attention suddenly shifted to the red phone ringing on his desk. He answered and heard the order for a system-wide emergency shutdown. He hit the emergency red button that relayed the order to all his station managers throughout Northern California and looked at the huge system map which covered the entire north wall of the office. The map marked individual substations, the status of each represented by tiny colored LEDs (light-emitting diodes). Normally, most lights on the map glowed green, with only a smattering of amber or red lights. Green lights signaled on-line substations, while amber indicated stations on standby, while off-line stations glowed red. Joe watched in dismay as the lights changed from green to red in a wave that cascaded across the board until the entire map glowed red. Never before had he witnessed such a massive shutdown, nor was he prepared to manage a system-wide catastrophe. He called each of his dozen yard managers to confirm that they had shut down, and several reported that oil fires enveloped their yards.

A company memo, issued the day before, advised operators to expect surges and minor brownouts if the CME powered through the Earth's protective magnetic field on the evening of September 6. However, this outage was beyond anything suggested in that memo. At the start of his shift, Joe called in two other controllers to help him, should there be a system-wide brownout. Now, all three controllers stood gaping at the red glow of the system map, not knowing what they should do next. When the first warnings came in over the teletype, at 6:57 p.m. Pacific Time, Joe issued a system-wide standby advisory to all substation managers. Joe's shut-down order came too late to be effective. One station after another went off-line as overloaded transformers burst into flames and the green lights on the master board turned red. Joe realized the power grid was in serious trouble and called the general manager. Seconds before, in the middle of his dinner, the lights in the manager's home had winked out. The manager fumbled to find his ringing cell phone in his darkened dining room and identified the caller.

"Joe, what's going on with the system?" he asked.

"Mr. Briton, the entire system has shut down," Joe explained. "No sir, I cannot initiate restart procedures. Many of the yards are reporting transformer fires. I think we are in big trouble. No sir, I issued a standby advisory at 6:57 p.m., but when the shutdown order came in at 7:03 p.m., it was too late to save most of the substations from fires." Mr. Britton responded with "Damn! It'll take months to replace all those transformers. Meanwhile we will lose millions of dollars."

Mr. Britton knew the huge power transformers that convert transmission line voltage to local distribution line voltage would take months to manufacture. There are only two companies that do so in the United States, and they would have to depend on emergency generators to remain in business. He realized that other power companies on the western grid had probably suffered similar losses, but he did not yet realize the nation-wide extent of the damage. With so many orders for power transformers, the manufacturing companies would take months to replace all the damaged transformers for PG&E alone. Until all the damaged transformers could be replaced, a civilization addicted to electricity would be without it and would have to find a way to deal with all the problems such a disaster suggested. He knew California would be chaotic without power for an extended time. It frightened him to think of his fellow Californians without power for months, and what might occur in such an extensive blackout. The next few months would try men's souls and be a struggle for survival. He could only imagine the consequences.

CHAPTER SIX:
A FARM IN NORTH DAKOTA

Peter and Judy Dexter were accustomed to the power outages common in North Dakota. Some outages in rural areas could last for hours or even several days, but not even floods caused disruptions that lasted for weeks. The Souris River flows out of Canada, circles Minot and then surges back into Canada. In the springtime, sometimes it floods Minot and parts of the surrounding counties. A major flood, in 1997, caused power outages throughout the county. Ottertail Electric, the local power company, had restored partial power to Minot within a week, yet some towns including Willow Creek had gone without electricity for a couple of weeks. Extended blackouts were more than an inconvenience for the citizens of Willow Creek. For instance, without power, the small service station in town could not pump gasoline, and the only operating gas stations were on the Minot AFB or in Minot. Retired military folks like Peter could buy gasoline on the base, but nonmilitary folks had to drive to Minot and wait in line for an hour or more to fill their tanks with a limit of fifteen gallons. A week into the 1997 flood and power blackout, Peter ran out of gasoline for his car, tractor, and emergency generator. Even the air base was short of fuel and so were all the gas stations in Minot. This experience convinced Peter that he should prepare his farm for such extended blackouts. He stored food and extra fuel on the farm, so when the September 6 power outage came to Willow Creek, the Dexter farm could manage without power for several weeks. They were able to feed themselves and their animals from their own stock of food and fresh farm produce. Because of his preparations, Peter would even be able to finish the fall harvest. He stored diesel in a 500-gallon fuel tank, which he used to run a 7.5 KW generator and fill his tractor and truck. A month into the blackout, Peter's supply of diesel ran low and he was forced to conserve. Drinking water was the most important item for the farm. The generator supplied power for the house and water well, but to conserve diesel, Peter only ran it intermittently. Fortunately, water stored in a 1,000-gallon water tower next to the barn could supplement the well. It had been unusually hot September, and the only air-conditioning available was the afternoon breeze that blew across the fields. Loose-fitting clothes and lemonade helped keep the family cool.

The memory of the previous blackouts was still fresh in Judy's mind, and she voiced her concern to Peter that first evening of the outage.

"Pete, I think this outage will go on longer than the one back in '97."

"Yes, and possibly even a lot longer," Peter regretfully answered. "Tonight as I passed by the power substation outside Minot AFB, I saw that the entire yard was in flames. I think the power surge damaged most of the transformers. It will take months to replace them."

"Months?" Judy repeated. "Do you think we will be without power for that long?"

"Yes, I do. It will take Ottertail Power months to replace those blown transformers at the Minot AFB substation."
"Do you think we will have enough diesel to run the generator and pump water?"

"Well, the water tower should provide enough water for a while. We can run the generator to charge our batteries and fill the water tank. If we conserve, we should have enough to last through several months. We should conserve the little gasoline and diesel we have. No more weekly trips into town for church."

Judy frowned.

"Well, not so fast mister. We are not going to give up going to church on Sunday. You could hitch the wagon to Buddy and Molly (the farm mules) and they can pull us into town," she insisted.

Peter smiled. He knew it would take more than a blackout to keep Judy away from church services. And she was right. Molly and Buddy could pull them into town. Peter had also stored three fifty-five gallon drums of gasoline in the tool shed. His SUV normally used 50 gallons each month, so the family would have to restrict travel to necessities and cut short their monthly trips to the AFB Commissary and shopping trips into Minot.

Harvest time was just about the worst time of year to be without power and have a limited supply of diesel for the tractor. Fortunately, Peter had almost finished harvesting before the September 6 blackout and had either delivered his crop to the grain dealers or stored it on the farm. He hadn't yet harvested the corn planted on the back forty acres and had barely enough fuel to finish the job. He decided that fuel for harvesting was more important than fuel for their cars or generator, and they could get along without electricity for the several months of winter it might take to restore power. It would be difficult for the family to go through the harsh North Dakota winter without power, but they would somehow manage. Peter installed a pellet stove last year, and had over two tons of pellets stored in the barn. In addition, they had a full propane tank holding 800 gallons.

The lessons learned in the '97 power outage had encouraged Peter to prepare their 420-acre farm for winter early in the fall. Last month, he had filled the 500-gallon fuel tank with diesel and the 55-gallon drums with gasoline at a time when fuel costs were unusually low. He also had filled the propane tank and plumbed the farmhouse to use propane for cooking and heating. That summer, their half-acre vegetable garden had produced tons of vegetables and Judy canned the vegetables and fruits from their orchard to feed the family through winter and most of spring. The corn bin would be full after harvesting the back forty. The root cellar was stocked with ten sacks of potatoes, five sacks of squash and four sacks of beans. North Dakota winters were harsh. Between November and April, temperatures mostly hovered between freezing and subzero. Relentless icy winds blew across the plains for days on end, building huge snowdrifts along fence lines. They could keep their freezer running part-time on the generator, until those cold temperatures arrived, and then frozen items could be stored in the barn. The side of beef, two butchered pigs, and three lambs could remain frozen until spring. A plentiful supply of hay to feed the four cows, three horses and two mules, filled the barn. Peter also stocked winter fodder for their six pigs, five sheep, and two she-goats. He bought two dozen 100-pound sacks of grain for the chickens and geese, and stored it in the tool shed. He was certain the animals and his family could make it comfortably through the winter, and in a few months, certainly by spring, Otter Tail Electric would restore power. He worried for his friends in town and especially his fellow parishioners. Those folks were not as well prepared and could not survive months without power. He would find a way to help his friends, although he couldn't feed the entire town.

Peter's concern grew for Dan Justin, his buddy in California. Peter and Dan had been close friends since their days together in the Air Force. They had met while at the Air Force Academy in Colorado, and all through the years at the Academy and in the service, they kept in touch. Dan was Best Man at Peter and Judy's wedding, and in turn, Peter was Dan's Best Man, when Dan and Nora wed in Santa Cruz. Each spring, the families took turns visiting one another. Last May, Dan and his family drove to North Dakota and spent two weeks on the Dexter farm. The two families got along well together. Scott and Trevor were the same age, and Penny and Pam became good friends. Keith was big brother to all four. Every time Dan and Nora visited the farm, Peter and Judy tried to talk them into moving out to Willow Creek. Dan was hesitant to leave his job and uproot his family from their California roots. Peter persisted in his offer and Dan left the door open by saying, "Perhaps after I graduate from Law School we will move, but now is not a good time."

Two days after the blackout, and before the telephone service went down, Peter called Dan and again encouraged him to bring his family to the farm.

"You folks need to get out of California. The power disruption will go badly in places where folks are unable to cope. The nuts will come out of the woodwork and make it a dangerous place for you and your family. Come and live with us on our farm in Willow Creek. Folks around here are friendly and self-sufficient. They are not like city folks, who have no idea what to do when they have no power. Anyway, I need your help on the farm and we can work together to protect and feed our families." Dan said he would think it over, but before he could get back to Peter and accept his offer, the telephone system throughout the country went down, and there was no way to contact him.

Peter's concern for others also included his church community in Willow Creek. Many townsfolk and parishioners had not yet prepared for winter. It would only be a matter of time before some of their friends would come asking for help, and he knew he couldn't refuse them. He could provide food for a few, but couldn't feed the entire Lutheran Church community, let alone the entire town. If the town folk learned the Dexter family was giving out food, some wouldn't hesitate to come to the farm and demand it, and even try to take it by force if necessary. During the first month of the crisis, thieves had robbed two farm families who attended their church, and worse was yet to come. Peter had an answer for those with criminal intent: a large caliber rifle and a twelve gauge shotgun should do the trick. Peter's nature was nonviolent and mild-mannered, yet he wasn't afraid to use either weapon to protect his family and farm. He prayed it would never come to that; yet he knew people could become violent when desperate or acting in a mob. "Just let them try to harm my family or my property," Peter vowed to friends. "If anyone tries to attack us they will get a belly full of lead." Folks knew he was deadly serious about this threat: a vow that would result it trouble.

CHAPTER SEVEN:
ESCAPE FROM THE CITY

In the three weeks that followed the power disruption, the entire country struggled to cope with the blackout. Unprepared for a long-term disruption, Federal, State and local governments lacked contingency plans to deal with a collapsing infrastructure. Cities large and small depend on a continuous supply of electricity to provide critical services. For the first two weeks of the blackout, portable electric generators powered hospitals and a few critical city services, such as water and sewers. A few homes and businesses with access to portable gasoline generators continued to function, yet as fuel ran out, one by one the generators shut down and businesses closed. Hospitals, radio stations, emergency services and a few stores functioned as long as possible; but after three weeks, services and business began to close down. A few generator-powered gas stations continued to fill customers' gas tanks and even pumped gasoline with hand pumps until the underground tanks ran dry and the refineries suspended tanker truck deliveries. Before long, without fuel, owners abandoned their automobiles by the side of the road and it became rare to see a car or truck driving down the road, street, or highway. After a month, delivery trucks and vans ran short of fuel and couldn't make their deliveries to stores. Looters stole whatever items remained on the mostly empty shelves. All public transport, including trains, airlines and buses, suspended service. Initially, critical services such as police, fire and other emergency services responded to priority calls; yet when their vehicles eventually ran out of fuel, all services ended.

Communication devices, such as cell phones and remote telephones, began failing within the first week of the blackout, and by the end of the month, most were out of service. So were the companies that provided such services. Initially, diesel generators kept local and limited long-distance telephone services working; however within a month, all of them had ceased operations. Electronics in satellites are sensitive to radiation and failed when the first burst from the solar storm hit the ionosphere. Their failure disrupted TV, GPS navigation, and satellite communications. Services that most citizens take for granted, like city water and sewage disposal, depend on electric pumps that now couldn't function. Water taps soon ran dry and sewage backed up into homes. Some towns that use water towers to store and pressurize their water systems continued to deliver water for a few weeks, yet without pumps to refill the tanks they ran dry and so did the town's water spigots. Initially, Santa Cruz, like other cities and towns, stationed water trucks at convenient locations, yet without a reliable supply of gasoline, the tankers eventually couldn't make those deliveries. Fires inevitably broke out throughout Santa Cruz. An entire block near the Santa Cruz beach and boardwalk caught fire, and with dry hydrants all the firefighters could do was watch. After the garbage trucks ran out of fuel, refuse collected in the streets and alleys. Lacking overhead lights, downtown Santa Cruz became a darkened, smelly, ghost town littered with abandoned cars, sewage, and rotting garbage. Rats crawled out of the sewers to invade homes. Public schools and colleges closed. For two weeks, local hospitals remained open by using emergency generator power; nevertheless after two weeks, the generators ran out of fuel and hospitals curtailed services and discharged their patients. Families forced to retrieve sick relatives cared for them at home, as best they could. Patients, who were dependent on mechanical life support equipment, died. There was nothing the hospitals or their relatives could do to prolong their lives

After delivery trucks ran out of fuel, food couldn't be delivered to grocery stores. Without working freezers, perishable foods and produce thawed and the stores either gave it away or threw it out. By the end of the first week, panicky shoppers had emptied store shelves of all canned and nonperishable packaged items. The few hardware stores that remained open, sold out of flashlights, batteries, candles, and kerosene for hurricane lamps. At the end of the third week, serious trouble broke out in many California cities, especially in Los Angeles, Fresno, San Diego, San Francisco and Oakland. As people ran out of food and water, looting became a survival necessity. With the police unable to keep order, packs of criminals and looters controlled the streets and anarchy reigned. Desperate people broke into downtown and mall stores and stole anything and everything not bolted down or secured. Once the thieves had emptied stores, they began breaking into private homes to steal whatever foodstuffs or valuables they could carry off. Some homeowners hung warning signs on their front doors, promising they would shoot any intruder, and many desperate thieves ended their criminal careers on the front or back doorsteps of neighborhood homes. Robbers also carried weapons and used them to force their way into any unprotected home. Rape, robbery and murder were commonplace. Human and animal bodies littered the streets, and with no city services to collect and bury them, they rotted where they fell. The smell of decaying flesh permeated city streets.

Unfortunately, Santa Cruz was not immune from these societal breakdowns. They just took a bit longer to develop in smaller cities than they did in the larger ones. Criminal behavior in each city was proportional to its size and condition. Those municipalities with large inner cities experienced more robberies, killings and rapes per capita, than did smaller towns or villages; yet, even in the smallest California hamlets, criminals acted without restraint.

Nationwide, the blackout created serious situations that not only shut down industry but threatened life. The power blackout disrupted nuclear storage facilities and chemical processing factories, and they soon became dangerous time bombs. The AEC maintains depository sites where they store spent nuclear power rods collected from power plants and submarines. Dozens of these storage facilities throughout the nation store radioactive materials in carefully monitored repositories. Fissionable materials and radioactive byproducts can remain dangerous for centuries. Spent fuel rods are either reprocessed or stored in deep pools of circulating water that absorbs emissions and keeps the rods from overheating. Unless the electric pumps continue to circulate water, the rods will eventually grow hot enough to boil off the protecting water and melt down, releasing clouds of radioactive materials into the atmosphere. Standby diesel generators at these sites, designed to supply power for several days or even two or three weeks, immediately went on line. These generators eventually ran out of fuel and became the top priority for the government to supply fuel to them from the strategic reserve gasoline storage facilities.

Electric pumps are also critical for the safe operation of many manufacturing plants. Without power, deadly fumes will gather and vent into the atmosphere. Aluminum smelting plants depend on a continuous supply of electricity to keep the aluminum in crucibles molten. Without power, they will solidify into a lump of useless metal and the smelting equipment will be beyond repair. Sewage processing plants are also dangerous. Without power, the plants cannot exhaust explosive methane into the sky or prevent raw sewage from spilling into the water system polluting groundwater, streams, lakes and oceans.

The government initiated priorities to manage the extended power failures and to make diesel fuel available to keep critical generators running. It became rare to see an airplane in the sky. Commercial flights were grounded throughout the continent and Air Force bases, including the base at Minot, suspended flight operations to conserve their dwindling supply of jet fuel.

Dan and his family were able to survive in relative comfort for the first two weeks of the blackout. They had enough water and food, and Dan had 110 gallons of gasoline stored in two 55-gallon drums in his garage. Before the power crisis, gasoline prices varied wildly. One month, pump prices would be over $4 per gallon, and then the next returned to under $2 per gallon only to rise to $3 weeks later. To save money, Dan filled those drums when the price was low. After the blackout started, he ran his electric generator for a few hours each day to keep his freezer cold and batteries charged. When he realized the noise from the generator could attract thieves, he stopped using it. He also wanted to conserve the extra fuel for a possible trip to the Dexter farm in Minot. Since the blackout began, Peter's offer to move his family to the Dexter farm weighed heavy on Dan's mind. Day by day as Santa Cruz grew more and more dangerous, Peter's offer looked better and better. Every night after dinner, the Justin family gathered around the portable AM radio to listen to news and hear stories about dangerous travel on the highways, the lack of gasoline everywhere, and lawlessness in American cities. Although reluctant to go on the road, Dan knew he would have to get his family out of the state, and the time to do so was running out.

One of Dan's hobbies was amateur radio. He worked a 100 watt station on the 40 and 80 meter HAM radio bands, and contacted fellow HAMS throughout the country. His station was not powerful, yet he was able to reach stations throughout the nation and sometimes even overseas. He covered his wall with QSL cards (proof of contact) sent to him by dozens of HAM operators throughout the world. He was especially proud of a QSL card he had received from Tibet, one of only two HAM radio stations that operated in that country. In an emergency, HAM radio operators formed a critical communications network. Volunteer HAM radio operators were the backbone of an emergency communications network, critical during disasters. In the first week of the power outage, Dan spent several hours each day relaying and receiving messages from around the country. He also owned a high frequency emergency services mobile transceiver, which he used to communicate with local emergency agencies. He relayed messages to State and Federal agencies and after the landline telephone system shut down, neighbors and friends came to his front door, asking him to contact friends or relatives. Dan sat by his battery-operated station hour after hour, relaying messages for friends and neighbors as well as for Homeland Security, local police, and the county sheriff's department.

By the second week of the disaster, all television stations went off the air. Several clear channel AM radio stations continued to broadcast on a limited schedule. Portable AM/FM and shortwave radios were the only source of news from the world outside Santa Cruz. The blackout did not affect Europe; thus, the BBC was Dan's best source of international news. A few clear channel stations, such as KGO in San Francisco, KFI in Los Angeles, and KSL in Salt Lake City, continued to broadcast local and national news on a limited schedule. From 7-9 p.m., each evening, KGO broadcast local and national news as well as government advisories. The news was not good, especially concerning road conditions. Lawlessness in major urban areas was rampant, and the government seemed powerless to stop it.

In San Francisco gangs of armed thieves roamed the streets committing theft, rape, and murder. Dead bodies and garbage littered sidewalks and alleyways and abandoned automobiles and trucks clogged the streets and avenues. Mobs ransacked businesses and looted whatever remained on shelves.

Throughout the nation desperate citizens panicked as food and water ran out and some began killing pets and looting their neighbors' homes. No one was safe. Mayors pleaded for federal or state aid to help quell the riots and fires that soon erupted throughout their cities. They could not protect their citizens or provide basic needs or critical services such as police, emergency care, fire, or water. The governor of California sent the National Guard into Sacramento. Overwhelmed by the extent of lawlessness and unable to restore law and order, the troops withdrew. The federal government was as ineffectual in California as it was in other states. Even when federal officials offered to send in troops, citing Posse Commentates, many state governors refused their help and some even banned federal troops from enforcing state or local law.

The evening dinner conversation around the Justin dinner table grew more and more depressing.

"Did you hear that PG&E claims it will take nine to ten months to restore power to just half of their six million customers in Northern California?" Nora asked.

"Yes, and all the TV and most radio stations have gone off the air," Scott added.

"The worst part is the mayhem on city streets right here in Santa Cruz," Nora complained. "People are killing one another over food and survival items. Today I watched a bunch of hoodlums break into Jim and Betty's house . . . you know . . . the blue-trimmed house down the street. I heard shots, and shortly after that, those thugs came running out of the house carrying all sorts of stuff. Dan, you should go down there and see if they are all right."

Dan said he would check on the neighbors, but was quick to reassure his own family that he would keep them from harm.

"Well, don't worry. Come hell or high water, I will protect you. If anyone tries to break in here, they will end up digging a bullet out of some part of their body."

Nora looked shocked and stared at Dan. It was unlike him to threaten violence. He always avoided a fight or tried to negotiate out of one; yet these were extraordinary times that stressed even pacifists.

"It would be better to let Chester frighten off those looters than shoot them," Nora suggested. Chester was the family's German shepherd dog. At the sound of his name, Chester's ears perked and he uttered a throaty growl from under the table.

"A well-placed bullet would be faster and more effective than Chester," Dan argued.

"Things are getting as bad in Santa Cruz as they are in the major cities," Nora complained. "The headline in the San Jose Mercury last week shouted, "NATIONWIDE DISASTER: THE COUNTRY IS POWERLESS TO ACT."

Keith scowled and said, "Well, that's a play on words. The power may be off, but the country is certainly not powerless."

"You're right Keith," Nora said. "Nor are we powerless, not as a family. Our future is in our own hands. For instance we can leave Santa Cruz."

"Leave Santa Cruz . . . and go where?" Scott whined.

"To Judy and Peter's farm of course," Nora declared.

Dan looked long and hard at Nora. Would she be willing to leave her parents, Jim and Dee, and all her friends in Santa Cruz and move to North Dakota? Previously, whenever Peter and Judy suggested this, Nora quickly rejected the idea. Now it was Dan who was dragging his feet about leaving. Nora looked determined.

"Nora, you are right. Perhaps we should consider leaving . . . while it is still possible to leave," Dan said. "Any day now, we will be stuck here . . . for good! We have enough gasoline to get out of the state, perhaps all the way to Judy and Peter's farm in North Dakota. We could take the trailer and live in it along the way. They say rural towns and villages are doing better than the large cities. Peter and Judy keep asking us to move out to their farm, yet realize that such a journey would be dangerous."

Keith smiled but Penny and Scott looked bewildered.

Nora brightened. "Yes it would be a dangerous journey, but it is even more dangerous to stay here in Santa Cruz. I know Judy wants us to come. For the sake of the family, we should pack our stuff and go."

"While we still can," Keith added.

"Peter repeated his offer when we talked by telephone after the blackout," Dan admitted. "I told him I would think about it; yet with the phones out, I haven't been able to talk with him for the past several weeks, and things are much worse now than they were when we last talked. I relayed a message to him through my HAM radio contact in Minot, but I never heard back if Peter received my message. I would feel better if Peter and Judy knew we were coming. With all that is going on, I am not sure they would welcome us under these drastic circumstances."

"Of course they would," Nora argued. "Last spring, Peter and Judy begged us to move to North Dakota and help them run the farm. We should leave . . . NOW."

Scott wasn't so sure. "All my friends are here. I don't want to leave. How about Grandma and Grandpa? We can't just leave them here."

"Last week I told Dee and Jim we were thinking of moving to North Dakota," Nora admitted. "Of course, at first they were against the idea, but then Jim said it would be best for us."

"Couldn't they come with us?" Penny asked.

Judy smiled and gave Penny a hug. "No, they said they would never leave Santa Cruz. For better or worse, this is their home. This is the way it is with older folks."

Dan looked amazed. "Nora, you mean to tell me you had this discussion with your parents, and they agreed that we should leave? Why didn't you tell me?"

Nora frowned. "I was looking for the right opportunity to tell you. Dee and Jim want what is best for us. It's time for us to stop procrastinating and decide. I say we should go."

Dan was still not convinced. "KGO keeps advising about closed interstate highways, and they warn everyone to stay in their homes and keep off the roads. They warn that gasoline is not available anywhere and gangs roam the countryside. At best, it would be a difficult and dangerous trip to Minot, and unless we can buy gas and food along the way, we may never make it to the farm."

"Let's put it to a vote," Nora suggested. "I vote to leave."

"I vote no," Penny said. "It isn't right to leave Grandma and Grandpa here all alone."

Keith said to count him in. Scott said he didn't care one way or the other, but he really wanted to stay.

"Scott, decide. Should we stay or go," Nora chided.

"OK then, I vote we stay," Scott said.

"Well Dan, I guess we are split. Keith and I say to go, and Scott and Penny want to stay. Now it's up to you".

Dan was torn. He knew it was not safe or wise to travel on the open road. It would be especially difficult with winter just around the corner. Many roads, especially the main highways and the interstate system, had closed down, and once winter hit, few if any roads would remain open. Trees, slides or abandoned cars and trucks already blocked many roads. Rioters and looters roamed state highways and city streets. Desperate refugees clogged the highways. A road trip to North Dakota would be a dangerous gamble; perhaps the safest plan was to remain in their home.

"It's 1,900 miles to Peter and Judy's farm, and we can't expect to buy food or gasoline along the way," Dan warned. "I am not sure Peter would welcome us at his farm. I haven't talked to him since the first week after the blackout. For now I vote we stay."

Nora shook her head. "Well, I know that Peter and Judy would find room for us in that big farmhouse of theirs."

"And if not, we could live in the trailer," Keith added.

Dan stood by his decision. It was just too dangerous to make such a journey. Yet it wasn't long before circumstances forced him to change his mind.

A week after Dan decided against traveling to North Dakota, three men unsuccessfully tried to break into the Justin home while the family was away visiting friends. The thieves were unable to break into the house, because someone or something chased them off before they gained entry. It could have been Chester or the Justin family returning home that frightened the looters off. Someone had jimmied one of the bedroom windows and another thief tried to pry open the attached garage side door; but for whatever reason, the thieves had failed to get inside. Had they been successful, the family would have lost their stash of food, water, supplies and gasoline. They would not only be in dire straits, but such a loss would end any thoughts of escape from Santa Cruz. Dan and Nora thanked God the thieves had been unable to break in. Their next door neighbors did not fare as well. Thieves broke in and trashed the entire house, taking whatever they could carry off. They stole the neighbor's food, water, tools, and clothes. As a result, their neighbors now had nothing, so Judy shared with them what little her family could spare. Had the thieves discovered Dan's stock of freeze-dried foods, water and gasoline, the debate over escaping from California would be academic.

Dan knew that after the looters trashed their next door neighbors' house, it would be only a matter of time before robbers forced him to defend himself and his family. He didn't want to kill anyone, yet he vowed he'd shoot anyone who threatened his family. Most of the citizens of Santa Cruz were good, law abiding folks, but a few desperate people were acting like brigands. Mobs roamed downtown Santa Cruz and looters even broke into well-protected and guarded homes. Judy was still concerned about their friends Jim and Betty, who lived down the street. She insisted that Dan check in on them, so he went over to their house. The front door was ajar, and some household items lay on the front lawn. Inside the house, Jim and Betty were on the bedroom floor, each bound and shot: in a random and senseless murder. The murderers had then ransacked the house. Most disturbing, there was no sign of their two small children. Dan and Judy visited the police station and filed a report, but the police could do nothing except offer to see that the bodies were buried. The police had received so many missing persons reports that they wouldn't commit to conduct an investigation to find the children. The best they could offer was that the children were probably with some relative or friend.

The next day, some folks down the street shot a group of looters and then dragged them out into the street, where they remained to rot. Already people lay dead in the streets of Santa Cruz, and without services, their bodies began to rot in the gutters and alleyways. It was too terrible to describe. There was no honor among thieves as they began robbing and shooting one another. With almost no police protection, the criminals became more and more brazen and Santa Cruz was now a dog-eat-dog town, with everyone looking out for themselves. Dan kept his guns loaded and handy. This was no way to live.

The attempted break-in of their house and their friends' murder forced Dan to change his mind. The prolonged decision was made. It was time to get out of Dodge, while they still could. Dan gathered his family and spread road maps out on the kitchen table. They had enough gasoline stored to get out of California, and with a little luck, possibly all the way to Peter and Judy's farm. Even if they did not make it that far, small towns in Oregon, Idaho, or Montana would be a safer place to stay than Santa Cruz. They would avoid major roads and the interstate highway system.

Some years ago, Dan and Peter Dexter had hunted elk together in Idaho and Montana. As a result, Dan knew about the back roads in those states. Idaho and Montana were mostly rural states, populated with small farming and logging communities. Self-sufficient, conservative, and private described most residents of these states. Dan learned through his hunting trips that those folks wanted nothing more than for others to respect their private property. On one hunting trip to northern Idaho,

Dan and Peter knocked on a rancher's door to ask for permission to hunt on the man's ranch. The rancher stuck a two-barrel shotgun in their faces and told them to "git". They "got" as fast as they could.

Folks in rural states hadn't yet experienced the riots and mayhem as those residents of California and New York cities had. Small towns were more independent, self-sufficient, and more welcoming than the big cities. Rural folks did for themselves, and unlike city folk, they did not depend on others to provide for them. After years of living off handouts from the government, many inner-city folks were so dependent on government aid that they couldn't do for themselves. Generation after generation of government subsidies including welfare, food stamps, free medical care, and other support had taken a toll on urban incentive. Seventy percent of the citizens living in inner cities were dependent, in one form or another, on government handouts. When the infrastructure failed and free handouts ended, most city folk did not know how to survive. Many reverted to the only thing they knew: crime. A few hardy souls tried to make do, yet many others considered the answer was a life of looting and crime. Without the police or sheriff to stop them, criminals ran amok.

Rural folk were fundamentally different, and Judy and Peter were good examples of people who knew how to fend for themselves. After years of running their own farm, they could live without modern conveniences and knew how to depend on their own knowledge and abilities. If equipment or buildings on the farm broke down, Peter didn't call a handyman, he fixed it himself. If a farm animal needed medical attention, he didn't call the vet; he and Judy doctored the creature themselves. Judy never bought prepared foods from the store. She fixed all the family meals from scratch. Other than a few staples, the farm provided most of their needs: milk, cream and butter from their cows; eggs and meat from their chickens; pork from their pigs; wheat, corn and vegetables from the fields; everything they needed was on the farm. They learned survival from their farming neighbors, whose self-sufficiency had impressed Dan and Nora on their visits.

The Justin family debate had ended. Now the task was to prepare to leave. Dan welded a spare thirty-five gallon gas tank onto the truck and piped it into his fuel delivery system, and then filled both truck tanks with gasoline.

In addition, he filled two 15 gallon gas cans with another thirty gallons of fuel. Judy and Penny prepared enough supplies to last two weeks. Even if they didn't make it all the way to the Dexter farm, there were many places along the route where they could camp or small towns in which to stay.

On the maps of California, Oregon, Idaho, Montana, and North Dakota, Dan marked their route with a yellow pen: a route that would take them through five states and cover 1,900 miles. The plan was to avoid major highways and cities and keep mostly to back roads and county highways. They would drive east of Santa Cruz to central California, then north crossing over into Oregon, and then through Oregon to Idaho. The route continued north to Montana, then across northern Montana into North Dakota and Minot. Normally, such a trip should only take two or three days, but Dan figured that under the circumstances, it might take them several days or even a couple of weeks to make this trip.

Dan, Judy and Keith packed the F150 truck and trailer with clothes, camping gear, Dan's HAM radio and batteries, a chain saw, tools, guns, and enough dried food to last several weeks. The 18-foot Aristocrat Trailer would be their home for the next several days or even weeks if that is what it took. Nora packed items she thought critical for the family's survival. Dan expected they wouldn't be able to buy gasoline or food along the way, so they had to carry enough supplies to last them the entire two week trip. A pickup pulling a trailer and equipped with two thirty-five gallon gas tanks could travel almost 1,300 miles without refueling. However, they would need an extra thirty gallons of gasoline to make the entire 1,900 mile trip. Dan and Keith strapped the two fifteen gallon cans of gasoline to the back bumper of the trailer. They carried another five gallons in a small can inside the trailer. The truck got twenty miles a gallon on the open road, slightly less when pulling a trailer. Since it was unlikely they would be able to buy gasoline on the road, they hoped the 100 gallons would take them the full distance. Driving conservatively, they could stretch the range, and perhaps they would be able to buy a few extra gallons somewhere in Idaho. They filled the trailer water tank and one 15-gallon jug with water. The trailer's two 10-gallon propane tanks were full from a previous camping trip.

Dan carefully planned a route that would take them to North Dakota. The interstate highways were rumored to be the most dangerous, so his route would avoid them. Since the blackout, most state and county road departments had shut down, and rural road conditions across the nation were questionable at best. They could only pray the roads along the route Dan chose were open and would remain so throughout the next couple of weeks. They planned to inquire about local road conditions along the way; it was late in the summer, and their trip must be finished before the first heavy snowfalls closed the mountain passes. This would happen in late October or early November. No highway crews would be out to plow those roads, so they had to get through before the snow blocked them. Rumors of rock slides and washouts made travel on the highways across the Sierra Nevada dicey and were certain to be impassable after the first snowstorm hit. Dan chose an indirect route, one that depended on back roads and avoided the Sierra Nevada and its 7,500-foot passes. The radio reports claimed that the large cities were chaotic and closed to through traffic. The radio also reported the interstate highways were congested with refugees and mobs of frenzied looters. They were considered unsafe and it would be wise to entirely avoid them if possible. He avoided interstates and main highways, and marked the route along less traveled state and county secondary roads. His route was much longer than the Interstate across California, Nevada, Utah, Wyoming, Montana, into North Dakota. They couldn't depend on buying supplies along the way, so it was imperative that they carry extra supplies for a trip that could take two or three weeks.

*   *   *

Dan and his family left Santa Cruz on the morning of October 15, six weeks after the blackout began. As expected, landslides and abandoned autos and trucks blocked the main highway over the Santa Cruz Mountains to San Jose. Dan already decided to bypass the chaotic Bay Area, so he headed south on county roads through Watsonville and then east, bypassing Gilroy, to Interstate 5. The road from Watsonville to the outskirts of Gilroy was a mess. They drove around the rock slides and abandoned vehicles that blocked the narrow two-lane county road. Several times, Dan and Keith had to get out of their truck and clear rocks and tree branches from the road. A large tree blocked the road west of Gilroy. Dan used his chain saw to cut the tree into small logs, and then he and Keith pushed the rounds off the roadway. Even in normal times, few people used these back roads. Now with most cars and trucks out of gas, they only met two other cars along the mostly deserted road. The radio reported Interstate 5 was cluttered with refugees, abandoned cars, and other debris and some portions of the highway were impassable. Dan had to use this highway for a few miles, until it met a county road that would bypass Merced, Modesto, Stockton, and Sacramento. To Dan's amazement, the highway was open, clear of people and cars. Since it was a more direct route than the back roads, Dan decided to chance taking Interstate 5, at least until they came closer to Stockton. They only met a few cars plying the highway, all traveling south from Stockton, but as they got closer to the city they had to weave around folks using the highway as a foot path. The highway soon became choked with refugees trudging south along the highway in an ant-like procession, packs strapped to their backs and small children in hand. A few folks pushed or pulled carts or wagons loaded with all their worldly possessions. The inside lanes were empty, except for a smattering of bicycles and an occasional horse or mule drawn wagon piled high with household items. The picture reminded Dan of the roads in war-torn Vietnam, crowded with thousands of refugees carrying all their possessions on their backs or in overloaded ox carts and wagons.

"These refugees are escaping Stockton and Sacramento, much as we are escaping Santa Cruz," Dan commented. "We dare not drive through either of those cities. The reports warn everyone to stay away. There are no police or other law enforcement to keep the peace in those cities. People are shooting one another, and mobs roam the streets. If any of those looters suspected we had food and water, they will try to take it by force."

Dan detoured around Stockton and Sacramento, keeping to the county roads that skirted both cities, and arrived outside Yuba City later that afternoon. Refugees crowded the shoulders of the highway that led north from the capitol. As they drew closer to Yuba City, the crowds increased in size, eventually clogging both sides of the road intending to get away from Sacramento, away from the chaos. Dan locked the car doors, closed the windows, and used his horn to clear a path for his truck and trailer. He slowed down to a crawl but dared not stop. He knew that some of these folks might try to hitch a ride or climb onto the back of his pickup truck. People seemed surprised to see a truck and trailer moving along the highway, and only reluctantly moved aside. When a few men tried to climb into the back of the truck; Dan increased his speed so they could not do so. On the outskirts of Yuba City, an overturned tractor and trailer with a load of spilled onions blocked both sides of the highway. The accident forced Dan to drive on the shoulder. He honked the horn, yet people hiking along the shoulder only reluctantly moved aside and others deliberately stood their ground and tried to block the truck. To avoid running over one particularly stubborn man, Dan was forced to stop the truck. The minute he did so, four men tried to open the truck doors and three other men climbed into the bed of the truck. Another man climbed up onto the hood and began pounding his fists on the windshield. Nora screamed. Dan blasted the horn and sped through the crowd scattering people left and right.

"Dan . . . you are going to hit someone," Nora shrieked.

"I damn will if they don't get out of our way."

The three men in the bed of the truck pounded their fists on the top of the cab and on rear window. Terrified, Penny began to cry. Intent on breaking the windshield, the man on the hood lay spread-eagled, holding on to the windshield wiper with one hand and pounding his fist on the glass with the other.

Dan hit the brakes. The man flew off and tumbled into the barrow ditch next to the shoulder.

"He fell off.," Nora yelled, "stop and see if he's all right."

"No way in hell," Dan said. "If I stop, those people will be on us like fleas on a dog." Dan continued to blast the horn and dodge his way through the crowd.

"Stop the car," Nora screamed.

He ignored her. "She doesn't have the foggiest idea of how much danger we are in," Dan said under his breath. He knew these refugees were desperate and a mob will do things that individuals would never think of doing. Dan bumped into a man who was slower than the others to get out of the way. The man fell onto the shoulder only inches from the truck wheels. Dan didn't know if he was hurt or not, but he was not going to stop to find out.

"Stop . . . you hit him," Nora screamed. Dan kept on going, laying on the horn and dodging groups of people. Nora glared at him as if she were seeing her husband for the first time.

A large group of refugees crowded the shoulder immediately ahead. After they saw Dan almost run someone over, they jumped aside. Some people dove into the barrow ditch, while others ran onto the highway. As soon as the pickup was safely beyond the onion truck and wrecked trailer, Dan maneuvered his rig back onto the crowded roadway. People scattered as the truck accelerated. One man refused to step aside, pulled a gun from his waistband, and pointed it at the truck. Dan zigzagged, brushing the man aside before he could get a shot off. Meanwhile, the three men in the truck bed continued to pound on the rear window and then began to throw objects out of the truck bed.

"Dad, those guys in the back are throwing our stuff out of the truck," Keith cried.

Dan drove several hundred yards down the road, until he was clear of the mob, and stopped. He took his revolver out of the glove compartment, jumped out of the truck and pointed it at the men. They stopped pounding on the window and stared at Dan.

"Get out of my truck or you will be digging a bullet out of your body. The men didn't move, so Dan fired a warning shot intended to go over their heads but the bullet ricocheted off the truck cab with a loud twang.

All three men jumped off the truck and ran back down the highway toward the onion truck.
Dan ran down the highway and rescued his toolbox, a box of canned goods, and a suitcase the men had thrown out of the pickup. He threw the items back into the truck bed, climbed back in the cab, and stomped

on the gas peddle. Tires squealed as they drove down the highway toward Chico. Nora, more shocked than angry, silently shot daggers at Dan. Was this the same man she married all those years ago? She had never before seen Dan act like this. How could he show so little regard for these unfortunate people? She tried to say something, but words failed her. Dan ignored her cold stare and concentrated on the road.

Scott was the first to break the silence. "Dad, were you going to shoot those men?"

"You bet I was. It was either them or us. Nora, you and the kids have to realize that we have to protect ourselves. This is not a time for Christian charity. These people are desperate and will do anything to survive. They are insane with fear. You don't realize it, but a mob will do things no individual would ever think of doing. They will steal everything we have, and might even kill us or hurt the kids. I don't intend to give them that chance."

No one spoke for the next several minutes as they drove along side streets that avoided downtown Yuba City. Signs of rioting and looting were everywhere. Garbage and refuse littered the streets and glass from smashed storefront windows covered the sidewalks. Burned-out smoking car hulks and blackened brick buildings smoldered throughout the town. Nora gasped when she saw a dead body crumpled like a rag doll in the street with a horde of flies buzzing around his bloodied head. Dan drove down another side street, where the dead bodies of men and women cluttered the sidewalks. Nora looked away and Dan averted his children's gaze from the dead bodies by calling attention to a deserted Burger King restaurant on one corner. The city seemed abandoned; no one was on the streets and theirs was the only vehicle moving through town.

Outside Yuba City, more crowds of folks heading north clogged the road, yet in a few miles the heavy foot traffic began to thin out. As they neared Chico, fewer and fewer folks walked or pulled carts along the road. The foot traffic disappeared altogether at the city limits.

Dan was reluctant to drive into Chico, yet since the main highway went through downtown and he was unfamiliar with the farm roads that skirted the city, he had no choice but to drive through as quickly as possible. Considering the growing mayhem south of here, the city of Chico seemed unusually tranquil and orderly. A few citizens walked along the downtown sidewalks. No abandoned cars, garbage, or dead people cluttered the streets as they had in Yuba City. No one tried to stop them or even wave to them as they sped through town. Walnut trees and irrigation ditches lined the highway north of Chico as it coursed through fields of yellowing cornstalks interspersed with flooded rice fields.

Twenty miles north of the city, they came to a small roadside RV park and gas station. A large "CLOSED" sign blocked the entrance to the Richfield gas station. A relic of bygone years, the abandoned station was complete with a service bay, lift, and rusting signs that advertised Valveoline oil and Goodyear tires. Three lone sentinels, old glass top pumps, guarded the service island, and a hand-painted sign reading "NO GAS TODAY" leaned against a flatbed truck parked in the service island.

"No gas today or any other day," Dan mused.

Across the street from the station an overhead sign announced "CHARLIE'S RV PARK".

It had been a long, nerve-racking day. Everyone was tired and begged to stop for the night. Dan pulled his rig into the entrance to the RV park and got out of the truck to have a look around. The park was empty; not a single tent, trailer, or RV was in any of the spaces. Eerily quiet and with no one around, the place seemed abandoned. Yet it appeared neat and clean, so he assumed someone must be around to take care of the place. He walked over to the small building at the park entrance to register. The office was empty. A note pinned to door read:

Everyone is invited to stay in the park without charge.
Sorry there is no water or electricity.
Please respect this park and treat it as private property.
Take your refuse with you when you leave.
Charlie Jones, manager

He wrote his name in the register and then pulled his rig into a pull-through space at the back of the park, where a stand of Aspen trees hide them from the main highway. He left the trailer hitched to the truck, in case they needed to make a quick get-away. It made Dan edgy to stay in an empty trailer park, with no other folks around and an advancing mob of refugees only thirty miles away. Nevertheless, this park seemed safer than simply pulling off the main road or camping on a side road. Besides, the mob probably would not make it this far until the next day. He didn't want to worry Nora or the kids, so while still outside he loaded his rifle and shotgun, and then locked them in the truck. Keith watched him load the guns and asked why he had locked them in the truck. Dan claimed it was just a precaution.

After a dinner of canned hash covered with fried eggs, Nora the kids climbed into their bunks and fell fast asleep. Sleep did not come that easy for Dan. He remained wakeful throughout the night and kept a loaded handgun under his pillow. Chester curled up on the floor, beneath Dan and Nora's bunk. Even the slightest outside noise caused the dog to raise his head and perk up his ears. In the middle of the night, he growled softly. Dan fingered the handgun ready to snap into action should someone try to break in. He heard nothing but realized that dogs can hear sounds that humans cannot. He lay still and strained to listen for the sounds that had disturbed Chester. After a few minutes, Chester buried his head in his legs and went back to sleep. Dan remained awake all night. At the first sign of dawn, he opened the trailer door and took a short walk over to the Aspen grove. Chester followed on his heels. Dan unzipped his trousers and Chester lifted a leg and they both and began to water the grass.

"Hey, fellow . . . !"

Dan spun around and peed on his boot. Chester stood his ground and barked. A grizzled old man in overalls, a red shirt and straw hat stood not ten feet away. At that moment, Dan realized he had left his handgun in the trailer and his other guns were locked in the truck.

"Good . . . good morning," Dan sputtered as he zipped up his trousers.

He grabbed Chester by the collar and told him to quiet down.

"Welcome to Charlie's Park," the man muttered, looking down at Dan's wet boot. "Ya pissed on yer boot," he said, half laughing.

"You startled me. I signed in on the register last night, but no one was around to take my money."

"Well, like the sign says, there's no charge." The man said, extending an open hand. "The name's Charlie."

"You keep a well maintained park," Dan said, as he shook the man's extended hand. Charlie pumped Dan's hand like he was working the handle of a well pump.

"Well, it's all I can do nowadays. Not much for me to clean, you folks being the first guests I've had for nary on a week now."

Dan and Charlie chatted for a while, until Nora and the kids stepped outside the trailer.

Dan took Charlie over to the trailer and introduced his family.

Charlie tipped his hat to Nora, then looking back at Dan said, "You'll wanna be careful 'bout those folks out on the highway. I heard tell they are a desperate, mean bunch of sons-o'-bitches. Some would sooner slice your ears off than talk with you."

"Yes," Dan agreed, "we ran into a bunch of refugees yesterday, about five miles south of Yuba City. They gave us a bit of trouble. They'll probably be here in a day or two."

Charlie looked at the California license plate, with its Santa Cruz Ford frame.

"I see from your plates and the register you signed you are from Santa Cruz. Where are you heading"

"North Dakota," Dan answered.

"North Dakota you say," Charlie repeated and uttered a long whistle. "That's a long way from here. I don't think you can make it all that far."

"Why not?"

"Well, I heard talk on the radio that those roads north of Redding are closed, blocked by landslides, abandoned cars, butchered cows and other such crap," Charlie explained.

Dan frowned. "I thought we would go through Alturas and follow Highway 395 to Burns, then east from there. Hear anything about those roads?"

"Nope, but I expect they'd have similar problems," Charlie warned. "Some folks in Oregon are hungry and the hungrier they get, the nuttier they act. There's no law enforcement around to stop 'em neither. I heard the National Guard is keeping the peace in Idaho and Montana, so if you folks can get that far, you might have a better chance to get all the way to North Dakota. There's a back road north of Alturas that runs across Nevada and Oregon into Idaho. Look for signs to Adel and Highway 140, just north of Lakeview. The road mostly crosses open desert and dry lakes and then winds through the mountains. Ain't many folks liv'in there and those few that do aren't inclined to mess with you, providing you don't mess with them."

Dan thanked Charlie for his hospitality and advice. After breakfast, he raised the trailer jacks, and then headed his rig north, avoiding the main Highway Interstate 5. At Red Bluff, he took a roundabout northeast route, bypassing Redding by driving through Mt. Lassen National Park to Susanville, then north through Alturas and into Oregon. All the roads from Chico north and east of Red Bluff were open, with only an occasional abandoned truck or car cluttering the highway. In some places, landslides or fallen trees narrowed the road to a single lane, yet Dan was able to maneuver his rig around these few obstacles.

They met only two other cars along the way. It was customary that whenever cars driving on lonely roads met, both drivers would stop and exchange information about the road ahead. Both times, they stopped and exchanged information with the other drivers who said the roads ahead were clear. Dan told them about the roads he had just traveled. "Where y'all headed," a man asked. When Dan said North Dakota, he shook his head and said "no way" or something to that effect. "You won't find any gas for sale, and many main roads between here and there are blocked." Dan ignored the warnings and drove to the next stop at Lakeview, north of Alturas, where he intended to ask about the local roads into Idaho.

CHAPTER EIGHT:
HART MOUNTAIN

As in Chico, Lakeview looked peaceful and tidy. Main Street was clean, uncluttered, and deserted except for a young couple strolling unconcerned down the sidewalk. They didn't meet another car until they saw one driving out of the large parking lot at the end of the street. The lot was filled with hundreds of cars and trucks parked side by side and arranged in neat, orderly rows. Dan stopped at a small coffee shop, located the road split into westbound and northbound highways. As he entered the shop, his mouth watered from the delicious aroma of bacon and fresh coffee that permeated the restaurant. A portly woman stood over a wood stove, carefully filling coffee cups from a large pot that had been perking on top of the stove. He walked over to a booth where half a dozen ranchers sat sipping steaming cups of coffee. He introduced himself and asked about U.S. Highway 395 to Burns

"Ya might not wa'na go to Burns," one man warned in a throaty voice. Dressed in a red-plaid shirt, greasy overalls, and wearing a weather-beaten Stetson, the man's unshaven face and gray handlebar mustache completed his rancher persona. As he took another noisy sip of coffee, Dan noticed the cup shook slightly in hands, hands tanned and marked by deep folds and calluses, attesting to many years of hard fieldwork. He lowered his coffee cup, and squinted at Dan through tinted glasses, as if to judge if the stranger was friend or foe. Finally he put the coffee cup down and croaked, "Heard tell Burns is a dangerous place nowadays. Those folks up there are plain nuts; a bunch of real loonies. Well . . . it don't matter. Ya can't get there from here anyhow 'cause the road's washed out." Nodding toward a man wearing a maroon Washington State University baseball cap, he continued, "and as far as old Orin here tells me, it'll prob'ly stay washed out until the road department hires their crew back."

Orin looked up from his breakfast and added, "Yep, Pete's right. The road's closed and it's gon'na stay that way. It be closed for two weeks now . . . ya can't get to Burns on Highway 395."

Dan smiled . . . warily.

"I didn't intend to go to Burns; but it's on our way to Idaho. How about Highway 140? Is it clear all the way to where it meets Highway 95 in Nevada?"

"Yep, heard tell it is," a third customer offered. His portly body, baggy brown pants held in place by red suspenders, shiny bald head, twinkling eyes, and full white beard made him look like a rancher's version of Santa Claus. "But, I heard tell they closed Highway 95 into Idaho between Jordan Valley and the Idaho border. You shouldn't go that way neither."

The man cleared his throat and continued. "Best ya take east U.S. 140 outside Lakeview, and follow the county road that goes through Plush and the Hart Mountain Antelope Refuge. After Plush, follow the signs to Frenchglen and Malheur Lake. The road also goes to Burns, but Pete's right, I wouldn't be goin' there if I were you . . . unless yous got a death wish," he warned with a nod of his bald head.

Santa Claus took another noisy slurp of coffee and then leaned in toward Dan and said in a hushed voice, "I drove up there last week and Burns was in shambles. Garbage, dead animals, and abandoned cars everywhere, and streets full of litter. Glass from broken storefront windows and crap was strewn all over the sidewalks and streets. I even saw a man's body lying in a side street. The crazies took over that city two weeks ago. I was lucky to get out of that place with my life."

"Well, we don't intend to go to Burns if we can avoid it," Dan repeated. "Have you heard if Highway 20 from Burns to Boise is open?"

Orin eyed Dan suspiciously.

"One of our breakfast bunch said he went to Boise on that road last week. He ain't here today, but if he was he'd tell you Boise is as bad off as Burns.

He claimed he was fortunate to escape that city with his wallet and shirt. Why do you want to go to Boise anyway?"

"Just passing through Idaho on our way northeast," Dan answered.

"Northeast . . . where to?" the man persisted.

"North Dakota."

On hearing that, Pete let out a long, slow whistle. "That's a fair piece from here. I hear most of dem roads up der is either closed or blocked, and even if not blocked, dey will be as soon as der snow flies. And when the snow flies in dese parts, it gets deep . . . real fast like. You can't buy gasoline or food anywhere along the way . . . least not that I heard of." Pete took off his tinted glasses and squinted at Dan as if staring into bright sunlight. Dan thought this gesture must be out of habit, for the room was only dimly lit by the storefront street window on the opposite side of the restaurant.

After a few seconds Pete asked, "Ya got a good Oregon map on you?"

Dan shook his head no.

"Well then, I think I can help ya," he offered.

He walked over to the counter, reached behind it and brought back a road map and spread it out on a table, close to the window. With his nicotine-stained index finger, he shakily traced the route to Frenchglen and Burns.

"Don't take the road all the way into Burns," he repeated. "After Frenchglen, follow the county road to New Princeton, and at the town of Crane, follow the signs to Juntura and Highway 20 east. Those roads are open, leastwise as far as I know, and the Indians up there are a friendly bunch but I'd not mess with them if I were you." He folded the map and handed it to Dan.

"The woman behind the counter says you can keep it."

"Thanks much for the advice and the Oregon map," Dan said, with a nod to the woman behind the counter.

"Well, now you've got one," she shot back. "I sure as hell don't need it any more. I'd be out of my mind to go anywhere on those roads."

"Why are towns like Lakeview and Alturas calm and peaceful, and Burns and Boise so chaotic?" Dan asked. The breakfast bunch snickered in unison.

Orin took off his WSU cap and squinted at Dan through hazel eyes narrowed by years working in bright sunlit fields. With half a smile, he said, "Well, hell fella, those folks in Burns are just plain crazy . . . always thought they were one fencepost short of a whole coral. Now they've gone out of their way to prove it. I heard tell the folks in all those big cities in Idaho are just as wacky. If I were you, I'd avoid all of them . . . from Ontario to Boise to Lewiston."

Dan thanked the men for their friendly advice and left the café. He gave the map to Nora and drove north a few miles to the junction of Highway 140, which led east. The road climbed out of the valley and wound into mountains forested with juniper and stunted pine trees. After a steep climb, the truck tumbled onto a high desert mesa peppered by sage brush and speckled with an occasional lone juniper tree. After a few miles, a weathered sign pointed to a gravel road leading to the town of Plush. A fifteen mile drive on the washboard road took them to the edge of town, which reminded Dan of one of those hamlets featured in a Spaghetti Western movie. Hitching posts and warped plank sidewalks lined the main street ruled by a dozen false front buildings. Plush seemed like a ghost town, with no sign of man or beast. A large whitewashed building, with a covered front porch, stretched along the west side of the street and displayed a large faded sign suspended by chains from the main-beam that read:

Plush Mercantile.
Groceries, Tobacco, Hardware and Liquor

The store appeared closed, but then Dan noticed a box of watermelons and a few sacks of dog food stacked on the porch. On the double-wide front door, a smaller sign read:

Open seven days a week, 7 to 7

Dan parked in front of the store with the intention to ask if he could buy a few groceries, but he thought better of it when two rough looking ranchers came out of the store and threw an unfriendly stare his way.

"These folks do not look very friendly," Nora commented.
"It's all right," Dan said, "I'm not going in. They most likely wouldn't sell food to us anyway."

Tumbleweeds rolled down the street, pushed forward by a small dust devil that entered from the opposite end of town. Dan waited in front of the store for the dust devil to pass by. The miniature whirlwind violently pitched the Plush Mercantile sign to and fro and rocked Dan's truck as it slid down the street, flinging papers and dust high into the air. The sign threatened to tear away from its chains, but gradually settled down. Dan waited for the dust devil to finish its business in town and then drove through Plush, continuing down the severely washboarded and rutted road that led to a sign announcing the boundary of the Hart Mountain Antelope Refuge. Once through the entrance flanked on each side by a rock pillar, Dan followed the gravel road, surrounded by an expansive desert peppered with sage brush. Not a tree, building, fence, windmill, or any sign of humans graced the desolate tract. They made good time on the well maintained gravel road, complete with culverts and side ditches to prevent washouts. A few miles into the refuge they came to a sign nailed to a sawhorse blocking the road.

"WASHOUT . . . ROAD CLOSED"

A hand-lettered "DETOUR" sign nailed to a fencepost pointed to a nearby dirt side road. Dan tightened his grip on the steering wheel and drove down the dusty side road marked only by the detour sign. A far cry from the well maintained main road, the bumpy road led across a rocky flatland. Dan slowed to 15 miles per hour, and even at that speed, the truck kicked copious clouds of red dust into the desert as it bounced across ruts and potholes. After a few miles, the so called "detour" deteriorated into nothing more than a rock-strewn trail marked by two ruts and bordered by sagging lines of barbed wire loosely held off the ground by leaning fenceposts.

"This can't be the road to Frenchglen" Nora said, as she looked at the map in her lap and held onto the door handle. "The map doesn't show this road, and it doesn't look like it has been bladed since last spring . . . if even then."

Dan said that he hadn't seen any other road leading from the detour sign and with the main road washed out this must be the only other road to Frenchglen.

"Anyway," he said, "What else should you expect from a detour except dust, ruts and rocks?"

Nora wanted him to turn around, yet the narrow road offered no turnouts that would allow them to turn around without jackknifing the trailer. They drove several more bumpy miles, before coming to a potential turnout and the first sign of human habitation. Perched on top of a small knoll, a lonely farmhouse and barn overlooked the recently plowed acres wrestled from the sagebrush-covered desert. Nora suggested they use the farm driveway to turn around, but Dan had visions of a rancher greeting them with a shotgun, so he didn't drive into the farm. A couple of miles further on down the road, Nora spotted a wide turnout shaded by a grove of Aspen and Birch trees.

"That might be a good place to turn around," she suggested.

As they came closer, a station wagon and silver trailer parked under the trees appeared through the pall of dust. The opened hood of the car signaled an automobile in trouble. Dan parked his rig a few feet into the turnoff and then walked over to the trailer. The trailer door opened and a man pointed a shotgun at Dan's belly.

"Git," the man shouted as he waved the shotgun at Dan.

Dan stopped dead in his tracks. Miles from the nearest civilization one didn't argue with a man holding a shotgun. Dan offered an explanation.

"Hey . . . don't shoot . . . . it's okay," Dan shouted. "We just wanted to see if you needed any help."

When the man saw Nora and Penny climb out of the truck, followed by Keith and Scott, he lowered his shotgun, but kept it cocked. He must have thought a man with a family was unlikely to be dangerous, yet wary he kept the gun cocked. Chester jumped out of the car, spotted a jackrabbit in the ditch beside the road and bounded off into a field of sagebrush as the rabbit ran for his life.

"Sorry about the gun," the man finally apologized, as Dan's family joined him, "you just can't be too careful way out here in the middle of nowhere."

Everyone stood awkwardly frozen in place for a few seconds, until the man engaged the safety and stood the shotgun against the trailer. Walking away from the trailer, he offered Dan his hand.

"The name is Martin Sorrel," he said, "and this is my wife, June." A young woman carrying an infant strapped in a harness stepped out of the trailer, followed by a towheaded boy, three or four years old.

Dan took the man's hand and introduced himself. "Dan . . . Dan Justin. This is my wife, Nora, and my kids Keith, Scott, and Penny. If there is anything we can do to help, just ask," as he shook Martin's hand.

Martin beamed a broad, relaxed smile.

"Well now, if you have any extra gasoline, we'd sure appreciate it. We've been stuck out here since the old gas-guzzler ran dry three days ago. We're short on food and have no milk for the baby. As well as being out of gas, something is wrong with my car."

Dan was reluctant to give a stranger some of his precious gasoline, yet he could not refuse this needy family. He walked back to his trailer and wrestled the spare five-gallon gas can out of a side locker.

"Where are you folks heading," Dan asked, as he handed the can to Martin.

"Lakeview," Martin explained. "The wife has relatives there. We left our home in Burns a week ago. It's just crazy there . . . in Burns I mean. People are ransacking stores and breaking into each other's homes. Dead people line the streets and no one is even trying to bury them. Things got so bad in Burns that we decided to leave and take our chances out on the road. The folks in Frenchglen told us a washout had closed the main road to Plush, so we took this terrible detour, a much longer drive than the main road from Frenchglen to Plush. This is far as we got before the car ran out of gas."

"Well, you're just about 20 miles from Plush and another 40 miles or so to Lakeview. A few gallons should be more than enough to get you to Lakeview," Dan suggested.

"I'll have to fix my car first," Martin objected.

"What's wrong with the car?" Dan asked.

"I don't know, but it started acting up after we hit a rock a few miles back. It keeps pulling to the left and the differential makes grinding sounds."

"Well, I'm not a mechanic but perhaps I can have a look at it later," Dan suggested.

The baby cried and squirmed in June's arms, as she introduced herself to Nora.

"Why don't you and your family come inside and sit a spell," June offered.

Nora and the kids piled into Martin's trailer, scooting around the dining table seats to make room for everyone. Dan remained outside and talked with Martin. Nora and the kids sat around the table as June gave each a glass of water.

"Sorry, but all I can offer is water," June apologized. The baby continued to cry and Penny asked the baby's name. June smiled and said they called him Pepper, although his given name was Jonathan.

"We can offer you folks some food," Nora suggested, "but not very much. We are trying to get all the way to North Dakota and barely have enough for the trip."

"We would appreciate any amount you can afford," June said. "Especially milk," she added.

"I'm sorry, but we don't have any milk," Nora said.

Dan remained outside, talking with Martin, who reached out and rubbed the towheaded boy's head. "This is my other son, Bart." Bart formed a shy smile and then hid behind his father's leg.

"Do you have a rifle?" Martin inquired.

Dan looked puzzled. "Yes, I do. Why do you ask?"

"I saw a herd of antelope drinking at the pond up the road a piece yesterday. I can't hunt antelope with a shotgun. Perhaps you could shoot one. An animal like that would provide food for both families."

Dan didn't answer and changed the subject. The idea of guns and shooting animals made him nervous. He took out his road map and spread it out on the table. "This unmarked detour we've been following is about here," Dan said, as he traced a phantom line on the map

"Well, this is the detour all right," Martin said. "For most of the way, it is little more than two ruts across the desert, though with the main road closed, it's the only way to get from Frenchglen to Plush. The folks in

Frenchglen told us that a washout made the main road impassable. One of the culverts, choked full of sagebrush, caused the creek to overflow and took out both the culvert and the road. The county laid off the road crew a month ago, so there's no one around to fix the road."

"How bad is the road ahead and how far is it to Frenchglen?" Dan asked.

Martin scowled. "Well sir, towing your trailer will be a problem. The road was passable three days ago when we came through, but you folks are the first car we've seen while camping here. The road is rough: mostly washboard and filled with rocks. It's almost impassable in several places. Two weeks ago, a flash flood washed over the road and there is a large creek you will have to ford. The road will take you around Beaty's Butte to the hamlet of Berdugo, just a few miles south of Frenchglen. It's about 85 miles to Frenchglen from here."

His brow wrinkled. "I think the rough road damaged our station wagon. Unless you can help me fix it, I'm not sure we can make it to Lakeview, even with your gas."

"Like I said, I'm not a mechanic, but I'll have a look in the morning," Dan offered. "If it's okay with you, we will camp here beside your trailer for the night."

Chester ran from the field with a dead jackrabbit in his mouth and dropped the unfortunate animal at Dan's feet. Dan patted Chester and thanked him for his generous offer, but Jackrabbit was not on tonight's menu. He gave the rabbit back to Chester. It was good that Chester hunted his own food, for only a single bag of dog kibble remained in the trailer.

Martin directed Dan's rig to a flat parking spot under the trees, a few yards away from his own trailer. Dan pulled his trailer into the spot, unhitched it from the truck, and set the stabilizer jacks. Nora reminded Dan that they needed water. A small creek ran out of the field behind the Aspen trees and passed through a culvert pipe under the road and into a field opposite the turnout. Dan assigned Keith and Scott the task of filling the trailer water tank. Keith carried several full buckets to the trailer, yet after delivering only one bucket, Scott wandered off down the road, leaving the task to Keith. Dan noticed Keith working alone and asked him where Scott was. Keith shrugged his shoulders and pointed to the road. Dan hiked a quarter mile down the road and found Scott sitting alongside a pond, watching a flock of geese.

"Scott," Dan hollered, "Why aren't you helping your brother like I asked?"

Scott jumped to his feet and the startled geese took to the air.

"Well . . . Keith was doing just fine by himself," Scott whined.

Dan took his son by the arm and marched him back to the trailer.

"Keith, you can stop getting water. Scott will finish the job."

Scott gave his brother a dirty look as he grabbed the bucket and trudged off to the creek.

Nora and June had become instant friends. As they chatted, June's one-month-old baby cried constantly, yet June was unable to comfort him.

"He's really hungry," June said remorsefully. "We ran out of milk yesterday and I have been unable to nurse him."

"I'm so sorry that we don't have some," Nora said.

"Mom, I saw some goats in that farm we passed a couple of miles back," Penny offered. "Maybe Dad could milk one of them."

Nora smiled. "Penny, do you know how to milk a goat?"

"I saw a guy do it on the Survivor TV show one time," Penny said. "It didn't look too difficult."

"Well, it would be easier to have Dad ask the farmer for some milk," Nora said.

Nora asked Dan if he would drive down to the farm and ask for some milk for Pepper and he agreed to do so. He placed a bucket in the truck and drove with Penny and Martin to the farm. A sign announcing "The Wilson's" hung from a log archway over the driveway. A large red barn dominated the crest of a small rise a hundred yards down the gravel driveway. West of the barn stood a weathered two-story clapboard house and separate three-car garage. Both buildings were in sorry need of a fresh coat of paint. A spreading oak tree shaded the house from the noonday sun and a single-seat swing hung from one of its large branches. A sandbox sat under the tree and a toddler's tricycle upside-down in the box indicated children lived here. Dan and Martin walked to the house as a few chickens and a rooster scattered before them. They climbed the few squeaky front steps that led to the covered and screened front porch. Martin opened the screen door and knocked several times, yet no one answered his persistent raps. Dan climbed down from the porch and peeked inside the three-car garage. It housed a John Deer tractor and a truck, but no car. Apparently, the family had gone into town for the day. Several cows grazed in a field behind the house and a few recently plowed acres looked ready for winter wheat. A well-kept corral with three horses and a fenced yard with a dozen grazing goats and two Alpacas were situated next to the barn. Upon seeing the goats, Martin suggested they could milk one of them.

"Well, I am sure that under the circumstances, the Wilson family wouldn't mind if we milked one of their goats," Dan assumed. "Do you know how to milk a goat?" he asked.

"No, I thought you did. I don't even know how to tell a she-goat from a Billy goat," Martin admitted, with an impish smile.

Dan shrugged his shoulders.

"Wouldn't the female goat be the ones without horns?" Penny asked.

"Perhaps, but all six of these goats have horns," Dan observed.

Penny made an obvious suggestion. "Look for teats. Try the one with the spike horns."

Dan looked under the goat and discovered an udder and teats.

"This one's a mama," he announced.

Penny placed her bucket under the she-goat and sat on a stump as Martin positioned himself in front of the animal and held on to its head by the horns. She squeezed on the teats and watery milk squirted into the bucket. After five minutes, the bucket was one-third full, enough milk to feed the hungry baby and then some. Meanwhile, Dan went into the shed beside the barn and raided the henhouse, stuffing a dozen fresh laid brown eggs into a sack.

When they returned to the trailers, June poured the warm milk into a bottle and stuck it into Pepper's mouth. Pepper stopped crying and sucked the bottle dry. After a burp louder than one Dan could conjure after a beer, he smiled for the first time since Dan and his family arrived.

Penny was especially taken with Pepper, and offered to watch him so June could rest. She suffered from post-partum exhaustion, and she appreciated Penny's offer. Over the next two days, Penny spent most of her free time playing with Pepper, while June caught up on her sleep. Penny had a way with small children and babies. Back in Santa Cruz, she baby-sat for their neighbors' six-month-old baby and four-year-old boy. She also volunteered to help at the day care nursery run by Nora's friend, Janice. Janice marveled at how good Penny was with the children, reading books and playing games with them. Janice had told Nora that she was lucky to have such a responsible and dedicated daughter.

"It might not be such a bad idea to stay around here for a day or two," Dan had suggested to Nora. "I could help Martin fix his car and perhaps even shoot and butcher an antelope. We have enough food for two weeks and there is clean water here. Chester can hunt rabbits and you could even take a bath across the road where the creek spills into a cistern. As long as we get to North Dakota before snow closes the roads in early November, we can take our time."

Nora agreed, and so they would stay another day or two. That evening before the sun set, Martin and Dan prepared to go antelope hunting.

Martin told Dan that each evening a herd came to drink from a small pond a few hundred yards down the road from their camp, and suggested that would be a good spot to wait. Dan tied Chester to a tree so he would not follow them and spook the antelope.

Before the sun touched the horizon, Dan and Martin trudged down the road and hid behind a few tule bushes, twenty yards downwind from the pond. The pond was small, partially filling a shallow depression only thirty yards across. A gentle wind ruffled the water and formed an opening across the duckweed and algae-choked surface. A pair of ducks spied the open water and after plashing onto the pond, began diving for small fish. The men sat on the damp ground and waited in the bushes for the antelope to appear. The sun turned the sky and desert crimson as it disappeared over the western hills. The wind died and except for the muffled sound of quacking ducks, the pond and desert beyond grew silent.

Dan noticed movement on a ridge a few hundred yards to the west of the pond. A few seconds later, a herd of a dozen antelope appeared over the ridge and then cautiously climbed down to the pond. Small canine prints around the pond suggested coyotes were occasional visitors, so the antelopes, nervously sniffing the wind, remained ready to run at the slightest hint of danger. The largest animal warily tiptoed to the pond, looked around, and seeing no evidence of danger, put his head down and drank. When he finished, the rest of the herd crowded around the muddy shoreline and took their turn to drink. Although a quarter-mile away, Chester smelled the antelope and began to bark. In unison, the entire herd immediately jerked their heads up from the pond and even before Dan had time to aim his rifle the herd scampered up the bank and stampeded into the desert. Dan uttered a curse and blamed himself for not locking Chester inside the trailer. "We'll try again tomorrow," Dan promised, "and next time I'll make sure Chester can't spook them."

The men returned to camp and gathered their families around a fire ring for the evening campfire. Bathed by flickering flames, they listened on their radio to the nightly news from KGO, in San Francisco. The station broadcasted news twice each day, for a half hour at noon and 8 p.m. The radio reports from San Francisco were disturbing. Two weeks after the blackout, fuel depots and trucks began running out of gasoline and diesel.

Although the local warehouses still had supplies, delivery trucks could not deliver them to stores in the city or on the Peninsula. A train wreck on the Southern Pacific line in San Mateo had blocked the tracks and the track clearing equipment was busy keeping the line open in the Sierras. Freight trains remained stuck in the San Jose yards and could not haul goods to the distribution centers in the city, and even if they did, there was no way to deliver goods.

Panicked San Franciscans soon emptied the store shelves, so the Mayor ordered the local warehouses to open to the public on Wednesdays. The news spread fast, and at dawn, Wednesday, people began gathering outside the main warehouse near Hunters Point. A few on duty police tried to keep order but were unable to control the growing crowd. Pushing and shoving soon escalated into fistfights, and gunshots rang out. The crowd panicked and stampeded into the street, trampling several people in their panic. When the warehouse doors finally opened at 8 a.m., the crowd stormed the building, grabbing whatever they could carry. It was pure mayhem. Before ten, the warehouse was empty and the crowd scattered.

Because of the shortage of gasoline, two weeks into the blackout, car and truck owners had begun abandoning their autos on streets, lots, driveways, and highways, wherever their vehicle happened to be when it ran out of fuel. Within the first month of the blackout, people parked cars and trucks anywhere, blocking the streets. Street thugs set many on fire. A month after the power outage, the city's water system, sewage, hospitals, and other civic services and emergency responders could no longer provide services. Empty buses and streetcars littered the streets or remained parked in their yards. Because people could not get to work, most businesses and factories had closed their doors. Schools and colleges also shut down. Out of fuel, San Francisco police cars, fire trucks, and ambulances were parked. Without fire protection, blazes ravaged parts of the city, especially in the avenues where homes and apartments were built next to each other. Even if the fire trucks had been able to reach a home or business fire, the water hydrants were dry. Without water, there was no way to control fires.

The multitude of homeless grew larger and many people camped out in city parks and parking lots. Garbage trucks no longer could make their rounds, so garbage, refuse and sewage littered the streets. Since the coroner was unable to gather dead bodies, corpses rotted in the streets and alleys. Without police protection, mobs roamed the city, stealing whatever items they could pilfer. Theft, rape and murder became rampant. Citizens became virtual prisoners in their own homes. It was unsafe for anyone to be out on the streets.

By the fifth week, the rule of law became "every-man-for-himself". Based on basic survival instincts, people devised their own laws. The strong preyed on the weak and lawlessness prevailed in the city. As food and water became increasingly scarce, gangs of thieves raided private homes, killed whoever got in their way, and looted everything not nailed down or locked away. Some home and business owners shot looters on sight, but many homeowners fled and looters rampaged through their homes and made off with whatever they could carry. In the sixth week of the blackout, the Mayor of San Francisco finally ordered the California National Guard into the city, with instructions to restore law and order and quell the mayhem that had erupted into outright anarchy. After two days, the National Guard formed some semblance of law and order to parts of the city, including Chinatown, the Avenues, and Pacific Heights. Thieves and looters still roamed unchallenged on many downtown streets, yet there was little left for them to loot.

Since it was unsafe for citizens to leave their homes, the city became a community of shut-ins. Those walking on streets of San Francisco were apt to be robbed, raped or shot. Those who still could live in their homes were among the more fortunate of San Franciscans. Thousands of others made homeless by the fires or looters found shelter in churches and public buildings. The city opened office buildings and hotels in downtown San Francisco for emergency shelters. The thousands of refugees fled to the Presidio or Golden Gate Park, where the army had erected tent cities; potable water, food, and sanitation were the main issues. Everything from tents to tarps to packing crates served as shelter from the constant San Francisco fall drizzle. Fortunately, with their experience in providing shelter in other countries wracked by disaster, the army had the necessary experience to raise and maintain a tent city.

The radio news reports did not give the impression that things would improve in the near future. A spokesperson from PG&E claimed that it would take a year to restore electric power to the city, and the National Guard had been unable to police the entire city. Reminiscent of the aftermath of the1906 earthquake, there was nothing to stop the flames from advancing across the city. San Francisco burned and people fled down the peninsula.

Dan tuned the radio to another clear channel AM station in Boise, Idaho to listen to the local road report. The Boise news was as disheartening as that from San Francisco. Many roads and streets in the capitol city were blocked by abandoned vehicles, accidents, and other debris. Mobs roamed downtown streets, as well as surrounding state and federal highways. Muggers barricaded the interstate highway, stopping the rare car that still plied the road. Occupants would be dragged outside, beaten, and then robbed. Dan congratulated himself for planning a route that avoided the interstate system and other major highways. He knew they would be unsafe, especially for a pickup truck dragging a trailer behind it. His original plan was to drive to Boise, where rumor had it he could find gasoline for sale, then drive north on Highways 21, 75 and U.S. 93 to Missoula, Great Falls, and then on to Havre, Montana, and follow U.S. Highway 2 to Minot. On hearing the bad news from Boise, he spread his maps out on the table and traced a new route from Hart Mountain to North Dakota, one that avoided the interstate highways and Boise. The revised plan would take them through Ontario, Oregon, then north through Idaho on U.S. 95, east on U.S. 12 to Missoula, then to north Havre and U.S. Highway 2 to Minot.

After eating breakfast the next morning, Dan crawled under Martin's car to have a look at his undercarriage. It took only a few minutes to decide that he could not repair it.

"Martin, I have some bad news," Dan began, as he shook his head. "You said the sedan was difficult to steer, and I now know why. Your left front steering-rod is bent. I can remove it and bend it back into shape so that you can maneuver, but I think you have a bigger problem than the rod. That grinding sound you heard is coming from your rear differential. You must have hit a rock, which cracked the rear differential housing and caused lubricant to leak out. Some of the gears are badly damaged. There is no way I can fix the differential. I can fix the bent rod, patch the cracked differential and lubricate it with a bit of grease I have with me. With these temporary fixes, you can drive to Lakeview, but there is no way you can pull your trailer over these roads and down the steep mountain grade to Lakeview."

"I was afraid you might say that," Martin said with a sigh. "You should take care that the same misfortune does not happen to you when you leave. The road to Frenchglen is rough and full of boulders. I bounced on a big one several miles back. I think that rock could have cracked the differential. I hate to leave our trailer parked here. It was to be our home when we arrived at June's cousin's farm, and most of what we own is inside. I guess now we have no choice but to pack as much in the car that it can carry and leave the trailer. Perhaps June's cousin can bring his truck back up here and drag the trailer down to Lakeview."

At sunset, Dan locked Chester inside the trailer, and he, Keith, and Martin walked down to the pond and hid in the tule bushes. It wasn't long before the antelope herd wandered into the water hole.

The leader buck stayed on the ridge to keep watch as the others drank. Dan stood up, shouldered his rifle and sighted in on the young buck closest to him. The rifle explosion startled the herd. They instantly stampeded into the desert. The buck took a dozen steps, staggered and then, mortally wounded, fell to the ground. Dan walked to the dying animal and dispatched him with his hunting knife. The hunters spent the next half-hour butchering and dressing the animal. Keith helped by carrying half of the hind quarter back to the trailer. The animal was small but when properly prepared and smoked, he could provide enough meat to feed both families for the better part of a week. The antelope meat solved another of Dan's problems. They didn't have very much food for Chester, and the last of the dog food would be soon gone. Chester had caught rabbits from the day they arrived at Hart Mountain, yet a diet of rabbits could cause nutritional problems even for a dog. The antelope would provide nourishing food for the families and Chester. Keith took the antelope liver and fed it to Chester. He wolfed the liver down in a single gulp, and then begged for more.

"Save the heart and other innards for Chester to eat tomorrow," Dan cautioned Keith. "No telling what there will be for him to eat in the coming days."

The following morning, they said good-bye to Martin, June, Bart, and Pepper. Martin & June loaded most of their possessions from the trailer into the back of their sedan.

"Perhaps my cousin in Lakeview will let us use his bunkhouse," June expected. "Otherwise, we can live in our trailer, providing we can get it down to Lakeview."

Keith and Nora helped Martin and June pack their car as Penny watched Bart and Pepper. After a fond farewell, they gaze at Martin's sedan as it disappeared down the road in a cloud of dust. Nora prayed that they would make it safely to Lakeview, but she would never know if they did.

It was time for the Justin family to continue their trip to North Dakota. Dan hitched the trailer to the truck and carefully drove down the washboard road leading to Frenchglen, eighty-five miles distant. It was easy to see how this road had damaged Martin's car. Littered with potholes and boulders, the road consisted of two parallel ruts. It was a challenge to negotiate all the sharp rocks, soccer-ball sized boulders, and potholes that threatened to destroy their truck and trailer. Along the way, they forded two shallow creeks and dragged the trailer through several washouts. The culvert pipes that once protected the road lay bent into useless piles of scrap rested alongside the road. After a few miles, the road disappeared into a deep, 30-foot-wide creek. Dan and Keith got out of the truck and waded into the creek, testing the depth and solidness of the bottom with stout sticks. Worried, Dan told Keith, "I'm afraid we might get stuck in this creek. It is two feet deep in the middle and the bed is soft and sandy in spots."

"It should be ok, Dad. Martin crossed over it."

"Martin didn't say anything about crossing such a deep, wide creek. I suspect it wasn't this big when he crossed over it several days ago."

Dan looked across the flat desert toward the mountains to the east and noted a line of dark clouds that extended across the horizon.

"I think this creek is rising, because of a recent flash flood," he surmised. "See those black clouds over the mountains? It is raining over there. We had better try to get across this creek before it gets any deeper."

Dan put the truck into four-wheel drive and compound low gear, and then ventured out into the creek. The water soon reached the truck bumpers. Halfway across the creek, the truck front wheels began to slip and spin out on the sandy creek bed. Dan could make no further progress. He knew if he continued to spin the wheels, the truck would only dig itself into the soft creek bed.

"Nora, take the wheel. When I yell, gently step on the accelerator. Once the truck begins to move, keep going until you reach the opposite bank. Whatever you do, do not stop. Keith and Scott . . . come with me."

Dan, Scott, and Keith jumped into the water. Dan noticed the creek had already risen a few more inches from the time he first saw it.

"Keith, Scott . . . grab some of those willow branches along the bank and place them under the truck and trailer wheels."

They both grabbed an armful and jammed them under the front and rear truck wheels.

"OK, Nora," Dan yelled, "now ease it out."

Nora gently stepped on the accelerator and the truck began to inch forward. Dan, and Keith pushed from behind while Scott moved the branches from behind the truck wheels and placed them under the front and rear wheels. The rig slowly moved forward. Nora was doing a great job, sensing just how much to encourage the truck forward without spinning the wheels.

Past the halfway point, a firmer bed of cobblestones and gravel covered the river bottom. Once the truck reached that part of the creek, it easily gained the opposite bank and climbed onto the embankment. Dan gave Keith a big hug.

"Son, you did a great job out there."

Keith beamed, but Scott stood on the bank and scowled. "Daddy's little fair-haired boy," he mumbled under this breath. Dan looked around for Scott, and seeing him standing on the bank, ran over to him and threw his arms around his son. "I am proud of you too, Scott. You did a great job out there. Without your help, we would never have made it across." Scott managed a weak smile. Keith and Scott climbed into the backseat of the truck with Penny. "You're both soaking wet," she complained. "Well, if we didn't help dad, you'd still be sitting in the middle of the river as the water rose to drown you," Scott said defensively. Nora turned around. "Boys, go into the trailer and change out of your wet clothes. You too, Dan."

Although they didn't have to cross any more rain-swollen streams, the pothole and boulder-strewn road made for a slow, bumpy drive. Nora marveled that Martin and his family had pulled their trailer over this road with a low clearance sedan. The towns of Berdugo and Sageview were a big disappointment, being little more than a few deserted shacks and broken fences. The road was graded after passing through Sageview, and a few miles further on, it merged with county Highway 205, the main road between Plush and Frenchglen. Dan paused to look at the barriers placed across the main road leading to Plush. A sign warned that the road was closed because of a washout. A detour sign pointed to the washboard road they had just successfully navigated. The detour sign warned that only four-wheel drive cars and trucks should attempt the road and trailers were not recommended. Dan stifled the urge to get out of his truck and pen an even stronger warning on the detour sign, perhaps something like:

"The Road from Hell. Good Luck, Sucker."

Anyone who ventured even a few miles down this road would certainly have the good sense to turn around at the first turnout and go back. Little wonder that over the past three days, they hadn't even met anyone except the Martins on that terrible road. A few miles before reaching Frenchglen, a sign advertised they would find a bar, motel, mercantile, and gas station in the town, yet when the arrived nothing was open. Like Plush, the town appeared deserted. It had taken six hours to drive the bumpy eighty-five miles from their camping spot in the Hart Mountain Refuge to Frenchglen, which turned out to be only a bunch of weathered wood buildings with no one around. Dan thanked his lucky stars that they hadn't depended on Frenchglen for anything more than a signpost. Outside of town, a sign marked a fork in the road: one fork leading to Burns, 65 miles distant, and the other to Malheur Lake, New Princeton and Highway 20.

As Martin suggested, they avoided the highway to Burns and took the Malheur Lake and New Princeton road, which 50 miles later merged with U.S. 20 at Juntura. Unobstructed, Highway 20 took them to the outskirts of Vale, Oregon. Dan noticed a sign pointing to the Oregon Trail RV Park, and after a short drive west of town, they drove through the entrance marked by a large hand painted "WELCOME" sign. A dozen trailers filled the front of the park. In the back, several parking pads remained empty. Dan pulled alongside the office, honked his horn and rolled down the window. A man with a gray beard, generous handlebar mustache, and wearing a crumpled cowboy hat stepped out of the office.
Noticing the California license plates, he greeted them with, "Welcome folks, to the Oregon Trail RV Park. I am the manager, and my name is Frank. Where in California are you folks from?"

Dan told him Santa Cruz.

"Santa Cruz you say . . . Damn . . . I have a cousin who lives in Watsonville. How are things going down there?"

"Not good," Dan said. "That's why we left."

"How long do you want to stay?"

"Just overnight," Dan replied.

"Well, that will be $40 then, in advance. You're the first out-of-state visitors we've seen in a week. Where in the hell did you find enough gasoline along the way to drive all the way here from Santa Cruz?"

"We didn't find any gasoline," Dan said. "We are driving on the same tank we filled up back in Santa Cruz."

"All that way on only one tank-full you say?" Frank was skeptical. "You must know how to get good gas mileage out of this rig of yours."

"I drive very carefully, but now the tank is on empty," Dan replied, not telling him about the extra gas tank.

"Where ya heading?" the manager asked.

"North Dakota."

Frank let out a long, slow whistle. "North Dakota, you say? That's a long way from here," he commented, as he slowly shook his head. "I don't know how you folks figure you'll get from here to North Dakota. It's unlikely you will find any gas along the way."

"We'll manage," Dan replied.

Dan glanced down at his gas gauge. The needle pointed to the empty mark. They had come almost 700 miles and used most of the 35 gallons in the main tank while getting better than 20 miles per gallon. *Not bad for this rig,* Dan thought. He knew he could switch to the spare 35-gallon tank whenever the main tank ran dry, and he also had two 15-gallon cans of gas strapped to the rear bumper of the trailer. He calculated this could be enough to get them to Minot, but it would be a close call. A few extra gallons in the main tank would sure help.

"I understand there might be gas available in Boise or in Grangeville, north of here," Dan said.

"Well, perhaps. I heard a rumor that some gas may be for sale in Grangeville, but I wouldn't count on it. I can tell you one thing for sure. There isn't a drop for sale anywhere around here. If I were you, I wouldn't go anywhere near Boise."

"Yes, we heard on the radio that people are going crazy in Boise," Nora added.

The manager leaned in the window and looked at Nora. "A bit more than crazy, lady . . . Boise is a trap for travelers. It's like the Roach Hotel, where folks check in but don't check out." He backed out of the window and stood tall beside the truck. "I suggest you folks avoid Boise and follow Highway 95 north to Grangeville. I saw your extra gas tanks on the back of the trailer; you had better guard them with your life. Don't depend on buying gasoline in Grangeville. Even if they have some, which I doubt, given your California license plates, I wouldn't expect those folks will sell you a single gallon."

Dan handed the manager $40.

The manager took the money. "You can park your rig on any empty pad in the back. Don't bother hooking it to water or electricity. We have neither. You can get water from the water truck parked next to the playground."

He then added, "When you leave in the morning, you'll pass through the towns north of here, but whatever you do, don't stop. Don't go into Nampa or Caldwell. Roving gangs of hoodlums have been stopping cars on city streets, dragging folks out of their cars, and then beating and robbing them. Ontario and Weiser are not as bad, but also dangerous. If you drive through early in the morning and don't stop, you should get through all right."

"How are the roads north of here? Are they open?" Dan inquired.

"I heard tell that U.S. 95 and U.S. 12 are open, but there is no guarantee of that. Some fellow came through here a couple of days ago and said he drove down Highway 12 from Missoula to Grangeville, and from there to here. He didn't mention anything about road closures. He said they were selling gasoline in Missoula for $15 a gallon, but I sure wouldn't depend on that if I were you. He had Idaho license plates. Those two 15-gallon gas tanks on the back of your trailer should get you to Missoula, but not much further. You'll pass through Grangeville on your way north, so you might as well try to see if they will sell you some gas, but I wouldn't count on it."

Dan parked his rig on a pad toward the back of the park and walked to the little store at the front of the park. Bare shelves stressed the lack of food and other items. Scott topped their water tank off with five gallons from the water truck. Later, the manager wandered over to their rig and said the water wasn't free. It cost $5 a gallon. Dan paid him $25 but complained the manager was unfairly gouging his customers.

Early the next morning, they drove down U.S. 95 toward Ontario. Nora unfolded the map and traced their route north with her finger. "After Ontario, the highway crosses over into Idaho, and then through Weiser and north toward Grangeville. We should be in Grangeville by this afternoon." As expected, the car started to sputter, and Dan switched from the now empty main tank to the spare tank.

Neither Dan nor his family had prepared themselves for the adventure that awaited them.

CHAPTER NINE:
WILLOW CREEK, NORTH DAKOTA

Five-hundred-and-fifty souls, mostly of Scandinavian descent, lived in the little farming town of Willow Creek, north of Minot, North Dakota. Names such as Johansson, Iverson, Olsen, and Peterson were common. Most locals, conservative and hardworking folks, attended one of the three churches in the town that included a Lutheran, a Methodist, and a Catholic church. The Lutheran church of St. Paul formed the largest congregation in the town and surrounding area. The Dexter family worshipped at St. Paul's, where Peter was an Elder. Their pastor was the Rev. John Helming, a popular and loving shepherd. St. Paul's Church and hall, two blocks east of the town center, sat next to the city park.

The folks of Willow Creek struggled with the effects of the blackout. As September faded into October, the Mercantile ran out of food and city water could not serve homes, nor could the city move sewage to the waste-water treatment plant. The folks who lived on farms outside town coped without electricity better than townsfolk, who depended on a constant supply of electric power and water. North Dakota winters are harsh, and even in early October folks depended on electricity to run their fan-driven oil furnaces to heat their homes. Without electricity, the furnaces were useless. As the outside temperature dropped to freezing, many homes became iceberg cold. Those folks who depended on wood stoves or fireplaces to heat their homes counted themselves fortunate, while the rest of the townsfolk wore extra clothing and shivered in their unheated homes.

By the end of October, six weeks into the blackout, it was rare to see an automobile or truck moving along Willow Creek streets. The only gas station in town, the BP service station, initially rigged a hand pump to fill the townsfolk's cars from their underground tanks, yet it wasn't long before their tanks ran dry. In late September, the British Petroleum refinery in Minot had made the last delivery to Willow Creek. BP warned the station manager that he should not expect further deliveries, at least not until the local utility restored power to the refinery. By the first part of October, all the gas stations in Minot and surrounding towns had run out of diesel and gasoline, forcing folks to park their cars and trucks.

As usual, North Dakota farmers spent the later weeks of summer preparing their farms for the long winter months ahead. The same was true on the Dexter farm, this year being no exception. For the entire month of August, Peter's wife, Judy, canned vegetables, cooked preserves, and stored food for her family as she had done every year since they moved here. Peter filled the barn cribs with corn, squash, bush beans, and potatoes. He filled the loft with hay and other fodder for his animals. By early September, the Dexter family and their neighbors were ready for another North Dakota winter.

In rural farm communities like Willow Creek, folks were much better off than the citizens of large cities, yet eventually even small towns were forced to deal with shortages and civil unrest. Potable water soon became a main concern in Willow Creek. The town's municipal water company normally pumped groundwater into a 100-foot-high water tower. The silver tower, emblazoned with "WILLOW CREEK" painted in huge block letters, dominated the town's skyline. Gravity pressurized the town's water system and electric pumps filled the tank from wells. Without these pumps, the water tank ran dry, and so did the town's faucets. The water company borrowed a 5,000-gallon, stainless steel water truck from a milk farm. When the water system failed, they filled the truck gas-tank with gasoline borrowed from the fire department and ran the tank truck to nearby Lake Darling, filled it with clean, sanitized water, and then parked it in the town square. The company rationed the potable water, allowing each family to fill a five-gallon jug each day. Showers and baths were out of the question, although despite the cold fall weather, many folks bathed in the Willow Creek swimming hole, east of town.

Accurate, current information is critical in a time of crisis. Battery-powered portable radios were the only means to keep in touch with the outside world, yet by the end of October, the batteries in most portable radios were dead and the Merc had long sold the last battery. Peter owned a wind-up radio that did not rely on batteries. He brought the radio to the church hall and together St. Paul members listened to the nightly news broadcast from Fargo and Bismarck. The government signed contracts with every heavy electrical equipment manufacturer in the country, from Raytheon, to General Electric to Westinghouse. The government supplied gasoline to run the manufacturers' generators and ordered them to build replacement power transformers as fast as possible. They estimated that by April most of the grid could be functioning again. Yet April was still six months away, a long time to go without power especially through the winter months.

The government bureaucracy could not deal with a prolonged crisis. Storehouses of food, gasoline and emergency supplies were available, yet getting them to where they were needed seemed an insurmountable problem. Rail is the most fuel-efficient way to deliver food and goods to cities, yet the bickering and bumbling between local bureaucrats, and disagreement with railroad unions, disrupted efficient transportation. Supplies didn't get to those who most needed them. Many folks, especially those in large cities, were starving. Potable water wasn't readily avaliable and an epidemic of dysentery and typhoid broke out. A steady supply of gasoline and diesel to trucking companies could have eased the situation, but Capitol Hill only debated and delayed opening the strategic national gasoline and oil reserves. State governors and local politicians demanded the federal government do something about the fuel crisis, yet as usual, the administration dragged their feet, claiming they could not deplete the military oil and gasoline reserves.

In a move to reduce the country's dependence on foreign oil, the government had subsidized ethanol production and encouraged farmers to grow corn in place of other grains. When corn production wasn't sufficient to meet the increased demand for ethanol, they had used the federal corn reserves which now were empty. Wheat and grain production dwindled when farmers planted field after field in corn. The limited reserves of wheat, oats and rye soon disappeared. Without fuel for tractors and harvesters, farmers could not plant and harvest the winter wheat crop, and little hope remained for planting and harvesting next year's grains.

Supplying food to the hungry townsfolk of Willow Creek became a major challenge. The local mercantile ran out of food during the second week into the blackout. Niles Olsen, the grocer and owner of the Willow Creek Mercantile, made several trips into Minot during the first few days of the disaster and brought back as much hardware and nonperishable food as his truck could carry. Unfortunately, the supplies did not last long. Kerosene and batteries were in high demand, and those commodities had run out after the first few weeks. Despite strict rationing, by early October, the Merc shelves were empty and their delivery truck had no gasoline. There would be no more trips to Minot for food or hardware. Accustomed to keeping a well-stocked food closet, most Midwestern households were able to feed their families throughout September and October. However by November, supplies began to run short for most townsfolk.

Fresh milk was especially critical for those families with small children. Each day, farmers hand-milked their cows and brought the raw milk to the Merc and distributed it to needy families. They also brought along any produce that they could spare. Despite such neighborliness, food distribution at the Merc was not enough to meet the town's needs, and at times disorganized and chaotic.

Peter Dexter knew that it would not be long before some of the members of his Lutheran congregation and other townsfolk would have nothing at all to eat. Each farm had stored supplies of food for the winter, and all the parish council needed to do was to collect and make this food available. To help feed parishioners and townsfolk, Peter proposed a food bank at St. Paul's hall. He and a few other parishioners visited the surrounding farms and asked for contributions of food to stock the food bank. With donations from Peter's farm and the farms of most of his neighbors, no one in Willow Creek would starve.

Judy milked their cows each morning and every other day, brought milk to the food bank and shared it with families who had babies or small children. Peter contributed whatever food he thought his own family could spare. The generosity of local farmers amazed Pastor Helming. Peter, with the cooperation of the Pastoral Committee, ran the food bank with efficiency and fairness. Soon, non-church members outnumbered the parishioners who visited the food bank, and Peter gave food equally to everyone, parishioner and non-parishioner alike. The food bank opened every other day and gave out whatever food they could put out on tables.

Available on a "first come first served" basis, the tables were usually bare by midmorning. Most families came for food once or twice a week, but Peter noticed three men who showed up every other day to carry off as much food as they could fit into their tote bags.

It soon became clear that the unrestricted food distribution policy could not be sustained. They had to impose some controls, for if the blackout continued for many more weeks, the food bank would be unable to feed church members, let alone the entire community.

The news on the radio was not encouraging. The government expected the blackout could last six months or longer in the Midwestern states, yet without placing some restrictions on the food bank, Peter and the local farmers couldn't keep food on the shelves at St. Paul's Church. The Pastoral Committee debated closing the food bank to those outside the Lutheran community, but Peter and Pastor Helming passionately argued the food bank had an obligation to serve the entire Willow Creek community. The Pastoral Committee voted to keep the food bank open to the entire community, yet open it only on Tuesdays and Saturdays, and set a limit on the amount of food individuals and families could take. Mayor Peterson, a member of the Pastoral Committee, strongly disagreed with the proposed food rationing policy and insisted such limits wouldn't be necessary if they limited distribution to only St. Paul church members and a few "special cases" in the community. The Pastoral Committee disagreed and he angrily stomped out of the meeting.

As expected, the rationing policy was unpopular with just about everyone. A few parishioners resented a rationing policy designed to allow enough food for the entire community. Likewise, most townsfolk objected to the increased rationing and restricting distribution to two days each week. The first sign of violence erupted shortly after the first major snowstorm of the year in early November October buried North Dakota under two feet of fresh snow.

Folks whose cars had long since run out of gas made the trip to the food bank, trudging through the heavy snow that blanketed the countryside and the clogged unplowed roads. Peter, Judy and other food bank workers gave out canned goods, milk, eggs, and other fresh produce strictly within the limits set down by the Council. They set items out on a table and allowed folks to help themselves, according to their needs, but they strictly oversaw whatever each family or person carried out.

Most folks cooperated with the limits imposed by the Pastoral Council, yet there were notable exceptions, especially with the three men who visited the food bank each Tuesday and Saturday. The men were not church members and one of the three, a tall blond-headed chap, had given Peter a hard time whenever he came for food. Haughty, belligerent, and full of himself, he would fill his tote bag with as much food as he could carry out the door, much more than he could possibly have needed for himself or his family, if he had one. His two friends did likewise. After the Council imposed rationing, the next time the man and his friends came for food, Peter explained the new rules for food distribution. The man argued with Peter about the limits. Peter said each man could fill only one tote bag and tried to explain the need for rationing. The men left with half-full bags and grumbled as they went. A few minutes later the blond headed man came back in and asked Peter if he could help him fix a flat tire. Still angry about the argument the men had given him and surprised that the men had gasoline for their car, Peter went out to the parking lot anyway and got some tools out of his own car, and changed the man's flat tire. Even as Peter fixed the tire, the man continued to insist that he had a right to more food. Their discussion soon became heated and the man threatened to "punch Peter out." Several parishioners came to Peter's rescue, and the three men eventually left with only a few ears of corn, summer squash, and a few canned goods.

One of the parishioners who helped rescue Peter claimed that he saw the same three men selling food in town. The next time they appeared at the food bank, Peter confronted them. They denied selling food, but another member of the Parish Council stepped forward and claimed he also had seen them selling food near the Willow Creek Mercantile. On hearing this, Peter told the three men they were no longer welcome at the food bank, and after a brief scuffle, several parishioners helped Peter escorted them off the property.

Mayor Peterson, still fuming over the policy to ration food, watched as Peter and his helpers ran the three men off church property. He went face-to-face with Peter and accused him of being in his words a "tinhorn Gestapo". Peter stood his ground. He reminded the mayor that the Pastoral Committee had initiated the food policy and told him to "go pound sand". Jim Peterson took his complaint to Pastor Helming, but the Pastor supported Peter and the Council's decision. Mayor Peterson cursed and said he and his family would no longer be coming to Sunday services at St. Paul's. A few days later, he began bad mouthing Peter and Pastor Helming in the town council meetings and claimed the Lutheran Church policy was designed to discriminate against nonmembers. Many townsfolk believed the mayor's accusations and resentment against Peter and the Lutheran community grew.

Despite the limit to only open the food bank on Tuesday and Saturday, Judy Dexter continued bringing eggs and milk to the food bank every other day for families with small children. The dwindling supply of gasoline to fuel the Dexter truck concerned Peter. To conserve fuel, he asked Judy to take eggs and milk to the food bank only on Tuesday and Saturday, rather than every other day. She argued that some families depended on fresh milk and eggs, but Peter insisted on a twice a week delivery policy.

It wasn't long before folks began to appear at the Dexter farm, asking for milk, eggs and vegetables. They came on horse-drawn wagons or pushed handcarts down the snow-covered county road. Some folks walked to the farm, filled backpacks or tote bags and then carried the food back to their homes. The Dexters turned no one away, yet as more and more folks came each day to the farm, Peter realized that he could not continue to give out food and still have enough to feed his own family. When he finally announced the only place to get free food would be at the food bank on Tuesday and Saturday, some townsfolk grew indignant. A few even cursed him. As in the big cities, people were scared, frustrated and angry, and the more desperate some townsfolk became, the more they might resort to violence. As incidents grew commonplace in town, Peter considered plans to protect his family and farm. He kept a dozen domesticated white geese penned in his barnyard. Geese make excellent intruder alarms. When a fox or other marauders, human or animal, invade the property, the geese make a ruckus loud enough to wake the entire household. If their honking did not scare a trespasser away, Peter would do so with a shouted warning and a shotgun blast in the air. One evening, the Dexters were eating dinner, when the goose-alarm sounded. Expecting to find a fox in the henhouse, Peter grabbed his shotgun and hurried out onto the porch, where he witnessed three men trying to pry the lock off barn door with a tire iron. He yelled for the trespassers to get off his property, but they ignored him and continued to pry on the latch.

Peter pumped his 12-gauge shotgun once and fired a warning shot over their heads. Two of the men stopped what they were doing and fled into the woods behind the barn. The third man stood his ground and glared at Peter. Dressed in coveralls, boots and wearing a ski hat pulled down over his forehead, the man walked menacingly through the snow toward Peter, with the tire iron still in his hand.

At first, Peter didn't know what to do. The man had an angry look of determination on his face and raised the tire iron over his head as if he intended to crush Peter's skull. Loudly cursing and swearing he moved toward the porch. Peter shouted a second warning and pumped the shotgun, but the man paid no attention. With the intruder only twenty yards away and closing fast, Peter fired a second warning shot over the man's head. Rather than back off as Peter expected he would, the man hesitated for a second, and then quickened his pace toward the house.

Judy stood in the front door, watching the assault unfold. When the second shot didn't deter the man, she shouted at Peter.

"Shoot him, for God's sake, shoot him," she screamed.

By now, the man was only a few yards away from the porch steps and showed no sign he intended to back off. Peter yelled a third time to get off his property, yet the man kept on coming. When only a few feet from the bottom step, Peter lowered the shotgun and pulled the trigger. The pellets struck the man in the torso and lower legs. His look of anger turned to one of shock and surprise as he stumbled backwards a couple of feet, dropped the tire iron, and fell to the snow-covered ground. Peter ran down the steps, stood over him and watched as a widening pool of blood stained the snow. The man's legs jerked convulsively as he gasped for air. The shotgun blast had mortally wounded him.

Peter turned to Judy and asked her to fetch a blanket. The man's lips moved as he tried to say something, but words failed him. The pellets had shredded his pants and shirt, and blood and intestines oozed from a gaping hole in his belly. He stared blankly into the sky and gasped for air. Peter knelt beside him, but there was nothing he could do. He took a closer look at the man. He was young, perhaps in his late twenties, with a week's growth of reddish-blond beard covering a pockmarked face. A lock of blond hair escaped from beneath his ski cap and hung over his forehead. The man looked well-fed and powerfully built. Peter bent over and removed the ski cap. He recognized the man he had confronted at the food bank a couple of weeks earlier, the same person that Peter accused of selling donated food in town. The wounded man stared into space, then turned his head toward Peter and with a mixed look of fear and hatred, uttered a curse, shuddered, and then exhaled a lengthy groan. A few seconds later, his eyes clouded over, his legs stopped twitching, and he slowly breathed out his last breath.

Judy ran out of the house with a blanket but stood at the bottom of the steps, frozen by the realization that a man had just died in their front yard. Trevor followed his mother out onto the porch, but Peter quickly told him to go back inside and take care of his sister.

Peter took the blanket from Judy. His hands shook as he fumbled with the blanket and tried to cover the body. Judy stood beside the body. Tears stained her cheeks. "Why wouldn't he stop? Why wouldn't the damn fool just stop?"

"He must have been desperate, insane or both," Peter said. He didn't cover the man's face and asked Judy if she recognized him. She knelt down beside the body. Her eyes widened as she recognized the pockmarked face and reddish-blond hair. "This is the same man who threatened you when you refused him food at the church a couple of weeks ago."

Judy paused for a second. "Jake . . . the man's name is Jake."

Peter turned to her. "Jake . . . that's right. When folks grow desperate there are always those who will try to steal food from the farm. It's only been a few weeks since the blackout began and already some people are acting like brigands. Jake was probably desperate and driven to thievery, and now I've killed the poor man."

Judy shuddered, covered the man's face with the blanket, and began to cry.

"Peter, it wasn't your fault," she said between sobs. "He wouldn't stop, and he was ready to hit you with that tire iron. Did you see the madness in his eyes? He would have killed you and possibly me and the children as well. You did what you had to do to protect your family."

Concerned that the man's accomplices might return, Peter asked her to go inside and lock all the doors. Before she turned to go back inside, he said he would take Jake's body into town, to the sheriff. He handed her the shotgun and said to use it if the other men came back. Peter got his pickup truck, backed it to where Jake lay, and lifted the limp body into the truck bed. Then he covered the body with a tarp and drove into town. A few minutes later, he arrived at the sheriff's office, went inside and told the desk officer what had just happened. Bill Eisner, the local sheriff, came out to the truck and lifted the blanket off the man's face.

"That's Jake . . . Jake Brevick," Bill said. "He's a bad one . . . been in trouble more times than I care to count. Most of his crimes were misdemeanors, such as petty larceny, small-time theft and the like. Last year he stole a car. A jury convicted him of a felony and he became a guest of the state prison. In fact, because of the power outage, the state released most of their nonviolent convicts, including Jake, just two week ago."

Bill looked hard at Peter and asked, "Were his friends with him when you shot him?"

Peter said two other men were with Jake, but they fled into the woods at the first warning shot.

"Do you know who they were?"

"No, but I think I've seen them at the food bank."

"Did they witness the shooting?"

"I don't think so. They ran into the woods before I shot Jake."

"Did anyone else witness the shooting?"

"Just Judy," Peter answered.

Sheriff Eisner sent a deputy down the street to ask the coroner, Darren Jenkins, to meet them at the Restful Valley Mortuary, across the street from the coroner's office. The sheriff and Peter drove over to the mortuary and carried Jake's draped body into the morgue. The coroner was waiting for them in the preparation room. Coroner Jenkins directed them to lay Jake out on the examination table.

Then he asked the deputy to go get Mayor Peterson to come and identify the dead man. The sheriff did not want Peter around when Jim Peterson came to the mortuary, so he told Peter to go back to the office with his deputy and file a written report of the incident. Bill told Peter that most likely an inquest wouldn't charge him with manslaughter. It seemed like an open-and-shut case of self-defense. Peter was eager to go back home and make sure Judy and the kids were all right, so he hurried back to the sheriff's office, filed a short statement with the deputy, and drove home.

"I'm troubled that this is an example of what we can look forward to," Peter told Judy, after arriving home and repeating what the sheriff had said. "I won't be charged, but when other folks become desperate, we can expect more attempted break-ins. Tomorrow, I am going to put another lock on the barn door. We will have to keep all the house doors locked and the guns loaded and listen for the geese to raise a ruckus. You and the kids must remain on the farm. I hate to live like this, but I fear it may get worse before things get back to normal."

Later that day, Sheriff Bill Eisner and his deputy visited the Dexter farm to investigate the shooting scene and examine the barn door for evidence of an attempted break-in. They confiscated the spent shotgun shells and Peter's shotgun. Bill took pictures and tape measurements of the distance between the barn door and the porch. He took a statement from Judy and quizzed both her and Peter about the tire iron. Despite a careful search in the snow, he couldn't find the iron. He walked over to the woods and searched for evidence of the other two men. He found footprints in the snow at the edge of the woods, where someone had stood. He also found and a couple of cigarette butts. He noted there was no clear view of the front of the house from this location.

The Willow Creek Sheriff's office was unprepared to investigate a murder. Before the power outage, the worst incidents that Sheriff Eisner had to deal with were town drunks, domestic disturbances, neighbor disputes, and petty thievery. From the first week of the blackout, Sheriff Eisner had had his hands full, investigating petty thefts and responding to various complaints. He could see that the townsfolk were growing restless and he expected trouble was brewing. In many small towns and villages throughout the country, townsfolk banded together to help one another through the crisis. In Willow Creek, everyone knew their neighbors and lent a hand to those who needed help. No one could remember the last time there had been a murder in Willow Creek.

Yet now things were different. Over the past few weeks, the sheriff had a difficult time keeping law and order in the community. In recent days thieves broke into three local businesses and several homes. Sheriff Eisner found evidence left behind in two of the break-ins, and based on his findings, he arrested the Hansen brothers and charged them with two felony counts of breaking and entering. The county jail in Minot was full and could not accept more prisoners. Willow Creek had neither a courthouse to conduct court nor a jail to house prisoners. Lacking gasoline, the sheriff could not transport those he arrested to Minot, to appear before a judge. Last month, the Willow Creek City Council members Jerry Reeves and Mayor Jim Peterson named the Olsen boardinghouse as a temporary jail and appointed two deputies as guards. The City Council appointed Sam Jameson as acting judge. Sam, a lawyer and president of the Willow Creek Cattleman's Association, practiced litigation law in Minot, yet had no experience as a judge. Judge Jameson held court each Thursday afternoon, in the Willow Creek Community Hall. He jailed the Hansen brothers in the Olsen's downtown boardinghouse to await trial. For the first few weeks, the Olsen jail had only housed a few overnight drunks and a man for domestic abuse, but now the Hanson brothers became guests.

A few days after the Brevick shooting, Sheriff Eisner arrested Mike Graves; one of Jake's suspected partners in the aborted Dexter farm robbery. The sheriff caught Mike red-handed as he tried to break into the Willow Creek Mercantile. He imprisoned him at the boardinghouse, in an upstairs bedroom next to the Hansen brothers and scheduled him to appear in Judge Jameson's court the following week.

The folks in Willow Creek adjusted to life without power even as some parts of the country were able to restore their power systems. Peter and his family listened to the radio reports that power companies in some northwest cities, namely Seattle, Spokane, and Portland, had managed to restore limited power to their customers. The Grand Coulee Dam power generation plant was one of the few that had shut down before the solar storm hit, and their quick action saved their transformers from major damage. The Ottertail Power Company did not take such preventive action, and the resulting fire damaged their transformers beyond repair. Peter knew that Ottertail Power was on a long list of those waiting for new transformers.

It would be weeks, or even months, before Ottertail Power could restore service to Willow Creek—a much longer wait than folks anticipated.

CHAPTER TEN:
ON THE ROAD TO MONTANA

An orange-tinted sun rose over distant mountains as Dan's truck sped down the highway leading from Vale to Ontario. The thermometer read 22 degrees, and as the sun's rays hit the dark macadam, wisps of mist rose into the crisp morning air and coated nearby tree branches with a layer of hoarfrost. A faint breeze floated across the fields, carrying with it the smell of fresh cut hay and alfalfa. Tinged with the hoarfrost, bushes and small trees alongside the road sparkled in sunlight like a million diamonds. Aspen, birch, oak, and sycamore trees displayed brilliant yellow and red fall colors, warning of the winter soon to come. Herds of cows roamed the fields, munching on the last summer grass. Their warm breath condensed in the crisp morning air and floated above the pasture, creating a faint cloud that hung over the herd.

Heeding the warning from the manager of the Oregon Trails RV Park, Dan slowed down to a crawl as they entered the town of Ontario. The city showed more signs of mayhem than any other place they had visited. Scores of abandoned cars and trucks littered the roadside. An overturned tanker truck blocked the road ahead, forcing Dan to detour onto a side street. Garbage, broken furniture, ruined appliances, cardboard boxes, and hulks of burned-out cars littered the streets forcing Dan to weave his rig around the clutter. The early hour suggested most folks would still be in bed; yet he spotted several early-risers meandering along the sidewalks. Alert for thugs who might block his way and pull him and his family from the truck, Dan searched for a street that would take him back to the main highway. People walked in a stupor, looking neither right nor left and pretended to ignore their truck. As he turned a corner into a street he hoped would take them back to the main highway, two men jumped out of the shadows and defiantly stood in front of the truck. One man held a piece of rebar in his hand and the other waved a baseball bat. Penny screamed and Dan honked the horn and accelerated toward them.

Cursing and waving their weapons, they jumped out of the way at the last moment.

"Dad, were you going to hit them?" Penny asked.

"If I had to . . . , " Dan answered without hesitation.

Scott leaned over the front seat to get a better view. "Good thing those jerks got out of the way then, otherwise . . . splat . . . like bugs on our windshield."

Nora clearly disapproved of Scott's comment and her icy glare caused him to shrink back into his seat. Dan drove back onto the main highway and accelerated as he picked his way through downtown Ontario. He knew that, unlike the confrontation outside Chico, if he hit someone, Nora would insist they stop and see what could be done to help the unfortunate soul. Fortunately, there were only a few people on the street as they drove downtown, and the few folks who were, quickly got out of the way of their rig.

Dan zigzagged down Main Street, avoiding the piles of garbage, overturned cars, and dead animals that littered the street. Smashed storefront windows in the center of town had covered the sidewalks with shards of glass. Crumpled shopping carts, empty cartons, piles of cardboard, and loose papers fluttering in the wind indicated riots were responsible for such destruction. Wisps of white smoke curled from buildings, and the blackened brick walls and collapsed roofs of some testified to fires that had ravaged this part of town. A half-mile from downtown, a block-wide shopping center had been reduced to a smoldering ruin, with the collapsed roofs still puffing clouds of black smoke. They didn't see any sign of firemen, police or National Guardsmen patrolling any part of the city. Nora nervously grasped the armrests and breathed in shallow gasps as they drove past the devastation that had once been a thriving city. Once safely outside the city limits, she released her iron grip on the armrests and began to cry. Dan started to pull over to see if she was all right, but she told him to keep going.

"I'll be fine," she exclaimed, "just keep going. It's just all so terribly dreadful."

They passed under Interstate 84 and then continued north on State Highway 95, and hurried through the towns of Payette and Weiser, neither of which had escaped damage. The 190 miles of serpentine highway that led north to the small town of Grangeville passed through several small towns, but none showed the signs of destruction as in the larger cities. They arrived in Grangeville early that afternoon.

Contrasted with Ontario, Grangeville was clean, neat and orderly, with no signs of the lawlessness and carnage evident in Ontario or Weiser. Since leaving Ontario, they met only a handful of trucks and cars along the highway, yet much to their surprise, as they approached Grangeville they passed several pickup trucks and sedans traveling south from the city.

"Perhaps the rumors that gasoline is available in Grangeville aren't exaggerated," Nora said hopefully.

In the town center, they came to a gasoline tanker truck, with a green dinosaur logo and the letters BP painted on the side. Next to the tanker, a large generator housed on a flatbed truck rumbled and belched grey smoke. Thick power cables snaked across the street from the generator to a store. An "OPEN" sign hung in the front window of the Grangeville Market. Lights were visible from inside.

Dan parked his rig across the street from the store and as he and Nora climbed out she told the children to stay in the car. As they entered the store, a clerk standing behind the cash register greeted them. His friendly smile revealed a set of yellow teeth.

"Howdy folks," he croaked, "My name is Pete. What can I do for you?"

The low counter and a stained apron did not hide the man's bulging belly. Well built, muscular, and wearing a red tartan shirt the man seemed friendly. Yellow suspenders held up his size 44 jeans, and a few locks of hair escaped from beneath a black cowboy hat. A gold ring adorned his left ear. The man's weathered and furrowed face betrayed years of work in harsh sunlight and his gray-tinged, handlebar mustache added to the illusion that he had time-traveled from the 1890s. Dan said nothing but acknowledged his friendly greeting with a nod. Nora returned his smile and uttered a friendly "hello".

"What can I do for you folks today?" the clerk repeated.

Dan and Nora glanced around the store. Several shoppers casually strolled up and down the aisles, pushing carts or carrying hand baskets. Canned and packaged nonperishable items filled the shelves and several freezers were packed with frozen goods.

No one in any other town they passed through had been willing to sell food to strangers even if they had any, which few did. Given the present circumstances, it seemed like a foolish question, but it was worth a try.

"Your shelves look well stocked," Dan said. "Would you be willing to sell us some food?"

"I take it you folks are not from around here," Pete said, without answering Dan's question.

"No, we are from Santa Cruz in California," Nora answered.

Dan knew that Californians were not well-received in Idaho and frowned at her for offering this information. "How is it that you have electricity and food on your shelves?"

"Well, it's a small town and folks around here ain't crazy like those folks in the cities south of here. We help one another in times like this. The power company loaned us the generator across the street and the gasoline company brought in a tanker truck full of diesel so we could have a few hours of electricity each day. It's enough to keep the freezers cold, water flowing, and a few lights lit. Next door is the telephone company and our radio station. The generator provides local telephone service that operates 24/7 and the radio station broadcasts two hours each day." He delivered the news with obvious pride.

Nora was perplexed. "Where did you get all this food? We've seen nothing like this since we left Santa Cruz. Within a week after the blackout started, all of our store shelves were bare."

"Well folks, besides managing this mercantile, my brother and I own a large distribution warehouse in the center of town. Until the blackout, our business delivered food to stores throughout northern Idaho, from Sandpoint to Riggins. Now we can't get gasoline for our delivery trucks, so we have a warehouse full of food and no way to deliver most of it, so I am selling it to the locals. Because we have power, we can carry fresh produce and dairy products, but most of what we have is canned and packaged foods . . . stuff that will not spoil."

"I noticed milk and eggs for sale in the cooler," Nora commented, as she looked down the main aisle.

"Yep, we have a few cows and chickens around here. They don't need electricity to provide us with food," Pete said with a sarcastic smile.
"Amazing," Dan commented. He asked a second time, "Would you consider selling food to some poor travelers?"

Pete thought for a moment, and then with a broad smile said, "Do you have children with you?"

"Yes," Nora replied. "Two boys and a girl . . . they're outside in the truck."

"Well, I don't have any kids myself, but I have a soft spot for young-ones. We don't usually sell to outsiders, but there haven't been many visitors around here lately. In fact, you are the first outsiders to stop in town for over a week now. I can sell you some food; but I have a strict rule to sell only as much as each of you can carry out of the store in a paper bag."

He handed each of them a large paper sack and said, "Pick out your food carefully and then come back to the counter."

Nora wandered up and down the aisles picking out cans of salmon, hash, vegetables, baked beans, flour, salt, rice, chili, and Spam. Dan filled his bag with coffee, milk, bread, butter and eggs. When both bags were full, they returned and placed their items on the counter.

"I see you picked practical stuff," Pete commented as he rang up each item. "You would be surprised at what some folks put in their bags: prepared foods, cigarettes, liquor, beer, pop, dog food, and other nonessentials. That comes to $56.23."

Dan commented that this was not much more than he would have expected to pay for the same items in a Santa Cruz supermarket before the blackout.

"Well sir, we're not in business to make a big killing off of folks who are in need. I just hope the warehouse food doesn't give out before the blackout ends."

"I hear that might be months away," Dan commented.

Pete frowned. "Some of the folks around here will not survive if electricity remains out through the winter months. Without that generator running across the street and a supply of diesel, we won't be able to store and sell perishable food. Soon it will turn cold and the snow will fly. We get a lot of snow around here. When our warehouse runs out of food, things might go from bad to worse. If that happens, I think I'll leave town and live in my hunting cabin near Elk City."

Dan leaned in closer to the counter and in a low voice said, "I saw a few trucks and cars on the road, while driving into town. That makes me think there must be gasoline for sale around here."

Pete shrugged his shoulders and then looked at Nora. "You say you have three kids in the truck out there?" She nodded. "Well, the BP station down the road is selling gas, but only to locals."

"Do you suppose the station owner could be encouraged to sell us a few gallons? It would sure help us get to our destination" Dan asked.

"Don't think so," Pete said, matter-of-factly.

"Well, perhaps they will sell us some gas in Missoula."

Pete looked long and hard at Nora, and then glanced at the rig across the street "Three kids you say?"

"Yes," Nora replied.

"Well, good luck trying to buy gas in Missoula. A friend of mine, George Pintos, owns the BP station down the road. He only sells gas to locals, but I might persuade him to sell you a few gallons. There's a limit of eight gallons, but that might help get you and your family to your destination. Where you folks headed anyway?"

"Well, right now . . . Missoula," Nora answered.

Pete sensed that Missoula was not their final destination. "And then, after Missoula?"

"North Dakota," Dan said.

Pete stared at the rig and noted the California license plates and the three kids standing on the sidewalk next to the car.

"How much gas do you have in that truck?"

"About 25 or 30 gallons," Dan answered.

"And those are your kids out there?" he asked, pointing to the truck.

"Yes, all three," Nora answered.

Pete studied Dan for a few seconds, looking for some sign of deception. "I doubt that you will find anyone who will be willing to sell you gas between here and North Dakota, and you will certainly need more than 25 gallons to get there," he said, slowly shaking his head.

"You're right. We don't have enough to get there," Dan replied. "Right now, my primary tank is empty and we are running on the spare tank.

Unless I can find some gas along the way, we probably can't make it all the way to North Dakota. Another eight gallons would sure be a big help though."

"Where in North Dakota are you heading?"

Dan stared at the clerk for a few seconds. This fellow seemed unusually curious about their business, but he might help them, so he answered "We're trying to reach our friends who live on a farm north of Minot."

"Minot you say . . . that's a long drive from here. I have a cousin in Dickenson. It will take more gasoline than what you are carrying to get to Minot. Rumor has it that some stations in Montana are selling gasoline, probably because the BP refinery in Missoula is still operating. Most likely they won't sell gasoline to strangers, and unless you can fill up in Missoula, you're apt to run out along the road, way before you get to Minot. It wouldn't be good for you and your family to run out on some Montana or North Dakota road, stuck in the middle of nowhere."

"It would really help out if we could buy a few gallons here," Nora repeated.

"Well, you folks seem like a nice family, even if you are from California. I'll make a call to George, but I can't guarantee that he will agree to sell gas to you."

Then he added, "Be aware that the road from Grangeville to Missoula passes through 150 miles of wilderness and there aren't any services between here and there. In fact, there aren't any towns either. Make sure your rig is in good shape before you leave Grangeville or you might find yourselves stuck on the road, with no hope of rescue."

Nora thanked the man for his advice and groceries. As they returned to the truck, Pete made the call to his friend. They drove down the highway to the BP Station located on the other side of town. Several cars waited in line for their turn in the service island. Dan noticed a BP tanker truck with Montana license plates parked alongside the station. The rumors of an operating refinery in Missoula must be true and this tanker truck was proof that gasoline was available in this part of the country. A hand painted sign announced:

Regular gasoline, $7/gallon.
Eight Gallon limit. No diesel.
Gas only sold between 3 and 5 PM
Locals only

It was 4 p.m. as Dan pulled his rig into the line. After a fifteen minute wait, he pulled alongside a pump. A man knocked on the driver's window and Dan rolled it down.

"We don't sell gasoline to outsiders," he announced acidly.

"Pete at the grocery store said he would call and put in a good word for us," Dan pleaded.

The man went in to the office and then returned. "Well, George says to make an exception for you folks, but you can only have eight gallons. That will be $56 . . . cash . . . in advance."

Dan took $56 out of his wallet, paid the attendant, and handed him the gas cap key. The attendant then began pumping eight gallons into their empty main tank. After the gauge indicated 8 gallons had been pumped, Dan took another look at the spare tank gas gauge. It registered ¾ full. He calculated that the 25 gallons remaining in the spare tank should take them another 500 miles or so, and the additional 8 gallons in the main tank would add 150 miles to the total. They still had 30 gallons in two cans tied to the back of the trailer. So far, the car had been getting about 20 miles per gallon, very good for a truck pulling a trailer. Dan figured that it was another 1,100 miles from here to Minot, and 40 miles more to Willow Creek. Even if they did not fill up in Missoula, an additional 8 gallons added to the 55 gallons they already carried should be enough to get them to Peter's farm, but there would be little gas to spare.

The attendant finished pumping and returned the gas key to Dan.

"I noticed the two 15-gallon gas cans tied to the back of your trailer. You'd better take care that no one steals them. Folks can get pretty desperate you know."

Dan thanked him and drove out of the station.

It began drizzling as they left town and headed down U.S. Highway 12 toward Missoula. The rain continued as they traveled through a few small settlements. The road climbed into the mountains, following the Lochsa River for mile after twisting mile. Although it was only a light drizzle, the dancing windshield wipers and the rain made it difficult to see the road as the sun set. Dan looked for a place to camp for the night, and about 30 miles west of Missoula, he saw a sign announcing Lolo Campgrounds and pulled into the campground.

The Forest Service campground provided two-dozen camp sites, all empty except for a tent erected in a site next to the only outhouse. Dan pulled into a site at the back of the campground. Despite the light drizzle, the kids and Chester were anxious to get out of the car, and as soon as Dan stopped, everyone climbed out. Chester ran off into the woods and the kids and Nora headed to the outhouse. As Dan knelt to adjust the leveling jacks, a man came over from the tent site and introduced himself. Over six-feet tall, well built, balding and sporting a bushy red beard, the man smiled as he bent over to greet Dan.

"The name's Lloyd Donaldson. I'm from Washington," he announced as he offered his hand. "Where are you folks headed?"

"Minot," Dan said as he stood to shake the man's hand.

Lloyd shook his head in disbelief. "Minot is a long way from here and I understand a few roads between here and there may be close."

"Yes, I know. We intend to take U.S. 2 across Montana into North Dakota. Last time I checked it was open."

"Well, it is good to see your family camping here. I've been the only person camped here for several days and have to say I'm getting mighty lonely.

Other than a few cars that stopped to use the outhouse, you folks are the first to stop and camp. I'm pretty much stuck here, as there isn't much gas left in my old Buick's gas tank, probably not even enough to get me down to Missoula, so here I stay."

"Well, I can let you have enough to get you to Missoula, if two gallons would do you," Dan offered.

"I'm not asking for any gas. I'm quite satisfied to stay here until things get better. I have plenty of food. Thanks, but I'm quite happy here."

"Well Lloyd, we can spare 2 gallons, and it would be a privilege to help you. Please bring your Buick over to my trailer."

Lloyd did so, and Dan unstrapped one of the 15-gallon gas cans from the trailer and pored two gallons into the Buick's tank. "There, that ought to get you into town whenever you decide to go. It is mostly downhill from here."

Lloyd thanked Dan and they talked a while longer. Dan introduced him to the rest of the family and Nora invited him to have dinner with them—an invitation which Lloyd readily accepted.

Chester was happy to be outside and after his run in the forest he returned soaking wet, with a squirrel clamped tightly in his jaws. He shook off the water, spraying everyone within ten feet, and then dropped the squirrel at Nora's feet as if to say, "Here's dinner."

Lloyd laughed. "That's quite a hunter you have there."

They sat in the trailer and exchanged pleasantries with Lloyd. He was a very interesting fellow, a veteran who had served as a medic in Vietnam. After dinner, Lloyd said he had better turn in for the night and excused himself.

It rained hard all that night but by morning, it had stopped. The campground was cold and damp. The fire ring looked inviting, so Keith asked if before they left he could start a campfire. Dan thought that was a good idea and sent Scott and Penny out into the woods to gather dry firewood, while Keith prepared kindling.

"Don't go far," Dan warned. "There is plenty of dry wood under the fir trees. Scott, watch out for your sister."

"Why do I always have to look after her," Scott said defiantly.

"Just do as I ask," Dan said.

Although there was plenty of wood scattered about the forest floor, most of it was soaking wet. Scott ignored Dan's warning and wandered deeper and deeper into the forest, in search of dry wood.

"Dad said not to go too far," Penny warned as she trailed behind him.

Scott ignored her and kept on walking until he came to a small clearing. A large pile of rocks in the center of the clearing caught Penny's attention. The pile looked as though someone had deliberately stacked rocks in the shape of a pyramid, one upon the other, with the bigger ones at the bottom. A ground level two-foot high fissure extended a few feet inside the pile.

"Scott, we don't have to go any further, Penny called out. "There is lots of dry wood in this little cave."

Scott ignored her and continued to walk across the clearing and disappeared into the woods.

Chester stayed with Penny as she began to gather sticks and branches from inside the fissure. As she reached into the back of the dark cave for a stick, she felt a sharp pain in her finger. She quickly withdrew her hand and screamed when she saw two puncture marks in her index finger, each dripping blood. She cried, as the pain shot along her finger, into her hand, and then traveled up her arm like a hot knife. Sobbing, she sat down on a boulder and Chester, sensing her anguish, nuzzled against her.

Nora began to worry the minute Scott and Penny left to gather wood. When they hadn't returned in ten minutes, she followed the path into the forest and met Scott wandering back to camp with a few sticks of wood in his arms. He was alone.

"Where's Penny?" Nora asked.

"She's with Chester. She was right behind me just a few minutes ago," Scott answered. But the truth was that Scott had ditched his sister and followed another path that skirted the clearing and rock pile.

Nora called out, but Penny didn't answer. Then she heard Chester barking. Nora and Scott rushed toward the sound and found Penny sitting on a boulder near the rock pile, with Chester protectively sitting at her feet. She held her hand and wept. "Mom, it hurts," she cried. Nora took her hand into hers examined it. Blood dripped from two puncture marks in her index finger. "What happened?" Nora asked.

"Something bit me," Penny sobbed.

Nora told Scott to go find his father, but Dan and Keith were already running toward the sound of the barking. They stumbled into the clearing before Scott even got to his feet. Dan took Penny's hand and examined her finger.

"It looks like a snake bite. What happened?" he asked her.

"I was reaching under a boulder for a stick, and something bit me," Penny sobbed.

Scott stood apart from the group with his head down and stared at the ground.

Keith spied a snake slithering away from the rock pile and about to disappear into the grass. He picked up a rock, squashed its head, and then held the withering animal by its tail. It was a 4 foot diamond-back rattler.

"Put that snake down," Dan yelled. "It could still bite you."

"Dad, I think it's pretty dead," Keith said. "It's a diamond back rattle snake."

"Dead or not, get rid of it, right now," Nora ordered.

Dan carried Penny back to the trailer and put her on the couch. Her finger began to swell and turn black.

Lloyd heard all the commotion and came over to see what was going on. He examined Penny's finger. "I treated snake bites like this in Vietnam. I'll need to extract some of the poison," he said. Dan nodded his head. Lloyd took Penny over to the sink, washed her hand with soap and warm water, and began to suck on her wounded finger, spitting the blood out into the sink. Then he took out his picket knife, sterilized it with a match, and made two small incisions below the bite and sucked more blood from Penny's finger. The child was brave, but when Lloyd made the incisions she screamed, sending a chill through everyone. After a few minutes of alternately sucking and spitting blood into the sink, Lloyd put a band-aid over the punctures and cuts. Her finger was twice the size it normally should be, and her hand was turning purple as well. Lloyd traced the vein under her forearm. It also was turning purple.

"You're going to have to get her to a doctor as fast as possible," Lloyd whispered to Dan. "The snake bite is a bad one, and she is reacting badly to the venom. There is a hospital in Missoula."

Dan retracted the trailer levelers, and hitched the trailer to the truck and locked Chester inside. Keith took the passenger seat, as Nora climbed into the back seat with Scott and cradled Penny in her lap.

CHAPTER ELEVEN:
MONTANA

Dan drove down the highway as fast as the wet, slippery road allowed. The rain began to fall again and then turned into a mushy snow as they climbed over Lolo Pass. They crossed over into Montana and followed the twisting highway down the mountain and into the valley. Penny's entire forearm began to swell and turn an ugly purple and her delicate hand had swelled to twice its normal size. Her pale face and sweat-drenched body suggested she was in shock. Nora did all she could to keep the child awake, yet Penny kept drifting off. Dan pulled into a roadside restaurant at the junction of Highway 12 and U.S. 93. A "closed" sign hung on the door but a weak light from inside suggested someone was there. He banged on the door until an elderly woman cautiously opened the door a crack and said that she was sorry, but they were closed. Dan asked directions to the nearest clinic or hospital.

The woman opened the door a bit further and stared blankly at him.

"A snake bit my daughter. Where can I find a doctor?" Dan pleaded.

"Oh," she said, detecting the desperation in Dan's voice, "there is a clinic just ten miles from here on Highway 93, just as you come into town, but I heard that it closed because of the power outage. St. Patrick's hospital is on the other side of town opposite the park and I am sure it's open," she said. "It is two or three miles further than the clinic, and that's where I think you should take her. Just stay on Bridger Street as it passes through town."

Dan thanked her and drove down Highway 93, which became Bridger Street as they passed the city limit sign.

"This is the road to the hospital, just like the lady said," Dan commented as they passed a blue "H" hospital sign.

Nora noticed a small brick building with a car parked in front and a sign that read:

Missoula Emergency Medical Clinic

An "Open" sign hung in the window.

"Screw the hospital, pull into that clinic," Nora insisted.

The boys remained in the car as Dan carried Penny into the waiting room. Nora followed close behind and took a seat in the waiting room. Dan handed the limp child to her and went over to the receptionist to explain the accident. After hearing the word "snakebite" and seeing the child in Nora's arms, she immediately went inside to find the doctor.

A few seconds later, he stepped into the waiting room and ushered Nora and Penny into an examination room. Nora placed Penny on the examination table and held her good hand while Dan filled out paperwork in the reception room. The doctor leaned over the stricken girl, felt her forehead and examined her finger and arm.

"Not to worry little lady," the Doctor said, "We'll have you fixed in a jiffy."

Penny was pale and clammy and only mumbled unintelligibly in response to the doctor's questions as he examined her finger and arm. He took her pulse and blood pressure and frowned. Her pulse was slow and her pressure was 80/35. After giving her medication to stabilize her blood pressure, he placed an oxygen mask over her face.

"Are you positive it was a rattlesnake that bit her?" the doctor asked Nora.

"Yes, our son killed it. It had rattles," Dan said as he entered the exam room.

The doctor searched through his cabinet for a vile of rattlesnake antivenin, but unable to find any, turned on the transceiver that substituted for the out-of-order phone lines and called St. Patrick's hospital. The pharmacist on duty said the hospital had several vials of rattlesnake antivenin on hand, but someone would have to come to the hospital and pick it up.

The doctor shut off the transceiver and turned to Dan.

"Sir, I am going to have to stay with the child and stabilize her. You will have to go to the hospital and get the antivenin. It's critical for Penny to receive antitoxin as soon as possible," the doctor insisted.

The snake neurotoxin had already caused her little arm to swell and it had turned purple all the way to her elbow. The poison would soon attack her internal cardiovascular system. The doctor frowned. "I will stay here and monitor the child's vitals. St. Patrick's hospital is in midtown, next to the park. I have talked to the resident pharmacist and the medicine is waiting for you at the front desk."

The boys had moved Chester to the car and were obediently waiting in the car with him. Dan drove down Bridger street as fast as he dared. The traffic lights inoperative and with almost no traffic on the streets, it only took fifteen minutes to drive to the park. Several cars and trucks passed them along the way, suggesting that gasoline must be available somewhere in Missoula. They found the hospital, a five-story, brown brick building on the east side of the city park, and pulled into the Emergency Parking lot. Dan told the boys to stay in the car and ran up the ramp leading to the emergency entrance. The reception room was empty except for a receptionist dressed in a white nurse's uniform and wearing the traditional nurse's hat. She sat at the front desk with her head resting on one hand as she flipped pages in a Vogue magazine. She didn't look up from her magazine to acknowledge Dan as he ran breathlessly through the lobby and stood in front of her at the front desk. He loudly cleared his throat. She casually glanced up and then returned her gaze back to the magazine. "Can I help you?" she asked with obvious boredom.

"Yes. Do you have antivenin medication ready for pickup?" Dan inquired.

Without even a superficial search of her desk she answered, "No . . . who ordered it?"

"I don't know the doctor's name. He is the doctor on call at the Missoula EMC across town. He sent me to get this medicine."

She looked at him and asked, "When did he call?" Her eyes casually drifted back to the magazine.

"The doctor called about 15 minutes ago," Dan replied, with growing irritation. "He sent me to pickup antivenin medication. It's a matter of life-or-death. The hospital pharmacist told him the package would be waiting for me at the emergency desk. This is the emergency desk, isn't it?

The receptionist put the magazine aside. "It is . . . and what's **your** name?"

"Dan Justin. A rattlesnake bit my daughter. Her name is Penny."

"I came on duty a few minutes ago and there were no notes about a medication pickup or a package."

"Please look . . . my daughter needs that medication as soon as possible."

Acting annoyed, she sighed and after shuffling through papers stacked on her desk, looked up and said, "I'm sorry, but there is no such order here, and besides, we cannot admit your daughter. The hospital is no longer accepting patients. At least not until they restore the electricity."

Clearly exasperated, Dan raised his voice.

"I am not here to check my daughter in. She is with the doctor at the Missoula Emergency Medical Clinic. He sent me here to bring him the antivenin that will save her life. Did you listen to what I just told you?"

The receptionist exhaled noisily and then pushed an intercom button. She beeped the pharmacist on call and when he answered, he claimed he knew nothing about an antivenin order.

The receptionist frowned. "I'm sorry, but we do not have any medication on hold for you. Perhaps it's in the doctor's name."

"I told you, I don't know his name. He is the doctor on call at the Emergency Clinic. All I know is that he called here, talked to the pharmacist on call, and ordered some antivenin for my daughter. He told me to pick it up at the front desk. Call the clinic and talk to the doctor."
"What is his transceiver channel?" she asked.

Dan seethed with frustration. "Transceiver channel . . . how would I know? I am just passing through town. Call someone and find out. It is the Missoula Medical Emergency Clinic. Do you understand the word *emergency*, because this sure as hell is one."

She pushed several buttons on the intercom and asked about the doctor on call at the Missoula Emergency Clinic. Finally with a deep sigh, she said, "His name is Dr. Wooster, but no one knows his transceiver channel nor does anyone remember taking a call from him about snakebite antivenin."

Dan's frustration turned into rage.

"Call the clinic; it must be on your list there," as he pointed to the rolodex on her desk.

She fingered through the rolodex file, and finally found the proper channel for the clinic.

"Oh . . . they're on the 'all call' channel," she said, without apologizing.

Just then, the hallway door opened and a technician in greens stepped into the room.

"Pickup for Dr. Wooster," he announced.

"That would be for me," Dan sighed. "Why did it take twenty minutes to bring the medication to the front desk? Dr. Wooster expected it to be waiting for me."

The man stared at Dan but ignored his question. "You are not Dr. Wooster. Let's see your prescription."

"Dr. Wooster didn't give me a script. He sent me to pick up the medication he ordered."

"Unless you have a written prescription signed by Dr. Wooster, I can't give this to you. No script, no medication. I can't just hand medication to a stranger. Rules are rules you know."

"Damn your rules! My daughter is dying and Dr. Wooster is trying to save her life. A rattlesnake bit her and she desperately needs the antivenin. Call him on the transceiver and get his permission to give the medication to me."

The man looked at the receptionist and shrugged his shoulders. The receptionists shrugged hers in response.

"I don't care what Dr. Wooster might or might not say on the transceiver. No script, no medication," the technician said, with a faint hint of a smirk. "Go back and get a script."

Dan put his face as close to the technician's as he dared and hissed, "I don't have time to go back. Call the clinic . . . now . . . before I strangle you. My daughter is dying while you people shrug your shoulders and hide behind your damned rules."

Clearly intimidated, the technician nodded to the receptionist and she switched the transceiver to 'all call' and paged the clinic. Dr. Wooster immediately answered. She handed the transceiver to the technician.

"Some guy is here at the hospital demanding I give him antivenin without a script. He claims you ordered it, but he has no script. You know I cannot just hand medication to a stranger. Now he's threatening me," the technician complained.

Dr. Wooster burned up the transceiver with a series of swearwords.

"Quit screwing around and give the medication to Mr. Justin . . . NOW. I spoke with the resident pharmacist, Dr. Martin, just a half hour ago. He knows Mr. Justin is coming to the hospital to pick up the medication. Mr. Justin's daughter needs that antivenin immediately."

"You know that I can't do that," the technician insisted. "You should have sent him here with a signed a script."

"Let me talk to Dr. Martin," Dr. Wooster demanded.

"Well, he left a while ago," the technician said.

"Then patch me through to the pharmacist on call," Dr. Wooster demanded. The receptionist patched him through to Dr. Benedict. Dr. Wooster explained that Dr. Martin had left a note on his desk saying that he had filled an antivenin prescription and told the technician to take it down to the lobby at the front desk. A Mr. Justin would arrive shortly to pick it up. The pharmacist found the note and then asked to speak to the technician, who admitted that on the way to the lobby he stopped by the cafeteria for a cup of coffee. "I expected Mr. Justin would have a script, but . . . he doesn't have one," he whimpered.

Dr. Benedict hung up and went down to the reception room, took the package from the technician, and handed it to Dan. Then he turned to the technician, "If you had taken this medication to the reception desk immediately and left it there as a 'will call' as Dr. Martin instructed, we wouldn't be having this conversation."

The technician tried to excuse his actions with, "I would have given him the medication **but . . .**"

Dr. Benedict froze him in mid-sentence with a cold stare. "In the middle of every butt is an ass hole. Before Dr. Martin left for the day, he told you to take the medication to the lobby. He said nothing about demanding a script. You knew that and your lackadaisical attitude created this problem."

It had been fifteen long, frustrating minutes for Dan. With the medication finally in hand, he thanked Dr. Benedict, ran out the door, and climbed into his car. It had snowed while he was in the hospital, and an inch of new slush covered the streets. Ice coated Dan's windshield as he hurried across town as fast as the slippery road and limited visibility permitted. Fifteen minutes later, he ran into the clinic and rushed into the examination room. Keith and Scott followed their father inside and sat down in the clinic waiting room. Dan barged into the room and handed the antivenin to Dr. Wooster. Nora was standing alongside the examination table holding Penny's hand and softly talking to her.

Penny looked terrible. Her breathing was shallow, her eyes glazed over, and her hand and arm were swollen to twice their normal size. An oxygen mask was strapped over her puffy, purple face and an IV dripped into her good arm. Dr. Wooster injected the antivenin into the IV and increased the drip rate. After a few minutes she hadn't responded to the medication, so the doctor inject a second vial directly into her arm. Twenty minutes later he administered a third vial of antivenin. Fifteen minutes passed before Penny slowly opened her eyes and squeezed her mother's hand.

Smiling, Dr. Wooster turned to Nora and said, "I think she is going to be just fine. Normally, we would admit her to the hospital for observation but they are not taking patients right now. She has some necrosis on her index finger, yet I think it will heal. We will keep her here overnight, and if by the morning she shows steady improvement, I will release her. Is that your trailer outside?"

"Yes," Nora replied, "but I am not going to leave her side."

"Well, I don't want you to," the doctor said. "You can stay right here with her and sleep on the cot." He turned to Dan and suggested, "You and the boys can stay in your trailer overnight, and we will see how things are going with Penny in the morning."

Penny had a difficult, restless night, but by morning her arm and hand were still discolored but almost back to normal size, and her breathing and pulse were regular.

Dr Wooster was of a mind to release her, yet to make sure there was no permanent damage to her arm or hand he suggested they remain in town for a few days so he could check on her condition. Dan was reluctant to remain in town. Overnight, two more inches of wet snow had fallen and slush covered Missoula's streets. An early fall snow in Montana is not unusual, and travelers could expect heavy snowfall anytime between mid-October and early November. More than a few inches would clog the highways all across Montana. With no highway workers to plow the roads, they would soon become impassable. They had to leave now or remain in Missoula for the winter, and Dan was unwilling to do that. Penny's accident had already cost them a travel day, and Nora thought that Penny was well enough to travel. The doctor reluctantly agreed.

He handed Penny's medication to Nora saying, "Just keep her warm and quiet. If she is not doing well by tomorrow, stop at the Wolf Point Clinic. I will radio the doctor on call and alert him."

They thanked Dr. Wooster for his help and compassion. Penny even managed a weak smile as they said good-bye.

Dan piled his family into the truck and drove across town, looking for an open gas station. He finally found one near the Interstate. A large sign announced that gasoline was $9 per gallon and the limit was ten gallons. A line of cars waited for their turn at the pump. When Dan finally pulled alongside the pump, the service station attendant noticed the California license plates and knocked on the car window.

"Sorry, but we do not sell gas to out-of-state folks," he stressed.

Dan pleaded his case, but the attendant was unrelenting. "No gasoline for out-of-state cars." That was that. Dan asked if any other stations were selling gas. The attendant said there were, but he would get the same answer wherever he went. "You must have Montana plates to buy gasoline here in Missoula," he said. "No exceptions."

Such a discriminatory policy was not only unfair but probably illegal, yet under the present circumstances, there was nothing Dan could do. He angrily drove out of Missoula and onto the highway leading northwest to Great Falls as more snow flurries added to the slush already gathering in piles alongside the road. Nora sat in the backseat, with Penny sandwiched between herself and Scott, and Keith sat in front with his dad. Chester sat on the floor. By late morning, the snow turned to rain and melted the three inches of slush on the highway. They drove through Great Falls, looking for an open gas station, but couldn't find one. By late afternoon, another 116 miles of road was behind them. They arrived at Havre, where the state highway merged with U.S. Highway 2 which would take them across Montana and North Dakota and into Minot. A few miles east of Havre, Nora spotted a trailer park with an "Overnighters Welcomed" sign hanging over the entrance. Nora thought Penny had had enough travel for one day and suggested that they stay there for the night. Dan pulled into the park and walked into the office. After Dan answered the usual "Where are you folks from and where are you going" questions, the manager slowly shook his head.

"Well sir, I sure hope you folks are prepared for winter weather; you'll need chains and a full tank of gasoline. A snowstorm is due in tomorrow, and there are no gas stations or services open between here and Williston, North Dakota." Williston, a distant 310 miles, is the only town of any size between Havre and the Montana-North Dakota border.

That night the temperature dropped to 20 degrees and it snowed six inches. Dan untangled his chains, and in the morning, he and Keith put them on the truck as Chester wandered around the park searching for a snow-free spot under a tree where he could pee. Dan made slow progress along the snow covered road. The temperature remained below freezing and 30 miles east of Havre, a herd of sheep crossing the highway blocked the road. The sheep meandered along the road and the flock seemed endless. The Basque sheepherders, mounted on mules and dressed in serapes and wide-brimmed hats, seemed in no hurry to move the sheep along or even create a break in the flock to let Dan's truck pass through. Dan turned off the motor and waited a half-hour for the herd to move on.

Well-known for large herds of sheep, Montana is also infamous for its relentless winds. The wind blew across the featureless, flat countryside in gusts that shook the truck and plastered the windshield with sticky snow. The windshield wipers could not keep up with the onslaught and Dan had to stop every few miles to scrape ice from the windshield and peel the frozen wipers from the glass. Even after the snow stopped, the persistent wind blew powdery snow across the road making it impossible to see the blacktop. Snow piled in deep drifts alongside the highway, covered fenceposts, and filled drainage ditches. Concerned that he might drive off the road into a ditch, Dan crept along at twenty-five miles per hour. On a long straight stretch, the wind had blown the dry snow off the pavement. Worried that his chains would wear out on the dry pavement, Dan pulled over and removed them.

Ten miles further on, they entered hilly country where the high roadside bluffs protected the highway from the onslaught of wind and allowed the snow to again accumulate on the roadway. In some places, it piled into foot-high berms that blocked the roadway. Dan plowed through the first few of these drifts, yet without chains, it would only be a matter of time before they became stuck. Dan and the boys put the chains back on and continued down the highway, only to find more miles of snow-free pavement. They repeated placing chains on and then taking them off for the better part of the day. As Dan predicted, one of the links on the front left tire chain finally broke and the loose chain began beating against the wheel well. Dan spent the next hour trying to replace the broken link, a task that forced him to remove his gloves. By the time he finished repairing the chain his fingers were almost frostbitten. Nora took his frozen fingers into her hands and gently blew on them. As feeling came back, it felt as if 100 pins were piercing his flesh. Dan couldn't drive, so Nora took the wheel. By late afternoon, the snowstorm subsided and the sky cleared, allowing Nora to make better time. Exhausted from taking the chains on and off, Dan's eyes felt heavy and he dozed off. When he awoke, the sun had set and they had only made it to Wolf Point, about 240 miles from Havre and 70 miles from the Montana-North Dakota border. Penny was doing well, so Nora decided they didn't need to visit the clinic. She stopped at a roadside park outside town, and they agreed to make camp here for the night. Dan realized that the small progress they made that day had disheartened his family. They needed a diversion. He took out his harmonica and played a ditty, interspersing the tune with bawdy limericks. Everyone laughed and even Nora, who disapproved of these rogue lyrics, cracked a smile. Dan had not played his harmonica since leaving Santa Cruz and the music improved their mood. He promised that tomorrow would be a better day, and assured them that the weather and road conditions would improve. By tomorrow night, they would make it all the way to Minot. Then he cooked a treat for dinner: a pizza baked in the propane oven. The tune, Dan's promise, and pizza lifted everyone's spirits. Their luck could only change for the better.

That was wishful thinking.

CHAPTER TWELVE:
NORTH DAKOTA

By morning, Penny felt much better. Her arm had returned to a normal size and color, and this morning she was her usual cheerful self. After a quick breakfast, they drove down the snow covered U.S Highway 2. Three hours later, everyone cheered when Keith first spotted the "Welcome to North Dakota" sign. Dan pulled over and studied his map, which showed that after passing through Williston, U.S. 2 would merge with U.S. 85 and then continue north for a few miles, before leaving U.S. 85 and heading eastward. As they traveled north on Highway 85, Dan missed the snow-covered U.S. 2 turnoff sign and drove for several miles, before he recognized his mistake. He turned his rig around and headed south, looking for the turnoff. Scott was the first to notice a vibration coming from the trailer and looked out the back window to see what was wrong.

"Dad, the trailer wheel is wobbling," Scott warned.

Dan looked in his outside rearview mirror and noticed the wheel on the trailer was indeed wobbling; in fact, it looked like it was ready to fall off. He pulled over and walked back to the trailer and noticed the left side tire leaned outward at an awkward angle. Smoke drifted from the axle and a closer look revealed the overheated wheel bearing had frozen and caused the axle to break in half. Only the wheel-well prevented the wheel from falling off altogether. This was more serious than a flat tire. He had an extra tire but did not have an extra bearing or a spare axle. He chided himself for not repacking the wheel bearings before they left Santa Cruz. He had intended to do so, yet in the last minute rush to pack, he forgot to do it. Now he would pay for such carelessness. Dan unhitched the trailer, jacked it up, and then placed blocks under the broken wheel. He removed the axle and one of the bearings, which he placed in his pocket, but was unable to remove the other bearing. He threw the wheel and the broken axle with the burned bearing into the truck bed. Nora and the kids watched from the car.

"Keith and I are going to drive back to Williston and try to get this wheel fixed," Dan said. "Nora, please take Penny and Scott and wait for us in the trailer. Lock the door. Scott, take care of your sister and mother, and don't open the trailer door for anyone until we return. We will be back as soon as possible."

The drive to Williston was uneventful though finding an open garage or service station in this town seemed hopeless. The garbage-strewn main street showed no signs of life. Boarded up stores and abandoned cars lined both sides of the street. The Oregon ghost town of Plush showed more signs of life than did Williston. Labor Day banners hung limply from lampposts and the sidewalks were littered with boxes and broken glass. They drove to the end of Farm Bureau Street and then explored a side street. From one end of the town to the other, they didn't see a single human being or pass another car, until Keith spotted a truck emerging from a side street. Dan turned around and followed the truck a few blocks until it parked outside a shack with an overhead sign that announced:

"Santa Catalina Cantina"

Several mud-covered trucks were parked on the street across from the Cantina. A cream colored, rusted-out 1955 Chevy short bed, with the front bumper hanging on by a single bolt, stood out from all the others. A sign painted on the door read:

Charlie's Garage

Parked in front of the Cantina were two recent vintage Ford trucks; with dents and spattered with red mud, and a mongrel dog in the truck bed, each waited for the return of its owner.

Dan pulled in between the two pickups, climbed out, and told Keith to wait in the truck. As Dan passed between his car and the neighboring truck, a pit-bull leaned out of the truck bed and growled a warning. He climbed the wood steps leading to the Cantina front porch and opened one of the swinging doors. Taking a hesitant step forward, he remained in the doorway for a few seconds as his eyes adjusted to the dimly-lit bar, thick with cigar and cigarette smoke. A Hank Williams tune twanged from a jute box in the back of the bar.

The interior reminded Dan of a scene from an old Western movie. Early western furniture on sawdust-covered floors, rough-hewn wood support beams, a knotty pine slat ceiling, and log walls with farm tools haphazardly nailed here and there. Two stacks of baled hay guarded an upright piano hugging one wall. The single front picture window admitted a weak beam of sunlight that provided barely enough light to guide customers to the oak bar that extended across the entire back of the establishment. The only other source of light came from flickering candles stuck on a wagon-wheel chandelier hanging from one of the roof beams. Several cowboys sat on bar stools, downing glass mugs of frothy beer and chasing them with shots of amber whiskey. A few other patrons sat at small tables, with their legs and mud-covered boots spread across the aisles. The clientele, dressed in rumpled hats, muddy boots, leather vests, flannel shirts, and soiled jeans looked like a tough bunch. Certainly not a group Dan cared to mess with.

He stood in the doorway for a moment, then took a deep breath and stepped inside. The noisy swinging door pivoted back and forth in a series of decreasing thuds. Customers stopped whatever they were doing and watched as Dan stepped over the gauntlet of sprawled legs and made his way to the bar. He felt conspicuously out of place but bravely strode over to the bar. The bartender, dressed in a baggy, long-sleeved shirt, held in place by red arm bands, suspiciously eyed Dan as he climbed onto an empty stool.

"What will you have?" he drawled. His tone sounded downright hostile, as if to say "strangers are not welcome here."

Dan took a deep breath and replied, "I was wondering if there is an open garage in town? I have a broken wheel that needs fixing."

A hushed groan drifted across the room.

"Nope," the bartender replied, the word coming from deep inside his throat. "All the garages in town closed down after the blackout. There's no gas for sale in Williston, and without gas, most cars are parked and there's little need for a garage."

Dan looked disappointed. After all, several cars were parked out front. The bartender lowered his voice and nodded to a man slumped over a table next to the front window.

"Could be that Charlie over there owns a garage . . . anyhow, he use'ta own one." The bartender indicated a customer sitting alone at a table next to the lone window.

"He's short of drinking cash, and his bar tab is over the limit, so if you offer to cross his palm with silver . . . he might be willing to open for you." Dan thanked him and walked over to the table. The man's eyes remained closed and he didn't stir as Dan approached. An empty beer glass sat on the table. Dan gently shook the man. He immediately sat up, and with steel blue eyes, glared at Dan. Short and overweight, with wisps of gray hair protruding from a moth-eaten ten-gallon hat loosely held in place by two enormous ears, the man's face morphed into a frown.

Dan cleared his throat. "Charlie?"

"Yep . . . who's askin'?" the man replied, and then intentionally turned away from Dan to stare out the window.

"The name is Dan . . . Dan Justin. I need a wheel fixed and understand you own a garage down the street."

The man's head jerked around and he gave Dan a blank stare. Even in this dim light, the man's large eyes were the deepest shade of blue that Dan had ever seen. A handlebar mustache hid his mouth, and his stubble-covered face, sculptured by deep set wrinkles, testified to years of hard labor.

"Yep . . . owned a garage some time back . . . closed it down weeks ago," he said as he looked into his empty beer glass.

Dan baited him. "I hear tell you could use some drinking cash. I would be willing to pay if you could fix a wheel for me."

The offer perked Charlie's attention. His eyes pierced Dan and a wry smile spread across his face. "How much cash you talkin' 'bout?"

"How about 30 bucks?" Dan proposed. He took a twenty and a ten out of his wallet and laid it on the table.

"Hows about $50 . . . plus parts," Charlie countered.

Dan knew that $50 was a lot to ask for fixing a wheel, yet he was in no mood to haggle. "Okay, fifty it is, but that includes parts." Dan added another twenty to the pile of cash.

Charlie scooped up the money, pushed his chair back and stood up. Once on his feet, he measured a full head shorter than Dan. "Foller me," he said, and staggered toward the front door. Dan followed him outside onto the sun-drenched porch. After the dark bar, the bright sunlight forced him to squint, and his eyes watered. Charlie staggered off the bar porch, adjusting the brim of his hat to shield his eyes from the sun. "Which truck is yours?" he asked.

Dan nodded to his truck.

Keith was still in the backseat as the two men climbed in. "Keith, this is Charlie. He is going to fix the wheel for us."

Charlie turned around and gave Keith a mumbled "hello" and a nod and settled into the front seat.

"Go down Farm Bureau Street and follow it west for three blocks," Charlie instructed.

A weather-beaten gas station, with an attached garage, stood at the end of the third block. Both the station and the garage were in bad need of a coat of paint. Two yellow and white gas pumps filled the service island and a large green and white "Sinclair" sign, complete with the familiar dinosaur logo, sat on top of the island canopy. The hulk of a dented Chevy truck blocked one of the island pull-ins, and trash blocked the other side.

Dan pulled in front of a sign over the garage that announced, "Charlie's Garage". Charlie climbed out of the truck and mumbled, "Let's have a look at that damn wheel."

Keith took the wheel out of the pickup, placed it on the ground, and then handed Charlie the broken axle, with the outside bearing still attached.

"What did this come off of?" Charlie asked.

"My 1979 trailer," Dan answered.

Charlie grunted, unlocked a side door, and then stepped inside and began working the chain that lifted the garage door. Once the door opened, Dan rolled the wheel inside and Keith trailed behind him. The garage looked as if a cyclone had struck it. Rusty frames of gutted automobiles, oily engine blocks, car doors, hoods, and various other auto parts lay strewn about the oil-stained floor. A full-length workbench covered with various tools and parts rested against the back wall. A hodgepodge pile of various engine parts, including water pumps, pistons, crankshafts, radiators, and dead batteries lay in a jumbled pile on one side of the garage, and a grease pit under a hydraulic car lift occupied the center. Two engine blocks supported by four-by-fours straddled the retracted lift.

"Looks like ya broke the damn axle," Charlie muttered, commenting on the obvious as he placed the broken rod in a bench vice. After a few whacks with a hammer, the frozen bearing slid off the shaft. Charlie examined the bearing and tossed it on the workbench. "Did ya tink ta bring da inner bearing along?"

"Yes I did," Dan answered as he reached into his pocket and handed Charlie the scorched inner wheel bearing.

Charlie frowned. "Y' knows ya got to pack dese t'ings w'id grease once in a while." This was not exactly news to Dan; even so, he sheepishly nodded his head.

Charlie placed the scored bearing in the vice and pried off the retaining ring with his pocketknife. "Well, dis bearing is done fer, and so's the other one. Dem balls and races 'been scored' till dey's all but useless." He picked up the axle and examined it. "Looks like dis axle came from a late '70's Ford; I prob'bly don't have a proper bearing and axle like dis one, but I'll 've a look around."

Charlie went over to the back bench and began to open drawers filled with various greasy parts. Not finding what he wanted, he took off his hat, scratched his head and took a closer look at the burned wheel bearing. Then he went over to the pile of junk and began to throw parts right and left. As he worked his way down into the inner depths of the pile, he let out a whoop and held up a half-inch diameter ten-inch long steel rod.

"It's a '73-79 Ford truck axle," he proudly announced as he jabbed the rod into the air.

Then, he went over to the workbench, opened several drawers, and rifled through the contents, until he came up with a handful of various bearings.

"Ain't got no proper Ford wheel bearings, but I kin build a set for ya from dese parts."

He examined Dan's damaged bearing housing and removed the scored balls and races. Then he replaced the ball bearings and races with parts that he salvaged from the other bearings, carefully packed the repaired bearing set with grease, and then installed the retainers. He slid both bearings onto the axle shaft and handed it back to Dan.

"Thar ya go," he said with pride.

Dan thanked him.

"How's 'bout a ride back to Santa Catalina?" Charlie asked.

Dan and Keith dropped Charlie off at the bar and then drove the 30 miles back to his stranded trailer and family.

Nora was overjoyed to see them. They had been gone for over three hours, and in all that time, not a single car or truck had passed by. It was late afternoon and soon would be dark. Black clouds on the western horizon promised another snowstorm. Dan spent the next hour replacing the trailer axle and wheel, and while he was at it, he removed the other trailer wheel and repacked those bearings with grease. When he examined the other set of bearings, he congratulated himself for taking the time to repack those wheel bearings, as they also showed early signs of overheating and scoring and would have eventually failed.

The sun had set and snow was falling as they prepared to leave. Chester had gone off into the farmland to chase rabbits and Dan's whistle didn't bring him back. They couldn't leave Chester stranded and Dan did not want to travel on snowy roads at night, so they decided to camp right where they were. They could make it to Minot, only 120 miles distant, in the morning. Chester returned fifteen minutes later, with another jackrabbit in his jaws.

The snow continued to fall off and on throughout the dark, moonless night. A pack of coyotes howling in the nearby hills frightened Penny and made Chester restless. The dog growled and scratched at the trailer door. The coyotes sounded close, yet Dan assured Penny that they were a long way off and would not come near the trailer. About three in the morning, Nora woke Dan saying she heard a noise outside the trailer. Chester growled and anxiously paced back and forth. Dan opened the door a crack, taking care to keep Chester inside. His flashlight startled three coyotes sniffing around the trailer. At first, the light caused them to back away, but eventually they ignored the flashlight and went on sniffing around the trailer for food. Chester kept trying to push past Dan and squeeze through the partially opened door, but Dan grabbed his collar and pulled him back inside. He closed the door, found his pistol, and then opened the trailer door a crack and fired a shot into the sky. At the sound of the gunshot, the coyotes ran off into the darkness. The sight of fleeing coyotes was too much for Chester. He squeezed through Dan's legs, pushed the door open, and then jumped to the ground and rushed into the night while barking madly. The fleet-footed coyotes had a head start and easily outdistanced Chester, who came back after Dan called him. A half hour later, the coyotes came back again and scratched around the trailer. Penny began to cry and even Scott admitted he was scared. Dan decided that it would take more than a pistol shot to frighten these animals away, so he loaded his 12 gauge shotgun. Nora placed her hand on Dan's shoulder.

"Dan let these creatures be, and I don't want you outside. Just lock the door and let the animals sniff around. There is nothing out there that they can take or damage. When they grow tired, they'll go away."

The coyotes continued to sniff and scratch around the trailer and truck for several minutes, and then after finding nothing to eat, as Nora predicted they ran off into the night. Soon the howling started gain, but this time from a good distance away. Nevertheless, Penny and Chester did not go back to sleep for some time afterwards.

Dan rose about 8 a.m., dressed and opened the trailer door to let Chester outside for his morning pee. Overnight, new snow had covered the ground to the door's bottom step. Chester barked and then bounded through the powdery snow. The morning sky was clear, yet during the night another 15 inches of the white stuff had blanketed the surrounding farmlands and highway. Before trying to drive back down the highway, Dan and Keith put the chains back on the truck. The warm pavement had melted some of the previous night's snowfall and a layer of ice now covered the highway. Despite the added traction of chains, the truck slipped and skidded down the highway. Their truck made fresh tracks in the new fallen snow and made it difficult for Dan to find the edge of the highway. The best he could do was to position his truck between the fence lines that bordered opposite sides of the road. The trackless road confirmed that no other vehicles had driven this way since last night's snowfall. The narrow shoulders bordering the highway gave Dan little room for error, and he knew there would be no hope for a rescue should he slip off the pavement and end up stuck in a roadside ditch.

Fighting strong crosswinds and blowing snow, the truck crept down the highway at barely ten miles per hour. It took over an hour to reach the U.S. 2 turnoff. To their relief, a set of dual truck tire tracks marked the highway and provided added traction for his truck and trailer.

Nora wrinkled her nose. "Dan, I think I smell gas."

Dan took in a deep breath, but said he didn't smell any.

The tracks continued east for forty miles, ending at a truck stop near the township of Ross. A Peterbuilt truck and trailer was parked outside the café. Dan parked and went inside. A lone customer sat at the counter sipping a cup of coffee. Dan introduced himself to the truck driver, who then shook his hand as if Dan was a lost brother.

"The name is Sean, Sean Martin. I watched your rig drive up. Where are you folks headed?"

"North of Minot," Dan replied. "We have been following your tracks for the last 40 miles. I hope you don't mind if we continue to follow you."

"Not at all," Sean replied. "I am heading to Minot myself." He placed two dollars on the counter and put on his sheepskin coat and cowboy hat.

"The road has been a bitch since Willington," Sean mumbled as they left the café together, "and it is slippery as snail snot. Despite my heavy rig I'm having a hard time fighting the crosswinds, and it has been a bitch to keep away from the edge of the snow-covered road. I dare not go over twenty-five miles per hour, and the only way to judge where the damn road is, is to stay halfway between the fence lines. The only good part is the snow has finally stopped."

To avoid the snow and ice kicked up by Sean's truck tires, Dan stayed about 25 yards behind and followed the fresh truck tracks down the highway. The wind blew in bursts so strong that it shook their truck. Blowing snow caused a white-out that made it difficult to see the truck's rear brake lights and after a few miles, Dan lost sight of the truck lights altogether. He continued to follow Sean's truck tracks until they wove back and forth across the highway in ever increasing arcs. Barely visible through the white out, the outline of Sean's jackknifed truck lay askance in a ditch. Dan pulled alongside the disabled truck as Sean appeared from behind the trailer, fighting against the raging wind to make his way to their rig.

Dan rolled the cab window down. "I misjudged the edge of the road," Sean yelled over the howling wind, "and I couldn't keep my truck under control on this slippery patch of ice. Now it's stuck in a ditch and without a tow truck, there's no way to get it back on the road. Can you please take me to Minot?"

Dan moved Penny to the front seat with Nora and made room for Sean in the back, with Scott and Keith.

"Sure glad you folks happened along," Sean said. "It would have been a long walk back to the diner, and I have yet to see another car or truck on this road."

"Yes, it would have been a long walk all right, and a cold one at that. I think the diner is five miles back and the next town is at least ten miles from here," Nora advised, looking at her map.

Sean smiled and said, "I don't know what I am going to do about the truck though. I was bringing a load of food from Spokane to Minot, and folks badly need that food in Minot. Perhaps I can get a wrecker from my company in Minot to come out and pull the truck out of the ditch."

They rode in silence for a few miles, and then Nora said, "Dan, I think I smell gas again."

Dan looked down at his gas gauge. The needle was well below the quarter-full indicator.

"That's odd," Dan commented. "The tank was half full when we left Williston and we haven't come far enough to use a quarter tank of gas."

Dan pulled over and shut off the engine. He had emptied the last fifteen gallon can of gas from the spare gas cans into the main tank back in Havre. With the added eight gallons he bought in Grangeville, he figured the gas in the main tank would be enough to take them all the way to Willow Creek. They should have used less than twenty gallons to drive the 365 miles from Havre, yet now the gauge pointed to less than five gallons remaining in the main tank. With the gas gauge reading less than a quarter full, he questioned if he now had enough gas to complete the trip.

Something was dreadfully wrong. Dan turned to Sean in the backseat.

"I don't know Sean, I thought I had more than enough gas to complete the trip. When we left Havre, we had more than 25 gallons in the main tank. Throughout the trip from California, we have been getting 20 miles to the gallon, but somehow we are getting much less than that now."

"Dan, some miles ago I told you I smelled gas," Nora reminded him.

"I think I smell it too," Sean added.

Sean and Dan got out of the truck and opened the hood. The smell of gas was overpowering. Dan waved to Nora to start the engine. The moment she did so, a thin stream of gasoline spurted from the short black rubber hose that connected the fuel pump to the carburetor.

"Turn off the engine!" Sean shouted to Nora.

Sean examined the fuel hose and discovered a tenth-inch slit on the underside. "The hose is split. It has to be replaced."

"I don't have another hose," Dan lamented. "Could we use some electrical tape to repair it?"

Sean thought about it for a minute, and then replied, "I don't think so. This hose develops a lot of pressure and I doubt electric tape would hold for long. You cannot afford to lose any more gasoline. Do you have any duct tape?" Dan didn't have any.

Keith had been listening to the conversation and climbed out of the truck.

"Dad . . . we could use the propane tank hose that leads from the spare tank in the trailer to the regulator. I think it's about the same size and length as the gas hose."

Sean and Dan went back to the trailer and examined the black rubber propane hose. Keith was right; the propane hose was about the same diameter as the broken fuel hose, and long enough to replace the damaged one. Sean disconnected the fuel hose and replaced it with the propane hose, carefully tightening the hose clamps at either end. Then he checked the new connections for leaks, and finding none, both men and Keith climbed back inside the truck.

"That's a clever son you have there," Sean said to Nora, after they were underway. Keith beamed and Nora smiled.

Dan mentally estimated if there was enough gasoline left to make it all the way to Willow Creek. The remaining five gallons in the main tank would take them to Minot, now only 65 miles away, but Willow Creek was another 40 miles north of Minot. If they made it to the farm, they would arrive on fumes. Dan asked Sean if he could buy gasoline at his company's truck depot in Minot.

Sean was not hopeful. Trucks use diesel and the depot usually don't carry much gasoline. Nevertheless, he promised to ask when they arrived.

CHAPTER THIRTEEN:
BACK AT THE FARM

The morning after the shooting, Peter was in a funk. The shooting weighed on him like a 60-pound sack of potatoes. He went about the farm doing his chores, but Judy sensed his mood had changed from optimistic to pessimistic. That morning, Peter went to the food bank to help prepare for that afternoon's opening, yet he couldn't keep his mind on the work and returned to the farm before noon.

After lunch, a persistent knock at the front door startled them. Peter grabbed his gun and opened the chained front door a crack. Sheriff Bill Eisner, hat in hand, stood on the porch with his deputy. Peter invited them inside.

"I hate to bring you bad news," Bill began, "but based on new information, Mayor Peterson convinced Judge Jameson to issue a warrant for your arrest. I am here to serve it."

Peter was incredulous. "My arrest . . . for what? Based on what new information?"

Sheriff Eisner said nothing as he handed the warrant to Peter. He read it and stopped at the phrase "manslaughter" and "for the investigation into the death of Jake Brevick."

Peter couldn't believe his eyes.

"The warrant says "manslaughter". How can that be? You told me that you wouldn't arrest me for shooting Jake. It was a clear case of self-defense."

Judy cried, unable to believe her ears. "Manslaughter . . . a warrant for manslaughter?"

"Well, based on some new information from Mayor Peterson, Judge Jamison signed this warrant," the sheriff explained.

Peter's head was spinning. "Based on what new information? Mayor Peterson has no new information. I told you everything that happened and just the way it happened. There's nothing more to tell you or the judge."

Judy was close to tears. "Bill, this warrant makes no sense whatever. Tell us what new information you have to justify Peter's arrest."

The Sheriff looked perplexed.

"Look . . . I can't tell you anything more right now. You'll learn the details at a hearing scheduled on Thursday afternoon. Judge Jameson issued the warrant at Mayor Peterson's insistence. I know this may seem unfair, but I am just doing my job." The sheriff took out a pair of handcuffs and placed them on Peter's wrists.

"Peter, you are under arrest. Anything you say can and will be held against you, you have the right to remain silent and be represented by an attorney, if you cannot afford one the court will appoint one for you. You will appear before the judge at Thursday's court hearing."

"You say I have a right to a lawyer, but where am I going to find a lawyer before the hearing on Thursday? This only gives me two days and the only lawyer in town is now the judge."

"I regret it but I can't help you with that . . . I wish I could," Bill said. "Judy, check with Pastor Helming. Perhaps he knows someone who could represent Peter on such short notice."

Bill led Peter out to the sheriff's car. Judy stood in the doorway, tears streaming down her face. Pam and Trevor stood by her side, too confused to ask questions.

The sheriff drove Peter into town. Along the way, Peter tried to make sense out of what could possibly motivate Mayor Peterson to demand his arrest. Then the truth hit him. Jake was Mayor Peterson's cousin. Most folks around Willow Creek were related in one way or another, and Peter only learned of the connection between the mayor and Jake after church services last Sunday.

Peter remembered the harsh words he and Jim Peterson exchanged over the policies he introduced at the food bank. Jim Peterson wanted Peter and Pastor Helming to drop all the limitations for food distribution at the food bank, but Peter firmly stood his ground. Mayor Peterson, also a member of St. Paul's parish and the parish board, claimed Peter didn't have the authority to make these rules. In his self-important view, Mayor Peterson's authority extended to the entire township, including St. Paul's church. He had never accepted the parish board decision on the food bank policy and continued to challenge Peter at every opportunity. Pastor Helming defended Peter, pointing out the board placed him in charge of the food bank, and Peter was carrying out the board's decisions, decisions that he as pastor supported. Mayor Peterson did not take such a defeat lightly. He seethed with anger and told another parishioner and a few town council members that Peter had overstepped his authority and would be sorry for his arrogance. Could Mayor Peterson be so vindictive as to demand Peter's arrest with some trumped-up charge? And what exactly was this "new" evidence? Peter knew that Mayor Peterson could be spiteful, especially when it involved his ego. No other explanation made any sense to him.

Since the town didn't have a jail, Peter wondered where Bill was taking him. He then remembered the rumor that he had heard about the Olsen boardinghouse.

Lars Olsen originally built the Olsen house in the late 1860's for his family, about the time Willow Creek incorporated. Lars and his wife raised eleven children in that house, and even now it remained the largest house in town. Mrs. Peters, the spinster granddaughter of Lars Olsen and sister of Niles Olsen, inherited the Olsen home. Some years ago, she convinced Niles to renovate the house built by their grandfather and she turned it into a boardinghouse. Downstairs, the house had a large sitting room, a library, kitchen, dining room, guest bedroom and master bedroom. Upstairs were seven smaller bedrooms. Lars farmed wheat on 1,000 acres, five miles outside town and around the turn of the century, he opened the downtown mercantile and hardware store. Niles inherited the Olsen businesses at the same time that his sister inherited the Olsen home. In the 1920s, Niles opened the Washington Savings and Loan Company across the street from his mercantile store. In recent years, the boardinghouse business had dwindled to a single resident, Miss Denardo, the local school's sixth grade teacher, who moved to Wahpeton after the school closed down in October.

Mrs. Peters leased the Olsen home to the town council and Sheriff Eisner converted it into a temporary jail and hired her as the resident cook and housekeeper. She continued to live in the downstairs master bedroom, next to the guest bedroom reserved for the warden they intended to hire. The first "guests" of the Olsen jail were the Hansen brothers and then Mike Graves, who Sheriff Eisner arrested the previous week for breaking and entering Nile's mercantile store.

Sheriff Eisner escorted Peter into the temporary Olsen boardinghouse jail and locked him in one of the upstairs bedrooms, down the hall from the Hansen brothers. As Peter walked down the hall to his cell, he saw Mike through the small window cut into the door and recognized him as one of the two other men with Jake the day he was shot. It was ironic and maddening that Peter now found himself locked up next to a member of the threesome who tried to break into his barn.

Thursday afternoon, Judy Dexter and a few members of her church gathered in the town hall for the weekly court session presided over by Judge Jameson. Present were Mayor Peterson, four other members of the town council, Pastor Helming, Coroner Jenkins, Niles Olsen, and Sheriff Eisner. Judge Jameson called the court to order and the court deputy ushered Peter Dexter and Mike Graves into the temporary courtroom. At first, Peter wondered why Mike was in the courtroom, and then he assumed Mike had to be there for his own court hearing.

Judge Jameson explained that this was an inquest about Jake Brevick's death. The judge read the complaint initiated by Mayor Peterson, which stipulated that Peter had shot Jake without justification. Judge Jameson then asked if a lawyer represented Peter.

Peter said that he had not hired a lawyer. "After the power blackout, the only criminal defense lawyer who lived in Willow Creek moved to Jamestown. The nearest defense lawyers are all in Minot, but since the phone lines are down, Judy hasn't been able to contact a lawyer."

Judge Jameson explained that since this was only an inquest, as such, Peter did not need legal representation and the hearing could proceed. Judy bristled. She felt it was illegal to hold a court hearing without legal representation for Peter and whispered her concern to Pastor Helming, who asked to be recognized and repeated Judy's objection. Judge Jameson claimed that since legal representation for Peter was unavailable, and because Peter was only "a person of interest", he didn't need a lawyer. Pastor Helming reminded the judge the sixth amendment to the Constitution guarantees all the accused legal representation in court. Judge Jameson repeated that Peter was only a "person of interest" and hadn't yet been charged with a crime; therefore, the sixth amendment didn't apply. Pastor Helming reminded the judge that Peter had been arrested. "You signed a warrant for Peter's arrest, he was read his rights and jailed, and now he stands accused before this court," Pastor Helming argued. "It seems to me that Peter is much more than a person of interest."

Judge Jameson ruled that Pastor Helming's objection was out of order. He repeated that the purpose of this hearing was only to determine if a crime had been committed. He then reminded Pastor Helming that he wasn't a lawyer and told him to sit down. Then he called Peter to the stand.

Peter kept his testimony short, explaining that the geese alerted him to someone on the property. He grabbed his shotgun and ran out onto the front porch to see Jake and his friends trying to break into his barn. He hollered for them to get off his property and fired a warning shot from his 12 gauge shotgun over their heads. Two of the men ran off but Jake ran toward the porch, waving a tire iron and screaming profanities. He fired another warning shot, but despite the repeated warnings Jake kept on coming. He shot Jake when he was a few steps from the porch. He claimed that he was only defending himself from a man with the clear intent to do him bodily harm. Afterwards, he covered the body with a blanket and then drove Jake's body to the sheriff.

The judge asked Peter why the sheriff had not found the tire iron that he claimed Jake had threatened him with. Peter supposed the iron ended under Jake's body, but didn't know why the sheriff hadn't found it.

The coroner took the stand and confirmed that pellet wounds to his lower torso caused Jake's death. There were no powder burns on his body, suggesting the shooting took place from some distance. The sheriff also testified that Peter brought in Jake's body and admitted shooting him in self-defense. Subsequent residue tests confirmed Peter had recently fired a gun. The sheriff had not yet performed the tests that would prove the fatal shot came from Peter's gun.

Then Judy took the stand and gave her testimony of the incident. She told the court that after Peter confronted three men trying to break into their barn, he fired a warning shot over their heads. Two of the men ran off, but one man came running toward the porch, cussing and waving a tire iron in his hand. She thought he intended to hit Peter. Terrified, she screamed for Peter to shoot him. Then Peter fired a second warning shot over the man's head and again yelled for the man to stop, yet he kept on coming. When he had nearly reached the bottom of the front steps, Peter fired the third and fatal shot. She said that neither she nor Peter initially recognized the man. However, as he lay dying on the ground and Peter removed his cap, she recognized him. He was Jake Brevick, the man who had Peter confronted at the food bank.

Mike Graves took the stand and contradicted Judy's and Peter's entire testimony. In his version, Jake, Mike, and another friend were passing by the Dexter farm when they heard a commotion and saw a fox attacking the geese. The geese continued honking as Jake and his friends ran down the driveway, intending to chase the fox away. Jake picked up a rock and threw it at the fox, which then ran off into the forest. Peter, on hearing the geese, came out onto the porch and began screaming profanities at Jake and his friends, while waving a shotgun at them. Jake went up to the house to talk to Peter, but as he neared the steps, Peter shot him at point-blank range."

"Peter fired two shots at us, and the pellets stung. Ed and I ran into the woods, but Jake walked toward the house to talk to Peter. There were no warning shots and Jake did not have a tire iron, as Judy testified. All Jake wanted to do was explain that he and his friends were chasing a fox away, but Peter shot him before he had the chance to do so."

He added that as Jake lay dying in the snow, Peter fired a fourth shot, which missed, and then as he stood over him fired a fifth shot into Jakes body. Furthermore, he denied that they were trying to break into the barn and repeated that Jake, "never had a tire iron or any other weapon in his hand."

Called to the stand, the sheriff testified he investigated the crime scene later in the day of the shooting. He examined the scene, confiscated Peter's shotgun, and gathered five spent shotgun shells from under the porch steps and surrounding area. The barn door latch showed signs of a forced entry, but the lock was missing. He did not find the tire iron, until he returned to the farm the following day to do a more thorough inspection of the property. Trevor then told him he saw the tire iron in the pigsty, and he found it there covered with blood and mud. He took it back to the office for completed fingerprint and blood type analysis.

Judge Jameson called Pastor Helming to the stand. The pastor testified that Peter was an outstanding member and deacon of St. Paul's church and told of his unblemished reputation in the Lutheran Church community. He related that it had come to his attention that Jake and his friends were selling food in town, and he cautioned Peter not to give these men anything more from the food bank. He related the confrontation that he witnessed between Jake and Peter. Pastor Helming said that when Peter told Jake he and his friends were no longer welcomed at the food bank, he overheard Jake say to Peter:

"We'll just see about that . . . someday your damned church may burn down to the ground."

Pastor Helming said the next week he and a parishioner put out a suspicious fire that started behind the back wall of the church. Someone piled brush and branches alongside the church and lit it. It looked like arson. He reported this incident to Sheriff Eisner and told him he suspected Jake tried to make good on his threat to burn down the church. However, as far as the pastor knew, Sheriff Eisner never followed up on his complaint.

Despite the contradictory testimony, Judge Jameson decided there was enough evidence to arraign Peter on homicide charges. He ordered the sheriff to arrest Peter. Sheriff Eisner reminded the Judge that he had already arrested Peter, on a signed manslaughter warrant.

"Well, then re-arrest him on a murder charge," the judge demanded.

The judge said he would preside over a hearing in this temporary courtroom, within three weeks. He set bail at $10,000 cash. Considering the present circumstances, he knew it was unlikely Judy could raise $10,000. The only bank in town was closed, and Judy didn't have $1,000 cash, let alone $10,000. She left the courtroom in tears, not knowing how she was going to run the farm with Peter in the Olsen jail.

Only Mike Graves, a known troublemaker and felon, had testified the killing had been anything other than self-defense, yet Judge Jameson had set bail so high that it ensured Peter would remain in jail until the trial. Since Peter was not a flight risk, the bail seemed unreasonable to many of his friends. Judy suspected that Mayor Peterson, still harboring a grudge against Peter, had influenced Judge Jameson to set such a high bail.

Pastor Helming caught Judy outside the courtroom and pledged his support for Peter and that of most of the Lutheran Church community. She complained that it was all so unfair and a clear case of vindictiveness perpetrated by the mayor. Pastor Helming knew a lawyer in Minot, and promised he would use the last of his precious gasoline to drive to Minot the next day and hire Josh Richards to defend Peter. Josh was a well-known criminal defense lawyer in Minot. In the past, he had represented Willow Creek citizens in the Minot court. The next day Pastor Helming made the drive to Minot and Josh readily agreed to represent Peter at the hearing next month. Pastor Helming complained about the high bail set by the judge, and since Peter was not considered a flight risk, asked Josh to speak to the judge about reducing bail as soon as possible.

Judy fixed dinner for herself and the kids that night, but she couldn't eat. She sat at the kitchen table and stared blankly at Peter's empty chair. Why did the judge set Peter's bail so high?

"The bastard," she thought. "He's just being revengeful."

Alone and defenseless, how was she going to run the farm without Peter? Trevor stopped eating and listened to a noise from the barnyard.

"Mom, the geese are making a ruckus. Someone is outside again."

Judy grabbed the shotgun and ran out onto the porch. Two men were trying to get the new lock off the barn door.

She shouldered the shotgun and screamed for the men to "git".

They ignored her warning and continued to pry on the lock. Judy cocked the gun and fired a shot. Lead pellets sprayed them but at this distance none penetrated the men's skin. Both men turned and ran down the driveway to the road.

Frustrated and frightened, Judy went back inside the house and locked all the doors. The next morning, she took the kids with her to visit with Sheriff Eisner.

"Two men tried to break into our barn last night," she complained. "I'm worried for the children."
"I'm sorry Judy," he said, "but there's not much I can do. I have no one who I could assign to protect you."

"Then, get Peter out of the Olsen jail," she demanded.

"It's not up to me. The only way to get him out is to pay the bail."

"Judge Jameson knows damn well I can't raise $10,000 dollars in cash," she said bitterly.

"I wish there was something I could do to help, but there just isn't. I understand Pastor Helming has hired a lawyer. Perhaps he can talk the judge into lowering the amount. I'm so sorry about all this," the sheriff said and added, "Peter is a good man."

Judy stormed out of the sheriff's office and went home and locked all the doors and windows, neglecting to even feed the animals.

Two days later, Josh drove to Willow Creek and took statements from Peter, Judy, Sheriff Eisner, and Mike Graves. He visited Judge Jameson and asked him to lower the bail, but the judge steadfastly refused to do so. Josh could not understand the judge's intractable decision and began to suspect something rotten was in play. Meantime, Peter languished in jail, next door to the room occupied by his accuser, Mike Graves.

CHAPTER FOURTEEN:
WELCOME TO WILLOW CREEK

Dan pulled into the Minot Trucking Company yard, and Sean went inside the office to report in and let his employer know where he left their truck. He also intended to ask for some gas for Dan, but never got that far. He came out a few minutes later upset and angry.

"The SOB fired me on the spot, and after working for this company for five years."

"Why?" Dan asked.

"They are pissed that I ran the truck off the highway. They claimed it was carelessness on my part. With all the blowing snow and ice, there was no way to tell the difference between the pavement and the shoulder, and unfortunately, I missed a curve and ran the truck into a ditch. My boss said I should have stopped in Havre until the weather cleared. I argued the folks in Minot were in bad need of the food I was carrying, and I was doing my best to get it to them, storm or no storm. He didn't give a damn about the starving people in Minot, but griped about having to rescue the truck."

Sean seethed with anger.

"I think the real reason he fired me is because there is no work for truck drivers until the power outage is over, at least not until we can get more diesel for the trucks. Sorry, but the company won't sell you any fuel."

Nora took his hand said that she was sorry about his misfortune.

Sean simmered down a bit, and then smiled saying, "I heard from another trucker there might be work at the Minot AFB. Could you drop me off on your way to Willow Creek?"

"Sure thing," Dan replied, "Our rig may make it to the Air Force Base, but I don't think there is enough gasoline in the tank to take us all the way to Willow Creek. I intend to stop at the AFB and use my influence as a former Air Force officer to buy a few gallons."

Dan tapped on the main gas gauge. The arrow pointed to the "empty" mark.

"Perhaps it would be better to look for some gasoline here in Minot."

"Fat chance of that," Sean said. "I was here two weeks ago, before my run to Spokane and back, and there was precious little gasoline for sale in Minot then. The chance of finding some around here is little and none. Your best chance is to make it to the Minot AFB rather than use what precious little gas you have left looking for some in town."

"You're right," Dan said thoughtfully, "and because I am a former Air Force Captain, there is a chance they would sell me some. It's worth a try."
As they drove through Minot, the town appeared neat and orderly. They could see no obvious damage to businesses along the main highway, no abandoned cars, no garbage in the streets, the store fronts were intact, and the townsfolk were leisurely walking along the sidewalks. They turned onto U.S. 83 that led north from the city to the Minot AFB and continued on into Canada. They passed a state highway patrol car and met a handful of other cars driving into the city. Dan reasoned there must be gasoline for sale in the area, otherwise, there would be no cars on the road. It was a good sign, and where better to ask for gasoline than at the AFB?

He pulled into the front gate of the Minot AFB, and two armed Marine sentries came out of the office to inspect the rig. One sentry asked Dan for identification, while the second sentry slowly circled the pickup and trailer. Dan produced his California driver's license, truck registration and his Air force ID card. The Marine carefully examined the documents, then returned them and saluted.

"Captain Justin. What is your business on the base?"

Dan put his documents away and said that he was dropping off his passenger to look for work.

The sentry asked, "Were you stationed here in Minot?"

"Yes, in fact this was my last assignment before I retired," Dan explained.

"Were you a pilot?"

"No, when I retired I was an air traffic controller."

The second sentry looked in the backseat and eyed Sean. "And who is this person?"

Sean took out his truck driver's license and handed it to the soldier.

"I'm looking for work on the base," Sean explained.

"Well, you may be in luck. I understand the distribution center is looking for a truck driver."

He returned his attention to Dan and said, "Since you are familiar with the base, please take Mr. Martin to the employment center at the base HQ. He can apply for work there."

The sentry finished his truck inspection and addressed Dan.

"Sir, please open the trailer for inspection."

Dan got out of the truck and unlocked the trailer door. The Marine entered the trailer and searched through the closets and drawers. Finding nothing unusual, he stepped outside.

"Sir, you are free to go on base," the sentry said, as he placed a green "Retired Officer" sticker on the truck window.

Dan thanked the Marine guards and asked, "I noticed while driving here a few trucks and cars were on the highway. We're going to Willow Creek, but I'm unsure if we have enough gasoline to make it that far. Is gasoline for sale on base?"

"Yes, but I'm not sure they can sell any to you. You can try at the Post Exchange, but your best chance would be to get permission from the Officer of the Day. Last week they were selling a few gallons to base personnel with special permission from the base commander, but seeing you are a retired Captain, the Officer of the Day might give you permission to buy a few gallons."

Dan drove past a long line of parked B-52 bombers, to the Post Exchange gas station. A large storage tank dwarfing the station usually stored several hundred thousand gallons of gasoline. He pulled alongside one of the pumps and an Airman First-Class came over to the truck. He took note of the California license plates and the green window sticker.

"Sorry Sir, but we cannot sell gasoline to anyone not assigned to the base," he said.

Dan showed him his Air Force ID. "I understood that I might buy a few gallons for emergency use."

The airman eyed Dan suspiciously. "Sir, what's your emergency?"

"We need to get to Willow Creek, and I would appreciate it if you could sell me five gallons. I would hate to run out on the open road."

"I'll see what I can do." The sentry took Dan's Air force ID, went into the office, and made a phone call. Less than a minute later, he was back.

"The Officer of the Day is Major Bret Riordan. He says he knows you, and to let you have five gallons. He says you should stop by Ops and say hello."

Major Bret Riordan! It had been years since he last saw Bret, an old drinking buddy who had worked with him in the flight ops center in the Azores. What a small world and what rare good luck that his friend was the Officer of the Day.

The airman pumped five gallons of precious high-octane fuel into Dan's main tank, saluted and wished them good luck.

"How much do I owe you?" Dan inquired.

"Nothing sir, the fuel is compliments of the Air Force."

Dan thanked him and drove to the employment center. Sean climbed out at the center and thanked Dan and Nora for the lift.

"I hope that we run into each other someday," Sean said.

"Good luck with the job, and if you are ever in Willow Creek, look for Peter Dexter's farm. We intend to stay there until power is restored to the country."

Dan drove down the street to the Operations Command Post. He and Nora left the kids and Chester in the truck and went inside. Major Riordan greeted Dan and Nora warmly and offered them a cup of coffee. After reminiscing about their stint in the Azores, Bret asked,

"So, what brings you Californians to North Dakota?"

Dan told him how crazy it was in California with all the crime, break-ins, muggings and roving gangs of hoodlums. He said they had to get out of Santa Cruz while they still had the chance.

"We are going to live on Peter Dexter's farm in Willow Creek, to escape that insanity."

"You don't mean Captain Peter Dexter do you?"

Dan nodded and asked, "Yes. Do you know Captain Dexter?"

"Well, I do not know him personally, but I know of him. I heard that he's in trouble in Willow Creek."

"Trouble . . . what kind of trouble?" Dan asked.

"Well . . . a couple of days ago, as Officer of the Day, I had a meeting with a Minot defense attorney, Josh Richards. Josh is a former JAG officer, and he stopped in here for permission to buy gasoline and see Captain Peter Dexter's service records. He mentioned he was going to Willow Creek to represent Peter on a murder charge."

Dan gasped. "Murder charge? Peter . . . no way!"

"Well, that's what Richards said, and that is all I know about it. I gave him a chit for the gasoline and the information he requested. With no newspapers or phones, I don't expect to hear how it went in court for Captain Dexter."

Dan now felt added urgency to get to Willow Creek as fast as possible. He thanked his friend, and hurried with Nora back to the truck. As they drove out of the base, Dan and Nora discussed what Major Riordan had told them.

"It is just hard to believe," Nora said, "there must be some mistake. Peter in jail? For murder? It must be hard on Judy and the kids."

Dan drove the remaining 25 miles to Willow Creek in less than a half hour and pulled into the driveway leading into the Dexter farm. The minute Dan pulled into the front yard, the geese began a ruckus, and Judy came out on the front porch with a shotgun. She immediately recognized the Justin pickup and trailer and came flying off the porch, Pam and Trevor close behind her.

Dan and Nora stepped out of the pickup and Judy threw her arms first around Nora, and then Dan.

"I am so glad to see you folks," she blubbered, as tears stained her cheeks. "I have been praying that you would come. You have arrived just when we most needed you. Thank God."

The boys and Penny climbed out of the truck and Chester ran out into the fields.

Dan let Judy have a good cry on his shoulder. "I heard that Peter is in jail."

Judy's head jerked away from Dan's shoulder. "How in the world did you hear about that?"

"We stopped at the Minot AFB for gas, and a friend of mine, Major Bret Riordan, told me. He met the other day with Peter's lawyer, Josh Richards. It is a small world."

"Josh visited with us the day before yesterday. He asked the judge to lower bail for Peter, but he refused."

Judy wiped away a tear. "I am so glad you folks are here. The kids and I have been frightened. Two men tried to break into our barn the other night, and the sheriff won't do a damn thing to protect us. I cannot run the farm alone. We have to get Peter out of jail. Can you help me raise bail?"

"How much do you need?" Dan asked.

"Almost $10, 000," she admitted.

Dan whistled. "Unfortunately, we don't have that much cash. Has there been a preliminary hearing yet?"

Judy nodded. "Last week."

"Why did the judge set bail so high?"

"There is something going on between the mayor and the judge. We suspect the mayor demanded this high bail so Peter couldn't get out of jail. The banks have been closed since mid-September. We can't cash a check or use our credit cards, neither can anyone else in town. I only have $600 in cash, and I wouldn't even have that much except before the blackout, I had been saving egg and milk money to donate to our church."

Dan grew angry. "What is wrong with that judge? He knows that no one can raise that amount of bail money with all the banks closed. I need to talk with Peter's lawyer."

Judy smiled. "Without phone service, there is no way to contact Josh . . . he lives in Minot. However, he'll be here again on Thursday morning, for the hearing scheduled that afternoon."

"You say the judge refused to reduce Peter's bail even when Josh spoke with him?"

"Yes, he met with the judge two days ago, but Judge Jameson refused to reduce bail. Josh could not understand why the judge acted so unreasonably, but I knew the answer. Mayor Jim Peterson is the problem. Peter confronted him some weeks ago, and Jim has not forgotten that Peter got the best of their argument. Jim thinks he owns the whole town and everyone in it. Jim and Peter exchanged angry words over Peter's food bank distribution policy at the Lutheran church. Judge Jameson is in the mayor's pocket, and I am sure that Jim Peterson is still seething over his altercation with Peter. I think Jim had the sheriff arrest Peter for manslaughter and then urged the judge to change the charge to murder. Peter was brought to court without a lawyer to represent him, which we all thought was illegal. Another complication is that the man Peter shot, Jake Brevick, is Mayor Peterson's cousin. The sheriff has said this was a clear case of self-defense. Peter is in jail because of the mayor's vindictiveness and small-town politics."

"There must be more to it than vindictiveness," Dan suspected. "Seems like too much trouble to go through for petty revenge."

He thought for a moment, and then said, "You say you have $600. Well, I have $6,500 cash. Do you think your friends and church members could raise another $2,900?"

"I'll ask Pastor Helming tomorrow morning when we go into town for Church services. I think some parishioners would be willing to help out," Judy said.

Judy led Dan and Nora into the kitchen and poured two cups of coffee from the "never empty" Dexter coffeepot warming on the stove.

"How was the trip out here?"

Nora took a sip of coffee. "Well, it was no picnic. It took us almost two weeks. We had to take back roads because the interstate was just too dangerous to drive. We avoided all the big cities. Fortunately, when we left Santa Cruz, we had two full gas tanks in the pickup and a couple full gas cans as well. We bought ten gallons in Idaho and thought we had enough gas to get here, but because of a leaky fuel pump, we almost ran out of gas near Minot. Fortunately, the AFB gave us five gallons, enough to get us here. Despite pulling the trailer, the pickup got good mileage."

"Penny was bitten by a rattlesnake in Idaho, and we had to take her to a doctor in Missoula," Dan added.

"A rattlesnake you say? What an ordeal. She looks ok now," Judy remarked sympathetically.

"Yes, Penny is fine," Nora said.

"How were the roads out here? I hear they closed most of the highways."

Dan put down his cup of coffee. "Many highways were closed, but we checked locally to find out which roads were open and closed. Most townsfolk were helpful, and in Grangeville they sold us food and gasoline. We ran into a snowstorm in Montana and western North Dakota, and of course no one is plowing the roads. Nonetheless, with much luck and a heap of prayers, we made it through."

"Where would you like us to park the trailer?" Dan asked.

Judy looked nonplussed. "Oh, behind the barn, but you needn't stay in the trailer," she said. "We have extra bedrooms in the house."

"Thank you, but we didn't want to impose," Nora interjected. "We'll be comfortable in the trailer."

"Well . . . suit yourselves . . . but I would feel better if you stayed in the house," Judy pleaded. "I had to chase two men off the property just a few of days ago. Quite frankly, we are all scared to death."

They sat around the table sipping coffee, and Judy related the circumstances leading to the shooting. She said that Peter shot Jake in self-defense, and related the details of the preliminary hearing. After listening to Judy's rendition, Dan wanted all the more to talk with Josh. However, that would have to wait until Thursday morning.

The next morning, Trevor and Keith hitched the two mules to the hay wagon and both families rode to St. Paul's Church for Sunday services. Pastor Helming warmly greeted Dan and his family and introduced them to the congregation. Mayor Peterson wasn't in church that day, and many folks already suspected that he had railroaded Peter and convinced the judge to set bail high to keep Peter in jail. After services, Judy explained that they needed help to raise $2,900 for Peter's bail. St. Paul's parishioners donated over $3,000 in cash and checks and gave the money to Judy. She now had enough cash to bail Peter out of jail.

Early Monday morning, Judy and Dan took the truck into town and confronted Judge Jameson. Judy surprised the judge when she handed $10,000 to him for Peter's bail, some of it in cash and some in personal checks. The judge refused to accept the personal checks, claiming because of the closed banks, he couldn't verify the checks and would only accept cash.

Dan could no longer contain his anger.

"You damn well know that we cannot raise $10,000 in cash. You and the town mayor have conspired to hold Peter in jail, for whatever reason I cannot imagine. I know the law, and the cash and promissory notes in the form of checks constitute legal payment of the bond. Checks are legal and there is nothing in the law to cover the case of closed banks. Accept this payment and release Peter or I will go to Minot and get a judge from the district court to come here and set you straight on the law."

Dan's fury unsettled Judge Jameson. He had managed to intimidate most of the Willow Creek townsfolk, few of whom knew anything about the law, but this Californian was not so easily intimidated. He could be trouble, and the last thing Jameson wanted was to have a district judge in his office.

He had no choice but to accept the bail money and release Peter from the Olsen house. He reluctantly signed the release form and handed it to Judy.

"We want a receipt for the $10, 000," Dan insisted.

"What's the matter, don't you trust me?" Jamison asked

"Not on your tintype," Dan said. "Now sign the receipt."

Judge Jameson seethed, yet he knew that Dan had him in a corner and signed the receipt.

Dan and Judy took the signed release papers to the sheriff's office, and Sheriff Eisner accompanied Dan and Judy to the Olsen jail to release Peter from custody.

The sheriff unlocked Peter's door and Dan and Judy entered the room. Peter stood slack jawed and wide-eyed, staring at Dan. He couldn't believe his eyes.

"Dan . . . what s-sight for sore eyes . . . w . . . when . . . h . . . how did you get here?" Peter stammered.

"We drove our trailer here and arrived Saturday night. With the help of your church friends, Judy and I have arranged bail," Dan said.

"You are free to go with them," the sheriff pronounced.

Peter hugged Judy, shook hands with Dan and thanked him for helping out with the bail money. Then they began the drive back to the Dexter farm.

"Mrs. Olsen fed us well enough, and the room was comfortable, but I am sure glad to be going home," Dan admitted.

"What is going on in this town?" Dan questioned. "I met Judge Jameson, and obviously, he's in the mayor's pocket. You ought to have seen his face, when Judy showed up with the bail money. At first, he refused to accept it, but I persuaded him otherwise."

Peter frowned.

"There is a town conspiracy all right, and it is between the judge and the mayor. Perhaps it includes Niles Olsen as well, the local mercantile owner. I haven't figured out why they have targeted me. After all, I am just a little fish in their big Willow Creek pond," Peter mused.

Dan took a deep breath and then said, "Well, you and I and your lawyer need to figure out what is going on . . . before the next hearing. Otherwise, such ignorance might just be your downfall. I hope your lawyer is a good one, because your enemies are a bunch of slimy snakes."

Peter sighed. "I have only met Josh Richards once, when he came to Willow Creek to talk with the Judge about lowering my bail and visited me in the Olsen jail. I liked Josh. He seems competent and reliable. You will have a chance to see him in action on Thursday."

"We can both talk with him when he arrives at the farm Thursday morning." Dan said."

CHAPTER FIFTEEN:
THE HEARING

Thursday morning, at 9:35 a.m., Josh Richards arrived at the Dexter farm, and Peter greeted him at the door. Josh wanted time to confer with Judy and her children, before the scheduled two p.m. court session.

"How did you get out of jail?" Josh asked, surprised to see Peter.

Peter smiled. "With the help of my friends," and introduced Josh to Dan and Nora.

Later that morning, Sheriff Eisner arrived at the Dexter farm to search for more evidence. He spoke with Josh for a few minutes and told him he had dusted the tire iron, found in the pigsty, for prints. Despite the encrusted mud, Sheriff Eisner found evidence of two different sets of fingerprints with blood on the iron. The blood was the same type as Jake's. One set of fingerprints belonged to Mike Graves and the other to Jake Brevick. No other prints were found on the iron.

Josh wanted to get a better sense of the shooting time-line and events, so he asked Peter, Dan, and Judy to reenact the incident, while he and the sheriff watched. Trevor, who had witnessed the attack from inside the house, played the part of Jake, and Keith and Scott were Jake's accomplices. Dan, Nora, and the sheriff watched from the porch, and Josh took careful notes.

The reenactment began with Trevor, Keith, and Scott walking down the drive that led from the county road to the Dexter home. As before, the geese began to make a racket when the boys turned into the driveway and came within two-dozen yards of the barn. The boys then went over to the barn and pretended to pry on the barn door latch, with a tire iron. Peter came out on the porch with a pretend shotgun and yelled at the three boys to get off his property. They initially paid no attention to Peter's warning, so he faked a shot into the air. Keith dropped the tire iron and he and Scott scampered into the woods. Trevor picked up the tire iron and walked toward Dan, who was still standing on the porch. Dan warned Trevor to stop but he kept on coming. Judy came out onto the porch and yelled for Dan to shoot. He fired a pretense warning shot into the air, but Trevor continued to come forward until he reached the bottom step.

When Trevor reached the bottom step, Peter turned to the observers and said, "This is the point when I shot Jake."

Sheriff Eisner nodded and asked, "What did you do next?"

Peter said that he went down to where Jake lay on his back, gasping his final breaths. Jake cursed him, shuddered, and then let out a long sigh and died. After a few minutes, Peter asked Judy to bring a blanket from the house to cover the body. Then he backed his truck up, loaded Jake's body into the bed of the pickup, and drove to the sheriff's office.

Josh took careful notes throughout the reenactment. At the conclusion, he put his notebook away and asked Peter about the tire iron the sheriff found in the pigsty. Peter couldn't explain how the iron ended in the pigsty. He surmised that Jake fell on top of it and the blood on it must have come from Jake as he bled to death. Anyway, he didn't notice the iron, when he lifted Jake into the bed of the pickup. The next day, when the sheriff came out to the Dexter farm to look for added evidence, there was no sign of the tire iron—at least not until his third visit, when Trevor told him he had seen a tire iron in the pigsty. Judy, Trevor, Pam, and Peter claimed that none of them had touched the tire iron, and since none of their prints were on the tool, their story was credible. No one could explain how the tire iron ended in the pigsty.

Josh carefully paged through his notes. "Sheriff, you visited the Dexter farm four times after the shooting: the first time, on the afternoon of the shooting; the second time, when you arrested Peter; then the following day, to do more investigative work; and finally, this morning. On your visits, did you find any shotgun shells around the porch?" The sheriff said that he found five empty 12 gauge Remington cartridges on his first visit and took them with him to his office.

"Five . . . are you sure you found five shells?" Josh questioned.

"Yes, I'm sure there were five shells," the sheriff said. "Two were on the porch, one more on the ground under the porch steps, and two on the ground in front of the steps. I sniffed them and confirmed that each had been recently fired."

Josh asked Peter again if he was sure he had only fired the shotgun three times.

Peter thought for a moment, then answered, "Yes, I am positive. I fired once to warn the men away from the barn; then a second time, to warn Jake as he came toward me; and finally, a third time, when I shot him. Yes; it was definitely only three times."

"Did you fire all three shots from the porch and the steps?"

"Yes. I fired the first and the second rounds from the porch, then the third, the one that killed Jake, from the porch steps."

"Sheriff, did you determine whether the five shotgun shells were all fired from Peter's gun?"

"No, I was unable to do so. The shells are missing."

"Missing you say. Isn't that a bit peculiar?"

"Missing or misplaced . . . whatever. Anyway, I don't have them," Bill declared.

Josh asked to examine Peter's shotgun that Sheriff Eisner held as evidence and had brought with him. Josh donned gloves and Bill handed the gun to him. Then Josh asked for five new shotgun shells. He placed a shell in the main chamber then tried to load four more shells, one at a time, into the tubular chamber that holds extra shells. Three shells easily slipped into the tube, yet when he tried to insert a fourth shell, it wouldn't fit.

"Why can't I get a fourth shell into the shell chamber?" Josh asked Peter.

"The tube has been plugged to allow only four shells in the gun at one time: three in the reserve tube and one in the main chamber. That's the law. Only four shells can be in the gun," Peter explained.

The sheriff looked puzzled. "Yet, when I came out to the farm later that day to look for evidence, I found five recently fired shell casings on and around the porch. Peter, did you reload the gun as Jake came toward you?"

"No, I had no time to reload. It all happened too fast. Anyway, I'm positive that I only fired three times," Peter insisted. "Sheriff, were any shells in the gun when you confiscated it?

"Yes, one shell was still in the tube."

Josh turned to Judy. "Judy, when you brought the blanket out to cover the body, did you notice the tire iron?"

"No, I didn't. Yet, if the tire iron was under Jake's body, I wouldn't have seen it," Judy surmised

"Did you notice it after Peter put Jake's body into the truck?" Again, she said she didn't, but the ground was muddy. Then she added, the pool of blood so upset her that she avoided looking at the ground where Jake had fallen.

"Did you see any shell casings on the porch or around the steps?" She said that she didn't remember seeing any shell casings, but then again, she wasn't looking for anything.

Peter said that when he returned from the sheriff's office, he remembered seeing some shell casings lying on the porch, yet didn't notice how many there were.

Josh asked the same question of Trevor and Pam, but neither of them saw the tire iron or remembered seeing the shell casings. Trevor said that he noticed the tire iron lying in the pigsty, when he fed the pigs the morning after the shooting. Fortunately, he did not disturb it, and when the sheriff came the next day, he told him about it. The tire iron was critical evidence needed to back up Peter's claim that Jake was threatening him with a tire iron, yet someone had tried to hide the iron in the pigsty.

The two extra shell casings found at the scene also remained a mystery. Both Peter and Judy claimed only three shots were fired, and since the gun could only hold four shells, then either Peter reloaded or someone compromised the crime scene. That same person could have hidden the tire iron in the pigsty and placed two recently fired shell casings onto the ground near the steps.

The sheriff had taken Peter's shotgun and shell casings as evidence on the day of the shooting. He had intended to test the shells to see if they all came from Peter's shotgun; however, he didn't properly protect the chain of evidence. He left the shells on his desk and the next day, when he went to test them, they were gone. A careful search of the office failed to find the shells, and the janitor said he didn't see them when he cleaned the office that night.

Josh asked to examine the lock and latch that Peter claimed Jake and his friends were trying to jimmy. The sheriff said that he had been unable to find the lock, but the scratched and bent latch showed evidence of tampering.

"Did you look around the barn for the lock?" Josh asked.

"No, I didn't think it was important at the time," Sheriff Eisner answered.

Josh made another note in his book. "Well, no matter. Whoever threw the tire iron into the pigsty and placed two shotgun shells on the ground, also probably took the lock."

Sheriff Eisner didn't comment.

Josh and the sheriff examined the barn door latch. Consistent with Peter's story, there were fresh gouge marks, suggesting that someone had recently tried to pry it open. Josh made careful notes of everything he saw, and then took the sheriff aside.

"Sheriff, I have one last question for you. Have you found the mysterious 'third person' involved in the alleged robbery at the Dexter home?"

Bill said that he hadn't. Josh looked surprised.

"He is a witness in the incident is he not? You have Mike Graves in custody; it shouldn't be too hard to find out who his accomplice was on that day . . . now should it?"

Sheriff Eisner admitted that he had not yet asked Mike about the other person, but had a good idea who it was. He promised to have that person in court for the hearing.

The sheriff drove back into town, while Josh wandered around the farm taking pictures. Judy and Nora prepared lunch and after they ate, everyone piled onto the hay wagon for the ride into town. The hearing was scheduled to begin at 2 p.m.

*   *   *

When the Dexter and Justin families entered the court at 1:45 p.m., interested spectators had almost filled the hall. The families split up and found separate seats wherever they could. Pastor Helming and eight of his parishioners sat in the third row and nodded. The Pastor nodded to Judy as she entered the room and showed her to a seat next to him. The bailiff reserved the front row for the participants, who entered the room from a side door shortly after Judy sat down. Peter and Josh Richards took seats on the right side of the room. Mike Graves and a man that Peter didn't recognize sat on the left side, next to Sheriff Eisner. Darren Jenkins, the coroner, Niles Olsen and Jim Peterson's wife sat in the second row, right behind the sheriff. Peter noted that Jim Peterson wasn't in the courtroom; a seat next to his wife remained empty. Betty Wyckoff, the judge's secretary and court recorder, took a seat at a table to the left of the judge's bench. A rectangular oak table placed on top of a two-foot high platform served as the bench, with a leather-padded chair. Lance Cantrell, the acting prosecutor, sat to the right of the Sheriff. Other than Judge Jameson, Lance was the only other lawyer in Willow Creek, and therefore, the logical choice to act as prosecutor. Peter whispered to Josh that Lance owned a family law practice in town and had no experience as a criminal lawyer. He was a close friend of both Judge Jameson and Mayor Peterson.

The hearing scheduled to begin at two o'clock came and went, but Judge Jameson failed to appear. The hearing room buzzed with chatter as folks impatiently squirmed in their seats and wondered what had delayed the judge. Twenty minutes later, the judge and Mayor Peterson finally entered the room, and the bailiff asked everyone to rise. The Judge took his seat behind the bench, and the Mayor sat next to his wife. Spectators murmured about the judge's late appearance, and Josh whispered to Peter that a real judge would not tolerate such tardiness. The sheriff gaveled the courtroom to order, and everyone sat down.

Judge Jameson did not explain his late appearance. He began the proceedings by stating that because of the inability to hold a trial in Willow Creek, this would be a hearing to determine if Peter should be held, pending a trial at a later date in Minot. He stated that the charge had been changed from manslaughter to murder in the second degree. There would be no jury, and the judge himself, based on a preponderance of the evidence, would decide if Peter should be bound over for trial. Peter whispered to Josh that if the judge bound him over for murder and revoked his bail, such an adverse decision could keep him in jail for months.

Judge Jameson said he would allow each side to present evidence, and then in contrast to a convened Grand Jury hearing, he would allow Josh to present his client's defense. Witnesses could testify under oath and evidence must be properly entered and marked. He would also allow cross-examinations. This hearing would follow all other normal courtroom procedures, testimony would be under oath, and he cautioned both sides to follow proper courtroom decorum and the rules of evidence.

Prosecutor Cantrell called his first witness, Coroner Darren Jenkins, to the stand. Mr. Jenkins testified that Jake died of traumatic blood loss, because of multiple pellet wounds to the legs and lower torso. His blood alcohol level was below .05 when he died.

The next witness was Sheriff Eisner, who testified Peter brought Jake's body into town and admitted he had shot him in self-defense. The sheriff also testified about his initial examination of the crime scene the afternoon of the shooting and another investigative visit the day following Peter's arrest. With Trevor's help, he found a tire iron in the pigsty and noted the damage to the barn door latch. He also testified that he had found five 12 gauge shotgun shell casings on and around the porch. He read his detailed report, including the tests he performed on the tire-iron and that Peter's shotgun had been recently fired. He entered his report and fingerprint photographs into evidence. Josh cross-examined the sheriff and asked if the five shotgun shells he found at the crime scene had been tested to see if they came from Peter's gun. The sheriff admitted the shells had not been tested and had disappeared from his office desk. Josh asked the sheriff about the fingerprint evidence found on the tire iron. He testified the only prints found on the tire iron belonged to Jake and Mike.

The prosecutor called Mike Graves. Mike testified that he, Jake, and Ed were innocently walking by the Dexter farm when, at the driveway entrance leading into the farm, Jake spied a fox breaking into the chicken coop. All three men ran down the driveway toward the barnyard to chase the fox into the woods.

Prosecutor Cantrell interrupted Mike. "Ed . . . Ed who?"

"Ed Lawton," he answered.

"Please continue."

". . . and then Peter came out onto his porch with a shotgun and began screaming obscenities at us. Next I knew, Peter fired a shot at us. The pellets stung, but none penetrated my skin. Ed and I ran toward the woods, but Jake stood his ground. I heard a second shot as we ran. We watched from the trees as Jake raised his hands and shouted not to shoot. With his hands still raised, he walked toward the porch and when he was within a few feet, Peter fired a third time."

Mike stared at Peter for a few seconds before he continued his testimony.

"The pellets tore into Jake's lower legs, and bleeding from multiple pellet wounds, he fell to his knees. Peter then fired a fourth shot from the bottom of the steps, but it missed Jake and tore a hole in the snow in front of him. Then, standing only a few feet away, he fired the fifth shot that ripped into Jake's belly. Then Jake fell on his back, and blood and guts stained the snow. Peter just stood over Jake's withering body and watched him die. Then he called for Judy to bring a blanket."

Lance asked, "Were you and Jake trying to break into the barn"

"No"

"Did Jake have a tire iron?"

"No, there was no tire iron . . . none of us had one. It all happened so fast . . . from the first shot to the last took less than 30 seconds. Part of that time Ed and I were running for the woods, but I'm sure Jake had nothing in his hands at the time," Mike testified.

"Describe again everything that you witnessed," Lance demanded.

"As we ran toward the woods, I looked back and saw Jake walking toward the porch, with his hands raised. Judy came outside and shouted for Peter to shoot Jake, which he did from the top of the steps. Then from the woods, I watched the pellets hit Jake in the lower legs and he fell to his knees in the snow. Peter fired again, but it missed Jake. And then, when Peter was only a few feet away from Jake, he fired a fifth shot, which hit Jake in the abdomen."

Lance asked again, "How many shots were fired?"

Mike hesitated for a few seconds, and then answered, "Five, definitely five shots. The first one that sprayed us as we stood by the barn; and then a second shot, as we ran for the woods; a third shot, that felled Jake; and finally, the last two shots. They came one after the other. Like BANG . . . BANG."

"How long did Peter take to fire off the final three shots, the one that hit Jake in the legs, the one that missed, and the final shot to Jake's stomach?"

"Just a few seconds, I'd say less than five or six," Mike estimated.

Lance continued. "What happened next?"

"As Jake lay sprawled on the snow, Peter stood over Jake and watched him die. Then Judy came out of the house with a blanket. At this point, Ed and I ran back to town."

Lance said he had finished questioning the witness, and it was then Josh's turn to cross-examine Mike.

Josh asked why Mike, Jake, and his other friend, Ed, just happened to be walking down the county road in front of the Dexter farm. Mike said that they were simply out for a walk. Josh asked why they chose to take such a long walk; after all, the Dexter farm was five miles outside town. Mike claimed they often walked this far for exercise.

"You testified that you saw a fox breaking into the chicken coop, but the coop is 50 yards from the road. Isn't that a long distance away to spot a fox?"

"Well, we could see the coop and the fox just fine," Mike answered.

Then Josh entered as evidence a picture he had taken from the road outside the Dexter farm and labeled it as "exhibit A". The picture showed the long driveway leading into the Dexter farmyard, as viewed from the main road. The barn and house were clearly visible, but a snow covered berm bordering the driveway hid the chicken coop from view.

"As you can see from the picture, the chicken coop isn't visible from the road. I repeat, how could you see a fox breaking into the chicken coop, when you could not possibly see the coop from the road?"

Mike squirmed in his chair, and then answered, "Well, I don't know. Perhaps at first we just heard the geese making a racket and then saw the fox from the driveway. I think the snow bank wasn't as high that day as shown in your picture."

Josh entered the tire iron into evidence as "exhibit B", with the sheriff's affidavit that proved two of the fingerprints found on it belonged to Mike and the deceased, Jake Brevick.

Josh again asked Mike if he was sure that Jake did not have a tire iron that day. He affirmed that none of them had a tire iron.

Josh moved close to Mike's face and asked, "How do you think a tire iron got into the pigsty?"

"Peter must have hidden that tire iron in the pigsty," Mike explained.

"Why on earth would he do that?"

"I dunno, perhaps he didn't want anyone to find it."

"Peter's fingerprints were not found on the tire iron, but yours and Jake's were. How do you explain that?" Josh persisted.

Mike smirked, "Well, last month when we visited the church food bank, we had a flat tire in the parking lot and Jake borrowed a tire iron from Peter to change it. My friend and I helped Jake fix his tire and I returned the tire iron to Peter."

"You returned the tire iron to Peter after you changed the tire?"

"Yes."

"So, wouldn't you expect Peter's fingerprints to be on the iron?"

"Not necessarily. Perhaps he had gloves on that day or he wiped the iron clean."

POWERLESS

"If he did that, he would have also removed your fingerprints and Jake's. Who was this friend who was with you when you borrowed the tire iron?"

Mike pointed to the man sitting next to Sheriff Eisner and said, "That fellow sitting next to the sheriff, Ed Lawton."

"Was Ed also the other man who was with you on the day Jake was shot?"

"Yes he was, both times."

Josh finished questioning Mike, requesting that he may wish to recall him later. The judge gave permission and then excused Mike.

Prosecutor Cantrell said that he had no further witnesses. The judge then asked Josh to present his defense.

Josh called Ed Lawton to the stand.

Ed wore a plaid shirt, dirty jeans and mud-caked cowboy boots. He had three days of stubble on his face and seemed disheveled. A wisp of black hair escaped from beneath his stained Minnesota Twins baseball cap and dangled across his forehead. Judge Jamison asked him to remove his hat. Ed clearly had not prepared himself to testify and squirmed uncomfortably in the witness chair, as Josh faced him.

"On the day of the shooting, how many shots did you hear?"

"Five," Ed answered, without hesitation.

"Are you sure you heard five separate shots, and not an echo coming from just three shots," Josh questioned.

Ed said he was sure he heard five separate, distinct gunshots. He went on to say the first and second shots peppered all three men with buckshot. Then he and Mike took off into the woods, but Jake stood his ground and walked toward the porch.

169

"Peter fired the third shot from the porch steps, and it hit Jake in the legs when he was just a few feet from house, just as Mike testified. Peter fired the fourth shot from the bottom of the steps and the fifth as he stood right over Jake. Five . . . I am positive there were five shots," Ed insisted.

"Mike testified the last two shots came in quick succession," Josh reminded Ed. How long would you estimate it took to fire all three last shots?"

Ed hesitated, "Including the shot that hit Jake in the legs?"

"Yes, the last three shots."

"Just a few seconds," Ed said.

"A few you say. How many is a few?"

"Well, fewer than five seconds for sure."

"How about the last two shots? How long did they take?"

"Well, BANG BANG. Just like that. Perhaps less than two seconds."

"You say you were hiding in the woods and watched as Peter shot Jake."

"Yes. I watched from the tree line, where I had a clear view of the front porch."

Josh asked the court recorder to read back the sheriff's testimony about the tests he performed on the shotgun, and then turned his attention back to Ed.

"The sheriff testified that Peter's recently fired shotgun was properly plugged and could hold only four shells. He found one shell still in the chamber. How could you hear five shots when the gun could only hold four shells and one remained in the chamber?" Josh asked.

"I dunno . . . Peter must have reloaded two shells as he was running down the steps toward Jake," Ed surmised.

"It would take several seconds to reload, wouldn't it? Yet didn't you testify that after you ran into the woods, the last three shots came in quick succession?"

Ed hesitated for a few seconds and then answered, "Yes, it would take a few seconds to reload, but I don't remember what I said about how long it took."

"As a matter of record, you testified the last three shots took fewer than five seconds," Josh said.

"Well, it doesn't take long to slam another couple of shells into the chamber. That must be what Peter did as he ran down the steps," Ed responded.

Josh went over to the evidence table and brought back Peter's 12 gauge pump shotgun, entered as "exhibit A", and then asked the judge if he would allow a brief demonstration. The judge agreed to allow it.

Josh asked Ed if he was familiar with a pump action shotgun.

"Yeah, I have one just like it," Ed admitted.

Jake made sure the safety was on and handed the gun to Ed, and then asked him to load four blank shells into the gun reserve chamber and one into the main chamber for a total of five shells. Ed could only fit three shells in the reserve chamber.

Josh repeated, "Like the sheriff said, the gun was properly plugged. So, if the gun can only hold four shells at a time, for there to have been a fifth shot, Peter would have had to reload. Isn't that right?"

Ed let out a sigh and said, "Yeah, I said so. I guess he must have reloaded."

Josh then asked Ed to pump the gun, and eject two of the four shells. Then he was to pretend to aim the gun and eject the third shell and then the fourth shell, load two more shells from his pocket into the empty chamber as fast as he could, and finally eject the fifth shell. Josh fingered a stopwatch as Ed performed the assigned tasks.

The pump action on the gun was stiff, making it impossible for Ed to pump this gun, with the stock firmly shouldered. He held the stock in one hand and pumped with the other. Each time Ed pumped the gun, he had to shoulder it and aim. Firing in quick succession was very difficult.

Ed took six seconds to pump, aim and then eject the third and fourth shells, and four seconds to load two shells into the chamber, and then, two seconds to aim the gun and eject the fifth shell.

Josh faced the court and said, "It took Ed twelve seconds in all to eject the third and fourth shells, and then reload and eject a fifth shell. He testified that it took about ten seconds for them to run to the safety of the woods, where Mike and Ed watched Peter shoot Jake. They also testified the final three shots came in quick succession: first, the third shot and then, less than five seconds later, the fourth and fifth shots, only two seconds apart. The demonstration proved that since only four shells could fit into the gun, had there been a fifth shot, it would take Peter several seconds to reload and fire the final shot. Under the best of circumstances, the last three shots would have taken more than twelve seconds."

Turning back to Ed, he asked, "How could Peter aim and fire five shots, the last three in fewer than five seconds, when it took you over twelve seconds to do the same thing," Josh asked.

"I don't know, perhaps he is faster than I am at pumping his gun. After all, he is experienced using his own gun, and I'm not," Ed answered.

"Is it your testimony that you had a clear view of the porch and barn from your hiding place in the woods?" Josh asked.

"Yeah, we could see the whole damn murder take place."

Josh handed Ed a picture of the woods, taken from the Dexter porch and entered it into evidence, as "exhibit C".

"Can you show me where you were hiding when you witnessed the shooting?" Josh asked.

Ed pointed to a spot along the tree line.

"You're sure that is where you and Mike were hiding," Josh persisted.

"Yeah, that's about where it was."

Josh gave Ed a red pen and asked him to circle the spot where he and Mike hid, and then excused him.

He recalled Mike to the stand.

"You previously testified that you witnessed blood and guts spew from Jake's belly when Peter shot him. How far is the tree line from where you and Ed watched the incident take place?"

"I dunno know, maybe it's 80 feet or so," Mike claimed.

"I measured it. It's 135 feet," Josh testified.

"And are you positive you had a clear view of the incident?" Josh then asked.

"Yeah, we saw it just as plain as day," Mike answered, showing irritation in his voice.

Josh pressed on. "And from that distance, you were able to watch the entire incident, including seeing blood and guts fly from Jake's belly?"

"Yep, I have good eyesight," Mike answered sarcastically.

"What did you and Ed do after that?" Josh asked.

"We got the hell out of there and ran back into town."

Josh handed Mike "exhibit C", the picture taken of the woods with the circle marked by Ed.

"Do you agree with Ed the place he circled along the tree line is about where you and he hid that day?" Josh asked.

"Yea, that's about the right spot," Mike agreed.

Josh entered a third and fourth photograph as exhibits "D" and "E". The first one, taken from the place along the tree line that both Mike and Ed identified as the spot where they hid that day, and the second, from several feet to the left of the spot. In the first photograph, a tool shed obstructed a full view of the porch and steps. All that one could see from that location was the south end of the front porch.

"In this photograph, neither the porch nor steps are visible. How could you see Peter shoot Jake from that location?" Josh questioned.

"Well, you didn't take that picture from the right spot," Mike claimed.

"I took this photo from the spot you and Ed just testified was the place where you hid," Josh said.

"Well, maybe I made a mistake. We were more to the left of the barn than that photo shows."

Josh gave the marked picture of the woods back to Mike.

"So, point out again where you now think you were hiding when the shooting took place."

Mike squirmed in his chair and took a closer look at the picture. "It was further to the left."

Josh persisted, "how much further?"

"Oh, I dunno, perhaps here." Josh pointed to another spot a few feet from the circle.

"Mark that spot with an 'x'," Josh instructed. Mike did so and handed the photograph back to him.

Josh then handed the second picture, "exhibit E", taken from the spot Mike had just identified on the photograph as their hiding spot, to the judge. The house and front porch were clearly visible, but a large bush hid the steps and the place where Jake fell. The judge examined the pictures and then returned them to the evidence table.

"Your Honor, it appears that this witness and Ed made a mistake when they testified that they had a clear view of the porch and could see Peter shoot Jake. I walked along the tree line shown in the photo, and nowhere along that line is there a clear view of the porch or porch steps."

Josh then asked his final question. "Mike, why are you now in jail?"

Prosecutor Cantrell objected, claiming the question was irrelevant, but the judge overruled him.

Mike admitted the sheriff caught him stealing goods from the tack and feed store.

"Doesn't that store belong to your uncle, Niles Olsen?" Josh insisted.

"Yea, it does."

"So then, you stole from your own uncle," Josh declared. Mike clenched his fists.

Josh said he had no further questions, and the judge excused Mike.

Josh called Peter to the stand, who repeated his version of the shooting. Josh quizzed him about his testimony that three men were trying to break into the barn and that Jake ran at him with a tire iron. Peter repeated that he only fired three shots from the porch and steps and did not fire a shot into Jake's body, as he lay on the ground.

"Did Jake or either of his friends ever borrow a tire iron from you?"

"Yes they did." Peter answered. "Jake once asked me for help to fix a flat tire in the church parking and I lent him my tire iron. He never returned it."

In Lance's cross-examination, Peter stuck by his story. He claimed he was protecting his property from three men who were trying to break into his barn and the shooting was in self-defense. Lance could not shake Peter's testimony. Peter insisted Jake threatened him with a tire iron and that he only fired three shots. Peter denied Lance's assertion that he had taken the plug out of the shotgun chamber and then later put it back in.

"It takes a special tool to remove the plug. I would have to take it to a gunsmith to have the plug removed," Peter testified.

Josh then called Pastor Helming to testify to the character of Peter Dexter. Pastor Helming said that Peter was an outstanding member of his parish, a deacon and a person of fine character. Peter developed the food bank and unselfishly served his community, in a time of need. He also testified about the altercations he witnessed between Mayor Jim Peterson and Peter, and that bad blood existed between the two men. He explained that Peter and three other parishioners ejected Jake and his friends from the food bank, because they were selling the food in town. He said that he heard Jake's subsequent threats to burn down the church and told about the fire that started behind the church building.

Josh also called Judy to the stand. She said that she saw Jake running toward the porch waving a tire iron in his hand and cursing Peter. Terrified, she told Peter to shoot the man, but rather than shoot him, Peter fired a second warning shot over Jake's head. The warning shot had no affect and Jake kept running toward the porch. When he nearly reached the front porch steps, Peter fired the third and fatal shot. There were only three shots fired, all three from the porch and porch steps. She was positive of these facts.

On cross-examination, Judy admitted that she did not see the tire iron again until the sheriff found it in the pigsty.

"Why were you screaming for Peter to shoot Jake?" Lance Cantrell asked"

"I thought Jake was going to bash Peter's head in with that tire iron."

Lance examined some papers on his desk and then asked, "You testified that Jake never reached the steps and Peter shot him while he was still some distance away. You were screaming for Peter to shoot him. Wasn't that an overreaction?"

Judy hesitated a moment and then answered.

"Peter first fired a warning shot, but then rather than flee as his friends did, Jake began running toward the house. Peter's second warning shot didn't slow Jake down even a bit. I saw a madman running toward my husband, wielding a tire iron and cursing. He would have been on Peter in a couple of seconds. I feared for Peter's life."

"What you saw in Jake's hand could just have been a stick rather than a tire iron, could it not?" Lance hinted.

"I know a stick from a tire iron. Jake was waving a tire iron," Judy said indignantly.

Lance couldn't shake her testimony. She continued to insist that Peter only fired three shots that day and that all three came from the porch. She was insistent that Peter never fired the shotgun from the bottom of the steps and didn't shoot Jake while standing over him.

Lance finished his cross-examination, and then Josh called his final witness, Sheriff Eisner.

The sheriff confirmed that the day after the shooting, he returned to the Dexter farm to collect evidence. With Trevor's help, he found the tire-iron in the pigsty and collected five shells from the porch and beneath the steps.

"I took the tire-iron, shotgun and five shells back to my office for examination and dusted both the gun and tire iron for fingerprints. The prints on the gun were Peter's, and the gun had been recently fired. Unfortunately, the five shotgun shells I found at the crime scene disappeared before I could perform tests to prove they all came from Peter's gun. When I went home that night, I left the shells on my desk. When I returned the following morning, they were gone. Despite a thorough search, the shells were never found."

Sheriff Eisner testified that one set of fingerprints on the tire iron belonged to Jake, and another set belonged to Mike. He was unable to find any other prints on the tire iron. All the prints on the gun belonged to Peter.

On cross-examination, Lance tried to impugn the sheriff's testimony by claiming that he was not a fingerprint expert, and thus could not clearly identify the fingerprints on the tire iron. The sheriff ignored the objection and referred to the pictures previously entered as evidence, showing the fingerprints on the tire iron and those taken from Jake's body to be identical. The judge reexamined the photographs and admitted the fingerprints were clearly identical, and it did not take an expert to see both Jake's and Mike's fingerprints matched those on the tire iron.

Then Lance rebuked the Sheriff for being careless with the evidence and not securing the shotgun shells.

Sheriff Eisner bristled at the accusation.

"I had control of the evidence from the moment I took it from the Dexter farm. I locked the tire iron and shotgun in a closet, but that night someone broke into my office and took the shotgun shells from my desk."

"Why didn't you lock the shotgun shells with the other evidence?"

"I intended to; a phone call that came into the office distracted me as I was about to leave for the night. The better question is who broke into my office and stole the shells?"

Finally, Josh called John Ulver, a parishioner at St. Paul's and one of the men who helped Peter run the food bank.

"Do you recall any time at the food bank when Jake asked Peter for help to change his tire?" Josh inquired.

"Yes, I do. I was with Peter each time Jake and his friends visited the food bank, and one time Jake asked him for help to change a flat tire. Peter let him borrow his tire iron." John also testified that he overheard the threats Jake made, when Peter denied him access to the food bank.

The defense then rested.

After a three-hour adjournment, Judge Jameson spoke to the court.

"Clearly, considering all the contradictory testimony and evidence presented to this court, the facts do not rise to the level necessary to indict Peter Dexter for murder in the death of Jake Brevick. Because of insufficient evidence, the judgment of this court is there will be no indictment for murder in this case and Peter Dexter is free to go."

The courtroom broke out into applause. Peter watched as Jim Peterson and his wife made their way out of courtroom. Niles accosted Jim in the back of the hearing room. Although Peter could not hear what Niles was saying, he was insistently poking his finger into Jim's chest as he spoke.

Peter hugged Judy and the kids, then shook Josh's hand, then went over to Dan and Judy.

"Thanks for being here for me. You don't know how much it meant to us to have you folks supporting us during this awful time."

"No problem," Nora said. "What are friends for?"

"It's over. Let's go home," Judy said, as tears streaked her makeup.

Yet, in Dan's mind, it wasn't over. Something was rotten in Willow Creek, and he was determined to find out what that was. Who placed the extra shotgun shells at the crime scene and hid the tire iron in the pigsty, and who stole those shotgun shells from the sheriff's office?

Why did the Mayor want Peter in jail, and how could the Judge jail Peter when he was only a person of interest? This was all very curious.

CHAPTER SIXTEEN: SKULLDUGGERY

In early November, the North Dakota weather turned bitterly cold, and daytime temperatures hovered in the low twenties. One evening after the hearing, both families sat in the Dexter family room to enjoy the warmth of a log fire and discuss some unanswered questions.

"I'm just so glad it is all over," Peter sighed.

Dan looked pensive. "Do you really think it's over?"

The question surprised Peter. "Sure it is . . . done . . . over . . . finished . . . kaput!"

Nora looked questioningly at Dan. "Of course it's over. Why do you ask?"

Dan chose his words carefully.

"Well . . . I was thinking about the skullduggery that led to Peter's illegal incarceration. I mean the false accusations, the lies, the conspiracy, the tampering with evidence, and worst of all, issuing a warrant for manslaughter; then jailing Peter, only to admit later that he was a "person of interest". The judge changed the charge to murder, which allowed him to set the bail unreasonably high. This was more than revenge by a self-important mayor. What did he and the judge have to gain by locking Peter in jail? I don't buy the story that Mayor Peterson wanted to get even with you, Peter. Sure, you questioned his authority and killed his cousin. There is something more fundamentally in play here, something that drove desperate men to do desperate things. Because their plan failed, it's not over." Dan looked around the room.

"Go on," Peter encouraged. Dan cleared his throat and continued.

"When we arrived, Judy told us about the shooting and the results of the inquest. This didn't make much sense to me. Were you arrested or not? The sheriff thought he was arresting you, according to a signed warrant, but then the judge admitted you were only a person of interest, and only after the inquest were you charged. What did Jake and his friends want to steal? There is nothing of real value in your barn and they were not desperate enough to steal food. Was there something of value in your barn, something of such value, the mayor hired Jake and his friends to break into your barn? And then, after their failed attempt, the mayor wanted you out of the picture so he could hire others to break into your barn unmolested. What were they searching for?"

Peter still looked puzzled, but Dan continued.

"The mayor pressured the judge to hold you on a charge of manslaughter and then changed it to murder and set a bail so high that under the circumstances, he knew Judy would be unable to post it. While you were in custody, two men came to the farm and tried to break in, but Judy chased them off. Someone took the tire iron and hid it in the pigsty, stole the barn door lock and dropped two more shotgun cartridges on the ground under the porch steps. Before the sheriff could test the shotgun shells, someone also broke into the sheriff's office and stole them. There are just too many unanswered questions for this to be 'over', as you say."

Peter looked confused for a minute, and then his face set in an expression of outrage.

"You know, now that you mention it, there has to be more to it. I just assumed Jim Peterson seethed over our altercation and because I shot his cousin. I thought it was his way of taking revenge. As a newcomer to Willow Creek, I challenged his authority—a real no-no in a town where most folks are related and are second or third generation citizens."

After a short pause, Peter continued.

"Your point is well taken. Mayor Peterson's motives must go way beyond revenge. Sure, Jake was his cousin, yet the two men were not on good terms. In fact, they hadn't spoken to each other for months. There must be a reason Peterson wanted me out of the way. Someone came out to the farm after the shooting, probably when I took Jake's body to town, and tampered with the evidence. Whoever did that was trying to make the shooting look like murder rather than self-defense. Why did Mike and Ed perjure themselves in court by falsely claiming they had a good view of the shooting, when they clearly didn't? Why insist that Jake did not have a tire iron? What was the purpose behind testifying there were five shots rather than the three?"

"Perhaps Mike was just trying to cover up his story at the inquest, and Ed was supporting his lie." Dan proffered. He thought for a minute and then asked, "When did you buy this farm?"

"Oh . . . about a dozen years ago, shortly before I retired from the Air Force, in 1995."

"Who did you buy it from?"

"Well, we bought it from Niles Olsen, the hardware and mercantile store owner. Come to think of it, Jim Peterson is his son-in-law. Do you think all this might have something to do with my purchase of the farm?"

"My rule is to follow the money," Dan suggested. "I suspect there is something in your barn they wanted, and after Jake and his friends muffed the break in, they needed you out of the way so someone else could have another go at it. I think Jim Peterson or Niles put Jake and his friends up to breaking into your barn, and then once you were out of the way, sent someone else to the farm to compromise the evidence. Then they hired a couple of men to break into the barn a second time, but Judy scared them off. There must be something inside the barn they desperately want, something that would be worth stealing."

"That would certainly explain the two men trying to break in while Dan was in jail," Judy said.

Peter's brow furrowed.

"There is nothing much in the barn except some stored food, farm equipment, animals, and hay—nothing worth stealing."

"Well, there must be something in there that you do not know about," Dan insisted. "Do you have a large mortgage on the farm?"

"You bet . . . almost $300,000."

"Who holds the mortgage?"

"The local savings and loan . . . Willow Creek S & L."

"And who owns Willow Creek S & L?"

"Like most businesses in town, Niles Olsen owns it," Nora answered.

"Are you delinquent on the mortgage payments?" Dan asked.

"Well yes. Since the blackout, when the banks closed, no one can make monthly mortgage payments to Willow Creek Savings and Loan or any other bank for that matter. However, before the blackout, my payments were always on time. In addition, I have a short-term loan with Willow Creek Savings and Loan for spring planting: a seed and fertilizer loan I took out before the blackout. For the last several years, I have taken a loan out with them every spring and paid it back after the harvest. Without power, Willow Creek Savings and Loan has been unable to accept my loan payments. The Federal Reserve has frozen all banking transactions, and since September, the banks have been ordered to delay all loan payments. In addition, until they restore electricity, financial institutions can't conduct foreclosures."

"Yes, I imagine the banks and S & Ls are hurting," Dan surmised. "Even the stock exchange is closed. Without computers and telecommunications to run their business, the financial markets in the country have ground to a dead stop. Has the Willow Creek Savings and Loan sent you a delinquency notice?"

"Well . . . yes they did. Every customer got one, but I assumed it was a formality and ignored it. I can't pay and they can't collect. The government has placed everything on hold. Everyone knows this."

"Is it possible that despite the moratorium, they were trying to foreclose on your mortgage?"

"They can't do that, especially without legal notice."

Dan pondered that thought for a minute. "Well, actually they can. I'm not a lawyer, and this is a question for Josh, but nothing in standard loan agreements provides for an extended power outage. No exception exists to allow payment extensions when the banks can't conduct business. They consider a mortgage delinquent if it goes unpaid for three consecutive months. I heard on the radio that a few unscrupulous banks were trying to foreclose on unpaid loans. Federal court circuit judges ruled that given the present circumstances, especially with an inoperative Federal Reserve, such actions are illegal. It is unquestionably unethical, but now it is illegal as well. Yet, that has not stopped some unscrupulous lenders from intimidating their customers. Let's look at that letter the S & L sent you."

Peter sorted through a stack of opened letters and handed the delinquency notice to Dan.

"It says here that unless you pay all your delinquent mortgage payments within ten days, they will start foreclosure proceedings."

"Yes, I read that . . . and ignored it. It is just a form letter. How can they hold foreclosure proceedings with the S & L institutions shut down?"

"It is a small town, and Niles owns the S & L that holds the mortgage on this farm. If he wants your farm, he might try to find a way to foreclose, power outage or not. How about that lawyer who acted as prosecutor at your hearing . . . I believe his name was Lance Cantrell, wasn't it?"

"Yes, folks say Lance is one sharp cookie, especially when it comes to finances," Peter recalled. "He is the attorney for Niles and most merchants in town. He completes their tax forms, prepares financial documents, and represents Niles and other business owners in town, in matters of law."

"Since Lance represents Niles and probably the S & L as well, it could be that Lance and Niles have access to your property documents. Without your knowledge, and despite the government moratorium, they could be trying to figure a way to foreclose on your property."

Peter and Nora sat speechless. Could Dan be right? Was all this about taking their farm away? There were many farms in financial difficulty throughout the county. Financial troubles were a normal part of farming. Have a bad year, take out a loan. Have a good year and pay it back. Local S & Ls and banks are in a virtual partnership with farmers.

"Why in God's name would this particular farm interest Niles and Lance?" Judy questioned.

Dan pondered Judy's question.

"I was curious about why Judge Jameson and Mayor Peterson came late to the trial. It's reasonable to assume they conducted business together for fifteen minutes before the start of proceedings."

Dan gave them a minute to ponder this. "I think the key is to find out what Jake and his friends were after in the barn. Let's go out there tomorrow morning and have a good look around."

Peter agreed, but he couldn't imagine there was anything of value in the barn. He thought he had visited every nook and cranny of that barn. Nonetheless, they would give it a go.

After breakfast, both families went out to the barn to have a thorough look around. Peter, Dan, and Trevor carried flashlights, so they could examine the darkest corners of the barn. Keith and Trevor poked pitchforks through the hay stored in the loft. Nora and Judy and the girls searched through the various barn cabinets and storerooms.

For the better part of an hour, nothing unusual turned up. Then Trevor shouted he had found something in a darkened back corner of the loft. Under a pile of loose hay, he discovered a locked storage trunk with Ophelia Olsen's name on it. Peter, Dan, and Nora climbed into the loft and examined the trunk. A padlock held the trunk lid fast, but Peter broke the lock with a hammer. Once inside, Peter moved some clothes to reveal a steel box wrapped in a moth-eaten purple cloth. He used a screwdriver to pry the locked box open. It was filled with yellowed papers and documents. They took the box inside the house where the light was better and set it on the kitchen table. Peter pulled a faded yellow document out of the box. It proved to be the original recorded deed to the Ingles property.

He carefully examined the document with a magnifying glass. "This must have been what Jake was looking for."

The deed stated that Henry and Clara Ingles purchased the 680-acre farm from the Northern Pacific Railroad Company, in 1887. The northern section of the transcontinental rail line once ran through Willow Creek, on its way to the west coast. The railroad abandoned that section of track years ago, in favor of a line that went through Minot. As an enticement to build the original line, the government granted the Northern Pacific Company alternate sections of land alongside the surveyed right-of-way. The county clerk in Willow Creek signed and dated the deed on June 16, 1887. The deed described a full section (680 acres) was transferred from the Northern Pacific RR to the Ingles, for a purchase price of $340. This was a complete surprise to Peter, because the deed conveyed to him from Niles described only a 420 acre plot. Nothing in the box suggested the status of the other 260 acres. Peter had always assumed his neighbor, Conrad Perkins, owned those fenced 260 acres. Conrad lived in a farmhouse two miles down the county road from the Dexter home and had farmed the plot in question long before Peter and Judy bought their farm from Niles. They had every reason to believe Conrad was the legal owner of that plot.

An aged brown newspaper notice announced Henry Ingles' death, in 1918, and another notice recorded Clara's death, in 1922. Henry's firstborn son, Lloyd Ingles, inherited the farm when his mother died. Other yellowed documents included death certificates for both Clara and Henry, a birth certificate for Lloyd Ingles, dated 1889, and a marriage certificate between Lloyd Ingles and one Arleen Smith, dated 1910. A newsprint article described a fire in 1921 that burned down the Ingles' farmhouse. Every member of the Ingles family, except Lloyd and his oldest daughters, Ophelia and Laura, died in that terrible fire. A 1927 invitation announced the wedding of Ophelia to Jonathan Olsen. Ophelia and Jonathan never had any children of their own. They purchased 420 acres of the farm from Lloyd in 1933. A 1935 obituary told of Jonathan's passing.

Another document was Ophelia's 1937 will. Ophelia died in 1942 and the Ophelia will that Lance Cantrell submitted for probate named Niles Olsen as Ophelia's heir. After probate, Niles became the sole owner.

Peter carefully examined Ophelia's will. "Dan, this will disputes Niles ever owned this farm. Ophelia Olsen left the farm to her sister's son, Samuel Gerhardt, not Niles." Dan took the document from Peter's hand and quickly read it. "So, the will submitted in probate must have been a forgery. No wonder Niles and Lance were so anxious to find this box."

One last document of special interest was a 1930 mining assay, properly recorded and notarized in the Willow Creek Assay Office. It stated a rich seam of coal lay under the 680-acre Ingles property. As mayor of Willow Creek and officer of the savings and loan company, Jim Peterson had access to a copy of this document and would have made Niles aware of the intrinsic value of the Ingles farm. This revelation occurred when WC S&L researched the history of the Ingles deed, to convey ownership and issue title insurance. Unfortunately for Niles, it came after he signed the purchase agreement with Peter and Judy. Peter remembered that Niles tried to back out of the purchase agreement and even offered more money than the Dexters had paid for the property, but Peter turned him down.

Peter handed the mining assay to Dan.

"Most likely, the 1930 mining assay was discovered when Lance Cantrell did the routine title search of the Ingles farm to convey the property to you and Nora. Niles Olsen's ownership of the Ingles property was obtained by fraud, and Lance was a party to this. However, no one would ever be the wiser unless the original Ophelia will was uncovered."

Dan read the document and handed it back. "If this mining assay is correct, the farm could be worth millions."

Now the conspiracy began to make sense. Unless Lance, Niles and Judge Peterson could find and destroy the original copy of Ophelia's will, their plan to gain the Ingles farm and the riches under it might someday be undone. Niles must have known about the box full of family documents and papers that his aunt Ophelia kept. He probably also knew about her will and that she had named her nephew, Samuel, as her heir. He hadn't thought about or seen that box for years, but if it was ever discovered it could prove his and Lance's undoing. Ophelia had contracted cancer in 1936 and spent months suffering with that terrible disease. She did not trust her brother, Orville, or his son Niles, so Niles suspected that before she died, his aunt hid the box somewhere on the farm, probably in the barn. Niles sent Jake to find the box of papers, and then when Peter shot him, Lance, Niles and the Judge conspired to imprison Peter. Once he was out of the way, they could search the property for those papers.

Peter carefully placed the documents back into the box. "This box must have been what Jake was after. The title and the other documents prove the property was valuable and the forged will disputes Niles Olsen's legal ownership of the Ingles property. Little wonder that Niles wanted to find this box. It also explains why he was trying to foreclose on my mortgage."

Peter and Dan searched through a leather box of papers for his deed to the farm. Peter found the Deed of Conveyance and purchase agreement between Peter and Judy Dexter and Niles Olsen. The Title Search disclosed Ophelia Olsen bought 420 acres of the 680 acre farm from Lloyd Ingles, in 1929, as part of a bankruptcy. Apparently, Lloyd lost part of his farm in the 1928 stock market crash, but held on to the remaining 260 acres that contained the Ingles farmhouse. Lance Cantrell represented Niles in probate court and presented the Ophelia Olsen will to the court, after her death in 1942. Yet that will was a forgery and the real Ophelia will named her sister's son, Samuel, as heir. Niles never legally owned the Ingles farm.

"This makes sense," Peter said. "There is a foundation of a burned-out house on the 260-acre property that Conrad Perkins now farms. After the original house burned down, Lloyd Ingles rebuilt the house on the southwest corner of that same property, about 100 yards from the old foundation. This is the house that Conrad now lives in."

"We should take these documents to the county recorder and register them," Dan recommended. "You also need to visit with the sheriff. Niles should be arrested if he is behind this fraud and attempted break-in by Jake and his friends. When the county government returns to normal, you can open another title search of the entire 680-acre Ingles property. Considering the intrinsic value of your property, Niles certainly didn't want you to find out about the fraudulent will, the Ingles farm title history, or the mining assay report."

"Well, if Niles didn't own the property when he sold it to me, it may mean that Judy and I are not the legal owners."

Dan thought for a moment. "When you bought the property, you also bought a title insurance policy, and whoever issued that policy researched and guaranteed clear title. There is nothing for you to worry about. Perhaps we should make a trip into town and look through the title company records ourselves. If the Ophelia Olsen will is a forgery, then it is true that Niles did not have clear title at the time he sold the farm to you. Nevertheless, your title insurance protects you. Clearly, Niles tried to take advantage of the power outage to gain title to your property, by foreclosure. It is also obvious that Jim Peterson and Judge Jameson were in on the conspiracy."

The next day Dan, Judy, and Peter rode their wagon into town and visited Sheriff Eisner. The sheriff looked over Peter's documents, sighed, and said,

"Well, I thought something was mighty suspicious about this case from the get-go. Jim's insistence that you were guilty of manslaughter and his deal with Judge Jameson to change the charge to murder and set the bail so high made no sense to me. It seemed as if something other than revenge motivated him. That coal seam on your property could be worth a lot of money."

"Only if I allow some damn company to come in and dig it up," Peter commented. "Have you ever seen what strip mining does to a piece of farmland?"

The sheriff frowned and then nodded agreement.

"Regardless, you need to show these documents to Josh Richards. With the telephones down, I don't know how you are going to get a message through to him, but you should try to do so," Sheriff Eisner added. "Meanwhile, let's go down to the courthouse and visit with our county clerk, Betty Wyckoff. She will record these documents for you, make notarized copies, and then store them in her safe."

"I don't know that I can trust Betty with the originals," Peter said. "After all, she works for Judge Jameson. If he has conspired with Mayor Peterson and Niles Olsen, they could destroy the documents."

Sheriff Eisner frowned.

"Don't worry about Betty. She's as straight as an arrow. She may work for the judge, but she is the only one with access to the safe, and no one else is going to get access to the contents of that safe without her permission. To be on the safe side, she should give you a receipt and I will witness that she has archived the original documents. I will also keep a notarized copy of the documents in my safe. The Minidoka Title Company will have archived the old records and the recorder's office will also have a copy. Betty will dig out the Minidoka title search records for you to give to Josh."

Betty was as cooperative as the sheriff expected and found the Dexter farm title documents.

"You know that Niles owns most everything in town, including the Willow Creek S & L," Betty explained. "The Minidoka Title Insurance Company, founded by Orville Olsen, issued your title policy. Unfortunately, the company went out of business after they issued your policy. Orville had appointed his son, Niles, to run the company years ago, but Niles' lack of management eventually bankrupted it."

Betty examined Peter's documents.

"I have to agree that the Ophelia will that Lance submitted in probate must have been a forgery. Given evidence of the original 1937 will, any court would rule that the submitted will is a forgery and that Niles never owned your farm. The Minidoka title search conducted when Niles conveyed the farm to you did not suggest any questionable ownership in the records. Nevertheless the title insurance company that issued you the title insurance is no longer in business and your insurance policy may be worthless."

"Ophelia Ingles survived that terrible 1921 house fire. She married Jonathan Olsen in 1927, so she was Niles's aunt by marriage. It is probable that she and Jonathan bought your farm from Lloyd Ingles and recorded it in Ophelia's name. It seems that Niles forged a will naming himself as heir. I cannot believe that Lance was a party to this fraud"

Peter handed Betty the assay report. She examined it and then said, "Your deed gives you full rights to water, timber and minerals. No one around here has any valuable minerals on their property, so when Niles conveyed your deed, he must not have known about this assay report and thus did not hesitate to include mineral rights in the deed. The mineral assay specifies your farm has a large deposit of coal beneath it. There are several coal and oil deposits in the Dakotas, but mostly to the southern and western parts of the states. Coal deposits in this county are rare. Your property is valuable."

"What about the Conrad Perkins farm, who owns that property?" Peter asked.

"The tax record shows a California relative of Niles Olsen has paid the yearly taxes on the 260-acre Perkins farm. Conrad Perkins is not the registered owner of the 260 acre Ingles farm. Conrad farmed it, but never owned it. It is unclear just how Conrad came live on that property. There is no record that he leased it from the owner, Miles Olsen, who inherited the property from Lloyd Ingles. Miles never showed any interest in the property, but he did pay the taxes. Miles died in 1995, and since then his trust has continued to pay the taxes."

Betty mentioned something about adverse possession, a legal term referring to uncontested continuous use of a piece of property that may convey lawful ownership to Conrad. Peter asked her what this meant, but she said that this was an issue beyond her pay scale, but Josh should research it.

As Dan and Peter left the county courthouse, Dan said, "I brought my HAM radio station with us from California. I need to install a good antenna, and if it is ok with you, I can install a temporary one on the farm. While we were still in Santa Cruz, I was trying to get a message through to you and contacted Jerry, a HAM operator in Minot. I have his call letters, W7TEM, and perhaps we can get a message to Josh through Jerry."

Dan and Peter returned to the farm and strung a quarter wavelength 40 meter transmission antenna on poles leading from the barn to the tool shed and connected the dipole to Dan's transmitter.

Dan hooked his transceiver to a car battery and turned it on. To test the radio, Dan called CQ and immediately raised a ham in Spokane, Washington. He said that Spokane now had electricity for 12 hours each day. The Grand Coolie Hydroelectric power plant, undamaged by the September event, continued to supply power to a major part of the Northwest. Most eastern Washington State cities had restored water and sewage services, and the local post office was again delivering mail. Even the Spokane Hospitals and various public services remained open for business. Gradually, things were returning to normal, throughout the Northwest.

Dan tried several times to contact Jerry in Minot, without success. Eventually, he raised a ham operator in Bismarck, who reported Dan's signal was loud and clear. Later that evening, he tried again and this time Jerry answered the CQ. He asked Jerry to contact Josh Richards and tell him that they wanted to set up a meeting with him in Minot as soon as possible. Jerry said the Minot telephone system was still down, but he would visit Josh's office in downtown Minot in the morning and give him the message. Jerry worked for the Minot police department, and each day he patrolled the city in his police car. Even though the Minot Police Department had a very limited supply of gasoline, they had enough to patrol the city and responded to emergency radio calls.

The following day, Jerry called back on the radio and said that he had met Josh in his downtown office and if Dan could drive down from Willow Creek, Josh would meet with them on Wednesday afternoon.

"We only have a few gallons of gasoline remaining; how are we going to get to Minot?" Dan asked.

"Just as our ancestors did," Peter offered. "We'll hitch the wagon and ride into town. It's only 30 miles."

The wagon ride to Minot took almost four hours. They met a few other horse-pulled wagons along the way but only passed two cars. Plainly, gasoline was still unavailable in Minot. They arrived at Josh's office late Wednesday morning.

After warm handshakes, Josh admitted he hadn't thought Peter and Dan would be able to get into town.

Peter smiled. "Look out your window."

Josh looked outside and chuckled, when he saw the horses and wagon parked between two abandoned cars.

"I forgot about horses and wagons." He then turned toward Dan and asked what was on his mind that he would undertake such a long journey.

Peter told him about finding the box in the barn, and handed Josh copies of the documents he found in the barn.

"I want to know if there is any legal question about my title to the farm and also about the ownership of the 260-acre Ingles or Perkins property."

Josh looked over the original title and compared it to Peter's title and title insurance paperwork.

"Even if there is some doubt about Niles' ownership of the property, there is no doubt you have clear title to 420 acres described in your title and guaranteed by the title insurance policy. "Yes," Peter said, "but I understand the company that issued title policy is bankrupt and it may not pay off if it turns out my title is flawed."

"I don't think you have anything to worry about in that respect," Josh said. "What is your interest in the other 260 acres?"

"Well, I want you to find out who the legal owner is. My neighbor, Conrad Perkins, has farmed it for years, and we assumed he owned the corn and alfalfa farm and the house on it. Nevertheless, at the Willow Creek courthouse, we were unable to find his title to the land or any record of his lease for that property. The courthouse records say the property is owned by the Miles Olsen Trust in California. Perhaps Conrad squatted on the property. Could he obtain title by adverse possession?"

"Well, if there is continuous use of a property for more than seven years without objections from the landowner, the user can claim title for the land. Sometimes this law applies to easements or even to small plots of land, but I have never heard it applied to an entire farm. This will have to be something for the courts to decide . . . when I can file an appeal that is," Josh said.

Peter handed Josh the mineral assay report. Josh looked over the single page report, then took out a magnifying glass and examined the county recorder's stamp and signature.

"This document appears to be genuine, as are all the other documents. The Ophelia will is also genuine," Josh commented. "Given this will, how did Niles Olsen obtain ownership of the property?"

"Niles doctored Ophelia's original will replaced himself as heir. His lawyer Lance Cantrell submitted the fraudulent will in probate court in 1942".

"Lance Cantrell, the prosecutor in your trial?"

"Yes, the same man."

"Did you record all these documents in the county records office?"

"Yes, we did so yesterday and left the originals with Betty Wyckoff, the county clerk and recording officer."

"Do you have a receipt for that recording and notarized copies of all the documents entrusted to the county recorder?"

"Yes," Peter answered. "And the Sheriff has a notarized copy," Dan added.

Peter produced the receipt and Josh looked it over. "This receipt should protect you. I hope the county recorder is trustworthy. She now has the original documents, and there is no telling how deep the corruption in the Willow Creek city hall may go. Without this receipt, your originals might have simply disappeared."

"We think the mayor, Judge Jameson, Lance Cantrell, and Niles Olsen, together committed this fraud," Peter surmised. "Niles had access to the title search documents that uncovered the title history of the Ingles property. It's likely he discovered the true value of the property and then conspired with Jameson to foreclose on the old Ingles farm.
Josh sighed deeply and sat down. "I suspect that is the case. After visiting Willow Creek and nosing around a bit, I surmise that Niles Olsen is the main character behind this conspiracy. These documents reveal his motive and confirm my suspicions. In fact, I think except for Sheriff Eisner and Betty, other town leaders could be in on this fraud. Lance Cantrell must have discovered the Ingle farm mineral assay in the county records office, and then Niles tried to use the power blackout as an excuse to foreclose on your property. Such an unethical foreclosure would not hold up in court, of course, but Niles must have thought it would or he would not have gone to such lengths. Somehow, Niles must have been aware of the original documents in your barn and desperately wanted those papers destroyed. I suspect he hired Jake and his friends to steal them. Then when Jake and his friends muffed the break-in, Niles had to make another attempt. Jake's shooting was an unintended outcome."

Josh continued. "As soon as the courts are back in session, I'll petition the Minot Court for an indictment, accusing Niles Olsen and Lance Cantrell of fraud and Mayor Peterson and Judge Jameson of fraudulent use of public office. Meanwhile, be careful when you go into town. By now, they probably suspect you have found the documents and there is no telling how far these folks will go to protect their interests."

Peter and Dan began to wonder if they could trust Betty, but realized it would be useless for her to destroy the originals, considering that Peter and the sheriff had possession of notarized copies. They thanked Josh and returned to the farm, arriving back home at twilight.

*   *   *

For the next few weeks and months, Peter, Dan, and their boys worked around the farm and Nora and Judy and the girls worked in the barn and house. Each evening after supper, they all gathered around the wind-up radio to listen to the brief news broadcast from Minneapolis. These nightly gatherings went on throughout the winter months. Fir instance in December they heard:

"This past week, the Minnesota governor gave permission for federal troops to help the National Guard restore order in our city," the KMIN announcer reported. "Under martial law, federal troops have entered Minneapolis and are restoring order in our city. We have other reports that gangs and rampant crime still plague the cities of Detroit, Cleveland, Boston, Los Angeles, Dallas, Miami, and San Francisco. The mayors of those cities are reluctant to ask the governors to invite federal troops to aid the National Guard to restore order. A report from our correspondent in Washington DC claims the city is so unsafe, the federal government has temporarily moved out. The President, his cabinet, Congress, and the Supreme Court, have moved to Philadelphia and are running the federal government from Independence Hall and the surrounding buildings. Ironically, Philadelphia, the first seat of American government, has now resumed that honor."

Then in early January: the families listened to a Philadelphia commentator critically report on the displaced federal government.

"The Philadelphia administration remains as ineffective in Philadelphia as they were in Washington. The President, a consummate politician, can't get Congress to make the bipartisan decisions necessary to get the country back on its feet. The usual bickering and endless debates between members of Congress, on both sides of the aisle, continue. After weeks of wrangling, they have not been able to agree on a course of action necessary to restore the nation. The usual government solution, to throw money at the problem, will not work. There is no money to throw. Solving this crisis will take leadership and decisive action, both qualities lacking in the Philadelphia administration and Congress. Americans are losing confidence in their government. Some generals have independently proposed action and are ignoring orders from central command. Prominent citizens and a few members of Congress have formed a ghost government based in Phoenix. They call themselves the American Republic or AMREP. A few Army generals, who are sympathetic to the maverick Phoenix government, formed a proactive militia and ordered their troops into the cities of San Diego, Phoenix and San Diego. As reported last week, these efforts have been largely successful and order is now restored in those cities."

The nightly broadcasts from Minneapolis and Bismarck in mid-Winter alarmed the families. Exacerbated by a scarcity of working TV and radio stations, and without newspapers, Federal government misinformation and rumors flourished. Citizens had little information about the Philadelphia government's activities. The KMIN nightly news reported that the Philadelphia government had lost credibility. Few Americans trusted government information. The communiqués from the American Republic government in Phoenix were more credible and detailed than those from Philadelphia. The country now had two governments, one in Philadelphia, which controlled the states east of the Mississippi, and a provisional government in Phoenix, that controlled the western states. The federal government began to unravel and the country was on the brink of anarchy.

One evening, Dan was able to contact his ham buddy, Mark, in Santa Cruz. Mark reported that last month, the mayors of the lawless cities of San Francisco, Oakland, and Los Angeles petitioned the California Governor to send in federal troops to assist the beleaguered National Guard troops. When he refused to do so, the National Guard generals revolted and appealed to the Phoenix-based American Republic government for help. AMREP sent troops into San Francisco, Oakland and Los Angeles, and San

Franciscans lined the streets and watched as the AMREP troops marched into their city, to restore order. The National Guard, who occupied the San Francisco city hall and the downtown areas, joined the militia troops. Within a week, order was restored, and the combined militia and National Guard troops patrolled the streets.

For the first time in weeks, law and order had returned to city streets, and the citizens of San Francisco could once again feel safe in their person, homes, and businesses. Trainloads of food and critical supplies from Phoenix entered the city for distribution by the National Guard. San Francisco General Hospital resumed operations and the National Guard and AMREP troops answered emergency calls, collected garbage, and restored water and sewer services.

In February the KMIN news report electrified their listeners.

"Under intensive public pressure, the Philadelphia-based federal government has opened the national oil and gasoline reserves and the Army Corps of Engineers will reopen four Louisiana and Alabama refineries. The priority is to manufacture and distribute diesel to the trucking and railroad industries. The nation's railroads and trucking industries will be able to move tons of food, gasoline, medicines, and supplies, from government and industrial stockpiles, to cities throughout the eastern half of the country. The western states are not part of this plan and are being directed by the maverick government in Phoenix. The Senators and Representatives from California, Nevada, New Mexico, and Arizona, who have not already defected to Phoenix, are protesting the illegal actions of the American Republic. As of this report, they have been unable to stop the unelected Phoenix government from carrying out their own restoration plan and sending troops into beleaguered western cities to restore order."

The following evening, KMIN reported, "Lacking direction from Philadelphia and encouraged by the maverick government in Phoenix, the Army Corps of Engineers has taken control of General Electric, General Dynamics and Sylvania. Their mandate is to hasten production of power transformers."

Within weeks, the companies sent replacement power transformers to hundreds of destroyed power stations. Slowly, city by city, the country's infrastructure came back on line.

On the last week of March, Dan received the following news broadcast from a station in Denver:

"Hydroelectric generators at Grand Coolie Dam have been electrifying Seattle, Tacoma, Salem, Portland and Spokane for months. With the Northwest grid only minimally damaged by the outage, these cities provide electricity to their customers, for eight hours each day. A few television and radio stations in these cities are back on the air, with a limited schedule. Some major hospitals have reopened, and after the militia and National Guard troops restored order to Oakland and surrounding cities, the refineries in Richmond, California, resumed gasoline production."

The Justin and Dexter families rejoiced over the reports but they knew that most cities, including Minot, remained low on the priority list and shouldn't expect to have their power restored for many more weeks. They would wait patiently for that day, but in the meantime they were doing fine on the farm.

The crisis had severely stressed the federal government to the breaking point, yet some States and local governments had pulled their act together and effectively served their communities. The same could also be said of individuals. Some folks managed quite well, even extending help to their neighbors. This was especially true in rural communities.

Because of earth's orientation at the time the CME struck, Europe, Asia and most of the southern Hemisphere were unaffected by the electrical storms that plagued the USA, Mexico and Canada. Yet North America could expect little in the way of help from the rest of the world. Some nations, ambivalent to problems beyond their own borders, remained aloof and noncommittal when asked for help, conveniently forgetting the hand they had received from the USA in their own time of need. While such narcissism irritated most Americans, they should have been terrified about the plans of Islamic terrorists, who viewed the power disaster as an opportunity to replace the constitutional republic enjoyed in the United

States with their version of an Islamic government. To bring about the downfall of America, they needed a big event; a man-made disaster so earthshaking that it would bring down the American government and fill the resulting void with a government of their own creation.

The terrorists had a plan, a terrible plan, to realize their goals.

PART TWO:
A CLEAR AND
IMMINENT DANGER

The power blackout throughout America provided a unique opportunity for radical Muslim's to advance their goal to spread fundamentalist Islam to the United States. For decades, various Muslim jihadist groups, such as Usama Bin Laden's al-Qaeda, had plotted attacks or made hollow threats of attacks against America. Any democracy based on Judeo-Christian principles represented a major block to their goal of world domination. Specifically, to achieve this goal, they must destroy the United States of America and then rebuild it with an Islamic form of government, one based on Sharia Law. The strategy was to ferment unrest, fear, and a distrust of their government, and then Americans would rise and demand a new form of government, one that could provide their basic needs and protect them.

With this strategy in mind, al-Qaeda designed the attack on 9-11, yet that plan failed in its ultimate goal. Designed to provoke American anger against a government unable to protect them, it had the opposite effect. Rather than attack their government, Americans supported the administration, which then enacted steps to root out terrorists at home and abroad. America gained the support of the United Nations and invaded Afghanistan and succeeded in removing the jihadist Taliban government. Although disrupted, Islamic terrorists in the mid-East continued to design minor attacks against America, yet not one of these assaults provided the impetus necessary to bring down the U.S. government.

With the Washington government focused on restoring the power-damaged infrastructure and insuring citizens that they could protect them against terrorist attacks, an opportunity presented itself. A well-designed attack on an entire American city, one that would make 9-11 appear mild in comparison, would bring that government to its knees and open the door to replace it with one based on Islamic principles. The decades-old plan involved placing operatives in high government positions and forming sleeper cells throughout the country, and this they had successfully done. Al-Qaeda was incredibly patient, yet the power blackout in America presented them with a unique opportunity, a gift from Allah. As America focused on recovery, their jihadist plans to blow up an American city moved forward. All they lacked was the bomb materials. It was time to fulfill their plan.

CHAPTER SEVENTEEN: THE THEFT

Nursal Furdusi felt miserable. After hours of travel on the lurching steam train that plied the poorly maintained tracks from Astana in Kazakhstan to Tashkent in Uzbekistan, nausea and general malaise lingered as a constant companion. A hawker staggered down the aisle, deftly balancing a tray of steaming bowls of rice as he made his way toward the back of the swaying coach car. He stopped beside Nursal and offered a bowl of rice laced with fish. Nursal waved off the offer but passed the bowl over to his seat partner, Abu Talib, who hungrily shoveled rice and fish into his mouth. The smell of fish forced Nursal to choke down his rising queasiness. Toward the back of the coach, his two other companions, Said bin-Taimur and Mitzal al Wahhab, slept as if they had not a care in the world. No matter, he mused, he worried enough for everyone.

Nursal and his travel companions made up one of two teams sent by al-Qaeda into former Russian countries to steal fissionable materials. Nursal's team had succeeded in the first part of their mission, and on a separate train, four pounds of plutonium and thirty pounds of weapons-grade uranium remained hidden in an innocent-looking crate filled with webs of silk cloth. With the object of their theft safely stowed aboard another train, Nursal daydreamed of his triumphant return home in Afghanistan.

The hawker passed by his sleeping friends and moved on to the last coach as the train lurched to a stop at the last town before crossing the Uzbekistan border. The food hawker climbed off onto the platform and Nursal watched as two uniformed policemen prepared to climb onboard. Were these two police officers looking for him and his companions? Thus far all had gone well for Nursal and his team; however, the sight of uniformed police climbing on board made his heart beat faster. He relaxed, knowing that their crate, sent yesterday on a separate train, would be waiting for them in Afghanistan. The police officers would find nothing incriminating on this train.

As the train chugged across the border into Uzbekistan territory, a government agent came down the aisle, checking passports. Wearing a colorful Uzbek cover and felt hat, he examined passports with one hand and held on to a seatback with the other to keep his balance as the train lurched on the undulating tracks. He stopped opposite Nursal and in guttural Russian, asked for passports. Abu interrupted his dinner and handed his passport to Nursal who then handed both his and Abu's documents to the agent. The Russian flipped through them, grunted, and then punched a hole in each. With a smile that caused the tips of his handlebar mustache to flip upwards, he handed them back. Nursal hid a smirk, knowing the smiling Uzbek agent had just allowed two wanted terrorists to enter his country. If the agent only suspected Nursal and his partners were terrorists returning from their mission to Kazakhstan, he would have sent for those two police officers in the other car. Nursal settled into his seat and daydreamed about the successful raid two days earlier and the daring way they stole an atom bomb right from under Russian noses. Yes indeed, someday Islam would honor him as a hero.

*   *   *

Five days earlier, Nursal and his team arrived in the Kazakhstan city of Astana and met with their al-Qaeda contacts. After a briefing on the nuclear depository built into a cave in the Tien Shan Mountains, fifty kilometers outside the city, Nusral rented a van and drove his team toward the depository. Leaving the van hidden in a cornfield about a half-mile west of the depository, they hid in the bushes outside the gate and waited for the cover of darkness. The depository sat at the bottom of a 300-foot high granite cliff. A guardhouse secured the gate and an eight-foot chain-link fence surrounded the one-acre compound containing three two-story brick buildings and a few nondescript, corrugated-metal sheds. Several trucks and jeeps remained parked in a lot next to the closest brick building and a large, iron double door guarded the entrance to the depository cave.

The al-Qaeda cell in Astana had thoroughly briefed Nursal about the depository layout and the nuclear storage room deep inside the cave. Still nervous about the details, he took out his laser flashlight and examined the hand-drawn map one more time. At exactly 9 p.m., a jeep drove to the entrance gate with two soldiers, the night shift relief guards. The relieved guards remained for a minute or two, chatting with their replacements, before climbing into the jeep and driving off into the night. One guard began his hourly inspection tour around the perimeter of the depository, while the other remained on duty at the entrance. Now that only one soldier guarded the entrance, it was time for Nursal and his team to act. Cloaked by a moonless night and the poorly lit depository grounds, the Afghan terrorists cut the fence and slipped undetected onto the depository grounds. Their mission was to find the nuclear storage room, pilfer enough plutonium and enriched uranium to build a single bomb, and then smuggle it by train across Kazakhstan and Uzbekistan to Afghanistan. If their raid remained undetected, it would be days before the Russians could take inventory and realize what had gone missing. Such a delay would be critical to ensure their safe return to Afghanistan with their loot.

The sentry stood in front of the guard shack, his rifle leaning against the shack as he lit a cigarette. Unseen, Mitzal snuck behind the shack, grabbed the guard by the neck and placed a cloth soaked with ether across his mouth and nose. The guard struggled for a few seconds and then collapsed into Mitzal's arms. Mitzal dragged the unconscious guard inside the shack and waited for the second guard to return.

A few minutes later the guard returned and noticed that his companion was not at his post. He called out, but when he didn't get a response, he drew his side arm and went inside the guard station. Mitzal grabbed the sentry as he crossed the threshold and put him to sleep with a second ether-soaked rag. Both guards would sleep soundlessly for at least thirty minutes. Mitzal took the guard's keys, and then ducking under the compound searchlight, the two men ran to the foot of the cliff and unlocked the double doors protecting the cave entrance. Nursal led his team into the tunnel dimly lit by a string of naked lightbulbs hanging from a pair of wires strung along the cave roof. The tunnel ran straight for a few hundred meters and then made a left turn and plunged into the bowels of the mountain. They walked 500 meters down the gently sloping passageway, until it split into left and right corridors. The map marked that the repository for the nuclear fuel was at the end of the corridor to the right. The left corridor led to the guard's quarters. The repository corridor ran for eighty-five yards and then made a sharp right turn. Nursal heard heavy boot steps approaching from around the bend and held his hand high for everyone to stop. He braced himself as the soldier rounded the corner. The man's eyes widened and his jaw slackened as he realized the men were intruders. He opened his mouth to yell; yet he was so overwhelmed by surprise that he couldn't utter a sound. Mitzal sprang on him like a cat on a mouse and placed an ether-soaked cloth over his face. Seconds later, the guard collapsed in Mitzal's arms.

The intruders walked around the corner and down the corridor that ended in a floor to ceiling steel wall containing a green door. Nursal tried to open the door, but finding it locked, sent Abu back to the unconscious soldier to search for keys. He found them on a chain attached to the man's belt. They opened the green door and entered a large well-lit room containing six rows of heavy metal shelves and cabinets. Nursal turned on his handheld Geiger counter and entered the first aisle. As he walked down the aisle, the steady click of the counter quickened, finally growing into a nonstop buzz. Nursal turned the detector audio switch off and watched the indicator meter rise to the halfway mark as he continued further down the aisle. The shelf in front of him housed several dozen metal canisters that resembled large thermos bottles. He picked up one of the heavy canisters and carefully unscrewed the cap. Styrofoam inside the canister protected eight silver-gray metallic wedges, each about three centimeters wide and ten centimeters long. The Geiger detector meter needle jumped into the red "danger" level, confirming that those wedges were highly radioactive plutonium. Screwing the cap back on, he wrapped lead foil around the canister and placed it in his backpack. Then he opened a second canister, which also contained eight plutonium wedges. The bomb needed 32 wedges to form a soccer-ball sized "pit", weighing about 10 kilograms, so he wrapped two more canisters with lead foil and placed them in a second backpack, which he gave to Abu. To conceal the four missing canisters, he moved the remaining canisters to the front of the shelf.

"We have the plutonium," Nursal called out, "now let's find the uranium." Several coffin-size crates lay stacked against the back wall. Said pried the lid off one of the crates and Nursal dug into a bed of foam beads. He pulled out a lead box, about 40 centimeters on a side, placed the heavy box on the floor, and then opened it. It contained a molded block of Styrofoam surrounding a silver-gray object machined in the shape of a half-basketball. His Geiger counter confirmed the hemisphere was uranium enriched with radioactive uranium 235. A second crate produced another box containing a matching hemisphere of uranium.

They placed the two lead boxes of uranium in separate backpacks, gave one to Said and the other to Mitzal. They retraced their steps out of the cave and back to the guard shack where both guards remained peacefully sleeping. The entire raid had taken less than thirty minutes. Nursal and the team hurried back down the road, climbed into their rented van and drove back to Astana, where they met with another al-Qaeda member who ran an import-export business near the train depot. They placed the boxes and thermos bottles into a shipping crate and covered them with packing material and layers of silk cloth intended for export.

The plan was to ship the bomb materials by train to Mazar-e-Sharif in Afghanistan. Nursal thought they would have at least twenty-five hours before the Kazakhstan authorities reported the missing materials to the Russian Nuclear agency; perhaps, with luck, they'd have even as much as a couple of days. With the poorly documented inventory records, it would force the authorities to make a thorough search of the depository before they could document exactly how much uranium and plutonium went missing. It was also likely that those in charge of the depository might delay reporting the robbery or even cover up the theft, rather than risk their careers by reporting they had lost enough materials to make an atom bomb.

"Ship the crate on the next train from Astana to Mazar-e-Sharif in Afghanistan," Nursal directed the exporter. "We will take a separate train tomorrow to Mazar-e-Sharif and retrieve our crate from the station master. Should the authorities detain us along the way, we don't want to be on the same train with the nuclear materials." The following morning, Nursal and his team climbed on the train heading to Tashkent, Termiz, and ending Mazar-e-Sharif.

*   *   *

Nursal snapped out of his daydream and watched as the Uzbek conductor worked his way down the aisle toward Said and Mitzal, who peacefully slept at the back end of the coach. The Uzbek conductor shook Said awake and demanded his passport. After Said produced both his and Mitzal's, the conductor punched each and then returned them. He opened the door and went on to inspect passengers in the next car. Nursal breathed a sign of relief as the coach door slammed behind the conductor.

Five hours after crossing the Uzbekistan border, the train slowed as it approached the Tashkent train station. Rather than pulling into the station, the train moved onto a siding beside a large freight yard and stopped. An army truck pulled alongside the train and six well-armed soldiers climbed out of the truck and boarded the baggage car. Nursal nervously looked out of the window and watched as two other soldiers from the truck climbed onto the first coach

Nursal whispered to Abu, "The soldiers are searching for the bomb materials with a Geiger counter. The Russians must have discovered the theft and are probing each train. Thankfully, they hadn't discovered the theft in time to search last night's train carrying the bomb materials. They'll find nothing on this train, yet they might be searching for us."

"What should we do?" Abu asked. Nursal didn't answer, but watched with horror as more soldiers from a second truck boarded the train.

"Follow me," Nursal said.

They walked toward the back of the coach where their other two friends, now wide-awake, watched as the soldiers boarded. Abu pointed out the window to the army truck and a dozen soldiers walking the tracks toward the front of the train. Two soldiers climbed into each coach in front of theirs.

"We're getting off this train," Nursal said. "Follow me."

All four men made their way to the last coach car, opened the back door, and then jumped off the train. As they ran across the tracks toward a freight train slowly moving out of the yard, shots rang out and both Abu and Said fell onto the tracks. Nursal kept running toward the freight train, with Mitzal following close behind. Bullets whizzed past their heads and kicked shards of track ballast into the air. Nursal ran alongside the moving freight train and reached for a boxcar handhold. The train had picked up speed and he was barely able to grab the handrail and swing himself into the open boxcar. He turned around and reached for Mitzal's hand as he made a last minute desperate attempt to board the accelerating train. Nursal yanked Mitzal into the empty boxcar and they both fell in a heap onto the straw covered floor. The soldiers sprinted across the freight yard firing their rifles at the boxcar as they ran. Bullets ricocheted off the steel walls, narrowly missing both men. Nursal slid the boxcar door closed and sat down on a bale of hay to catch his breath. The train sped up as it moved out of the yard and onto the main line.

The train rattled and swayed across Uzbekistan as the sun set over the western mountains and a moonless night enveloped the train in total darkness. About midnight, the train slowed, switched to a siding, and stopped. Nursal and Mitzal opened the boxcar door a crack and peeked out. The star filled sky reached from horizon to horizon, with no hint of nearby cities or towns to brighten the pitch-black canopy. Nursal looked up and down the line of cars and noticed beams from three flashlights moving from the front of the train and then progressing from one cattle car to the next in line.

"Train inspectors are searching the train," Nursal warned as he watched the men shine their lights under each car and then open each boxcar door and climb inside.

The two terrorists jumped down from the boxcar and crawled underneath and onto the undercarriage, suspending themselves from four iron bars that ran parallel to the boxcar axles. The distance between the bars and the floor of the car was only 30 centimeters, but they managed to wrap their legs and arms around the bars and hold on as the soldiers inspected the train. The terrorists' boxcar was only a few cars ahead of the caboose, and after a few minutes, they heard the boxcar door next to theirs open and then slam shut. A flashlight beam briefly swept under their boxcar, and then the door opened, and two heavy booted soldiers climbed inside and tromped about the floor of the empty car. Their boots sent straw and dust cascading between the floor slats and into their faces. Mitzal stifled a sneeze. The two-by-two boxcar floor slats spaced by a quarter-inch gap, allowed them to watch the soldiers' flashlight beams move across the car as they searched. Had either soldier shined his light onto the floor, he would have seen the fugitives hanging onto the undercarriage. The soldiers, finding nothing of interest in the car, climbed down and slammed the boxcar door shut. Nursal stuck his head out from beneath the car so he could watch as the soldiers inspected the next two empty boxcars and then moved to the remaining four fully loaded cattle cars. They did not open the doors of those cars because they were filled with cattle. Walking to the back of the train, they swung their red lamps to and fro, signaling the engineer that the train could now move on; they then climbed into the caboose. The whistle blew twice, and the train began to move. Nursal and Mitzal knew there wasn't time to climb back into the car, so they continued hanging onto the undercarriage as the train huffed and puffed onto the main line, only stopping briefly to allow the brakeman to reset the switch. After an hour, it became more and more difficult for Mitzal and Nursal to hold onto the undercarriage bars. Mitzal began to lose his grip.

"I can't hold on much longer," he cried.

"You must," Nursal warned. "If you let go, the train wheels will cut you in two."

Nursal's own arms burned and his foot, wedged between the bars and the bottom of the boxcar, was numb. Twenty minutes later, the train slowed, moved onto a siding, and stopped. Nursal loosened his foot from the bar and dropped to the ground. Mitzal also unhooked himself and fell to the ground. Cautiously, they crawled from underneath the train, got to their feet and looked up and down the tracks for soldiers. In the inky blackness, all they could see were the two red lights on either side of the caboose and a single flashlight beam belonging to the brakeman as he climbed back into the caboose, after closing another siding switch.

Nursal breathed a sigh of relief. "Our train went into this siding to allow another freight to pass, not for another inspection. Let's get back inside the boxcar."

However they couldn't open the door of their boxcar. The soldiers had sealed the boxcar door with yellow tape and wire straps. Nursal and Mitzal walked back toward the end of the train. A hint of dawn painted the sky and allowed them to find their way down the string of cars. Each boxcar door had been sealed, except for the last four cattle cars in front of the caboose. Nursal slid aside the door of the first cattle car, and two dozen nervous cattle stared back at him. As he swung into the car, the bull nearest the door bellowed and moved away, crowding against his neighbors. Nursal held out his hand to help Mitzal into the car, then closed the door and faced the cattle. The car smelled nasty. The odor of urine and cow dung was overpowering. The cattle backed away from Nursal and Mitzal who pressed themselves against the side of the car. The animals grew nervous and began shoving one another and shifting positions as they tried to get as far away as possible from their new travel companions. The closest animal to them, adorned with long, pointed horns, lowered his head and snorted. Nursal and Mitzal looked at the horns and squeezing themselves between the cattle and the side of the car, they shuffled to the bales of hay stacked in the rear. They climbed onto the stack and sat down, glad to be out from the undercarriage of the cattle car but not especially happy with their new travel companions. The cattle eventually settled down and ignored them. A few minutes later, a northbound freight train sped by and signaled with a loud, piercing screech that first increased and then decreased in pitch as it passed by. Their train whistle blew twice and the clatter of train car couplings rippled down the line as the train moved forward onto the main line, stopping briefly to allow the brakeman to reposition the siding switch and then climb back on board. Soon the train was heading at breakneck speed down the track and the terrorists settled down for a long, uncomfortable ride. Nursal peeked between the side slats of the cattle car and watched as the sun rose above a flat, treeless plain.

The train lurched and rattled on for mile after mile, passing through several small towns and occasionally pulling onto sidings, to make way for northbound trains. The siding stops usually lasted only a few minutes, but Mitzal became curious when one stop lasted for over ten minutes. He climbed to the top of the haystack, opened a trapdoor, and climbed out on the roof for a better view. The train had stopped on a siding and two men were struggling to fit a large hose into the tank car receptacle behind the engine. At the same time, two men filled large buckets with water and carried them toward the cattle cars.

Mitzal climbed back inside the car and warned Nursal, "We must hide. Two men are coming to water the cattle." They arranged four bales of hay to make a hideaway and then climbed inside and covered themselves with loose hay. The men opened the door, filled a water trough, and then after closing the door, went on to the next cattle car.

"This is why they didn't seal these doors," Mitzal commented. "They knew they would have to water the cattle."

Nursal prayed the track would lead south from Tashkent to the city of Termiz. Fifty kilometers beyond Termiz, he knew the line crossed over the Amu Myra River and into Afghanistan, ending at the town of Mazar-e-Sharif. The journey across Uzbekistan continued all that day, yet they had no way of knowing for sure if Termiz or some other city was this train's destination. If Allah was with them, the train would take them past Termiz and all the way into Afghanistan. Nursal thought the army might stop and search the train once again in Termiz, so they planned to jump off if they saw army trucks waiting in the freight yard.

Two hours later, the train slowed and switched to a track that headed westerly. Unsure if the train was headed to Termiz or some other destination away from Afghanistan, all they could do was watch the trackside signs for hints of where they were heading. Mitzal shouted for joy when he saw a trackside sign that proclaimed Termiz was 25 kilometers away. As they approached the Termiz freight yard, Nursal again climbed onto the roof of the boxcar, so he could see the freight yard ahead. The train slowed as it passed through the widespread freight yard. He relaxed when there was no sign of soldiers or army trucks and climbed back down inside the car. The train proceeded through the yard and stopped, where it waited for a northbound train to pass before rejoining the main line. From the railroad maps he had studied, Mitzal knew that once past Termiz, the line did not pass through any other sizable towns until it crossed over the river and into Afghanistan, terminating at the town of Mazar-e-Sharif.

"Allah has been good to us," Mitzal said thankfully. "We will soon be back in Afghanistan."

"Yet not so good to our friends Abu and Said," Nursal lamented. "They are either dead or captured by now."

The train chugged on throughout the afternoon and at dusk, crossed over the Amu Myra River and into Afghanistan. When the train stopped in the Mazar-e-Sharif freight yard, Nursal and Mitzal climbed through the trapdoor and left the cattle car. They walked to the passenger depot two miles further down the tracks and entered the station, avoiding customs and the UN inspection station located at the back of the terminal. They waited for the daily passenger train from Uzbekistan to arrive. Mingling with the arriving passengers, they passed through customs in single file. A policeman gave Nursal and Mitzal a hasty look, examined their passports, and then waved them through. They smelled like their travel companions and one inspector commented that they each needed a shower. The crate of textiles was waiting for them in the baggage room. A blue-helmeted United Nations sergeant opened the crate, dug through several layers of silk cloth, and without digging even halfway into the crate, hammered the lid back on and stamped their import paperwork. They borrowed a hand truck and moved the crate outside, where a truck waited for them. Nursal recognized his friends from the al-Qaeda cell in Almar and greeted them warmly. They loaded the crate onto the truck, already loaded with other crates filled with fabric and textiles, and then covered it with a tarp. Nursal said farewell to Mitzal, claiming that he had other business in Mazar-e-Sharif. Mitzal rode with the men to Balkh, where other team members assembled the plutonium into a "pit", encased it inside the uranium sphere, and then transported the bomb to Almar.

That evening, Nursal attended a meeting at the home of Amin Sharief, the head of al-Qaeda operations in northern Afghanistan. Sharief and six other high-level members sat around a table in Amin's home, drank sweetened tea, and listened to Nursal's story of his successful mission to Kazakhstan and theft of an atomic bomb. No one knew if the other al-Qaeda mission to steal a second atom bomb from an Uzbekistan depository had succeeded or not, yet this did not concern Amin. Nursal had done his part and now the terrorists had an atomic bomb, a cause for celebration. Amin poured each member a cup of unsweetened herb tea and they all congratulated Nursal for his courage and a successful mission. Suddenly in the middle of their celebration over Nursal's good news, half a dozen Afghan troops broke down the front door and burst into the room. The terrorists reached for their weapons, but before any of them could grab a gun, the soldiers opened fire, killing all six and severely wounding Amin and Nursal who took a bullet in his shoulder. Nevertheless, he was lucky to be alive. The troops lined Nursal and Amin against the wall and searched them. Bleeding from a head wound, Amin collapsed on the floor. Blood pouring from his shoulder wound, Nursal knelt down to help him and a soldier kicked him in the ribs so hard that he couldn't breathe. Two soldiers grabbed Nursal by each arm, dragged him out of the house, and threw him into the back of an army truck. They took Nursal to a downtown prison where, after a day of festering, his shoulder wound was finally treated. The next day, they led him to an interrogation room, where he was beaten and quizzed for five long hours. Despite the beatings, he told the interrogators nothing. He endured the torture with a smug smile, confident that by now Mitzal would have delivered the bomb to his al-Qaeda friends in Balkh, where they would assemble it and transfer it to Bashar al-Fulani, the leader of the al-Qaeda cell in Anar Darreh. Bashar had been trained by the Iranians about the workings of an atomic bomb, and it was his assigned task to smuggle the bomb into America and detonate it in a designated American City. Nursal was supposed to accompany Bashar to America, but considering his capture, that would not be possible.

Two days later, the Afghan soldiers loaded Nursal into a truck with other suspected al-Qaeda and Taliban prisoners and took him to the Ghurian prison in western Afghanistan, where he was imprisoned in a four-by-six cell without the benefit of a trial or formal charges. He knew that he would be held in Ghurian indefinitely, and from the moment he arrived, he plotted his escape.

CHAPTER EIGHTEEN:
THE PLOT

As the last rays of the winder sun disappeared behind the Afghan-Iranian Mountains, Bashar al-Fulani squatted to warm his hands by the fire and glowing embers of a courtyard fire pit. The climb in the dead of winter to this frozen mountain retreat, ten kilometers outside Anar Darreh, had exhausted and chilled him to the bone. A thousand needles pricked Bashar's fingers as the fire warmed his numb fingers. The low courtyard walls provided scant protection from the icy winds that constantly blew across the Afghanistan plains and lifted tons of reddish-brown dust high into the Afghan air. The dust tinged the sky with an iridescent pink glow, extending from the western mountain peaks to the desert that reached to the eastern horizon. A group of mud huts surrounding the courtyard served as the base camp for the el Mossel Militia (EMM), a small group of al-Qaeda affiliated insurgents based in western Afghanistan. Bashar commanded this mixed group of Wahhabi insurgents and Islamic dissidents dedicated to erasing Israel from the face of the map and chasing the American Army from the Moslem world. Bashar had fought his Jihad with the Americans for six years: six long years that had drained him in both body and soul. Yet enough hatred simmered within him to complete one last mission, the most important assignment in his jihad with America.

Six of his most trusted comrades sat around the courtyard fire and waited impatiently for the meeting to begin. Their loud chatter, a mixture of Farsi and Arabic, rose above the howling wind and echoed off the courtyard walls. Bashar's lieutenants had traveled from Egypt, Yemen, Iraq and parts of Afghanistan to attend this critical yet unexplained meeting. Bashar had concealed the purpose of this gathering from his lieutenants, and when he revealed it, they would be aware of their part in the most earthshaking al-Qaeda plan yet devised to create a worldwide caliphate. And he, Bashar al-Fulani, had been selected to fulfill this plan. His name would go down in history and he thanked his al-Qaeda superiors and Allah for such an honor.

The existing chaos created by the power outage in North America had provided Islam with a unique opportunity, and Allah had provided the means to punish the infidel Americans for their offenses against Islam. He was proud to be Allah's instrument of jihad. At his hands, the Americans would soon pay for their insolence, and an Islamic caliphate would soon be established in North America.

Bashar, born thirty years earlier in Egypt and raised in Afghanistan, was the son of a Saudi college professor and an Afghani mother. While a student attending Cairo University, he joined a group of "freedom fighters" loosely affiliated with al-Qaeda. Members were Sunni Muslims belonging to the Wahhabi sect of Islam, a faction formed in the 15th century and dedicated to spreading fundamentalist Islam throughout the world. The American Government stood stubbornly in the way of their Islamic goal, an enemy that must be dealt a mortal blow. The EMM methods sanctioned by Wahhabi fundamentalists were ruthless but effective. The American presence in Afghanistan and Iraq threatened the sovereignty of Iran and the new caliphate of Egypt-Syria. For years, Bashar had engaged in random EMM tactics designed to intimidate anyone who cooperated with the Americans. The EMM murdered elected officials and a terrorized American soldiers with roadside IED's, even attacking their own countrymen when it benefited their cause. Afghanistan, a prime target for EMM actions, still suffered under American occupation. First the Russians, then the Americans, and finally the United Nations tried to control this country, yet not one of them could defeat the EMM or Taliban insurrectionists. No one, neither Afghani nor foreigner, could feel safe in this sad, war-torn country.

After graduation from Cairo University, with a degree in Civil Engineering, Bashar rose within the ranks of the EMM, eventually to become the leader of the deadliest group of "freedom fighters" in Afghanistan. Since the end of the Iraq war, the U.S. had destroyed or disbanded most insurgency and terrorist groups. When Navy Seals killed Usama Bin Laden in Pakistan, al-Qaeda moved their headquarters to Yemen and the EMM became al-Qaeda's main terrorist arm in Afghanistan and Pakistan. Under the unofficial protection of Iran, the EMM conducted disruptive and intimidating raids and bombings within Afghanistan and Pakistan, while al-Qaeda carried out attacks in Iraq, Jordan, and Saudi Arabia. Recently the

EMM blew up a police station in Islamabad and damaged an American air base outside Kabul. They set fire to a hotel in Abu Dhabi, and their suicide bombers killed countless Afghani citizens in Kabul and Kandahar. Bashar was on America's list of the ten Most Wanted Terrorists. He swelled with pride and seethed with hatred and revenge at this news. In his distorted mind, he would be the most revered figure in Islam and would go down in history as the leader of the terrorists who destroyed an American city. He imagined a monument someday erected in his honor, perhaps a statue standing tall in the capitol of Kabul, Afghanistan, his adopted country, or perhaps now that Egypt was squarely in the al-Qaeda camp, in Alexandria, his Egyptian birthplace.

All eyes remained riveted on Bashar outlined in the glow of embers as he prepared to speak. He studied the bearded faces of his lieutenants sitting around the fire circle. His eyes darted from face to face, each bronze forehead reflecting a golden glow from the fire pit. These were his handpicked lieutenants, each of whom he knew and trusted with his life.

Two of the six, Kaleem Rahman and his cousin, Kaysan Hashim, had been Bashar's friends since their days together at Cairo University. Kaleem was 28 years old, six-foot three, handsome with a well developed and muscular upper body. Extroverted, often outspoken and confrontational, he had earned a well-deserved reputation as a troublemaker. His olive skin, deep-set dark eyes behind half-closed eyelids, neatly trimmed beard, and expensive clothes branded him as a wealthy Arab, yet he was neither wealthy nor Arab. A poor Hazara born and raised in western Afghanistan, Kaleem's family sold their home to send him to college. While studying at Cairo University, he met Bashar, who recruited him into the EMM. Kaleem disappointed his parents when he left the university without completing his studies. He returned to Afghanistan to help Bashar form the EMM cell near Ana Darreh.

Mild-mannered Kaysan was intelligent, soft-spoken, and deeply religious. Two years younger than Kaleem, he was the only member of his extended family who had earned a college degree. A generous crop of black hair partly covered his broad forehead, and his dark eyes surrounded by heavy glasses, marked him as an intellectual. His ivory-white teeth flashed behind lips constantly parted in a half-smile, while a full black beard and mustache covered the lower part of his face. At first glance, people would mistake Kaysan for a Pashtun; however, his almond-shaped eyes and a hooked nose betrayed his Hazara heritage. Born in Herat, he grew up in a mountainous village near the Iranian border and went to school in Ana Darreh. His Uncle, a rich Pharmacist in Farah, sent Kaysan to study in Egypt. Bright and inquisitive, Kaysan graduated from Cairo University with a degree in Chemistry and after graduation, he returned to Afghanistan to work for his uncle at his Farah pharmacy. Bashar recruited him into the EMM cell when he visited Kaleem in Heart.

At twenty-two years of age, Saheim al-Schishalsi, from Kirkuk, was the youngest lieutenant in Bashar's EMM cell. The son of a former Iraqi commander in Sadam Hussein's Republican Army, Saheim recently graduated with a degree in Electrical Engineering, from the University of California at Berkeley. He was small in stature, with brown hair and eyes, clean shaven, and wore a pencil-thin mustache. He walked with a slight limp, the result of a broken leg gained in a college soccer match. Composed and submissive, few EEM members knew much about him. He was a loner who seldom spoke unless spoken to. He avoided making friends but was devoted to Bashar and would do anything without question that his commander asked of him.

Cousins Sabur Hussein, 33, and Akram al-Filistine, 31, were born in Yemen and attended Islamic schools that limited their education to reading the Koran and the Haddith. Their faces hid behind coal black, wild and untrimmed beards. At first glance, people assumed they were twins rather than cousins. Both men joined the Taliban fighters in 2000. American soldiers captured Akram and Sabur in western Afghanistan in 2004 and sent them to Guantanamo prison, where they languished for six years, until an American court released them, in 2010. Those bitter years in prison taught them to hate all Americans. Embittered by their imprisonment, they vowed to extract revenge on their American captors. After returning to Afghanistan, they found their way to Farah, where they met Kaysan, who introduced them to Bashar. Bashar recruited both cousins into the EMM cell in Ana Darrah.

The last member of the group was Qasid Sachem, 42, a dark, brooding, uneducated Pashtun from Kandahar. Over 6 feet tall, with a wrestler's physique, he took pleasure in intimidating other members of the cell. With a mercurial disposition and able to win any fistfight, other members of the EMM cell carefully avoided him. His skin was dark brown, almost black, and a pair of beady eyes set close together suspiciously darted from person to person, never holding still on anyone for more than a brief second or two. Thick eyebrows outlining his brow met at the bridge of his rather large nose. Unable to grow a thick beard like others in the group, he could only manage a thin, straggly beard that hung in stringy patches from his chin. Qasid had earned a reputation as an assassin, someone who would just as soon plunge a knife into a man's back than talk to him, and no one doubted or cared to test his credentials. His father in Kandahar was a merchant of hashish and opium, with a nasty reputation of his own that matched that of his son. Rather than attending school, Qasid spent his teen years hawking drugs on the Kandahar streets for his father. Bashar met Qasid in a drug deal and recruited him into the EEM. His loyalty to Bashar was absolute.

Bashar finished his review of those around the campfire and greeted his comrades: "*Salaam alaykum*". Speaking in a combination of Farsi and Arabic, he began to explain why he had called them here.

"This is a momentous occasion for our jihad. The decadent people of the United States are now suffering from a crisis, one that they are unable to control. Allah has sent great suffering to America. An arrow from the sun has pierced the heart of that evil country. Allah has disrupted their electrical power systems and darkened the entire nation for many months now. The corrupt American Government is unable to deal with this catastrophe and anarchy threatens the entire country. A country in such chaos is ripe for revolution. Allah has provided us with a unique opportunity, one where we can deliver a mortal blow to that corrupt nation. The blow will be one of such devastation that Americans will reject their government and their corrupt Christian faith, a faith that has led them to the brink of hell. After the jihad, they will be open to accept Islam and Shari'a law. We will be there to lead them out of darkness and establish an American caliphate. The time for the New World Order of Islam has come, and you my trusted friends, have been chosen to deliver the critical blow."

Bashar looked at his smiling comrades and chanted "*Allah-u-akbar!* (God is great)." Everyone joined Bashar's chant, repeating it over and over as it echoed off the courtyard walls. Bashar then whispered something to Qasid, who got up and quickly left the courtyard. Bashar's face glowed as he stood facing the group.

"Now I will show you the means of our jihad, a gift from Allah," Bashar beamed.

Bashar went over to the first of three crates placed alongside the courtyard wall and lifted the lid from the first crate. He fished through the Styrofoam peanuts until he recovered a large metal birdcage. Inside the birdcage and suspended by a rubber net was a silver aluminum sphere about the size of a soccer ball. He struggled to remove the heavy sphere from the birdcage, and then placed it on top of one of the crates and unscrewed it. The ball was bright silver on the outside and coal black on the inside. Bashar explained the ball was beryllium, with the inside coated with a layer of graphite. Neatly fitted inside the sphere were two hemispheres of polished dull-gray metal, separated by a metal plate. If brought together, the hemispheres would make a ball slightly smaller than the soccer ball. He carefully placed each hemisphere on a table next to the fire pit. The polished parts glowed orange, softly reflecting the glow of embers from fire pit, yet at the same time appearing to emit their own intrinsic radiance.

"This is enriched uranium, the fissionable heart of the bomb," Bashar explained. "Each half fits within this beryllium sphere, coated on the inside with graphite designed to slow neutrons."

He opened the second crate and dug around in the Styrofoam peanuts until he found a metal container that looked like a large thermos bottle. He placed the bottle on the table and unscrewed the cap. Four wedge-shaped machined metal parts, each about ten centimeters long, fit inside the thermos. Bashar extracted one of the wedges and held it high for all to see. He struggled to hold the weighty object. The dull silver material seemed extraordinarily heavy for its small size, no bigger than a wedge of cheese,

"This is plutonium. Inside the crate are seven more containers, each with room for four plutonium wedges identical to this one. Like a giant jigsaw puzzle, we will assemble these wedges to form a plutonium sphere, about the size of a baseball. The assembled plutonium called a "pit" will fit snuggly inside the uranium sphere. The third crate contains the Semtex explosive charges and timing circuits."

Bashar placed the plutonium back inside the thermos, screwed the cap back on and returned it to the crate.

"This bomb is our instrument of death to America," he proudly proclaimed. "As atom bombs go, it is a small one, perhaps the equivalent of ten or 15 kilotons of TNT. Semtex explosive charges carefully placed around the sphere, and timed by a circuit board, will implode and create a critical mass of enriched uranium, which will fission and ignite the plutonium. Then boom . . . no more American city."

His smile widened. "We will take the bomb to America, and to the city of Minot, in North Dakota, where we will assemble and detonate it outside an American air base. The other crate contains other parts of the bomb, including the Semtex explosives, the electronics and detonators. Allah has given us the task of taking this bomb to America, and detonating it in one of their cities . . . *Allah-u-akbar!*"

Incredulous, Kaysan Hashim was the first to raise a question. With his degree in chemistry, he was the only member besides Bashar who even vaguely understood the workings of an atom bomb.

"Then the bomb is a kit?" Kaysan questioned. "We are not nuclear scientists. How can we assemble an atom bomb from these . . . these bits and pieces?"

"Actually, it is all quite simple," Bashar reassured him. "The Iranians trained me to assemble the bomb. Each hemisphere of uranium is a sub-critical mass and must be compressed by a carefully shaped charge, to form a critical mass. The wedges of plutonium cannot fission until they are assembled into a pit and then flooded by slow neutrons from the uranium. When fashioned into the pit and then bathed by neutrons from the fissioning uranium, the plutonium will also fission. When the bomb is ready, we will fashion the Semtex and detonators into a shaped charge surrounding the beryllium sphere."

Kaysan pondered all this for a minute, and then asked, "Where did we get this bomb?"

"We stole the enriched uranium and the plutonium from a storage depository in Kazakhstan. The Russians have not even admitted their bomb is missing. It is fitting that we will destroy an American city with Russian plutonium." Bashar beamed and broke into a crooked smile. He took delight that he could explain the workings of an atomic bomb to his comrades. The knowledge made him feel powerful.

Kaysan looked troubled. "Is not the bomb dangerous to transport? Won't we die from radiation?"

"No," Bashar explained. "The lead canisters will inhibit most of the radiation, and as long as we don't expose ourselves to the plutonium for more than a few minutes at a time, we will be safe."

"Do we have there more bombs like this one?" Saheim asked.

"No, I don't think there are any others," Bashar said. "Unfortunately, this is the only one we have. Al-Qaeda tried to steal two bombs, but the Iranians told me the Russians caught one of our teams in Turkmenistan and confiscated the stolen materials."

"So, the Russians must know there is a bomb missing," Kaysan assumed.

"Well, probably by now they know, but they are not admitting this," Bashar answered. "The managers at the repository where we stole the bomb quickly covered up their ineptitude. For the Russians, losing one bomb was bad enough, but heads will roll for loosing two . . . . they told no one about the missing bombs."

Kaysan persisted with his questions. "How will we detonate the bomb?" Bashar closed the lid of the crate and without answering Kaysan, sat down on top of it.

Saheim also seemed uneasy and repeated the question. "Yes . . . how will we detonate this bomb?"

"Ah, my engineering friend," Bashar beamed . . . "THAT is where you come in. Take a look in the third crate."

Saheim pried the lid off the remaining crate. On top buried in Styrofoam peanuts was the neatly folded assembly instructions printed from the "How to Build an Atomic Bomb" web site. Covered in more peanuts was the putty-like Semtex plastic explosive, bomb housing, batteries, and several circuit boards loaded with chips and other electronic parts protected by bubble-wrap.

Puzzled, Saheim picked up the various electronic parts, unwrapped and briefly examined them, and then returned them to the crate. "I don't see a timing device, just some batteries and assorted circuit boards and wires. There are no circuit diagrams indicating how to put all the electronics together, so I have no idea how to assemble the triggering mechanism."

"A complicated triggering and timing device will not be necessary," Bashar explained. "We will detonate the bomb on site. To ensure that our mission succeeds, Allah has willed that we sacrifice ourselves. Saheim, all you have to do is wire the detonators to the explosives that I will place at critical points around the sphere. A single switch from the battery to the detonators will ignite the bomb. I know how to fashion shaped charges; I have been making IEDs for the Iraqi insurgents for years."

Kaysan wasn't convinced. "How will we know if it will work? After all, we can't test it."

"Don't fret my friend, it will work," Bashar stated with conviction, "Allah will insure that it works."

"Then this is to be a suicide mission. We will all be killed . . . vaporized," Kaysan whispered.

"It is Allah's will that we sacrifice ourselves for the Jihad. We will receive our reward in Paradise," Bashar assured him.

Bashar's assurance of a reward in heaven did not change Kaysan's mind. "The Qur'an forbids suicide," he argued. "I cannot take part in such a mission."

"We are all Allah's soldiers in the Jihad," Bashar said. "He will reward our mission and each person's sacrifice."

Just then Qasid returned to the courtyard and whispered something to Bashar. Bashar did not react, but remained focused on his reluctant lieutenant. "Kaysan, you are either with me or against me. You must decide. This is Allah's work."

A tear formed a streak down Kaysan's dust-caked face. He looked for assurance from his cousin Kaleem, but as usual, Kaleem's face was expressionless and he said nothing.

"I cannot go against our faith," Kaysan explained. "Mohammed and the Qur'an forbid suicide. I cannot and will not take part in a suicide mission. If you force me to choose, then I am against you."

Basher's face turned beet red. "Leave us then . . . and hide yourself in the town of Herat like the Hazara coward you are. Allah will decide your fate." Looking for other signs of resistance, his eyes darted to each of his sullen lieutenants, but their faces were blank.

"Does anyone else want to leave with the coward Kaysan? If so step forward."

Everyone looked at the ground. No one stepped forward.

"Then is everyone except Kaysan is ready to die for Allah?"

"*Allah-u-akbar*," they all shouted in unison, everyone, that is, except Kaysan, who continued to stare into the fire pit.

Basher turned to Kaysan and shouted, "Go then . . . get out . . . . NOW!"

Kaysan strapped on his backpack and walked through the courtyard gate into the cold dark night. The sliver of moon that hung over the mountain barely lit the trail down the mountainside that led to the small village of Terkite, home of his cousin Moesha Hashim.

"Moesha will surely take me in for the night, and then tomorrow I can find my way to Herat," Kaysan told himself, as he trudged down the switchback path.

After Kaysan disappeared through the courtyard gate, Bashar turned to the rest of the group.

"Kaysan is a traitor and a coward. We are best rid of him."

Bashar motioned for Qasid to follow him outside the courtyard. "Go after Kaysan and kill him," Bashar whispered. "If the Americans capture him, they will force him to reveal our plan. After you have killed Kaysan, go to Kabul and tell the Taliban high command that our mission is underway. They will get word to the al-Qaeda leaders in Iran, who will arrange our transportation to America."

Qasid nodded and followed the path down the darkened mountainside. Bashar came back into the courtyard and sat down with his men to share the details of the mission.

"I have sent Qasid to tell the Taliban that our plan is underway. We will take the bomb by truck and jeep to the border, where Iranian soldiers will then drive us and the bomb to the port of Bandar-a-Abbas, where a fishing boat will be waiting to take us to the United Arab Emirates. Kaleem, Akram and Saheim will go with me to America. Sabur and another driver will stay behind and drive the truck and jeep back here. At Abu Dhabi, we will load the bomb crates onto a containership headed to Vancouver, British Columbia. Al-Qaeda members in that city will rent a van and drive us across Canada to Moose Jaw, in Saskatchewan. From there, we will cross the U.S. border and drive to our destination, Minot, North Dakota, where we will assemble and detonate the bomb."

The choice of Minot as the target city puzzled Akram al-Filistine. "Minot, North Dakota? I have never heard of this place. It cannot be a big or important city. Why is such an insignificant place our objective? Why not choose a much larger city, such as New York or Washington, where the bomb would kill millions, not just a few thousand Americans?"

Bashar turned toward Akram and frowned. "The U.S. Air Force has dozens of B-52 bombers and hundreds of atom bombs stored at the air base near Minot. Once we detonate our bomb, those other bombs will vaporize and spread a radioactive cloud throughout the area. It will poison hundreds of thousands of people in the Midwest and pollute millions of acres of farmland. Americans will come to know firsthand of death and starvation. The result will be fewer Americans alive to pollute our world, but even more important, after our attack Americans will come to know that their government cannot protect them. This bomb will be the straw that breaks the back of the American government. People will reject their ineffective government and the door will open for al-Qaeda sleeper cells to take over. The high command chose Minot not for its size, but for the impact this explosion will have on all Americans. This is to be a demonstration of our power and ability to devastate any American city of our choosing, even one in the heartland of that country. This is our only bomb, but we will make America believe we have many such bombs and that no American city is safe from jihad."

Bashar paused and looked around at each man. They all seemed mesmerized by his speech. Assured they were with him, he continued.

"Al-Qaeda will make many demands of the teetering American government, including bringing their troops home from the Middle East within two months. If our demands are not met, they will threaten to blow up New York, or Los Angeles, or any other city of their choosing. The Americans will panic and demand that their government protect them, but will realize that it cannot do so. They will then demand solutions, any solution, and insist for a recall of their elected Washington officials. As riots erupt and the present administration falters, our operatives in dozens of cells throughout the country will be ready to take over key positions. We already have our people in critical government and military positions in Washington D.C. and in most businesses and state governments. In the aftermath, al-Qaeda will carry out their plan to establish a caliphate in America. They will believe the caliphate can protect them, and America will one day awake to an Islamic government. There is nothing they will be able to do to stop it."

Akram remained troubled. "It will be dangerous to offload the bomb in Vancouver, for we cannot depend on Canadian Customs to ignore our shipment. And it is unlikely we can transport it undetected across Canada. It will be impossible to take the bomb by road, across the U.S. border to Minot . . . impossible," Saheim stressed.

"And what do you know about America, Akram?" Bashar rebuked. "You have never lived there, as Saheim has. I have been there and know the soft bellies of the Americans. Their interest is only in themselves and their comforts. With all the chaos caused by the power outage, the government is not protecting their borders. Al-Qaeda, in Vancouver, will help us get the bomb across Canada and past the ineffective American Customs. The FBI and Homeland Security departments are in shambles. They cannot even control the mayhem and violence within their own cities. Our operatives in Canada tell us that Canadian Immigration is in such turmoil that they are unlikely to inspect our cargo at the Vancouver port."

Bashar paused to let his words sink in. "Allah has provided this opportunity, an opportunity to put a final nail in the American coffin. This bomb will be the beginning of the end of the United States of America. With the knowledge that their government can no longer protect them, Americans will clamor for security. We will offer them a caliphate, and they won't even realize that it is actually run by al-Qaeda. Amid the resulting political turmoil we cause, our friends already imbedded in the military and government will move in and take over. With Allah's help, we will succeed in creating an Islamic caliphate in America and subject the American people to Shari'a law and Islamic courts."

"*Allah-u-akbar!*" "*Allah-u-akbar,*" they all excitedly shouted in unison

CHAPTER NINETEEN:
THE PLAN SPRINGS A LEAK

A small rock tumbled past Kaysan as he hurried down the switchback trail. He stopped for a moment and listened as another rock tumbled from the mountainside above him. Someone was following and would soon overtake him. In the dim moonlight, Kaysan spotted a small pile of rocks further down the mountainside and a few yards off the path. He climbed down to the rocks, wedged himself between two large boulders, and said a short prayer that Allah would protect him. More rocks tumbled down the trail and bounced past the pile of boulders. He watched and waited, breathing in shallow gasps. His heart pounded and sweat beaded on his forehead. A minute later, the figure of a man silhouetted against the dimly lit skyline appeared on the ridge above the rock pile. Even in the dim light, he recognized the distinctive headgear and coat worn by Qasid Sachem. Qasid hurried past the pile of rocks and disappeared over the ridge below.

"So," Kaysan thought, "my friend Bashar sent Qasid to kill me. The EMM doesn't entertain dissent, only blind devotion. Because I refused to join in Bashar's sinful plot, my friends have turned on me and now I am prey."

Kaysan remained in his hiding place until he was sure Qasid was gone, and then crawled out and climbed back up the mountainside trail. The assassin would eventually realize his quarry had eluded him and double back to the rock pile. Kaysan searched for another trail, a side path he remembered seeing as he trudged down the mountain. About a kilometer uphill from the rock pile, he found the side path. This trail might not lead to his cousin in Terkite, yet now that did not matter. He had to get away from Qasid. The plan to stay at his cousin's house no longer seemed like a good idea. If he asked for Moesha's help and Qasid found him, he would not only kill him but might kill Moesha and his family as well. He had to get as far away from this mountain as possible. He walked 100 yards past the side path, to make it look as if he had backtracked to the compound. Then he broke off a branch from a small bush, erased his tracks for several yards along the side path, and then hurried down the trail. The path wound down the mountainside in a series of switchbacks, but as he suspected, it led away from Terkite. He had no idea where this path would take him, yet it was his only escape route. Qasid was not very bright and Kaysan knew he was a poor tracker. In the barely visible light, he would think Kaysan had gone back up mountain. Kaysan needed a new plan. Perhaps he could make it to Kandahar, where his friends would hide him. Even though Kandahar was many miles away, it was far safer than either Herat or Kabul.

After walking for the better part of an hour, Kaysan picked out the ghostly outline of a small village far below. Although he grew up in Do Qal'eh, a city not far from Anar Darrah, Kaysan didn't recognize the village clinging to the ridge below. Because farming the shallow and rocky mountain soil often proved unproductive, villages in this area were few and drifted from place to place. Sometimes villagers would move an entire town to a more productive area. He could not remember a village on this mountainside, and he would find no friends there willing to hide him. He decided to bypass the village and head further east toward the town of Farah, which lay on the road to Kandahar, providing that he could find the road in the dark.

His people, the Hazara, had settled in this part of the country centuries ago and could trace their origins to the Mongols and Kublai Kahn. The Afghani Pashtun considered the Hazara a backward and inferior people, and only offered them menial work as servants and laborers. Kaysan's father was born in Farah and found work as a household servant in Kandahar, where he met and married Kaysan's mother. When Kaysan was a young boy, his father took him to visit relatives in the remote village of Farah, nestled in a ravine at the foot of Mt. Tondi. The walk to Farah, the largest village in the area, would be a long trek; if he could find his relatives in that village, they would surely take him in.

He walked all night, until a salmon-tinged sun rose over the flat eastern landscape. In the early light, he found the dusty main road that led toward Farah and Kandahar. By midmorning, exhausted, hungry, and thirsty, he came to a small roadside tearoom. He asked an old man sitting outside if he could get a cup of tea and a little something to eat, although he had only a few coins with which to pay. The man introduced himself as Motif Bandar and led him to a nearby hut. Motif invited Kaysan inside and offered him a seat at a large round table, where four other men sat sipping their morning tea. He ordered a woman dressed in a black burka to bring some tea and biscuits for their guest. Kaysan thanked Motif and savored the hot tea and freshly baked biscuits. Before he had a chance to finish his meal, a commotion erupted outside the hut. Motif rose to have a look outside and cautioned Kaysan to remain seated, but before Motif could get out the door, two American soldiers burst into the hut and demanded to see everyone's papers. Captain's bars decorated the helmet of the first soldier and two stripes labeled the other solider as a corporal.

The soldiers lined everyone against the back wall, and one by one, began to examine their papers. The captain stepped in front of Kaysan and demanded his papers. Kaysan handed him his forged passport. The dirt-poor people of this region normally carried ID cards but few had passports. Kaysan's passport immediately spiked the soldier's curiosity. The captain eyed him suspiciously, and then took a magnifying glass from his pocket and carefully leafed through the passport pages. Kaysan's passport was a good forgery, but not good enough to pass magnifying glass scrutiny.

"This passport is a forgery," the captain proclaimed. "Come with me."

Kaysan started to protest, but a rifle butt to his stomach cut his argument short.

An army 4x4 truck waited outside the village. The Captain dragged Kaysan to the truck, handcuffed him and forced him to climb into the back. Inside, an American private sat on a crate and nervously fingered a loaded AK-47 rifle on his lap. Heads down, five other Afghans sat on side benches. No one spoke to Kaysan or even acknowledged his presence. He found a seat on a bench across from the soldier and sat down. A few minutes later, the truck was bouncing down the dusty road leading to Farah. Kaysan tried to start a conversation with another prisoner; but the sergeant ordered him to shut up. They drove in silence for another hour and finally stopped beside a grove of orange trees for a latrine break. As Kaysan climbed down from the truck, he recognized the outskirts of Aurum in the distance, a small village outside Farah. One half hour later, the truck entered Farah and parked alongside a block-long walled prison. Blue helmeted U.N. soldiers escorted Kaysan and the other prisoners through the gate and into the interrogation room, where they were ordered to sit on wooden benches placed alongside one wall. Minutes later, two Marine guards entered the room, grabbed Kaysan, and escorted him down a long, dark hall to a windowless and stuffy room, dimly lit by a single naked light bulb. A civilian dressed in a blue pinstripe suit sat behind a large metal desk and looked up from his paperwork as the guards shoved Kaysan into the room. The man's stock of pure white hair, light blue eyes, and unusually pale complexion blended with the spartan room. *An albino*" Kaysan thought, *and despite his civilian attire, most likely an American officer* The lack of an overhead fan, no fresh air, and the bare white walls aggravated Kaysan's discomfort and growing panic.

The man invited Kaysan to sit down and adjusted the desk lamp so that it glared in Kaysan's face.

"My name is Mr. Karl. I am a CIA officer and it is my job to interrogate you," the man began. "It will go well for you if you tell me the truth; however you will regret it if you lie."

He examined Kaysan's passport, and then placed the document under a binocular microscope on his desk. After a few seconds, he tossed the passport on the desk in front of Kaysan.

"Are you a member of al-Qaeda, or the Taliban Militia?"

Kaysan silently stared at the floor and almost imperceptibly shook his head to and fro.

"Well, which is it then, al-Qaeda or Taliban?"

Kaysan took a deep breath. "Neither," he replied defiantly.

"That lie is your first mistake," the officer grumbled. "Why do you carry a fake passport? Where did you get it?"

"I bought it from a man in Kabul," Kaysan replied.

"A man in Kabul . . . , " the officer mimicked. "What man?"

Kaysan avoided the bright light and continued to stare at the floor. "Just a man in the marketplace," he mumbled.

The man's voice lowered. "I warned you that it would not go well for you if you lied and now you are lying. This passport is an excellent forgery, created by a professional and not by some Kabul street hawker with a photocopier. It is much better than the rubbish you could buy on the street for ten dollars. Only a few people in Afghanistan have the equipment and expertise to create such a clever forgery, and those people are all members of either al-Qaeda or the Taliban."

He paused, and then repeated his question, almost shouting. "So, which is it?"

Kaysan remained silent.

"Your silence tells me that you are Taliban."

"No!" Kaysan answered emphatically. "I am not Taliban."

The officer's eyes narrowed. "Al-Qaeda then."

"I told you . . . no, I am not al-Qaeda or Taliban."

Clearly, Kaysan's denials didn't impress the officer.

"I have the evidence of your clumsy lie right here before me. I repeat, where did you get this passport?"

Kaysan squirmed in his chair and didn't answer.

The albino asked, "Where were you going with such a cleverly faked passport?"

Kaysan silently stared at the floor.

Mr. Karl looked at Kaysan for some minutes, then pressed a button on his desk and the two Marines entered the room and took Kaysan to a smaller room down the hall, some distance from the interrogation room. The undecorated room was windowless, the walls, floor and ceiling painted a monotonous dull white. One of the Marines flicked a switch and an overhead, hooded lamp bathed the room in brilliant white light. The only furniture was a single chair, a rack loaded with electronic equipment that blinked small blue and red lights, and a metal examination table under the lamp. The Marines dragged Kaysan over to the table, forced him to lie down, and then strapped him to the table. They stood at attention as Mr. Karl and a man in a white doctor's coat entered the room. With a nod and a flick of his finger, Mr. Karl dismissed the Marines. The doctor produced a syringe and held it upside down while tapping it with his finger to remove trapped air bubbles, and then without a word, stuck it into Kaysan's arm. The plunger slowly moved downward injecting the contents of the syringe into his bloodstream. Within seconds, Kaysan felt light-headed and woozy, much as he did whenever he smoked too much hashish.

Mr. Karl moved back to the examination table and looked down at Kaysan. He nodded to the doctor, who then retreated to the back of the room. Kaysan felt the officer's penetrating gaze.

"If you don't cooperate and truthfully answer my questions, it will not go well for you. If you continue to lie . . . well then, there is nothing I can do to save you."
Kaysan looked away from the officer and struggled against the straps, but the leather belts dug into his flesh and the resistance only increased his discomfort. Mr. Karl's threat spun around in his fog-shrouded brain. What did he mean by "there is nothing I can do to save you?" Was a lifetime in some dark, dank prison, or worse, to be his fate? He shuddered.

Mr. Karl continued the interrogation, repeating the same questions as before, yet Kaysan averted the man's gaze and defiantly stared at a spot on the ceiling. Kaysan's extensive training allowed him to focus his mind and resist the effects of the drug, although as the drug took full effect, it became more and more difficult for him to concentrate. His head spun and he felt compelled to say something, so he replied to Mr. Karl's questions with rehearsed lies. He was only a poor uneducated farmer and knew nothing about the Taliban or al-Qaeda. The officer wasn't buying the lies.

He called the two Marines back into the room and they helped the doctor strap a copper cuff to Kaysan's right wrist and left ankle, and then inserted a rubber mouthpiece between his teeth. Mr. Karl asked Kaysan his name, and he replied truthfully. He asked where he was from, and again Kaysan replied truthfully. Then he asked where he bought the passport. This question took more concentration than Kaysan could muster. He seemed to be floating on a soft cushion, with no control over his body. His mouth was dry, his tongue thick, and a wave of nausea began to overwhelm him. He couldn't focus on answering Mr. Karl's question with a lie, and all he could do was to remain silent. Mr. Karl motioned to the doctor, who pressed a large red button on a breadbox-sized black machine that looked like a defibulator. A surge of pain shot through Kaysan as every muscle in his body contracted with the electric shock. The shock abruptly ended and his whole body shook uncontrollably for several seconds. Mr. Karl then repeated the question, and again Kaysan refused to answer. He watched Mr. Karl adjust a dial and then felt the electricity again course through his body. It lasted longer than the first shock and his muscles constricted with such force, he thought his bones would crack. His interrogator repeated the question a third, and then a fourth time. Each lack of response resulted in another twist of the dial and few seconds of torture. The electric shock treatment was beyond painful, and after each shock Kaysan's body twitched convulsively for several seconds. The drugs and electric shock had sent his head spinning and nausea overwhelmed him. He felt himself falling into a deep dark pit.

The doctor momentarily halted the torture as Kaysan coughed and began to choke. He released the strap on his head and let him heave into a bucket. The doctor measured his pulse and blood pressure and told Mr. Karl that further torture might result in the man's death. The questions then continued, yet this time without more electric shocks. The albino's questions seemed to come from the lip of the pit he had fallen into. The interrogation was repetitious and relentless.

"Where did you get this passport?" "What cell do you belong to?" "Where were you going?"

Finally, Kaysan's ability to concentrate and resist the albino's questioning faded. His willpower succumbed to the drugs and the dread of further torture clouded his mind. After almost fifteen minutes of relentless questioning and torture, he could no longer resist. He confessed to everything he knew about his membership in the el-Mossel Militia and the plot to explode a nuclear bomb in Minot, North Dakota. He couldn't believe he was confessing all of this. It was as if the words poured out from a stranger's mouth rather than his own.

"A bomb?" Mr. Karl asked incredulously. "An atom bomb? Are you sure? How do you know it was an atom bomb?"

"Yes, it was an atom bomb. I am positive. I saw it," Kaysan insisted groggily. Mr. Karl left the room for a few minutes and Kaysan's mind began to clear, but his resistance to questioning had evaporated. When the officer returned, he again asked about the atom bomb. Kaysan described the bomb in some detail.

The officer's eyes grew wide. He knew enough about atomic weapons to realize Kaysan's description of an atomic bomb was accurate.

"Where did you see this bomb and when?"

"Five days ago, at our headquarters, ten kilometers outside Anar Darreh."

Convinced that Kaysan's drug-induced story was no hoax, Mr. Karl continued the interrogation.

"How do the terrorists intend to transport the bomb to the United States?"

Kaysan said didn't know. He had left the meeting before Bashar disclosed those details. He did remember that Bashar had mentioned Minot was the target.

When Mr. Karl heard "Minot", he stiffened. He was familiar with the city, having once been assigned to the nearby airbase as an intelligence officer. "You are sure that Minot was mentioned as the target?"

Kaysan's head continued to swim. His own voice sounded like it emanated from a ghost. "Yes, that is what they said. I do not know of Minot. I had never heard of that city, but I am sure that is what Bashar said."

"And who is Bashar?"

"He is the leader of the EMM. He is the one who will transport the bomb to America."

Satisfied that he had extracted everything of importance, Mr. Karl ordered the Marines to take Kaysan to a holding cell and let him sleep off the effects of the drugs. Mr. Karl tried to interrogate Kaysan the following day, but now that he was awake and drug-free, he refused to cooperate. When confronted with the information extracted from him the preceding day, he denied everything. Mr. Karl asked again about the EMM cell, the man called Bashar, and an atom bomb. Kaysan claimed he made all this up so they wouldn't continue to torture him, but Mr. Karl decided that his denial was a lie and his drug-induced confession was credible.

The CIA had assigned Mr. Karl to Afghanistan as an information officer, whose job was to interrogate captured field combatants. He had been on assignment for almost two years and was aware of the terrorist group known as the el-Mossel Militia and their successful acts of sabotage. The EMM was the most fanatical and dedicated terrorist organization in the Middle East. They took their orders directly from the Iranian Imam, who supported and funded the al-Qaeda leadership in Yemen, Afghanistan and Pakistan. Kaysan's information seemed credible. Mr. Karl had attended several briefings on atomic weapons and realized Kaysan's description of a rudimentary fission bomb was accurate. The CIA knew the towns of Terkite and Anar Darrah quartered EMM cells and suspected those cells were responsible for several ambushes on UN and American troops. The Marines planned a raid on both cells, but concerned about stirring a hornet's nest of opposition within the local Hazara population, the Afghani government had resisted such raids.

Mr. Karl had hit the intelligence jackpot. The CIA long suspected that al-Qaeda or an offshoot group like the EMM would get their hands on a nuke and try to detonate it in the States. Last year, Iran successfully tested their own atom bomb, and the terrorists would eventually get a bomb from the Iranians, or they might steal the components from Russia or one of the former Soviet Union Republics. It was not a matter of "if" but "when". Iranian officials and other Middle East leaders habitually made threats against the U.S. and Israel, yet most intelligence officers discounted such nuclear threats as political posturing. Mr. Karl knew Kaysan's information was not posturing, it was real. The unthinkable had happened and an atom bomb was now in the hands of terrorists headed to North America. Given the opportunity, these al-Qaeda maniacs would not hesitate to wipe an American city off the face of the earth. Unless he could alert the proper authorities in his own organization, the terrorists would succeed in their mission. Right now, he was the only person who could prevent this impending disaster.

Mr. Karl picked up the telephone and gave the information about the EMM cell in Anar Darreh to the American Marine commander in Kandahar. With the help of Afghan troops, the Marines attacked the cell the next day and arrested everyone in the compound. Unfortunately, they did not find any evidence of a bomb. Under interrogation, one of the terrorists admitted Bashar and a few of his officers had traveled to Iran several days ago. None of those arrested knew anything about a bomb, or so they claimed. The Marine commander became convinced that Kaysan's information was a ruse, an attempt to save his own skin.

Mr. Karl knew otherwise. He wanted to cable this critical information immediately to his CIA superiors, in Washington D.C., yet there was a problem. The CIA headquarters was in disarray, and Mr. Karl didn't know who he could trust with this information. The President's staff had caused politically motivated turmoil in Washington government agencies. A crisis of leadership existed within the CIA. Months before the blackout, the President had initiated a campaign to revamp several agencies, including the CIA, FBI, and the Homeland Security Departments. Directed by the President, the Administration forced a shuffle within those agencies, firing or retiring many career managers and replacing them with political appointees. Many of these appointees had little or no experience within the agency they now directed.

The newly appointed CIA Director of Foreign Intelligence, former Representative James Coleman, had demoted or transferred Agency insiders, including Jim Murtha, Mr. Karl's former supervisor. He then filled the agency management positions with outsiders, mostly cronies of the President who knew little of the history or operations within government agencies, never having served a day in the State Department, Homeland Security, the CIA, or FBI. Director Coleman knew nothing about surveillance or interrogation techniques and opposed many longtime agency procedures. He appointed friends of his to fill other vacant positions, without regard to their experience or competency.

Chaos reigned in the CIA home office and adversely affected operations in the foreign field offices. Orders would come down from headquarters to the CIA Afghan office one day and be countermanded the next. Jim Murtha had been transferred to a different position within the Agency, and his successor had not yet been named. Mr. Karl didn't know who he reported to or who he could trust with this critical information. Regardless, the strict protocol about disseminating information remained alive and well within the revamped CIA. If he did not follow strict hierarchical procedures when passing on information, it would result in a career-ending reprimand. Worse yet, some overworked bureaucrat might dismiss or bury Mr. Karl's warning under a stack of papers. He felt the best plan was to contact Jim Murtha, and without being specific, tell him he had intelligence that needed immediate agency attention and ask for his advice. Mr. Karl knew that Jim and would understand that he had critical information that had to get to the right person within the agency.

Mr. Karl sent an encrypted cable to his former boss and patiently waited for a response. Two days, and then four, went by, without a response. He assumed Jim might be busy with his new job, or he had assigned a subordinate to intercept information cables and wires from Afghanistan. In addition, the de-encryption process often delayed information for several days. He grew more and more impatient when a week went by with no response to his cable. He considered resending the information, or even directly contacting his former boss. Timely action was essential in order to intercept and defuse the bomb, before it arrived on U.S. soil. The

Agency must alert Homeland Security and all U.S. ports of entry to be on the lookout for this shipment.

He reasoned the terrorists would transport the bomb from Afghanistan to the States by ship. That would take time, perhaps as much as three weeks, before it arrived. He judged it would be impractical for the terrorists to send the bomb by air, where inspection was strict. No, the bomb had to be somewhere on a ship, he reasoned. He placed no confidence in the hope that the U.S. Port Customs would detect the bomb. At best, the port authorities inspected only one out of every ten containers arriving in U.S. ports. More likely, the terrorists had shipped the bomb to Mexico or Canada, where inspections were even more lackadaisical than those in the States. Even in the best of times, Homeland Security considered Canadian and Mexican Customs lax; now, they considered those organizations a joke. Foreign goods unloaded in Canadian or Mexican ports were only occasionally inspected, and then with cursory interest. They seldom opened containers or crates and even when they did so, the inspection was superficial. Since the destination was Minot, Mr. Karl reasoned the terrorists most likely would ship their deadly cargo from some port on the Persian Gulf or Gulf of Oman to a Canadian port, and then into the States. On his computer he tracked all shipments originating from those ports to Canada. No shipments from the Middle East were due to arrive in North American ports for the next two weeks, so he felt he had some time to get his message to the agency. His information was incomplete however, because the Iranian, Abu Dhabi, Yemen and Qatar governments refused to share their shipping records with the CIA.

Mr. Karl's best guess was they would offload the bomb at the port of Montreal and transport it by truck to Winnipeg or Regina, and then finally cross the border to Minot. If the CIA acted quickly, they might intercept the bomb at a Canadian port or at the U.S.-Canada border. Homeland Security was especially suspicious of all shipments originating in the Middle-East, yet inspections remained haphazard. Customs should be alerted to inspect all cars and trucks crossing over from Canada for radioactive materials.

After a week went by, with no response to his cable, Mr. Karl felt that time was running out. Desperate, he decided to send the information to another former CIA supervisor, Josh Richards. Mr. Karl knew Josh and trusted him. The admiration and respect went both ways. Josh would not question Mr. Karl's credibility, and would act on the information. Another two days went by, before Josh responded in the form of an impersonal e-mail. Josh claimed Afghanistan intelligence was no longer his area of responsibility, so he forwarded the warning to the administrative assistant to CIA Director Coleman. This confounded Karl, because he knew Josh would never assume his information was anything but serious. It was not like Josh to forward messages from field agents to an administrative assistant. He replied to the e-mail and thanked Josh for his attention to this critical information. He hoped Josh would read between the lines and do something on his own volition.

Over the next few days, Mr. Karl continued to visit Kaysan in his cell, but each time, Kaysan refused to give him any further information or corroborate his former story. Mr. Karl decided to try a new strategy. He had Kaysan transferred to a better cell, one with a window, a comfortable cot with warm blankets, and a writing desk. He provided Kaysan with a Qur'an and writing materials and saw to it that he was fed and clothed better. However, the results were the same. Kaysan still refused to cooperate.

Ten days after Mr. Karl sent the original cable, he still had no further response from Josh or from anyone else at CIA headquarters. He assumed the information had been discredited or was sitting unread on some bureaucrat's desk. The bomb must now be only days away from its destination, assuming it was headed to a Canadian port such as Montreal. It would probably cost him his job, but he had to contact the State Department. He knew such a violation of protocol could result in a reprimand or worse. Nevertheless, he decided to ignore his own career with the agency and get someone in the State Department to take notice. Perhaps Ambassador Crosby would listen to him.

Mr. Karl had met Ambassador Miriam Crosby at a cocktail party in Kabul some months ago. Impressed by this newly appointed Ambassador to Afghanistan, he judged her to be smart, fair, and competent. He decided to make an appointment with Ambassador Crosby and deliver his information to her in person. He identified himself to the assistant ambassador, who immediately put his telephone call through to Ambassador Crosby. Mr. Karl explained he had important information to share and wanted to do so in person. It was unusual for a CIA agent to want to see her, but she immediately scheduled an appointment at 3 p.m., in three days.

Mr. Karl tried to book passage to Kabul on a military flight, but bureaucrats in the Air Force delayed his request. He called the Farah military attaché for passage on the army's precious Lear Jet, which flew to Kabul three times each week, but the attaché claimed the next available seat was the following week. He could not deal with the military bureaucracy, so he decided to travel to Kabul by jeep. It took Mr. Karl and his driver two and a half days to drive from Farah to Kabul, some 850 kilometers of tortuous roads that wound through a countryside infested with the Taliban and other brigands. Thankfully, the trip was uneventful. On the appointed hour, the ambassador's secretary ushered Mr. Karl into Ambassador Crosby's office. She offered him a seat and a cup of coffee, and then listened attentively to Mr. Karl's information. After he finished, she said nothing. Tapping her pencil on the desk, she pondered his information and stared out the window. Then after what seemed like an eternity, she stopped tapping her pencil, turned to him.

"Minot as a target for a terrorist bomb seems like an unlikely choice," she finally said.

Mr. Karl winced, but immediately responded, "Quite frankly, I agree. I don't know why the terrorists chose Minot, yet that is exactly what they have done. It could be that they are aware of the Strategic Air Force weapons depository at the Minot air base, or simply that they randomly chose Minot. Nevertheless, if we don't stop them, it will result in a disaster far greater than 9-11."

The ambassador sat quietly for several more seconds, searching Mr. Karl's face for some sign of deception or insanity. Finding neither she smiled.

"Your report seems credible, yet I can't understand why the Agency is not listening to someone with your years of agency experience and integrity. Perhaps you have lost favor with them. You understand that you have committed a breach of protocol by coming to me with this information. It will not go well for you."

Mr. Karl tried to explain. "The CIA home office is in such a muddle right now that I do not even know who I report to. Days ago, I cabled them that I have critical information; I have not had a response. This information is time-critical and I can't trust my office will handle it as they should. I know I can trust you and am aware that my career may be destroyed by coming to you, but this is of no importance. If the terrorists explode this bomb, tens of thousands of Americans will die. We must prevent this bomb from entering the country."

The ambassador frowned and nodded. She understood and sympathized with his dilemma. She had experienced the same frustration within her own State Department. "Still, I would like to better understand why they chose Minot, North Dakota."

Mr. Karl theorized that Iran was behind the bomb plot. He explained that Minot as a target made sense when one viewed terrorist tactics in the larger picture. After they destroyed Minot, al-Qaeda planned to intimidate U.S. citizens with more threats of nuclear bomb explosions. Months earlier, the Iranian government had tested their own atom bomb and enriched enough uranium to manufacture several more bombs. If the terrorists could convince the American public that they could destroy a small city in the heartland of America, then any U.S. city, large or small, was at risk. The panic that would result could destabilize an already dysfunctional government and make the country open to Iranian demands. Such demands would include the removal of troops, bases, and ships from the entire Near-East.

Mr. Karl told Miriam that he had studied the goals of fundamentalist Islam. He knew that Iran's strategic plan was to install a caliphate in America. He told the Ambassador that Iranian demands would go much further than a threat. The terrorists would insist that America withdraw its military presence in Afghanistan and Iraq, and revoke all support for Israel. Even more severe demands would follow, and Iran would appear to come to our rescue, riding in on a white horse and save the Americans from the threat of nuclear disaster. Al-Qaeda operatives already strategically placed in Congress and the Senate would lead an initiative to dismiss Congress, the administration, and the Supreme Court. Shari 'a law would replace the Constitution and Iran would install its own Islamic courts. Then Iran could appoint a new President and Congress, one sympathetic to Islam.

Ambassador Crosby thought Mr. Karl's theory was implausible, yet the thought of a bomb on its way to the States called for immediate action. She understood the clock was running and if Mr. Karl was right, any day now the bomb would arrive at some Canadian port. In fact, it might already be sitting on the dock awaiting transport to Minot. Mr. Karl listened as she contacted the State Department in Washington and asked to talk with her boss, the Secretary of State. He knew better than to question the ambassador's report and without hesitation, alerted the Homeland Security Secretary, who called for a cabinet level emergency meeting that morning. The next day, Ambassador Crosby called Mr. Karl to her office and explained the results of that meeting with the President.

In the emergency security meeting, the President ordered everyone to keep the information that the terrorists had a nuclear bomb confidential, "Or there would be panic in the streets". He ordered the Homeland Security Secretary to alert all ports of entry to be on the lookout for anything suspicious from ships sailing from the Near East and to contact the Canadian Port Authorities to do likewise. The next day, all ports on the American and Canadian coasts and the ports of entry along the Canadian-U.S. border were placed on red alert. All were told to be on the lookout for some unspecified shipment from the Middle East. Instructions went out to inspect all cargo and containers from every ship, bus, car, truck, and train. The order directed inspectors to use scintillation detectors on all shipments and vehicles crossing the border into the United States. No one in the government knew it at the time, but the bureaucratic delay gave the terrorists exactly what they needed most: time to transport the bomb to North America.

Escorted by the EMM terrorists, the bomb was already headed to Minot, traveling on a trans-Canadian train as it crossed over the Canadian Rockies into Alberta.

CHAPTER TWENTY: CANADA

The predawn darkness obscured the mountains surrounding the EMM compound as Bashar and his four top lieutenants, Kaleem, Akram, Sabur, and Saheim loaded the three bomb crates into their truck. They placed the bomb crates toward the front and then loaded six rows of identical crates filled with cabbages, leaving a narrow aisle down the center.

"The most dangerous part of our journey will be from here to the Iranian border," Bashar warned. "Kaleem will drive the truck and I'll ride in the cab with him. Saheim, Akram, Sabur and my driver will follow in the jeep. If UN or U.S. troops stop us, let me do the talking. Once we arrive at the border, the Iranians will escort us to the port of Bandar-a-Abbas, where a fishing boat is waiting to take us and the bomb across the gulf to Abu Dhabi, in the United Arab Emirates. We will then board a containership now loading for their voyage to Vancouver, Canada."

The orb of the orange-tinted sun rose above the eastern horizon as the small convoy careened across the dusty desert. The washboard dirt road, rough and marked with countless potholes, did little to slow Kaleen's reckless driving. He raced across the desert at breakneck speed, raising clouds of dust, visible for miles around. Bashar bounced against the unpadded bench seat and held on to a strap as Kaleem swerved to avoid a large pothole.

"Kaleem, for the sake of Allah, slow down," Bashar urged, "We don't want those 'cabbages' jostled and you are raising dust that is visible for miles." Obediently, Kaleem slowed the truck to a more reasonable 25 miles per hour, and the dust cloud behind them that had obscured Sabur's jeep settled back onto the desert floor.

After a couple of hours, they arrived at the village of Chakhansur. Unchallenged and waved on by soldiers at a checkpoint, they drove through the mostly deserted streets and arrived at a second checkpoint a couple of kilometers beyond the village. Gates barred the road and several soldiers guarding the checkpoint immediately shouldered AK-47 rifles. Kaleem stopped the truck at the gate and Sabur and his driver pulled up behind him. An American sergeant, followed by six armed U.N. soldiers, each wearing a pale blue helmet, surrounded the truck and jeep and pointed their rifles at the convoy. Bashar rolled down his window and smiled at the sergeant.

"Papers," the soldier demanded, without returning Bashar's smile. The sergeant examined the travel permit and Kaleem and Bashar's passports. After flipping through them, the sergeant seemed satisfied and returned the documents to Bashar.

"What's your cargo and destination?"

"We're taking a load of cabbages to Zaranj."

The sergeant looked skeptical. "Zaranj is a small town. A truckload of cabbages is more than a village ten times the size of Zaranj could use."

"The cabbages are for the city of Zahedan in Iran," Bashar explained. "We intend to offload them in Zaranj, where another truck with a proper permit will take them on into Iran."

The sergeant leaned into the truck. "Zaranj is only two clicks from the Iranian border. Your permit doesn't allow you to cross over the border, and if you attempt to take your produce on into Iran and sell them in Zahedan, you will be arrested at the border when you return."

"As I explained before, we don't intend to cross over the border. We're just going to deliver these cabbages to the market in Zaranj, and then return to Farah."

"Who are the people in the jeep behind you?"

"They are farmworkers. They will help us unload the cabbages."

"Let's have a look in the back of the truck," the sergeant barked.

Bashar climbed down from the cab and dropped the tailgate.

Two soldiers climbed inside and randomly opened crates. Bashar tried to appear nonchalant, but he broke into a sweat as the soldiers worked their way toward the front of the truck where he had placed the bomb crates. Finding nothing but cabbages in all the crates that they bothered to open, the soldiers seemed satisfied that the truck didn't contain contraband. They climbed down and told the sergeant everything was in order. He went to the jeep and examined Saheim, Akram, Sabur and the driver's papers. Satisfied, he waved the truck and jeep through the roadblock. American Marines were bivouacked in Zaranj, and Bashar knew they would have to pass through a major checkpoint only a mile from the border. The Marines at the checkpoint were certain to be more thorough in their inspection than the UN soldiers had been in Chakhansur.

Bashar studied his map. A side road marked a detour that meandered through the desert and farms surrounding Zaranj and then joined the main highway just beyond the Marine checkpoint, only a mile from the Iranian border. The detour wasn't much of a road, better described as two ruts marking a trail that zigzagged westward through rain-parched fields. They drove slowly so as not to raise dust that would betray their passage. After an hour traveling on the bumpy detour, Kaleem complained they were driving in circles.

"See that lone tree in the field? We have passed that same tree before," Kaleem announced.

Bashar consulted his map and assured Kaleem they were on the right road. After another bone-jarring 45 minutes, the detour emptied onto the main highway, within sight of the Marine border checkpoint to the East and the Iranian border to the west. Bashar focused his field glasses on the Marine border checkpoint just a few hundred yards away, and watched as a jeep sped toward them.

"The Marines have spotted us!" Kaleem yelled and gunned the truck down the highway. The truck was too slow to outrun the Marine jeep, which cut in front of them and stopped 50 yards ahead and blocked the road. Three Marines and the driver jumped out of their jeep and ran toward the truck, pointing AK-47 rifles at them as they ran.

"Gun it," Bashar shouted to Kaleem. The truck and Saheim's jeep sped past the startled Marines, collided with the Marine jeep and pushed it off the road. Bullets whizzed over Bashar's head and ricocheted off their truck and Saheim's jeep. The gunfire stopped as Bashar's convoy sped across the no-man's land before the Iranian border. Braking to a stop at the Iranian checkpoint, Bashar took in a deep breath and then climbed down from the truck. Alerted to pass the Bashar convoy through the checkpoint, the Iranian soldiers made a token check of Bashar's papers and waved the truck and jeep across the border, where a Revolutionary Guard jeep patiently waited for them. The Iranian officer in the jeep had orders to escort the EMM members to Zahedan and then on to Bandar-a-Abbas, on the Persian Gulf.

A recent revolution in Iran had changed that government from one run by Mullahs, to a sectarian government, although the Mullahs and Iranian Revolutionary Guard still held considerable power within that country and relations with the United States remained strained. In defiance of the UN, the new Iranian government program to enrich uranium progressed at an even faster pace. The U.S. administration suspected that they also continued to support fanatical groups such as the EMM. The Iranian government may have changed, yet the jihadist goals of those in key government positions had not.

After unloading their cabbages at the Zahedan market, they transferred the bomb crates to an Iranian truck and then followed the truck to an army base outside the city, where the Iranian Republican Guards fed them and provided sleeping quarters for the night. Rising at dawn, Bashar said good-bye to Sabur and his driver and instructed them to take the truck and jeep back to Anar Darrah by an alternate route. Traveling in a jeep driven by an Iranian soldier, Bashar and his team followed the Iranian truck across 400 miles of dusty, jostling road that crossed Kerman province to the port city of Bandar-e-Abbas. Arriving at the port docks, the Iranians transferred the three crates to a small fishing boat, the *Orestan*. The boat's captain welcomed Bashar and his men aboard and prepared dinner for them. The boat left port later that night and headed out into the Persian Gulf.

As the *Orestan* crossed the Gulf, lights from the American fleet assigned to patrol the gulf appeared on the port side. A shooting incident that occurred the previous week clearly worried the Iranian captain. An Iranian gunboat had fired on an American destroyer sailing in international waters. The destroyer returned fire as the outmanned Iranian gunboat sped toward the safety of Iranian costal waters. As in many previous incidents, the destroyer chased them but slackened off when close to Iranian territorial waters. The Iranian navy enjoyed this high stakes game of catch-me-if-you-can. They would provoke an incident in international waters and then head for home with the Americans in hot pursuit and then afterwards, accuse the Americans of invading their territorial waters. These naval provocations served a useful purpose for the Iranians. Following each incident, they would demand talks between the United States and Iran, yet the result of such talk was always predictable. The Iranians would accuse the American Navy of invading their territorial waters. The Americans would deny the charge and try to divert the discussion to Iran's nuclear bomb program. The Iranians pretended that they were enriching uranium for power plants, although they had built only one such plant that Russia supplied with fuel. They used the talks to obfuscate and stall for time as their centrifuges spun and enriched more uranium for nonexistent power plants. The charade fell apart when the Iranians exploded their first atom bomb and the UN published a report that claimed Iran had enough enriched uranium to produce several bombs. Talking had done nothing but give them time to further their plans to become the first nuclear power in the Near East. For years, Israel had wanted to attack the Iranian uranium enrichment facility as they had done to the Iraq nuclear plant years earlier. Despite their pleas, the American government prevented them from doing so. Frustrated with Iran's obfuscation and American inaction, the Israelis developed their own plan to silence the Iranian centrifuges and destroy their capacity to manufacture more nuclear bombs. And now, with the Americans focused on internal problems, the Israeli plan proceeded in secret.

At sunrise, the American Fleet was still within sight of their boat. A small fishing vessel such as the *Oristan* was unlikely to gain the attention of the American Navy. Nevertheless, that morning two Navy war planes buzzed them. After several passes, including one close enough to wave to the pilots, the airplanes returned to the carrier group. Convinced the American Navy would soon board them, the *Oristan* captain instructed his crew to throw two dozen bales of hashish overboard, and was about to do the same to Bashar's three crates when Bashar held a gun to the captain's head and ordered the crew to stand down. The captain had no idea what the three crates contained, but he instinctively knew it would not go well for him if the Americans boarded his ship and opened those crates. He told his crew to back off. The *Oristan* continued on course but no American vessels approached, and by noontime the American fleet had disappeared over the horizon. The captain began a zigzag course back toward Iranian waters searching for his jettisoned bales of hashish, but they were nowhere to be found. That evening, the *Oristan* docked in Abu Dhabi, where Arab stevedores loaded Bashar's three crates into a dockside container already filled with other Iranian and Persian Gulf export cargo, intended for Canadian and United States markets. A huge crane lifted the sealed container onto the deck of the United Arab Emirates registered containership, the *SS al-Gilan*, headed for the port of Vancouver, British Columbia. Bashar trusted that Vancouver Customs would ignore his three crates inside the container, filled with dozens of other crates of Persian Rugs, furniture, spices, and other assorted household items. That afternoon, the *al-Gilan* weighed anchor, sailed around the Arabian Peninsula, into the Red Sea, and through the Suez Canal to the Mediterranean Sea. Two days later, the ship docked in Naples, where stevedores off-loaded a dozen containers. The ship then steamed through the Straights of Gibraltar and crossed the Atlantic Ocean to Caracas, Venezuela, where the crew off-loaded several more containers. After taking on other cargo, they steamed through the Panama Canal and along the West Coast of North America to Vancouver, British Columbia. Fifteen days after Bashar and his companions loaded the bomb on a truck and drove out of Afghanistan, the *al-Gilan* docked in the port of Tsawwassan, south of Vancouver. Bashar watched as cranes offloaded dozens of containers, placing each onto a waiting truck. The dockside crane lifted Bashar's container from the deck onto a waiting truck, which then drove to the Canadian Customs warehouse and offloaded the container. Bashar, Kaleem, Akram and Saheim went into the Canadian Immigration office and presented their forged Iranian passports and visas. The immigration officer looked over the documents, and then stamped them after asking each person only two questions; "What is your business in Canada and how long do you intend to stay?"

Over the past 20 years, a large community of Yemeni, Egyptian, Iranian, and Pakistani immigrants had settled in Vancouver. It was not unusual for people from the Gulf region or Middle East to be traveling to or from British Columbia. In response to the Immigration Officer's query, Bashar claimed he and his companions had come to Canada to help build a new mosque in Vancouver. They intended to remain in Canada for six weeks and then return to the middle-East. The Canadian officer flipped through the pages of Bashar's passport, and then stamped his visa and work permit and handed the documents back without comment. He gave only a passing glance to Kaleem, Saheim and Akram's documents and stamped them without asking a single question. Kaleem's and Bashar's passports were high quality Iranian forgeries; yet Saheim and Akram's Afghanistan documents were of lower quality and would not have passed careful inspection. A second customs official questioned Bashar about the contents of his three crates stored in the customs warehouse. Bashar handed him the manifest and import documents that claimed the crates contained woven Persian rugs and fabrics. The official stamped the documents and handed them back to Bashar. He then made a call to the customs officer at the warehouse, but made no effort to go over there and inspect the cargo himself.

Bashar found a telephone booth and called Amit Penshaw, his Vancouver EMM contact. One hour later, Amit arrived at customs in a rented van and introduced himself. His dark eyes sparkled as he smiled and welcomed Bashar to Canada. Clean shaven and dressed in a pair of faded jeans, Hawaiian shirt, and Seattle Mariners baseball cap, he looked like any other Canadian local, but his olive skin and accent betrayed his Arab roots. The five men drove to the Port Authority Customs warehouse, at the end of the docks, to recover their three crates. Oman Imports of Vancouver, the owners of the other cargo that had shared Bashar's container, were already loading their ten crates into the back of a rented truck. Bashar and Amit left Kaleem, Akram, and Saheim in the van and went into the customs office. Bashar handed his stamped shipping and import documents to the officer behind the counter.

Although a posted list of Canadian Customs rules written in English, Arabic, and Farsi specified compulsory inspection of all crate contents, the customs official signed and stamped Bashar's manifest and import documents, without leaving his office. The three other customs officers continued to work at their desks and no one bothered to go with Bashar to inspect the contents of his crates. They ignored the posted compulsory inspection notice and didn't bother to verify if the three crates contained Persian rugs and fabrics as specified in the manifest. Bashar had been told about the cavalier attitude of the Canadian Port Authorities and this is exactly why al-Qaeda had selected a Canadian port to import the bomb. After Amit helped Bashar and Saheim load the crates into his van, he drove them to a safe house in Coquitlam, a bedroom community on the eastern outskirts of Vancouver.

The safe house, a single-story brick and shingle three-bedroom residence, looked like most other homes in this bedroom city, with little that would distinguish it from the hundreds of other cookie-cutter like residences. Amit's wife, Sasha, met Bashar and his companions at the front door and invited them inside, while Amit parked the van in his two-car garage. Sasha ushered her guests into the dining room, where four men sat cross-legged on pillows placed around a large, knee-high oblong table. She told them to make themselves comfortable and poured each a cup of strong tea sweetened with goat milk. Introductions were neither offered nor requested. The small amount of conversation that did take place remained nonspecific and guarded. No one asked about Bashar's business in Canada, inquired where they were from, or questioned them on personal matters. Bashar assumed the four men at the table were other members of the local el-Mossel Militia cell, yet he knew better than to ask if this was so. As soon as Amit joined his quests at the table, Sasha began serving a lamb stew and steaming bowls of rice curry.

The dinner conversation was formal, each person waiting for a slight nod from Amit before speaking. Discussion centered on gasoline rationing and how it made everyday life in Canada so difficult. They also talked about recent events in the newly formed State of Palestine and the current elections to form a Palestinian government. Neither Amit nor any other member of the el-Mossel Militia cell in Vancouver had been told of Bashar's mission. Amit's instructions were to rent a van and escort Bashar, his companions, and their crates to Minot, North Dakota. A devoted Muslim soldier does not ask questions but does as he is commanded, and Amit was a good Muslim soldier.

The dinner conversation abruptly ended, when another guest entered the room. Everyone stopped eating and lowered their heads as if Mohammed himself had joined them at the dinner table. Over six-feet tall, gaunt, and wearing a full-length white robe and a knitted lavender skull cap, the stranger stood motionless in the doorway, his black eyes darting about the room. A black, full beard streaked with gray hid most of his elongated face. A crescent-shaped scar marked his broad, furrowed forehead. The man seemed vaguely familiar to Bashar. He tried to place him but couldn't do so. Amit got to his feet and offered the stranger the reserved place at the table next to his own. The stranger accepted Amit's offer with a nod and a dismissive wave of his hand and sat down across the table from Bashar. His deep-set dark eyes continued to dart around the table, momentarily studying each guest, until his penetrating gaze rested on Bashar. "Shalom," he said, with a barely perceptible nod to Bashar.

"Shalom," Bashar responded, although he still didn't recognize the man. The visitor's stare penetrated the inscrutable facial expression that Bashar normally wore and made him uncomfortable. Unmasked, he didn't know whether to smile or frown. He tried again to recall when and where he had met this man, but nothing came to mind. Sasha poured a cup of sweetened tea and placed a plate of lamb stew in front of their new guest. He did not speak, nor did he eat, but his gaze remained fixed on Bashar.

"You don't remember me," the man finally said. It was a statement not a question. Bashar slowly shook his head no, he did not.

"Cairo University," the man said. "I taught economics. You were one of my students. Not a very bright one as I remember."

A glimmer of recognition spread across Bashar's face. The professor he remembered was thinner, without any gray in his beard, and missing that prominent scar on his forehead. Yet . . . it was the same man. "Professor Passhia bin-Alaheim," he whispered.

"Yes, but no longer professor, just Passhia bin-Alaheim."

Passhia took a sip of tea and signaled with a gesture that everyone should resume eating. They all ate in silence as Sasha served three more courses, ending with a persimmon jelly pastry. Passhia said nothing more until the dinner ended. He rose, turned toward Bashar and said, "Allah be with you and your mission." Then he addressed all those in the room. "*Allah-u-akbar!*"

Everyone repeated the phrase in unison as Passhia turned and left the room. Although no one told him who he was, Bashar knew that Passhia must be a person of great importance, perhaps one of the al-Qaeda leaders in Canada. Passhia had mentioned Bashar's mission, and such a significant comment indicated he had access to high-level information. Considering the respect shown to the man by the other dinner guests, his former professor must be a key person.

As everyone got up from the table, Bashar asked Amit what time in the morning they were to leave in the van, for Minot.

"There is a flaw in your plan," Amit advised Bashar. "I cannot drive you from Vancouver to Minot."

Bashar frowned, unprepared for such unwelcome news. "Why is this so?"

"For two reasons," Amit explained. "First, there is no petrol available along the route, and I cannot buy enough in Vancouver to drive all the way to Minot."

Bashar protested. "I saw dozens of vehicles on the road between the airport and this safe house, so there must be plenty of fuel available in this city."

Amit seemed offended by Bashar's skepticism; he patiently defended his explanation.

"Although Vancouver is slowly recovering from the power outage and a limited amount of petrol is now available, the Canadian government strictly rations it. The province of British Columbia issues a petrol ration card to each registered automobile owner. The card limits purchases to ten gallons of petrol each week. Ten gallons will not even take us from here to Calgary." Amit smiled and then continued.

"The second reason is that snow and avalanches have closed the highway through the Canadian Rockies. The Canadian Highway department stopped clearing and maintaining the roads back in November, and by now, the highways through the Rockies are impassable and will remain so until this spring."

"So how then are we to journey to Minot?" Bashar asked.

"By train," Amit explained. "The Canadian Pacific Railroad still operates daily trans-Canada passenger train service. I bought tickets for six of us, from here to Moose Jaw, in Saskatchewan, where we can rent a van and then drive the remaining 380 kilometers to Minot. I understand the road to Minot is open and the U.S. border surveillance on that highway is lax."

"Six of us?" Bashar questioned. "Including you, me, Kaleem, Saheim, and Akram, that's only five people."

As if by an afterthought, Amit explained, "Passhia will go with us to Minot." This was news to Bashar, and such an unexpected change in plans upset him.

"I wasn't told that anyone else besides the five of us was to be a part of this mission," Bashar protested. "What is Passhia's role and who authorized him to go with us?"

Amit looked surprised. "One does not ask such impertinent questions," he admonished. "Passhia has said he will go with us, and that is enough for you or me to know." Such a rebuke, especially coming from an underling, annoyed Bashar, and the change of plans deeply troubled him. The mission, hatched months ago by top al-Qaeda leaders in Iran, did not include Passhia. Bashar had been privy to the mission details from the moment they were hatched, yet no one had advised him of a sixth traveler. Nevertheless, what was he to do? Obviously, Passhia was someone important and Amit was right; a good soldier does not ask questions. Bashar decided to drop his objection.

The next morning, Amit drove everyone to the Canadian Pacific Passenger station and supervised loading the three crates from his van into the baggage compartment of the waiting train. Passhia, Bashar, and his team found seats in the upstairs observation car and made themselves comfortable in the plush seats. The train departed on schedule and made its way across southern British Columbia. They crossed the Frasier River and then followed the tracks north to Kamloops and eastward into the Canadian Rockies. By late afternoon, the train began a gradual climb into the two-mile high mountains that formed the spine of the continental divide. Passhia sat alone, ignoring the scenery and those around him and read his Qur'an. Bashar looked out the large picture window of the observation car and marveled at the snowcapped, craggy peaks that graced the eastern horizon. They reminded him of those in northern Pakistan, where he once vacationed. As they climbed higher into the mountains, a dark cloud settled in over the mountains and a drift of snow began to fall. At first, the snow only dusted the rails and track ties, yet within minutes, the train plunged into a whiteout. Curtains of wind-driven snow soon buried the tracks and forced the train to slow to a crawl. After moving at a snail's pace for almost an hour, the train suddenly stopped, with an unsettling lurch that caused those standing in the aisle to grab for the nearest handhold. Some items fell from the overhead racks and coffee spilled onto a few laps.

"Why have we stopped?" Amit asked a conductor, as he hurried down the aisle.

"There's been a report of a snow slide on the tracks ahead. We will have to wait here for a snowplow from Calgary to clear the rails," he explained. "This may take a while and until they arrive and remove the slide, we're stuck here. They're now serving dinner in the dining car, or if you prefer, you can go outside and stretch your legs on the path alongside the roadbed."

The conductor paused, reconsidering his suggestion to take a walk outside in a blinding snowstorm. He then added parenthetically, "If you go outside, be sure to stay close to the train. It's easy to become lost in such a blizzard. And don't go out onto the trestle just ahead of the engine. It will be slippery, and it is a long way to the bottom. Without warning, we might decide to back the train down the mountain to Revelstoke for the night, so listen for three short blasts of the train horn. No one will come looking for you when we are ready to go."

Kaleem, Akram and Saheim decided to go to the dining car for dinner. Passhia, as usual, said nothing and remained reading in his seat. Bashar and Amit weren't hungry, so they climbed off the train and began walking on the trackside path toward the engine. A group of passengers made their way toward the back of the train and Bashar and Amit were alone on their walk to the front. As they arrived at the front of the engine, it stopped snowing and the fog momentarily lifted, allowing a spectacular view of their surroundings. The snowcapped peaks, painted pink by the setting sun, towered far above the train. In the presence of those magnificent peaks, Bashar felt small and insignificant. Although the fog had lifted from the tracks and mountain summit, the valley below remained shrouded. The train had stopped just short of a long trestle that spanned a wide, bottomless chasm. A brilliant waterfall spilled from a cliff high above the trestle and in misty veils of water, disappeared into the chasm below. On the other side of the trestle, the tracks disappeared into a dark, smoke-stained tunnel.

Bashar walked out onto the trestle and motioned for Amit to follow.

"Let's go see how bad the avalanche is," he suggested. "The conductor said it was just on the other side of the tunnel across the trestle."

Amit looked at the narrow trestle, only wide enough to fit a single set of tracks. At the end of the trestle the tracks soon disappeared into a tunnel. Foot-wide planks on one side of the trestle provided a meager walkway, with no protective railing. One slip or a careless step into empty space would prove fatal. Amit wasn't at all eager to cross over this trestle.

"The conductor said to stay close to the train," he argued. "Besides, the trestle walkway looks icy and dangerous." Bashar ignored Amit's warning and stepped out onto the trestle. He had completed ten yards of the fifty-yard walk to the opposite side, when he turned around and yelled, "Amit . . . quit being such a fool and follow me."

Amit hesitated as he took a second look at the narrow slippery boardwalk, the lack of any safety features, and the bottomless chasm below. This was not a good idea, but he wasn't about to let Bashar's challenge go unanswered. Holding his arms straight out to maintain balance, and keeping his eyes firmly fixed on his feet and the plank immediately ahead, he ignored the abyss and gingerly stepped out onto the trestle, placing one foot carefully in front of the other. The planks were wet, covered by the windblown veils of spray from the nearby waterfall. Amit paused and let his gaze follow the path of the waterfall as it tumbled from the cliff far above and disappeared into the fog choked chasm, falling in twisting rivulets of water, foam, and spray. It was a mistake to look down. A wave of vertigo and nausea overwhelmed him. Returning his attention back to the boardwalk, he concentrated on placing one foot in front of the other and testing each step for a solid foothold. Shaking and drenched in sweat, he finally reached the far side of the trestle and stepped off onto solid ground.

Bashar had already vanished inside the tunnel. Amit stood at the entrance, trying to catch sight of Bashar, but the ink-black tunnel interior had swallowed him. A blast of dank, cold air, smelling of moss and rotting wood, drifted from the tunnel. He held his breath, not wishing to breathe in this noxious wind, but he was forced to take another lungful of air. The smell reminded him of a burial chamber. He tried to think of a good excuse not to enter, but he was not about to endure another rebuke from Bashar. Bashar would force him to face his two greatest fears: that of vast heights and inky blackness.

Bashar called out from inside the tunnel: "Come on Amit, I'm not going to wait for you any longer."

Wait for me indeed, Amit thought. "Go ahead. I'm going back to the train," he shouted.

He turned away from the tunnel and tried to make out the train, but couldn't see it. Most of the trestle, now blanketed in a thick foggy mist, made his return even more dangerous than his walk across. He thought it would be best to go into the tunnel with Bashar and hope the fog would lift by the time they got back.

Amit took a few cautious steps inside the tunnel. Painted coal black from a century of engine smoke, the tunnel walls swallowed the meager amount of daylight that penetrated from the entrance. After stepping only a few yards inside, Amit couldn't see the train tracks or even his hands. As his eyes adjusted to the darkness, a tiny sliver of distant light promised an exit. He stood for a moment and listened to Bashar's footsteps echo off the tunnel walls as he made his way down the passageway.

Walk toward the light, Amit told himself as he moved toward the small spot of light in the distance. It seemed to take forever, but the spot of light gradually grew larger and larger, until he stumbled out into the daylight. Bashar gave him a disgusted look but said nothing as he turned and walked alone down the tracks. The single track hugged a ledge barely wide enough to allow a locomotive and cars passage. Chisel marks on the facade recounted the work of 19th century Chinese workers who hacked the roadbed from the sheer rock face. Amit imagined hundreds of these laborers with chisel and hammer in hand, hewing away on the mountainside to excavate this narrow ledge. They followed the shelf until the tracks disappeared around a bend. On the other side of the curve, the rails plunged into a mound of snow blended with basketball-sized rocks and parts of trees. Amit couldn't judge the depth of the obstacle; yet it was clear the landslide had created a formidable blockade. Two railroad men, dressed in striped overalls and railroad caps, stood next to the pile of snow and rock. One of the men talked on a walkie-talkie and waved his hands in the air as if the person on the other end could see his animated gestures. Amit approached the second man and asked him how long he thought it would take to clear the tracks.

"Perhaps a day or two," the man estimated, and then introduced himself as the brakeman.

"The avalanche has badly damaged this section of track," he reported. "Not only will the Canadian Pacific folks have to clear off the snow and rock, but they will also need to replace 30 yards of damaged rail."

The second man finished his communiqué and introduced himself as the conductor. He said the train would have to back down to Revelstoke and wait there for the snowplows and a work crew to arrive from Calgary to clear the avalanche and replace the tracks. The clearing and repair would take them all the following day and perhaps most of a second. The train did not have enough food, fuel, and toilet facilities for an extensive stay in these cold mountains, so he radioed the engineer to prepare to back the train down the mountain to Revelstoke.

A cold gust of wind suddenly blew up from the valley and covered the men with a dusting of powdery snow. Amit felt the mountain chill and zipped up his jacket. Small rocks and snow began to fall from the cliff above, and bouncing off the ledge, disappeared into the abyss.

"Come on, let's get out of here before another slide buries us," the brakeman warned.

The four men hurried back to the tunnel, dodging fist-sized rocks as they ran. Amit and Bashar ran behind the train conductor and brakeman, following them into the pitch-black tunnel. Once inside, Amit ran toward the small speck of light emanating from the tunnel entrance but soon fell far behind the other men. At last he emerged along from the tunnel, the others having already disappeared in the fog that still cloaked the trestle. As before, Amit hesitated to step out onto the trestle. He could barely see the walkway planks, not alone to the other side. Startled by the "all aboard" horn sounded by three short blasts, Amit remembered the conductor's warning to stay close to the train. "No one will come looking for you when we are ready to leave," he had warned. The thought of being left alone high in these freezing mountains was encouragement enough for him to gingerly step out onto the walkway.

The return hike proved even more intimidating for Amit than the walk over. The train, invisible in the fog, again sounded three short blasts of the air horn. The fog dampened the sound, making the horn sound as if it had already moved down the tracks. Amit conquered his fear and quickened his pace. Almost to the end, in his haste he slipped on a slimy plank and fell to his knees. To steady himself, he grabbed on to the rail and searched for the train. He could make out the engine headlight ahead in the fog, but his heart skipped as he realized it was growing smaller. The rumble of the diesel engine echoed in the chasm as the train began to back down the tracks. Steadying himself by holding onto the track rail, he rose to his feet and avoiding the slippery access planks, jumped from tie to tie. He reached the end of the trestle and began running on the roadbed toward the train as it accelerated. He realized that he was not going to win this race and waved his arms and shouted curses as he ran toward the receding train. *Why in the hell had Bashar and the conductors allowed the train to start without him,* he thought. *Bashar knew he was behind them. Would he really allow him to freeze to death in these mountains?*

The conductor must have finally alerted the engineer, or possible the engineer saw Amit running along the tracks, but in either case, with a long blast of the horn, the train slowed and then came to a stop. Amit breathlessly reached the first passenger car and the conductor helped him climb on board. With all its passengers now safely on board, the conductor signaled the engineer to resume the retreat down the mountainside.

Amit found Bashar sitting alone in the observation car and took the seat next to him. He glared at Bashar but said nothing. Bashar knew Amit was miffed, yet he didn't offer an apology. Bashar's cavalier attitude puzzled him; for had the train left him behind, their mission would certainly have ended in failure. Amit was the only team member with a driver's license and therefore the only one who could rent a van in Moose Jaw and drive them to Minot. He also was the only one with enough cash and a credit card to rent the van he had reserved in Moose Jaw.

They arrived in Revelstoke about 11 p.m. The train backed onto a sidetrack, where it would remain until the workers repaired the track. The Canadian Railway folks invited the day coach passengers to spend the night at the Revelstoke Travel Lodge. Expecting only a two-day journey, Amit had bought the cheaper day coach tickets. It was difficult to get any sleep in day coach seats, so when the Canadian Pacific Rail officials offered the hotel rooms, Amit quickly accepted. Passhia took one room for himself, and Bashar, Amit, Kaleem, and Akram bunked in the other room. Saheim preferred to remain on the train and stretched out across two day coach seats.

At daybreak, Amit conquered his anger and invited Bashar to explore the town with him. Wishing for a cup of coffee, they walked down the cobbled main street of Revelstoke and asked a man sitting on a park bench where they might find a coffee shop. His answer was friendly but unintelligible. The directions he offered sounded vaguely like English, but it was so laced with a heavy Scottish brogue that they couldn't understand a single word he spoke. Bashar and Amit looked puzzled, so the man finally shrugged and pointed in the general direction of downtown.

"What language was he speaking?" Bashar asked, as they walked down the street. Amit said it was English, but the folks who settled this town were from Scotland and retained their distinctive brogue. They finally found a small bar and coffee house, "Dunbar Tavern", across the street from a three-story brick building marked by a "Masonic Hall" sign. A balding man dressed in a red plaid shirt and black coveralls stood behind the counter and smiled at them as they entered.

"G'day folks, waddle ye 'ave?"
Bashar order two cappuccinos. The man stared blankly at Bashar as if he didn't understand the order. Finally, he said something in a heavy Scottish brogue that neither Amit nor Bashar understood. Amit turned for help to a woman standing behind them, patiently waiting to place her own order. She smiled and shrugged. Finally, Bashar pointed to a cappuccino advertisement on the wall behind the counter and held up two fingers. The man nodded and filled two cups from the noisy machine. They retreated to a table to drink their coffee. Afterwards, like two tourists, they spent the day wandering around town. When they grew tired of exploring, they stopped at the Aberdeen Inn for dinner and found Passhia sitting alone at a table. Bashar and Amit sat down at a table next to his. He was talking on a cell phone and without acknowledging Bashar or Amit with so much as a nod, he finished his telephone call, got up from the table, paid his bill, and then left the restaurant.

"A bit of an unfriendly chap . . . that one is," Bashar commented.

"He is an Imam, and a very important one at that. He seems to know you," Amit observed.

"From another life," Bashar answered.

Later that evening, they returned to the Travel Lodge and went to bed. They did not see Passhia again, not until they took their seats back on the train the next morning. He had taken a seat by himself and again, did not acknowledge either Bashar or Amit.

The journey to Calgary resumed midmorning, 36 hours behind schedule. The train continued across the Canadian plains, arriving in Moose Jaw late that evening. After the baggage men unloaded the crates, Amit left his companions at the train station and went off to rent a van. He returned with a 1960's vintage Volkswagen bus, painted in psychedelic colors and belching black smoke from a exhaust pipe held in place by wires tied to the bumper. Probably resurrected from a local junkyard, the bald tires, dented side panels, and torn upholstery made Saheim question if the van could get them to Minot without breaking down. He didn't hesitate to voice his displeasure to Amit.

"Where did you get this van . . . from the local Rent-a-Wreck?"

"No," Amit said, insulted that Saheim would make such a comment. "From National Car Rental. This is all they had available that could carry our cargo."

They loaded the crates into the van and rented a Motel 6 for the night. At sunrise they headed for the U.S. border and Minot. Normally, a rented van would come with a full tank of gasoline, yet under the fuel rationing rules, the Volkswagen tank contained only ten gallons. When Amit rented the van, he failed to notice the sign, warning customers of the limited gasoline. As they left town, he noticed the gas gauge registered half-full, yet this didn't concern him. He hadn't yet used his weekly ration card and he assumed they could buy another ten gallons at the next open gas station: a mistaken assumption. From Moose Jaw to Estervan, a town twelve miles from the U.S. border, they did not see a single open gas station. Bashar leaned over and stared at the gas gauge. It showed less than a third of a tank remained. He thought that in the States they could find an open gas station, although he knew this was only wishful thinking.

"Are you sure we can make it to Minot on the petrol left in this tank?" Bashar asked.

"I think there is enough to get us to Minot," Amit said confidently. "Even a quarter of a tank should be enough to take us the remaining 160 kilometers."

At the North Portal border crossing east of Estevan, they stopped behind a long line of cars and trucks waiting their turn at U.S. Customs. Amit climbed out of the van and walked to the Continental Transport truck in front of their Volkswagen. He asked the driver if he knew what was causing the delay.

The man looked up from writing in his log book. "I heard on my CB that Customs and Homeland Security are on high alert. They are thoroughly inspecting every car, truck, trailer, and bus that enters through this port," the truck driver explained. "It would be good to have all your paperwork in order at the check station. They get real pissy when you are unprepared. Keep it out and ready when it becomes your turn."

This was not good news. Amit had been told the customs inspection would be superficial. They couldn't chance a thorough and complete scrutiny of their passports and cargo. In addition, the colorful van and their obvious mid-eastern origin would call more attention to them than they wished. Amit had no transit paperwork for the crates, and without such permits, the customs officers would certainly open them up and inspect the contents. Amit climbed back into the van and made a U-turn. "We have to detour and try to enter through a different port. They are inspecting every piece of cargo and paperwork at this one."

Bashar consulted his map. It showed only one other open port of entry between Estevan and western Manitoba, yet considering their short supply of fuel, they had to pick the one closest to Minot. Directly north of Minot, the map marked a port of entry along Highway 83, marked as a secondary highway. Perhaps there would be less scrutiny at this crossing than the one at North Portal. They backtracked to Estevan and then drove east, through Carnduff and Pierson, to the junction with Highway 83. The highway, a north-south road a few miles east of the Saskatchewan-Manitoba border, proved to have almost no traffic. Only three cars waited in line at the U.S. Customs inspection station at the border. Everyone climbed out of the van and went into the customs office to present their passports and travel documents. The only officer on duty seemed tired and mumbled something about being on duty for the past twelve hours. Despite their mid-eastern appearance and flower-child-painted bus, he only asked their business and length of stay in the United States. Amit said that they were tourists and only intended to visit Mt. Rushmore, "to see the Presidents". The officer wearily stamped each visa for a ten day stay. A notice prominently posted on the door warned visitors that Homeland Security was enforcing yellow level security measures. Yet despite the notice, the officer did not bother to inspect the van. Everyone breathed a sign of relief as the van crossed over the border.

As they drove toward Minot, Amit glanced at the fuel gauge. The detour to Highway 83 used more gasoline than expected and the gas gauge now hovered above the big red "E" empty marker.

"We have to find some petrol and soon," he said. "I don't think we have enough left in the tank to take us another 100 kilometers to Minot. We also have to find a place to stop and assemble the bomb."

Twenty-nine miles down the highway from the border, a sign marked a turnoff.

Willow Creek
10 Miles

"Take that turnoff," Bashar said. "Perhaps we can find a place to stop and find some petrol in Willow Creek."

Five miles along the road to Willow Creek, the van began to sputter. "Turn in there," Bashar said, pointing to a driveway leading to a house and barn. The sign hanging over the entry read DEXTER'S. "Look how well-plowed the fields are," Bashar commented. "This farmer must have petrol for his tractors. We will 'encourage' them to give us some."

Akram fingered the pistol in his back pocket as the van sputtered and coughed its way down the long driveway. The engine finally died fifty yards short of the house. Amit coasted to a stop and everyone climbed out of the van. Chester and Puck interrupted their afternoon slumber on the front porch and ran down the road to confront the strangers as they emerged from the van. Barking furiously, the dogs stopped ten yards short of the van. They stood their ground and dared the strangers to advance. The terrorists froze and tried to figure out how they could avoid the dogs.

Today, Peter and Dan were plowing the back 40 acres, no more than a quarter mile from the house. Judy, Keith and Nora had prepared lunch in the kitchen and were about to call the children in from the barn where they were playing. Alerted by Chester and Puck's insistent barking, Judy grabbed the shotgun and ran out onto the front porch to see what was causing the dogs such annoyance. Nora and Keith followed close behind. Judy grew alarmed when she saw six strangers advancing toward the house, and told Keith to go find his dad. He immediately scrambled off the porch and ran toward the field where Dan and Peter were working.

The dogs held the intruders at bay. Snarling, Puck began to move toward the men.

"I hate dogs," Kaleem spat. Passhia stood safely behind Bashar and shuddered. In his Islamic mind, only a pig was more despicable than a dog.

"Shoot those animals," he commanded.

Akram took the pistol out of his back pocket and placed two bullets into Puck. The dog yelped and fell dead on the driveway. Chester turned and ran for the safety of the house. Akram fired two shots at the dog but both bullets missed. Now that both dogs were out of the way, Bashar and his team resumed their walk toward the house, but Passhia retreated to the van. Judy stepped to the front of the porch and yelled,

"Stop right where you are."

The terrorists hesitated when they saw Judy standing on the porch with a shotgun in her hands.

"It is only a woman," Bashar hissed, "keep on walking." He couldn't imagine that a woman, even a woman with a gun, could possibly represent a danger.

Nora was standing behind Judy when she heard the shots and saw Puck fall. She stepped around Judy and knelt down to greet Chester as he bounded up the steps.

"The bastards shot Puck," Nora wailed as she searched Chester for wounds, "but apparently Chester wasn't hit."

The men were only two dozen yards from the house, when Judy shouldered the gun and shouted a second warning. "Stop right where you are or I'll shoot."

This time the men stopped and glared at the two women on the porch.

"What kind of country is this where a woman can threaten a man with a gun?" Kaleem asked.

"Keep moving toward the house," Bashar commanded. Passhia remained in the safety of the van.

Bashar took a step and Judy fired a warning shot over his head. Passhia ducked as the pellets pinged against the van.

"Split up," Bashar commanded. "Akram, you and Saheim circle to the back of the house. The rest of us will take care of this arrogant woman."

Akram and Saheim ducked into the bushes alongside the driveway as Bashar, Kaleem, and Amit sprinted toward the house.

Judy lowered the shotgun and shouted a third warning, yet the three terrorists paid no heed and broke into a full run. She pumped the gun, fingered the trigger, and sighted in on them, but she hesitated. Judy had yet to get over Jake's unfortunate death and the resulting trial. She didn't want to have another death on their farm.

"Shoot . . . shoot . . . for God's sake shoot them," Nora screamed as she held on to Chester.

The men were now only a few strides from the porch steps. Before Judy could pull the trigger, Bashar took the steps two at a time and ripped the shotgun from her trembling hands. The gun went off and carved a hole in the porch roof. Kaleem grabbed Nora, and Amit put a headlock on Judy. Chester grabbed Amit's pants leg and Bashar struck the dog with the stock of his shotgun and Chester fell senseless onto the porch. The three terrorists then dragged the kicking and screaming women into the house. After they were inside, Passhia got out of the van and trotted toward the house. He climbed the front steps, stepped around the prone dog and stood in the front doorway watching as Bashar and Kaleem bound the two women to chairs. Saying nothing, he entered the house, found a chair in the dining room and positioned it where he would have a good view of the living room, and then sat down.

Pam, Trevor, Scott, and Penny had been playing hide-and-seek in the barn when they first heard the gunshots. They peaked out from the barn hayloft door, in time to see two men dart into the bushes and three men running toward the house. Puck lay still on the driveway, a pool of blood drenching the dirt beside the dead dog. Their mothers stood on the porch, Judy holding a shotgun and Nora holding Chester and screaming for Judy to shoot. The strangers bounded up the porch steps, grabbed the gun from Judy, struck Chester, and then dragged Judy and Nora into the house.

"Who are they?" Penney whispered.

"I don't know," Scott said. "They shot Puck."

Pam started to cry. "What should we do?"

"Just stay put for now," Trevor said, "Dad and Dan must have heard the shots."

Dan and Peter had heard the gunfire and were already running back toward the farmhouse when they met Keith at the edge of the plowed field. He breathlessly told them that several men had piled out of a van in the front yard and one of them shot Puck. Dan told Keith to go hide in the barn with the other children and keep them quiet. Dan and Peter raced toward the house as Keith ran through the barn's back door and climbed into the loft with the other children.

"Everyone hide here in the loft," Keith said, "and be quiet." The children hid behind a stack of hay and Keith took refuge in the far corner of the loft, where he had previously found the footlocker.

Akram and Saheim circled to the back of the house and intercepted Dan and Peter as they ran toward the farmhouse back door. Brandishing weapons, the terrorists forced the two men to their knees and tied their hands behind their backs. They got them to their feet and dragged them into the house and through the kitchen. Peter and Dan stumbled into the front room, where Kaleem had finished tying Nora and Judy to chairs. Bashar and Kaleem took charge of Dan and Peter and forced them to stand against a wall.

"Who else is on this farm," Bashar demanded. Neither man answered. Bashar nodded to Kaleem and he punched Peter in the stomach. Peter doubled over and retched, but remained silent. Bashar glared at Dan and then went over to Judy and repeated his question. She angrily stared back at him and spit out, "No one else is here, you damn bastard."

He slapped her across the mouth, and repeated his question, "Who else is on the farm?" Blood trickled from Judy's lip and tears wet her cheeks; but she refused to answer.

The terrorists became more and more nervous and agitated. Akram went over to Dan and hit him as Bashar demanded again to know who else was on the farm.

"Where is the boy? We saw him run from the house."

Dan wouldn't say, so Akram again pistol-whipped him. Dan spat out blood and swore at the terrorist, but said nothing about the boy. Judy closed her eyes as blood trickled from her mouth, onto her lap. Kaleem went over to her, took out his knife and held it to her throat.

"Where is the boy? Where did he go?" Bashar demanded as Kaleem held the knife to her throat.

"Leave her alone," Peter shouted.

Judy looked at Bashar and said, "I sent the boy off to get help from the neighbors." She pointed toward the next farm house.

"Tell us who else is on this farm, or I will have Kaleem slit her throat," Bashar screamed at Peter. Peter repeated that no one else was on the farm, but Bashar didn't buy it. He looked at Kaleem and then dragged a finger across his throat, signaling for Kaleem to kill her. Peter knew this was no bluff and shouted, "Wait! Our children are in the barn," Bashar told Kaleem to lower his knife and Judy began to cry.

Nora glared at Peter and blurted out, "Pete, for God's sake don't tell these bastards anything".

"Children?" Bashar repeated. "How many children and how old are they?"

Peter ignored Nora and answered, "Four teenagers, two boys and two girls."

"And the other boy . . . the one we saw running from the porch?" Bashar insisted.

"As Judy told you, Keith went to get help from the neighbors," Peter said.

"How far is the nearest neighbor?" Bashar demanded.

"About three miles down the road, toward town," Peter answered.

Bashar turned to Amit. "Go find that boy. He can't have much of a head start. Stop him before he can get help."

Amit bounded out of the house and ran in the direction pointed out by Judy.

"Where are your farm workers?" Bashar snarled at Dan.

"We don't have any. There is no money to pay workers," Dan explained.

Bashar sent Akram and Kaleem to flush the children out of the barn. Five minutes later, they came back, pushing Penny, Scott, Pam, and Trevor in front of them.

"We found these whelps behind a haystack in the barn loft," Akram said.

Bashar confronted Scott. "There must be other people on the farm, farm workers perhaps."

"No, no others," Scott said, "We can't afford workers."

Bashar grabbed Penny and twisted her arm behind her back.

"Who else is on the farm?"

Penny screamed and began to cry and tearfully repeated there were no others on the farm.

"Leave the child alone," Passhia commanded in Arabic as he got up from his dining room chair and walked into the living room.

Passhia turned his attention to Trevor, and asked in a low voice,

"Who else is on this farm?"

Trevor glared at him and said, "Go to hell, you bearded prick."

Bashar was standing next to Trevor. "This man is an imam, and you must respect him."

Trevor looked at Bashar and sneered. "As I said, he is a bearded prick." Bashar and hit him across the face, and blood trickled from his nose.

"Leave him alone," Dan yelled. "Does the Qur'an teach you to beat up women and children?" He had already decided these men were Islamic terrorists.

Bashar smirked, but Passhia motioned for him to back off. He said to lock the children in an upstairs bedroom.

Bashar and Akram took the children to an upstairs bedroom. Bashar ordered Akram to stay and guard the door, and returned to the front room to get the men and women. He and Kaleem took them upstairs. They pushed the men into the main bedroom and marched the women to a second bedroom, shoving them inside. Bashar told Akram to stay in the hallway and keep his pistol out. Then he said first in Arabic, and then in English in a voice loud enough for everyone to hear, "If anyone tries to escape . . . shoot them."

Bashar returned to the front room and said in Arabic, "We need to assemble the bomb . . . NOW, before that boy brings help."

"Don't worry about the boy," Kaleem said. "Amit will catch him."

The terrorists went out to the barn, leaving Akram to guard the prisoners. Bashar sent Kaleem to find some gasoline for the van and then drive it into the barn. Kaleem found a ten-gallon can of gasoline in the tack room, took it down the road to the van and poured the contents into the gas tank. Then he drove the van to the barn and backed it inside. Amit and Saheim helped Bashar slide the van door open and unload the three crates. Passhia stood by and watched, but never offered to help.

Keith crept to the edge of the loft where he could watch the men yet remain hidden. The men spoke in Arabic and Keith strained to understand what they were saying.

"This barn is an ideal place to assemble the bomb," Bashar commented. "We must hurry. That boy could bring help if Amit does not catch him."

Bashar opened the first crate and took out the parts of the birdcage and the outer sphere housing, unscrewed the graphite-lined container, and removed each half of the hollow uranium inner sphere. He handed a diagram for the birdcage to Amit and told him to assemble the cage from the PVC pipe parts and glue in the second crate. He then removed the plutonium from the eight canisters and fit the 32 plutonium wedges into a softball-sized pit, and then carefully placed it inside the uranium sphere, screwing both halves together. Finally, he placed the entire soccer-ball assembly into the web, supported by the birdcage that Amit had just finished gluing together.

It took Bashar a few minutes to shape the Semtex explosive and attach it in predetermined positions around the outer housing. The placement had to be precise, so Bashar carefully consulted his diagram. Finally, Saheim inserted the twelve detonators into each glob of Semtex and wired them to the circuit board at specific locations described by the wiring diagram. Each detonator was designed to explode the charges in a precisely timed sequence. He then connected the circuit board to a battery and the master toggle switch to wires hanging outside the birdcage. As usual, Passhia stood by impassively, watching but saying nothing.

Keith continued to eavesdrop from his hiding place in the loft and watched as the men unloaded the crates and assembled the strange-looking device. Although they were speaking mostly in Arabic, some of the conversation was in English and Keith understood enough to infer that they were assembling a bomb. He distinctly heard the words "atomic bomb" and "Minot Air Force Base". Keith did not know what he could do, other than remain hidden in the loft and wait for his chance to escape and get help. Perhaps he could run to their neighbors and have them drive him to the sheriff, though he knew the terrorists would be long gone by then. He had to do something . . . and do it now, before the terrorists could drive off with the bomb.

Bashar inspected Saheim's work and then said in Arabic, "Make sure you do not complete the circuit until it is time to detonate the bomb. We don't want it to go off prematurely."

Saheim nodded and finished wiring the bomb, leaving one wire hanging unconnected from the circuit board to the switch.

Amit, out of breath, ran into the barn. "I ran all the way to the next farm, but no one was home and there were no trucks or cars around. I did not find the boy. Perhaps the neighbors and the boy went into town for help."

"In that case, we have less time than I thought," Bashar said. "The device is ready. We must now go into the house and prepare ourselves."

Up to this point, Amit only had a vague idea about the objective of this mission, except that he knew they were about to blow something up. Prepare themselves for what? He walked over to the van and looked at the device sitting beside it. It looked like a bomb all right. The purpose of the mission became clear. They were going to blow up and American city.

"It's an atom bomb, isn't it?" Amit questioned Bashar.

"Yes, it is," Bashar answered, without hesitation.

"Where is the timing mechanism?"

"There is no timing mechanism," Saheim said sardonically.

"Then how are we to get away before the bomb goes off?" Amit asked.

"We won't. By tonight, we will be in Paradise with Allah," Bashar explained, in an emotionless monotone. "This is why we must prepare ourselves."

Amit's heart pounded and sweat beaded on his forehead.

"No one told me that this was to be a suicide mission. I didn't sign up for this," Amit said, his voice quivering.

Tears wet Amit's cheeks as the full impact of this mission hit him. *What will become of my wife and two children? How can they manage without me?*

Moreover, he knew the Qur'an forbids suicide. He considered running, but where could he go? Bashar could see signs of panic in his face.

"Thinking of running away?" Bashar said, with a sly, half smile. "You fool! Do you really think you can outrun an atom bomb? It will wipe out everything within a ten-mile radius, and kill anyone within 20 miles. Remember Hiroshima and Nagasaki? When the Americans dropped those bombs, seventy thousand people died in each city. You cannot outrun an atom bomb, so forget it and help us load the bomb into the van."

"Where are we going to detonate it?" Amit asked.

"We will take it to the Minot Air Force Base, where the Air Force has parked B-52's and they store many atomic weapons. The bomb will wipe the base and Minot off the map and spread radioactive poison all around five states. It will do the most damage if detonated just outside the gate." Bashar smirked. "Allah will reward us in heaven."

"Why Minot?" Amit asked, switching to English. "Minot is a small, insignificant city. If you wanted to kill the most people, you should have selected a larger city like Chicago or Washington or the wicked city of Las Vegas." Amit's hands trembled as he spoke.

"The al-Qaeda leaders told me that Sin City will someday also be a target, but they chose Minot for a reason. It is not for us to question their decisions," Bashar said, "we do what we are told to do."

"Thousands will die in this explosion," Saheim said in Arabic, with less emotion than a Terminix exterminator preparing to spray for termites. "Allah willing, we will kill many, many Americans with this bomb."

"This is not the time for discussion. Soon that boy could be back with help," Bashar warned. "Load the bomb and then we will prepare ourselves to meet Allah."

Passhia nodded his approval, yet as usual, said little and did nothing to help.

Bashar, Amit, and Saheim carefully lifted the finished bomb into the van. Leaving the van side door open, the four men went into the house to shave their bodies. Passhia followed them.

Passhia remained downstairs as the other terrorists went into the upstairs bathroom and prepared to shave. The men first shaved off their beards, and then prayed out loud as they shaved their heads, arms, torsos, and legs. Amit did not join in their prayers, but shaved himself and prayed for Allah's forgiveness.

Saheim' was the youngest member of the group. His hand shook as the razor glided over his head and locks of his hair fell on the floor. His courage began to falter and tears ran down his face.

Bashar noticed the young man's tears.

"Saheim, do not be fearful. Allah chose us to do his work, and he will reward us in heaven. You know this to be true . . . do you not?"

Saheim stared at Bashar. His youthful face showed a mixture of sadness and misgiving. This was the day they had trained for, looked forward to, and prayed for. Now the time had come and he was unsure. Was this death and destruction something Allah demanded of them, or was it just al-Qaeda retribution? Would Allah forgive their destruction of thousands of innocent men, women and children? A lump in his throat prevented him from answering Bashar. The other men had stopped shaving and stared at the two men. Passhia had been standing outside in the hallway listening. He quietly stepped into the bathroom and faced Saheim.

"You should not be ashamed of your doubt at this critical time in history. It is natural to fear your death, yet you should not be afraid. You were chosen. Your mission is clear, and your family back in Kirkuk will celebrate your sacrifice. You will be honored for all time as a national hero."

Saheim looked at the tile floor but didn't respond.

Passhia turned to the other men. "Now, bathe yourselves, dress, and go back to the barn. We do not have much more time. We will meet again in Paradise."

As soon as the men left the barn, Keith saw his chance to escape and get help, yet on the barn floor sat a partly wired atomic bomb. He thought about his options, and knew that any help he might get wouldn't arrive in time to stop this. Could he possibly disarm the bomb himself? If the terrorists succeeded in detonating this bomb, it would wipe out everything within a large radius of the Air Force Base, including his mom, dad, brother, sister, and just about everyone else in Minot and Willow Creek. He had watched enough James Bond movies to know about bomb timing devices and detonation wires. He also remembered watching James Bond disable a bomb as the timer counted down to zero. He climbed down from the loft, found a pair of wire cutters in the tack room and a role of electrical tape on the workbench, and went over to the van and carefully examined the bomb.

Supported by straps, a soccer-ball sized sphere rested inside the birdcage. A dozen pair of twisted wires led from a circuit board, to each of the thumb-sized detonators embedded in globs of putty placed around the sphere. A six-volt lantern battery was connected to the circuit board, which rested on a rubber mat placed on the floor of the van. A red LED flashed on the circuit board and indicated the board was powered. Red, blue, and yellow wires connected from a printed circuit board to a toggle switch that hung from the birdcage. An unconnected black wire dangled from the switch, indicating the bomb was not yet fully armed. Keith knew from the James Bond movie that if he cut any wrong wire, the bomb might detonate.

He looked for a place to cut a few of the detonator wires leading to the putty-like explosives: sabotage that no one would immediately notice. He cut one of the twisted wires where it attached to a detonator. Noting happened and the red LED on the circuit board continued to flash. In similar fashion, cut three more detonator wires. Turning his attention to the circuit board, he pondered how to disable it. He knew that if he cut the connections from the battery to the circuit board, the LED would stop flashing and call attention to his sabotage. He decided instead to cut one of the three wires leading from the switch to the circuit board. He tried to remember the Bond movie. Was it the red or the yellow wire that James had to cut first? One wire would disarm the bomb, yet the other might detonate it. It was always the red wire that should first be cut . . . wasn't it? No, in the movie James cut the yellow wire first. "This is silly," he whispered. "It was only a movie." He took a deep breath and snipped the red wire. Nothing happened and the LED continued to flash.

As he taped the red wire back together, making sure the copper wires did not touch and that his sabotage wasn't visible. He heard the men returning and quickly climbed back into the loft as the six men entered the barn. Five beardless men had shaved their heads and bodies and wore wearing full-length white gowns. That is everyone, except one man.

Passhia still wore his beard and the same street clothes as before. He asked Amit if he knew where the family kept their truck. Amit said it was next to the barn.

Bashar turned to Passhia. "Are you are not coming with us?"

"No, I must remain behind. I have other work to do," Passhia explained. "I will take the truck and drive to Canada."

Passhia directed Amit to go get the truck and fill it with gasoline. Amit drove the truck into the barn and filled the tank from another ten-gallon gas can.

When he finished, Amit looked longingly at Passhia, as if to ask if he could come with him. He thought better of it and said nothing.

"You had better go then," Bashar warned Passhia. "When the bomb detonates, Minot and this farm will cease to exist and you must be at least thirty miles away by that time."

Passhia nodded, then turned to the team and said, "We will all soon meet in Paradise. "*Allah-u-akbar!*"

Everyone chanted, "*Allah-u-akbar!*"

Passhia climbed into the Dexter pickup and drove out of the barn. Amit watched as the pickup disappeared down the driveway and with it, his last chance to escape certain death.

If anyone besides Amit was frightened, they didn't show it. Even Saheim smiled; pleased he had been picked to complete this mission. They believed the promise Passhia offered, and this very day they would have their reward in heaven. Amit doubted he would have the promised virgins.

Bashar and Saheim loaded the bomb into the van and climbed into the front seat, while Kaleem, Amit, and Akram covered the bomb with a tarp, climbed into the van, and closed the side door. As the van disappeared down the driveway, Keith climbed out of the loft and ran into the house. He freed his parents, the children, and the Dexters, from the bedrooms. Keith told them about the bomb and how he had sabotaged it, or at least he prayed that he had done so. Dan congratulated him with a big hug.

Peter shook his hand. "You are a clever and brave boy . . . a hero. You will never know how many lives you saved this day." Nora and Judy each gave him a big hug.

Dan turned his ham radio on and called his friend in Minot. He told them about the terrorist bomb. His friend contacted the Minot police station by radio, and within minutes, the state police were searching for the van on Highway 83. Unfortunately, by the time the police could get to the Minot Air Force Base, it would be too late.

The terrorists arrived at Minot Air Force Base several minutes before the Minot police did. They pulled into a highway turnout a quarter mile past the west gate, and then said a prayer. Amit joined them in prayer, yet his only thought was for his family. His shirt, drenched in sweat, plastered itself to his body. He secretly wanted to run down the road, but knew such an act would be that of a coward and would accomplish nothing. He knew Bashar was right. How could he outrun an atomic bomb?

At the prayer's conclusion, Bashar said it was time. He and Saheim climbed out of the van, threw open the side door and removed the tarp. Whispering a prayer and with shaking hands, Saheim connected the black wire to the circuit board and cupped the detonation switch in his hands. Bashar nodded. Saheim closed his tear-filled eyes and flipped the bat handle toggle switch to the "on" position. Nothing happened.

"What is wrong?" Bashar asked.

"It didn't detonate," Saheim said.

"Well, that much is obvious. We are still here. Perhaps you didn't wire it properly," Bashar scolded.

"No . . . I know my wires are correct."

Saheim noticed the flashing red LED signaling the circuit was still alive, so he began to trace the other wires. Keith had done a good job hiding his sabotage, but Saheim found the cut red wire that lead to the circuit board.

"Someone has sabotaged the bomb," Saheim exclaimed.

"How is that possible?" Bashar asked. "We locked everyone inside the house as we prepared the bomb."

"Someone else was in the barn . . . probably that boy. No matter . . . I can fix it," Saheim said as he reconnected the copper wires.

"It is ready now," he said.

"Good . . . now let's do it," Bashar nodded.

Saheim said a prayer and threw the switch.

The bomb detonated in a huge fireball, vaporizing the van, the bomb and the terrorists. The explosion shook every building on the Air Force Base, shattering windows within a quarter mile of the van, an explosion heard as faraway as Minot. Parts of the van, the bomb, and bodies flew in all directions. The rear end of the van somersaulted high in the air and landed in a ditch. It was a powerful explosion, yet it was not a nuclear one. The detonator wires Keith had cut prevented all the Semtex explosives from properly sequencing to implode the uranium and form a critical mass. The bomb imploded on one side only and the uranium did not compress to a critical mass or start a chain reaction in the plutonium.

While the bomb didn't result in a nuclear explosion, the plastic explosive created an impressive fireball and spread radioactive U-235 and plutonium all over the Air Force Base and surrounding area. HASMET closed the base for several weeks, to allow their decontamination crews to make the area safe for humans again, but were finally unsuccessful. Forced to close down the Minot Air Force base, the Air Force moved their operations to another base in Montana. The prevailing northerly winds spread small amounts of radioactivity from Minot to Bismarck. Radiation forced those living in the northern part of Minot to evacuate and undergo decontamination. For weeks, decontamination crews, dressed in bulky safety gear and carrying Geiger counters, swarmed around Minot, listening for those telltale clicks that signaled the presence of radioactive materials. Fortunately, because of prevailing northerly winds, no radiation fell on the farms north of the Air Force Base, including those surrounding Willow Creek.

The blame game for the aborted nuclear explosion erupted in Washington D.C., where an unprecedented spate of government finger-pointing erupted between various agencies. The FBI blamed the CIA for ignoring a warning from one of their most reliable and trusted operatives. The CIA blamed the SNAFU on the President and his politically motivated directives, intended to replace key leaders with those favorable to the administration. These newly appointed but inept leaders in key positions created confusion and distrust within the agencies. The President rebuked his Homeland Security Secretary for failing to alert and equip all ports of entry with bomb detectors. Homeland Security blamed the Canadian port authority and claimed that had they had done their job they would have confiscated the bomb at whichever port the bomb had entered. Canadian Customs correctly blamed lax U.S. supervision at the Highway 83 customs port, for allowing the terrorists to cross over into the States. U.S. Customs senior management had done little other than send increased surveillance warnings to various ports of entry, and some port managers didn't act on the directives. The manager at the Highway 83 port was fired, for assigning a lone inspector to work fourteen hours straight. In short, the Canadian-U.S. border remained as it had for a decade: a sieve that terrorists easily exploited. There was enough blame to go around the entire government bureaucracy, and it bounced from agency to agency. In the end, the President had to accept that he and his Administration were responsible.

The American people thanked God for averting this disaster, yet they marveled that it took a 14-year old boy to save the country from the greatest terrorist attack since 9/11. Terrorists now had nuclear materials and fundamentally, folks understood that their government could no longer protect them. This was the only al-Qaeda object achieved by what became called the Minot Incident, but its psychological effect devastated the nation.

Al-Qaeda took full advantage of the turmoil and claimed they had more atom bombs and would not hesitate to use them. The threat resulted in complete chaos. America was just recovering from the distress brought on by several months without power, and now, when faced with a threat much worse than a power outage, the government had no clear-cut action plan to deal with it. Americans realized our way of life was under threat and their government couldn't protect them. Many folks deserted their city homes and moved to the relative safety of small towns. Part of the fundamental Islamic plan to destroy America was now in play. It was time for al-Qaeda sleeper cells, placed throughout America, to act.

CHAPTER TWENTY-ONE:
CHAOS IS SPELLED WITH A "C".

Leveraging from the Minot Incident, al-Qaeda continued their strategy of posturing and intimidation. Within days in a tape released to the BBC, al-Qaeda claimed they would soon announce a list of demands. They warned that unless the American government followed through on all of their demands, mushroom clouds of nuclear death would rise over several targeted U.S. cities, where various sleeper cells were poised to explode nuclear bombs. No Americans died in the failed Minot nuclear explosion, yet the incident convinced most folks that they were in imminent and mortal danger from other nuclear attacks: attacks that could take place anytime and in any major or minor city of al-Qaeda's choosing.

In July Iran tested their first nuclear bomb. The rumor persisted that they had enough enriched uranium to make several more bombs. CIA intelligence claimed the nuclear material for the Minot bomb did not come from Iran, as first suspected, but from a poorly guarded depository in Kazakhstan Russia initially denied the accusation, but traces of uranium 235 used in the Minot incident were traced back to the Astana depository. Faced with mounting UN evidence of missing nuclear materials, they admitted the loss and tightened security at all their nuclear depositories. It was unlikely terrorists could steal more material from these sites, yet the UN Nuclear agency suspected that Iran would soon share fissionable materials with terrorists.

Many in Congress secretly argued we should let Israel destroy the uranium enrichment facility in Iran, where thousands of centrifuges spun 24/7. Despite the growing danger, the President waffled on that proposal. As a result, Iran continued to enrich uranium, while claiming it was only for electric power generation. Anyone with a computer could research this obvious lie. Only one nuclear power plant existed in all of Iran, and Russia supplied fissionable materials for that plant, a fact that contradicted their claim that they intended the enriched uranium for power generation.

The terrorists did everything in their power to heighten America's fears. The threat that even one nuclear bomb could explode in a city such as New York or Washington had a devastating effect on the American psyche and shattered the people's trust in their government. A nuclear explosion in any of those cities would kill tens or hundreds of thousands of people, and thousands more would die from radiation poisoning, a disaster that would eclipse that of 9/11.

Two weeks after the Minot incident, an EMM spokesperson delivered a specific list of al-Qaeda's demands. Within 90 days, the U.S. must withdraw all troops and ships from the Middle East, release all terrorist captives, and transfer one hundred billion dollars to an offshore bank account. In addition, the U.S. must denounce Israel, end all financial and weapons support of that country, and abrogate their defense treaty. If America didn't comply, they would direct their sleeper cells in the States to detonate a second, and then a third A-bomb. As the administration considered various options, Congress deliberated, but that was all they did. Both sides of the aisle debated and argued, yet neither side could agree on a specific plan. The only item they could agree on was that they wouldn't accept the terrorist demands. Such action amounted to a surrender of the government. The President spoke to a joint session of Congress and although the he talked tough, his speech was naïve, partisan, and lacked an actionable plan. Few in Congress trusted him or his rhetoric. He accused the Republicans of being obstructionists, and the Republicans blamed the Democrats for the years of ineffectual foreign policy. As a result, the Congressional debate raged on without resolution. As the 90-day ultimatum approached, the American public became furious with the inept Administration and Congress. There were rumors of an insurrection.

The President took the brunt of the criticism. As the country edged toward anarchy, fear-driven anger spilled out into the streets. A half million protesters marched on Washington, and rioters filled the streets of Philadelphia, Los Angeles, and Chicago. Pressured by growing civil unrest, the President and his cabinet resigned. The Vice President took over the government but two days later he was shot as his limo drove to the White House.

The next person in the line of presidential succession was Ted Simmons, the recently elected Speaker of the House. The Chief Justice swore Representative Simmons in as President the same day the Vice President was killed. Ted was an honorable and decisive Congressional leader. A lifelong Independent, he had a reputation for spearheading nonpartisan legislation. At the same time, fellow legislators knew him as a politically astute congressperson. Ted desperately needed credible intelligence about those al-Qaeda cells embedded in the U.S.; but he required new Presidential powers to obtain such information.

For years, judges had viewed unsubstantiated warrants as desperate fishing expeditions that the courts wouldn't uphold. Judges debated the Patriot Act, which gave the President and Homeland Security power to seek and destroy EMM cells. Previous administrations and courts had effectively gutted the Patriot Act, and President Simmons needed to restore some of its provisions. He was not to be denied the powers he needed to protect this nation. Immediately after assuming the Presidency, he issued executive orders that enabled Homeland Security to find and destroy al-Qaeda cells. His executive order came to be known as the Terrorist Surveillance Order that restored many of the provisions of the Patriot Act. When Iran exploded a second nuclear device, Homeland Security intensified their search for sleeper cells. Within a month, the FBI found and disabled dozens of suspected cells, yet found no nuclear materials or evidence thereof. Homeland Security told President Simmons that the al-Qaeda threats were without merit, but Ted didn't buy their assessment and ordered the National Guard in all States to assist the FBI in their efforts to search out and destroy al-Qaeda and EMM cells and find any additional atom bombs.

*   *   *

Shortly after the Minot Incident, The Royal Canadian Mounted Police found the stolen Dexter pickup truck, abandoned in a railroad yard outside Medicine Hat, Alberta. The RCMP was unable to track down the driver of the pickup, who was suspected to be involved in the Minot incident. Two days after the Canadians discovered the truck, two FBI agents visited the Dexter farm and questioned Keith Justin in detail. Keith was the only person who could identify the man who had escaped in the Dexter pickup. He described him as a tall, lanky man with a high forehead, full black beard, olive skin and deep-set, dark, penetrating eyes. One of the terrorists had addressed him as Passhia. Keith identified a picture in their mug book. It belonged to a former economics professor at the University of Cairo, Passhia bin-Alaheim, now a suspected member of the underground EMM group functioning in North America. With little to go on, the FBI and RCMP issued an "all-points" bulletin for Passhia. The agents assumed he had escaped by catching a freight train and now could be anywhere in Canada or the States. Nevertheless, his mug shot was posted in every U.S. Post Office and he became the subject of "most wanted" TV programs.

*   *   *

Back in Afghanistan, the U.S. military had transferred Kaysan from his holding cell in Farah to the Zahra Prison, outside Kabul. When first imprisoned at Farah, Kaysan refused to share critical information with Mr. Karl or his captors. However, after two months in Zahra, he had a change of heart and offered to share critical information about his former EMM comrades. He told his captors that he could name several key EMM leaders, their cell locations, and plans to blow up A-bombs in the United States. He knew the names of supporters within the Afghanistan government who financed the EMM. Of most interest to the Americans, he knew the location of some of the sleeper cells within the States.

Kaysan was furious with his former comrades in the el-Mossel Militia, who had betrayed him. Worse than a betrayal, Bashar had conspired to murder him. News of suicide bombings and the atrocity of 9/11, committed in the name of Allah, caused him to question al-Qaeda and even his own Islamic faith. Misguided imams had seduced his former friends to participate in a jihad. In particular, he blamed the Wahhabi sect of fundamental Islam that most EMM members subscribed to. The 19th century form of Wahhabism was a step backwards for Islam, led by those who didn't follow the teachings of Mohammad. He was unable to find anything in the Qur'an that could justify the murder of innocent men, women and children. In fact, Muhammad's sayings in the Haddith forbade the violence espoused by Wahhabism. After months of pondering such contradictions, Kaysan wanted to talk, but not with just anyone.

He told his captors that he would only share his information with Mr. Karl, the only person that he felt he could trust. Kaysan kept silent and patiently waited for a visit from Mr. Karl.

The word that Kaysan wanted to talk filtered through to the CIA office in Kabul, and Mr. Karl received orders to travel to the Zahra prison outside Kabul and interrogate Kaysan Hashim. At the time, he was still stationed in Farah and hadn't visited Kaysan since his transfer to the Zahra prison. He tried to get space on a military flight, but couldn't get a seat until the following week. Surface travel across Afghanistan was slow and dangerous, but his orders demanded an immediate meeting with Kaysan. He decided that he and a driver would travel in his jeep to Kabul. The journey was uneventful, until they rounded a curve 250 miles from Farah and swerved to avoid a large bomb crater in the road. A smoking 4x4 truck lay upside down in a ditch, the recent victim of an IED. They parked the jeep and got out to see if anyone in the truck needed help. The truck driver was dead, but a Marine Sergeant in the cab groaned. No one else was around, so Mr. Karl lifted the injured soldier out of the truck and placed him in the jeep. The nearest town was Kadhir, about twenty miles away. They drove as fast as they dared, expecting at any moment to activate another IED, but the three men made it into Kadhir without further incident and stopped at the outdoor town market. The driver asked for directions to the nearest hospital. Pretending to not understand his request, the locals turned away and refused to provide any directions. They drove to the police station in the center of town and went inside. The policeman at the front desk ignored their presence, until Mr. Karl pounded on the desk.

"Where is the closest hospital or U.S. army base?"

The desk sergeant just stared at him and did not answer. Mr. Karl asked the question a second time, adding that he had a severely wounded soldier in his jeep, but the policeman still didn't answer the question. Then Mr. Karl took his sidearm out of the holster, pointed it at the man's forehead and repeated the question a third time. A police lieutenant charged out of the office and confronted him.

"Put your weapon away," the Afghan lieutenant commanded. "There is a U.S. army base just the other side of town, a mile from a bombed-out church."

The trio drove to the outskirts of town, where an American and U.S. Marine flag flew from a single flagpole, next to a stucco-covered hotel pockmarked with bullet holes. Two Marines came out of the building and helped Mr. Karl carry the wounded soldier inside to the infirmary, where an army doctor examined him. The Marine Commander thanked Mr. Karl for bringing the soldier in and offered them lodging and a meal.

Mr. Karl and his driver resumed their journey the following morning, arriving at the Zahra prison near Kabul, two days later. After signing in at the front office, a Marine guard escorted Mr. Karl to Kaysan's cell, locked him inside and left. The cell was clean and comfortable, sparsely furnished with a bed, a table and chair, and a small writing desk. A beam of sunlight streamed in from a barred, open window, over the desk. The window overlooked the exercise yard and brightened the otherwise drab room. Smelling of fresh paint, the cell looked more like a college dormitory room than a prison cell. A portrait of Ali el-Fashial, the new President of Afghanistan, adorned the south wall, and much to Mr. Karl's surprise, a picture of former President G.W. Bush hung over the bed. Kaysan got up from the chair and greeted Mr. Karl. He appeared genuinely pleased to see him, and after shaking his hand, he moved the table over to the bed and offered Mr. Karl the only chair in the room. Kaysan sat down on the edge of his bed and pulled the table closer to him. For the moment, Mr. Karl stood with both hands leaning on the back of the empty chair, studying Kaysan, whose shaved head, bright eyes and neatly trimmed beard confirmed that he had received humane treatment while in this prison. It was evident that he had gained weight since Mr. Karl last saw him, yet the orange jumpsuit still hung loosely on his frail frame.

"Please, Mr. Karl . . . sit down," Kaysan pleaded, with a warm smile. "I've been expecting you."

Mr. Karl sat down and stared at the smiling prisoner across the table from him. Kaysan's tan skin and muscular arms and shoulders suggested many hours of exercise in the courtyard below. His broad smile displayed a mouthful of white teeth and the deep-set eyes sparkled as he spoke. All in all, Kaysan looked healthy, relaxed, and cheerful. Not the same man he had interrogated in Farah, months before. Evidently, the orders to treat Kaysan with respect had been followed.

"I came to see how you are doing," Mr. Karl began. "I understand you have something new to tell me."

Kaysan's smile broadened as he leaned across the table, drawing closer to Mr. Karl. "Yes, I have some critical information to share with you, but first I have to explain something." His soft voice was barely above a whisper. Mr. Karl listened intently.

"When we first met, you drugged and tortured me, and I hated you for what you were doing to me. But much to my surprise, afterwards you treated me with kindness. You saw to it that I got proper food and clean clothes, and you visited me several times. Others tried to interrogate me, but I focused on avoiding their questions, just as I initially did with you. The EMM trained me well for this. At first, out of loyalty to my friends and because of my training, I remained silent. I have come to believe my "friends" do not deserve my allegiance. My treatment in Zahra has been compassionate, and I slowly changed my opinion of the EMM and grew to respect my American captors. I have been reading the Qur'an and the Haddith, and believe my former friends betrayed me and Islam. The EMM trained and taught me to hate all westerners, which until recently I did with passion. Determined to be a good al-Qaeda soldier, I obeyed all their orders and did as they commanded. Yet, because I refused a mission of suicide, Bashar and my friends turned against me and even ordered a former comrade to murder me. These are evil people who have perverted Muhammad's teachings and no longer deserve my loyalty. I learned to read and write English in the prison school. They won't let me have a newspaper, but I have read many books and magazines in the prison library. Some speak of President Bush's policy to bring freedom to the people of Iraq and Afghanistan. America made many blunders in this terrible war, yet I believe their intentions were good. My thinking has changed. My former friends are now my enemies and my former enemy is now my friend."

Mr. Karl wanted to build on Kaysan's trust, so he shared details about the Minot incident and how Bashar and his friends had died in the unsuccessful attempt to explode their atom bomb. Obviously, no one had told Kaysan about the failure of Bashar's mission. On hearing this news, his brow furrowed.

"So . . . they failed," he said, with no hint of anger or regret. "Driven by ideology and hatred, Bashar dedicated himself to kill thousands of Americans and fulfill his agenda of death and suicide. He and his friends were eager to die for their cause, but I was not. This is why I left Anar Darreh. Bashar thought Allah would reward him for this terrible act, just as our comrades who destroyed the World Trade Center believed Allah would reward them. They were all wrong. Allah does not reward the murderers of innocent people, or those who commit suicide. These are evil acts forbidden in the Qur'an. It is good that Bashar's mission failed and innocent people did not die. Such a senseless act would not help spread Islam, and I have come to believe that Allah will punish rather than reward such acts of violence."

Mr. Karl said nothing, and waited for Kaysan to continue.

"It is a pity that Bashar and his comrades died as they had lived . . . filled with hatred and revenge," Kaysan reflected. "Allah be praised, I have buried that hatred that so filled my heart. I have information that must be shared. It can save many innocent lives. This is why I sent for you."

Kaysan's calm, expressionless attitude stunned Mr. Karl. When told that his friends had died he expected more emotion from him. Kaysan didn't react. It was as if he already knew.

"Your friends are all dead," Mr. Karl repeated. "Dead . . . blown to smithereens . . . their atoms scattered to the wind. Does this not matter to you?"

"Yes . . . it matters," Kaysan said, turning toward the window. "And yet . . . the saddest part of their mission was that Allah would not reward them as they expected. If there is a hell, I am sure they are roasting in it."

Such a statement from a former member of al-Qaeda puzzled Mr. Karl.

"Why have you decided that Allah won't reward them?"

Kaysan looked intently at Mr. Karl. His answer was barely audible.

"Their mission was flawed and evil. Allah does not approve of suicide or killing innocent men, women and children. This goes against everything Allah has taught us. It is wrong and evil. Consumed with hatred for the Americans, Bashar executed a plan of retribution that he knew in his heart was wrong. I could see it in his face when he banished me. Al-Qaeda tried to convince him he was doing Allah's will but in his heart, Bashar knew better. I am happy that their mission failed, and I am ready to share the truth about the EMM and al-Qaeda. This knowledge will help save many innocent lives."

Mr. Karl searched Kaysan for some sign of deception; yet there was none. Was he really ready to share what he knew, or was this meeting a trick designed to spin the CIA and Mr. Karl into a blind alley? Kaysan's face remained expressionless. Then his gaze shifted to the scene outside the window.

After a minute of uncomfortable silence, Mr. Karl spoke.

"Then go ahead. I am ready to listen."

Kaysan looked away from the window and faced Mr. Karl. "You should know the atom bomb Bashar took to America was the only one the EMM had. Iran keeps promising us a bomb, yet their promises are empty, so the EMM leaders sent two teams into Uzbekistan and Kazakhstan to steal bombs from the Russians One team stole a bomb from a depository in Kazakhstan and transported it across the Turkmenistan border into Afghanistan. Had the Russians caught them, they would have killed them on the spot and we would have no bomb. There are no other bombs because the second team failed in their mission. Our al-Qaeda leaders in Pakistan begged Iran for nuclear bombs that they would slip into America, but Iran would only give us empty promises. I don't know why this is, for

Iran hates America as much as we do, or as much as I used to. Anyway, whatever their reasoning, they would not share their bombs with us.

The EMM planned to detonated their bomb in an American city, and then threaten America with more bombs. In fact we only had the one bomb but the EMM would make America believe we had other bombs planted with sleeper cells in various cities. Faced with such a threat, the weak U.S. Administration would eventually give in to EMM demands. Then our leaders, who are already imbedded in key positions within the American government, would take over in a bloodless coup. Your countrymen could awake one morning to a new government, one that will abrogate the Constitution and replace your courts with judges who will rule by Shari'a law." Kaysan paused.

"Please continue," Mr. Karl pleaded.

"That was their plan; yet it was fundamentally flawed. Since my capture, I have read and studied much about America. I doubt that such a coup could succeed. Your nation is conservative and ruled by Judeo-Christian laws, with a tradition of freedom and inherent rights. It is inconceivable that Americans would allow Islamic Imams rule their country. Even if the EMM destroyed several cities, Americans would never give in to the demands of al-Qaeda and the EMM. Al-Qaeda will threaten America and try to intimidate your people. Do not listen to them. Steadfastness in an enemy intimidates terrorists, while concession only encourages them. This is my belief. Tell your American friends to disregard the terrorist threats. They have no other bombs. Do not take my words as truth; test my credibility. In my notebook is the address of an al-Qaeda safe house in Washington. Send the FBI to that address and you will find an EMM cell thriving down the street from the White House. A Yemeni national named Bandi el-Caseini is in charge of that cell. He is also an ambassador from Yemen and has made many friends in Congress."

Kaysan handed Mr. Karl a spiral notebook. The address of the Washington EMM safe house was at the top of the first page. On the following pages, he had scrawled the names of two dozen al-Qaeda and EMM members embedded in the U.S. State Department and other government offices. On the last page, Mr. Karl recognized the names of many presidential advisers, several prominent Representatives, one Senator, and the Deputy Secretary of State. Also named, were CEOs of prominent American companies, leaders in the media, and professors from several American universities. Mr. Karl stared at the last name on the list. It was that of the new Director of the CIA, James Coleman. The last page contained the addresses of over a dozen sleeper cell "safe houses", strategically placed throughout the country. Kaysan's signature was at the bottom of the last page

"Where did you get these names and addresses?" Mr. Karl inquired.

"For many years, I worked for the EMM, recruiting well-educated English-speaking people to infiltrate American business and government. We sent them to American universities, and funded their political or corporate careers. I know them; they run large corporations and are embedded in key government positions," Kaysan stressed. "They are devils, intent on bringing Islam to America by force. In the name of Allah, stop them before they eventually get their hands on other atom bombs and kill many innocent people."

Mr. Karl stood up, went over to the window, and drank in the Afghan scenery. The outline of the snowcapped northern mountains dominated a horizon barely visible through the ubiquitous red dust that hung over the country in the summer. He took a deep breath and tasted the warm, humid air, which reminded him of the desert outside Zahra. Then, still looking out the window, he thanked Kaysan.

"I believe everything you have told me, and I appreciate your candor. I now need to get this information back to my superiors. You are a true friend and I thank you."

Mr. Karl hurried back to his temporary office in the Ambassador's compound. He could not trust this information with anyone in his own CIA department. Even the name of CIA Director, James Coleman, was on Kaysan's list. Despite his shock to see the director's name on the list, he wasn't all that surprised. It could explain why the CIA had ignored his earlier cable, warning that an al-Qaeda atom bomb was headed to the States. The only person he could now trust was Ambassador Crosby, so he made an appointment to see her the next day. She canceled another appointment, and after the usual greeting in her office, he handed her Kaysan's notebook. As she leafed through it her eyes grew wide. She read the list of prominent names.

"How do you know if this is credible information?"

"Send the FBI to the address in Washington listed as an EMM cell only blocks from the Whitehouse," Mr. Karl suggested. "If they find a cell there, it will prove that Kaysan has told us the truth and his list is credible."

Mr. Karl sat quietly as Ambassador Crosby picked up the red telephone on her desk and placed a call to The Homeland Security Secretary in Washington. The Secretary ordered Mr. Karl to escort Kaysan to Washington. Two days later, Mr. Karl and Kaysan climbed on a jet transport headed to the States. After a stop in Germany, they flew to Washington and arrived there the following day. Meanwhile, the FBI raided the Washington address in Kaysan's notebook, and as Kaysan promised, they discovered an al-Qaeda cell operating in a third floor apartment, only two blocks from the Justice Department. Inside, they found shortwave radios, satellite telephone transmitters, and sophisticated listening and surveillance equipment. The computer hard drives contained enough information to indict a dozen EMM workers in Washington, as well as several elected and appointed officials on Kaysan's list. The raid confirmed the authenticity of the information in Kaysan's notebook. That afternoon, the FBI arrested CIA Director Coleman and two of his deputies at the CIA headquarters.

The following Monday, Kaysan and Mr. Karl sat before a hastily convened Congressional hearing. Observers and media packed the room. Kaysan told the committee about the al-Qaeda plans to explode the stolen atomic bomb in Minot and then intimidate the American people with threats of more atomic weapons . . . weapons they did not actually have. He explained about EMM operations in Afghanistan and all that he knew about that organization, and how he obtained the names and addresses listed in his notebook. The notebook included the names of several members of Congress, including one Representative on the very committee sitting before him. When Kaysan named him, he rose to protest, but two FBI agents handcuffed him and led him out of the hearing room.

Armed with additional warrants, the FBI conducted raids throughout the country. The raids uncovered two dozen al-Qaeda cells and resulted in the arrest of over 100 suspected terrorists, yet those raids only uncovered conventional weapons and chemical bombs. There were no atomic bombs or even evidence of radioactive materials. The government charged the conspirators and terrorists with sedition, including one Senator, three Representatives, CIA Director Coleman, and Iranian Ambassador Bandi el-Caseini.

In the days following the hearings, backed by evidence garnered from the hard drive captured in the Washington EMM safe house, the FBI exposed the al-Qaeda members placed within the U.S. government, universities, media, and several corporations. With a fist full of warrants, the FBI raided the homes and offices of all those on Kaysan's list. The evidence gathered by those raids allowed the FBI to disable many sleeper cells and arrest dozens of conspirators within the government.

President Simmons went on the air and told the American people that even if there were no more atomic bombs, the country needed to act aggressively to rout out sleeper cells, traitors and saboteurs, in order to protect the public from al-Qaeda. He not only wanted to prosecute those on Kaysan's list but he needed congressional backing, to get evidence against other suspects not on Kaysan's list but listed on the Washington EMM hard drive. Congress hesitated, so President Simmons urged the Attorney General to indict these traitors and conspirators. The FBI raid on the EMM safe house in Washington provided a wealth of evidence, and with that evidence they broke up dozens of sleeper cells and arrested hundreds of terrorists. The date set by al-Qaeda for the U.S. to meet their threats came and went and nothing happened. The American people realized that the terrorist threats were empty. They could go back to their normal lives and feel safe again.

The new administration purged itself of inept appointees in the CIA, FBI and Homeland Security. They restored communications and dealt effectively with the various projects to restore services, provide electric power and transportation to the country. Power companies replaced damaged transformers and restored electricity to cities and towns, throughout the country. The Federal Government closed its borders and sent the National Guard and much of the Army to patrol them. They inspected all cargo arriving in U.S. ports and restricted shipments from unfriendly countries. The Terrorist Surveillance Order restored many of the provisions in the Patriot Act, gutted by the previous administration.

As demonstrated in the aftermath of 9/11, the terrorist's nuclear bomb threats only united the country and firmed U.S. resolve to wipe out Radical Islam that had infiltrated this country. In the years after the Iraq war and insurgency, Afghanistan and Iraq evolved into quasi-democracies. These were not the kind of governments envisioned by past American Administrations, but one where the citizens of those nations enjoyed a representative government and relative security. Many Moslem dictatorships in the near east and Africa fell and the rebels formed representative governments. The U.S. declared Iran and their jihad terrorist cells within that country responsible for much of the unrest in the Islamic world, and initiated a complete embargo of shipments to that country. Israel conducted air raids and destroyed their nuclear enrichment facilities. For the first time in decades, other countries, even Russia, China, and a few Moslem regimes, joined the U.S. in the fight against Radical Islam.

Before the Minot incident, the U.S. military forces had dwindled to less than 500,000 soldiers, and our naval forces and Air Force were skeletons of their former strength. The President's administration worked hard to restore our military might. Faced with the possible annihilation of their country, tens of thousands of young men and women eagerly joined the armed forces. There was no need to enact the military draft. Within six months, over 2.5 million Americans were in uniform. The mullahs in Iran began to lose their stranglehold on the Iranian populace. Faced with a possible invasion, the citizens revolted and deposed their tyrannical rulers.

As America repaired its damaged infrastructure, threats from terrorists and unrelenting internal political partisanship continued to stress the administration. The new President, Ted Simmons, was a centrist with no patience for radical right of left wing politics. Decisive, unafraid, and principled, he placed Harry Truman's sign, "The Buck Stops Here", prominently on his desk. He passionately promoted small government and respected State's rights. Ted was just what the country needed at this critical time. He sought Congressional approval and worked tirelessly with State Governors to gain their cooperation. He spearheaded and signed the Electrical Power Restoration Act, which hastened electrical power repairs nationwide. The country was finally recovering from the power outage and threat from al-Qaeda.

Al-Qaeda had failed to understand a fundamental attribute of Americans. When threatened, they do not roll over, they get angry. While diverse and often divided, when faced with real danger, Americans put their differences aside and work together to fight against a foreign threat.

CHAPTER TWENTY-TWO:
LIFE GOES ON

In the months after Peter's trial, Willow Creek had changed for the better. Mayor Jim Peterson and Judge Jameson sold their farms and moved to California. Niles Olsen sold his hardware and mercantile stores and his interest in the Washington Savings and Loan Company, and moved to Minnesota. Most folks assumed he moved to avoid indictment for his participation in the Dexter farm fraud and trial. However, the Dexters were still considering civil action against him and the former mayor. That summer, coroner Darren Jenkins won the election for Willow Creek mayor.

On August 17, the town marked the biggest event of the year, dubbed "Lights on Day" . . . the day that Ottertail Electric again delivered power to the town. To celebrate, the townsfolk marked the date with a parade and party. City lights sparkled, electric motors hummed, sewage moved to the treatment plant, cars drove down the streets, and water flowed into homes and businesses. For the first time in months, the downtown fountain gushed with jets of crystal clear water and the local bank opened for business. Under new management, the Mercantile opened, its shelves stocked with food and freezers packed with meat and frozen goods. Two days later, a gasoline tanker truck arrived from Minot and filled the empty BP underground tanks at the town's only gas station. Folks stood in line to fill gas cans, which they took home to fill empty automobile gas tanks.

Willow Creek celebrated with a dance in the community hall, and St. Paul's held a *lutefisk* and *lefse* feast. Pastor Helming drove all the way to Bismarck to pick up a shipment of frozen cod, flown in from Norway. The traditional Norwegian food, *lutefisk* (baked codfish) and *lefse* (flat bread), was a favorite of local parishioners, yet the oily fish failed to impress newcomers in the crowded hall. An acquired taste, Penny Justin took a bite of the fish, wrinkled her nose, and complained to Nora that it reminded her of the cod-liver oil her mother once forced down her throat.

Keith's heroic action to disarm the atom bomb made him into a local, as well as national celebrity. A few weeks after the Minot incident, two reporters and a TV crew traveled from Minneapolis to the Dexter farm and interviewed Keith. Across the country, newspapers, radio, and TV news programs featured Keith's story. He became known as the hero of Willow Creek. Without his brave efforts, thousands of people would have died in that explosion and much of the Midwest would be contaminated with radioactivity. Folks marveled at the bravery and ingenuity that enabled a high school student to disarm an atomic bomb.

A correspondent asked, "How did you know how to do that?" Keith modestly explained that he learned how to do it by watching James Bond movies. For the residents of Minot and the people of North Dakota, Keith became their own homegrown hero.

Both North Dakota Senators came to Willow Creek to help celebrate the "Lights on Day" and presented Keith with the Presidential Medal of Freedom, the highest honor the country can award a civilian. Mayor Darren Jenkins presented Keith with the keys to the city and Senator Irving read a proclamation from the Governor of North Dakota that included a four-year college scholarship to a university of Keith's choosing. Flanked by both North Dakota Senators, Keith proudly rode in Mayor Jenkins's classic Cadillac convertible that led the parade through town. Dan and Nora could hardly contain their pride. One week later, a team of investigators from the CIA, led by Mr. Karl, arrived to interview Keith. Keith told them about the men who had assembled the atomic bomb in the Dexter barn and repeated what he overheard them say. Mr. Karl recorded his statements and sent his report to the FBI.

One of Keith's recollections especially caught Mr. Karl's attention. He claimed the man addressed as Bashar boasted that another bomb would soon "wipe Sin City off the face of the map". Such a statement made no sense if al-Qaeda only had one bomb. Was it possible that al-Qaeda could have a second bomb? Although Mr. Karl's report included Bashar's boast, FBI analysis concluded that such a statement only amounted to posturing and the terrorists only had a single bomb.

*   *   *

Hard work kept the Dexter and Justin families busy on the farm. All summer, the men worked long hours tilling, planting and harvesting wheat and corn, repairing fences and caring for their animals. In August, they began preparing the farm for the coming winter. Each person had an assigned job. Once Keith completed his senior year studies and received his diploma, he helped Dan and Peter in the fields. Scott and Trevor were in charge of caring for the farm animals. Judy, Nora, and Penny spent long hours in the kitchen, canning fruit and vegetables and preparing meals for their families.

Dan and Nora often talked about returning with their children to Santa Cruz; even so, they continued to postpone this decision. At the same time, they felt that they shouldn't indefinitely impose on Peter and Judy's hospitality. When Dan talked to Peter about leaving, he wouldn't hear of it. He claimed the now-blended families should remain together and argued that he needed Dan, Keith, and Scott to help him run the farm. Even so, after they completed the fall harvest, Dan felt it was time to return to their home in Santa Cruz.

In early September, Dan hitched his trailer to the car, bid a tearful farewell to Peter, Judy and the kids, and the Justin family began the long trip back to Santa Cruz. Road crews had repaired the Interstate Highway system and last year's two-week journey now took only three days. When they arrived in Santa Cruz, the city appeared well on the way to a full recovery. Since leaving California, Nora had continually worried about her parents, but just last month, she had heard from Jim that he and Dee were doing fine. They drove to Nora's parents' home a block from the San Lorenz River. Their home looked just as it had when they left for North Dakota. Dee and Jim lived through the nightmare in Santa Cruz by relying on their friends, a network of seniors who banded together to take care of one another. The chaos had been tough on them, but with help from their friends they survived and took pride in the fact that their city was returning to normal. The streets were clean, electricity, and water systems repaired, the sewers running, emergency services restored, and most businesses had reopened. Jim and Dee insisted the family would stay with them, but this was not part of Dan's plan. He thanked Jim for his offer but explained that they wanted to restore their old home and move back in. The day after arriving in Santa Cruz, they drove from Jim and Dee's to the other side of town, to see their old home. Despite reconstruction, signs of destruction and neglect remained throughout the city. Deserted and damaged homes marred their old neighborhood, but they were truly shocked when they drove up to the wreckage that once was their home.

The house exterior was a total wreck. A jungle of foot-high weeds and vines covered the front yard. Gaping holes and missing shingles pockmarked the roof; storm shutters hung at a skewed angle from broken windows; and thugs had torn siding from parts of the house and garage. Inside, all the kitchen appliances, including the stove and the refrigerator, were missing. Not a stick of furniture remained and most rooms showed signs of water damage. Vandals had ripped out the central heating system, shredded the carpets, and removed all the fixtures. They left gaping holes in the walls and ceiling, and ripped copper wires and pipes out of the walls. Acoustic panels hung from the ceiling or lay crumbled on the floor along with broken window glass and pieces of wallboard. Rain had seeped in from holes in the roof and covered the front room and one bedroom with an inch of smelly water. The house was a total loss. The extent of damage devastated Nora and her family. Obviously, they could no longer live in this rubble. They would have to tear down the ruins of the house and rebuild it, and it would take money they didn't have to restore this house.

Penny cried as she sifted through the rubble that once was her bedroom. "Why did we ever come back here . . . to this mess?"

"We can't stay here," Nora declared. "Let's either go back to Mom and Dad's or go to the Wilsons' in Scotts Valley. Perhaps we can stay with them until we decide what to do."

They found the Wilsons' house abandoned, and a neighbor said the family had moved to Bakersfield. Dan parked his rig in the driveway and the Justins prepared to spend another night in their trailer. Dan asked everyone if they wanted to go back to Willow Creek.

"Our prospects in Santa Cruz right now look bleak. We could rebuild our old house, but I don't have the money it would take to do so. We could also stay with Jim and Dee, but I think life would be better for us back in Willow Creek."

Everyone wanted to go back, everyone that is except for Keith, who did not seem enthusiastic about the idea of returning to North Dakota. The next day, he asked his dad if, before they returned to North Dakota, they could visit Dan's alma mater, the University of California, at Santa Cruz campus. Dan asked Keith why he wanted to visit the campus, and Keith confessed that he had sent his transcript to the University and they had accepted his application, contingent on a face-to-face meeting between him, his father, and the Dean of the College of Science. Although pleased that Keith had chosen to apply to his own alma mater, Dan was irked that Keith had not shared his plans with him or his mother.

"You will need to explain this decision to your mother, but first let's see if this is what you really want to do."
Dan and Keith drove to the campus and met with the Dean of the College of Science, Dr. George Markey, who had Keith's application sitting on his desk, waiting for final approval. Keith's reputation preceded him, and Dr. Markley knew all about the boy hero from North Dakota. After a brief interview, Dr. Markey said it would be an honor to enroll Keith in the College of Science. The fall semester would start near the end of September, so Dr. Markey encouraged Keith to enroll right away. The North Dakota State scholarship awarded to Keith would fund his entire education. Dan had barely warmed to the idea that his son would be leaving home, when he found himself in the registrar's office signing papers, touring the science building and dormitory, and meeting several of Keith's teachers and classmates. Dr. Markey also introduced them to Keith's assigned mentor and roommate, senior Ron Passavente.

Returning to Scott's Valley, Keith struggled to explain his decision to Nora. Hurt and dismayed, she protested that the three of them should have sat down and discussed this together "as a family". She felt left out of the decision and angry with Dan for allowing Keith to enroll at UCSC, without her involvement.

"We can't just leave Keith here . . . alone and friendless. Why can't he enroll in the University in Minot, or in Fargo?"

"He will be fine in Santa Cruz," Dan argued. "Jim and Dee are here in town, and thanks to the scholarship, he has more than enough money to see him through four or five years at UCSC. Dr. Markey, the Dean of the College of Science, has promised to take Keith under his wing. He has already assigned a senior, Ron Passavente, as his roommate and mentor."

"It was a mistake to come back here," Nora sighed. "This is no longer our home and now you are asking me to abandon our firstborn here."

Dan threw his arms around her. "Nora, this has been Keith's decision. He won't be alone; his grandparents are here and he'll be in college with other live-in students. We cannot stay here, but Keith needs to find his own way and it was his decision to enroll in UC. I think this is a good decision."

"I suppose so," Nora conceded, "but the idea that our son will be 1,000 miles away frightens me."

Dan tried to comfort her. "We were wrong not to consult with you. Tomorrow, the three of us will go to the campus and visit with Dr. Markley and meet Keith's roommate. I think you will feel better about the decision when you meet the Dean and visit Keith's dormitory. The phone system is working again, and tomorrow I'll buy two cell phones, one for Keith and one for us. We can talk to him as often as we please. It is not as if Keith is alone. Dee and Jim are here in town, and will keep in touch with him."

The first call Dan made on his new cell phone was to Peter to tell him that they were coming home and that Keith had enrolled in UCSC. The phrase "coming home" sounded odd to Nora. California had always been her home, and now home would be in the Dakotas and without her firstborn son. She cried softly, as Dan spoke with Peter, and wiped the tears from her cheeks. It would take some time to adjust to being without her son.

Peter said he had exciting news of his own to share with Dan and Nora. Dan turned on the speakerphone so they both could listen.

"After you folks left Willow Creek, something unexpected happened," Peter said. "Conrad Perkins, the man who farmed the 260-acre farm next to ours, suddenly abandoned his house and farm and left town. I was interested in purchasing the property and visited with the county recorder, Betty Wyckoff. Together we researched the title history of the Ingles' and Perkins' farms."

"Lloyd Olsen kept 260 acres of the original 680 acre farm and farmed it until his death in 1945. Lloyd's son, Miles Ingle, inherited the farm. He lived in California when his father died and there was no record of any subsequent title transfer of that property. Conrad Perkins never had title to the property he farmed all these years. We think Conrad must have rented the farm from Miles, although there is no record that he ever paid a dime of rental. Miles died ten years ago and his heirs now own that property, but they have never shown interest in it nor have they tried to collect back rent, until recently. I guess that is why Conrad left so suddenly. He knew that a title search would show that he owed tens of thousands of dollars in back rent to the Ingles family."

Dan looked at Nora and shrugged his shoulders. "That's interesting, but what does this have to do with us?"

"As I said, I wanted to buy the abandoned Ingles property. Then I thought that you and Nora might want to buy it. I had a realtor in town contact a member of the Ingles family in California, and they are willing to sell the property at a reasonable price. Are you folks interested?"

"Interested? You bet we are . . . it is a perfect solution. I think there is enough left in our bank here to cover the earnest money and I will send it to you."

Dan took what remained of his savings out of the Santa Cruz bank and sent it to Peter to put down on the Ingles farm.

After a tearful good-bye to Keith, Dee and Jim, the Justins returned to Willow Creek and moved into the abandoned Perkins house. In September, the local schools reopened for the fall semester. Scott and Trevor enrolled in the local high school and Penny and Pam enrolled in the junior high school. The Justin family had occasionally attended a church in Santa Cruz but were not regular church goers. Since arriving in Willow Creek, they attended St. Paul's weekly with Peter and Judy, and now felt like accepted members of the Willow Creek community and St. Paul's parish. They met with Pastor Helming, who registered them as permanent members of St. Paul's. Strapped for cash after buying the Ingles farm, Dan found work in Minot as a payroll accountant. The long commute to Minot, the 40-hour workweek, and farming kept Dan over-committed, yet he loved the farm. The Justin family settled onto their farm and into the Willow Creek community and Keith thrived in his first year in college.

CHAPTER TWENTY-THREE:
IT'S NOT OVER UNTIL IT'S OVER

Mr. Karl sat in his temporary Washington DC office and pondered the Congressional hearings, in which Kaysan Hashim convinced Congress that the EMM had no materials for another atom bomb. Their threats were a ruse, intended to intimidate the country. Kaysan's testimony gained credibility when the FBI raided several terrorist cells on Kaysan's list and jailed dozens of al-Qaeda members without discovering any evidence of another bomb. Yet events taking place back in Afghanistan would eventually dispel this false sense of security.

Kaysan returned home, knowing that by dismissing the threat of another bomb and alerting America to imbedded terrorist cells and sedition within their own government, he had been true to his conscience and to Allah's will. Kaysan didn't believe that Allah wanted thousands of innocent men, women and children to die, and knew that Bashar's failed plan was inherently evil. He was proud of his collaboration with the Americans. All the same, many of his former al-Qaeda comrades denounced Kaysan as a traitor and targeted him for assassination. His testimony before the American Congress was a major news item in Kabul. Mr. Karl tried to talk him out of returning to Afghanistan, but Kaysan wouldn't hear of it. The idea that he wouldn't be safe among his own people was absurd, or so he thought.

The minute Kaysan stepped off the airplane at the Kabul airport, shots rang out across the tarmac. Bullets whizzed past his head and ricocheted off the portable airplane ramp behind him. The two Afghan guards who escorted him off the airplane grabbed his arms and rushed him into the terminal building. At first, he thought they were simply trying to save his life. Yet as they dragged him down poorly lit stairs and into the basement, he wondered why they were treating him so roughly. His feet bounced off the steps and he stumbled along the long hallway until the guards shoved him into a windowless, drab room, lit by a single bare light bulb and empty except for a rough-hewn wood bench.

The two Afghans were replaced by two Marines who forced Kaysan's hands behind his back, handcuffed him, and then dragged him over to the bench and told him to sit down. Kaysan refused to sit and struggled to remain on his feet. He glared at the Americans who had seemingly morphed from rescuers into captors.

"Why am I bound?" Kaysan demanded.

"Shut up and sit down," one Marine guard growled. Kaysan remained standing, until a kick to the back of his legs forced him onto the bench.

The Marines turned and walked out of the room. They shut the heavy steel door and he heard the clanking sound of a set of keys as they locked him in the cell. He sat alone in the cold, gloomy room and tried to make sense of such an unexpected turn of events. Rather than the hero's welcome he expected, the Americans were treating him like a brigand. What could motivate such conduct? He had done nothing wrong. The tight handcuffs dug into his wrists and cut off the circulation to his hands. He grew confused and angry. Neglected for several hours in the damp, dimly lit room, he fumed that no one came to give him food or water, to loosen his handcuffs, or explain why he was being held. He had been a friend to the Americans, even risking his own life for them. What did he do to deserve such treatment? Nothing made any sense to him.

He sat on that hard wooden bench for three uncomfortable hours and grew angrier with each passing minute. His fingers were numb, his legs cramped, and he shivered in the clammy, cold room. Finally, two security guards opened the door and escorted him down the hallway to the airport security office. Sitting behind a large oak desk, a well-dressed woman, flanked by two tall Afghan officers who stood on either side, looked up as Kaysan entered the room.

"Take his handcuffs off," she curtly ordered one of the officers.

"Please . . . sit down," the woman offered as the Afghan officer removed the handcuffs and the other officer tried to hand Kaysan a cup of hot tea. He badly wanted the tea but he couldn't take it. His cramped hands and numb fingers wouldn't obey his command to grasp the cup.

"I prefer to stand," Kaysan said, rubbing his numb hands together to bring life back to them. A thousand needles seemed to prick each finger as they awoke.

"As you wish," the woman conceded.

Kaysan stared at her and she stared back through a pair of oversized, tinted glasses. Her thin lips displayed only the faint hint of a smile as she studied him. She appeared to be in her late forties, her face unadorned with makeup but tanned and outlined with deep wrinkles. She wore a smart lavender suit complemented by a diamond necklace with her blond hair arranged in a bun. She wore no other jewelry, not even rings on her fingers or a bracelet on her thin wrist. She continued to look at him for a few more seconds, and then removed her glasses revealing a pair of lovely hazel eyes that revealed a soul imbued in wisdom and understanding. Her professional attire and mannerism declared she must be someone important.

"My name is Miriam Crosby," she finally said. Her eyes sparkled as she introduced herself. "I am the ambassador for the United States in Afghanistan. I owe you an apology."

Ambassador Crosby? He had heard of her but was amazed that they had sent an ambassador to interrogate him. Kaysan said nothing and continued to rub his sore wrists. Finally, after several seconds, he spoke.

"Why was I dragged into a cell and handcuffed like a brigand," he demanded. "I did nothing wrong."

She frowned as she tried to explain. "There was a terrible misunderstanding and I must apologize for your inappropriate reception. Please sit down."

He sat down. The cold room caused Kaysan to shiver. Miriam noticed his discomfort and told the Afghan officer to place a blanket over his shoulders and offer the tea again.

"I instructed the Afghan guards to protect you our on the tarmac from possible assassins, but somehow they misunderstood and thought you were Taliban. There is such a language and cultural barrier to deal with in this country. I'm so sorry this happened."

Misunderstanding my ass, he thought as the officer placed the blanket over his shoulders. He accepted the hot tea, which warmed his hands and calmed his fits of shivering. Her apology didn't convince him. His treatment in the Farah prison and in Washington had been humane and respectful, yet nothing this woman said could fully explain his welcome home to Kabul. Ambassador Crosby waited for him to finish drinking the tea, then smiled and congratulated him for his courageous help to America.

"Considering my treatment, your congratulation lacks sincerity," Kaysan said sarcastically.

"Again, I am sorry," the Ambassador repeated. "We intended to protect you, not jail you. It was all a big snafu."

Kaysan frowned. "Snafu, what is this . . . snafu?"

Miriam gave a little laugh and explained, "It means Situation Normal All Fouled Up."

"You Americans make many snafus," he mocked.

Miriam ignored the remark. "You have saved many innocent lives. We cannot thank you enough for what you have done."

Kaysan rolled his eyes and stared off into space.

"However, we have something else to ask of you," she added, nodding to the Afghan officer. He cleared his throat and looked down at Kaysan.

"Last week, the Americans in Aurum captured a suspected el-Mussel terrorist named Qasid Sachem. Under interrogation, Mr. Sachem claims he knows you . . . personally. Everyone in Afghanistan has heard of Kaysan Hashim and all except the Taliban and al-Qaeda consider you a national hero. However, Qasid is a terrorist and he doesn't share in your adulation. He called you a traitor to Islam and the Jihad, and claims the Taliban have declared a fatwa against you. He also bragged that al-Qaeda has a second atom bomb. He says he saw it in a safe house near Ghurian on the Afghan-Iranian border."

"He lies," Kaysan said, "there are no other bombs."

"This is what we want you to confirm. You must to go with us to the prison at Ghurian and talk to Qasid. Find out if his claim of a second bomb is credible or a self-serving lie."

"Talk to him?" Kaysan asked incredulously. "The bastard tried to kill me. He is the last person I want to talk to."

He looked away from the officer and stared at Miriam. "After the way you have treated me, why would I want to do anything more to help your country? Forget it and let me go to my home in Herat."

Ambassador Crosby leaned across the desk. "Kaysan, we understand how you must feel, but we desperately need your help. If there is another bomb, we must find it, and do so quickly. You are our best hope to corroborate Qasid's story about a second bomb. Please talk with him and ask about the bomb that he claims to have seen. Play on his arrogance and get him to talk. You will know if he is telling the truth. If he is lying or perhaps confused about what he saw, this will be apparent to you. Only you can tell us which it is: mistake, truth or lie. If there is a second bomb, your information will help us save more many innocent lives."

Still seething with indignation, Kaysan remained stone-faced and silent. Miriam smiled her friendliest and warmest smile, and then having made her case, leaned back in her chair.

"Kaysan, we know you are a good person, otherwise you would not have risked your life for us. Realize the Taliban will kill you as soon as you arrive in Herat. Three Taliban terrorists tried to shoot you the minute you got off the airplane, even here at the heavily guarded airport. Two of those assassins are now in our morgue and the other one escaped. Others are ready to take their place. You wouldn't last one day unguarded in Heart. Your only chance is to remain under our protection. Otherwise . . . . , " her voice trailed off as she drew her finger across her neck.

Kaysan's anger began to soften as he carefully weighed her words. She seemed sincere and he knew his choices were few. If he went to Herat, he probably would be dead within hours, as Miriam had warned. Sad but true, his former friends now wanted to kill him. Such was the way of the Taliban and their allies. He had not taken five steps on Afghan soil before they tried to murder him. Thankfully, they were poor shots.

Ambassador Crosby was persuasive, and Kaysan melted under her unrelenting yet kind stare.

Kaysan stood. "Yes . . . I'll talk with Qasid, but I don't expect the truth from him. He is a psychopathic liar and dedicated assassin. I would sooner talk with the devil himself. All the same, praise Allah, I will do it if only to save innocent lives."

Ambassador Crosby's smile faded. She looked serious as she said, "This information can save the lives of innocent persons. One of the assassins on the tarmac escaped. He saw us drag you into the airport, and will assume that you were arrested. Our plan is to make it look like you were arrested and we are taking you to Ghurian Prison. Qasid is a prisoner there and the al-Qaeda grapevine will get the word to him of your arrest. We will arrange a meeting between you and Qasid. Perhaps he will talk to a fellow prisoner."

Kaysan climbed into the back of a jeep, for the three day ride to Ghurian. When they arrived, the Marine guards rubbed some makeup on his cheek to make it look like he had been roughed up, dressed him in an orange jumpsuit, and pasted a realistic looking plastic cut on his forehead. They handcuffed him and led him blindfolded into the prison and placed him alone in a cell. Two days later, guards led him down the hall to a room, sat him down at a table, and removed his handcuffs. He recognized the man sitting across the table as Qasid, but he seemed thinner and older than the man he remembered. His gaunt face, unkempt black beard streaked with gray, and skeleton-like frame made him look less intimidating than the man who had chased Kaysan down the mountain, intent on placing a knife in his heart. Qasid's face contorted into a snarl as he glared at Kaysan. He hacked up some phlegm and spat at Kaysan while uttering a curse in Arabic. The spittle missed Kaysan but made a direct hit on the uniform of the Marine standing beside him. The Marine reacted by slapping Qasid across the face. As blood oozed from his lip, Qasid leered and vented curses in English at the Marine guard. He then returned his attention to Kaysan, and changed back to Arabic.

"So, the turncoat Kaysan dares sit here and stare at me. I heard you were in this prison and I asked to see you. It looks like the ungrateful Americans have rewarded your deeds with beatings and handcuffs. Allah be praised! The stinking dog has received his just reward, and now you are stuck in this hellhole with me. If I had caught you that night on the mountain, I would have plunged a knife deep into your turncoat heart."

Kaysan shuddered imperceptibly, yet his gaze remained fixed on Qasid. He softly replied, "That was not Allah's will."

Qasid grew even more belligerent and exploded with a string of curses. "Allah's will? What do you know of Allah's will? His will is to crush the Americans, and you have frustrated Allah's plan with your betrayal. You are a coward and a traitor to the Jihad."

As Kaysan expected, the conversation was not going well. Without defending himself, he sat impassively as Qasid continued his verbal assault. He was playing the game, coolly waiting for Qasid to calm down so he could bait him. He knew Qasid was an arrogant, self-righteous fool, with the intelligence of a Philistine brute. Now he would play on that arrogance.

After another minute of curses and insults, Qasid ran out of vehemence and simply glared at his former comrade. Kaysan waited and then asked in a calm, quiet voice, "Qasid, the Americans detained me because they think I know about a second atomic bomb. I know there is no second bomb. They tell me that you claim to have seen it, but I know that this must be a lie. Bashar had the only bomb, and the Russians caught those who tried to steal a second bomb. Anyway, you wouldn't know an atomic bomb even if you had actually seen one. You have no idea what an atomic bomb looks like. You told the Americans about a second bomb to gain some favor for yourself. You are a liar and fool who can no longer tell the difference between a lie and the truth."

Kaysan had struck a chord. Qasid knew what an atomic bomb looked like. Who was this turncoat to question him like this? Hatred clouded Qasid's better judgment, and he began screaming at Kaysan.

"Truth?" "Truth?" "You would not know the truth if it bit you in the ass, you stinking traitor. I know what I saw . . . it was an atom bomb."

"I don't believe you," Kaysan whispered. "You are trying to bargain with the Americans for better treatment, with this lie about another bomb."

Qasid looked stunned. "You think it is a lie? I saw the bomb. My friends showed it to me. I know what an atom bomb looks like."

"I didn't know you had any friends. Who showed you this so called bomb?" Kaysan demanded.

"The el-Mossel group in Terkite did, a cell led by your cousin Moesha. You remember Moesha, your long lost relative?" The snarl returned to Qasid's face. "He hates you even more than I do."

Kaysan had not heard the name Moesha spoken for many years, nor had he seen his cousin since they were teenagers. When he hiked down the mountain from Bashar's hideout he had considered seeking refuge with Moesha in Terkite, but then thought better of it. That turned out to be a lifesaving decision, for he had no idea that Moesha led another el-Mossel cell. Even as teenagers, Kaysan had never liked his arrogant cousin. Had he sought refuge with Moesha in Terkite, he would have handed him over to Qasid to be butchered. Qasid and Moesha had much in common: they were both Hazara and lifelong sociopaths.

Kaysan and his cousin never got along as children. Once they both entered a kite fighting competition; his cousin cheated and cut Kaysan's string with a hidden knife rather than fight with his kite. They traded punches and Moesha bloodied his cousin's nose. Even as a teenager, Moesha was a sadistic bully, and no love was lost between them. The mention of Moesha's name caused Kaysan to shudder.

Kaysan continued to bait Qasid. He remembered that Qasid had been sent out of the room before Bashar proudly showed off the bomb to his lieutenants. Therefore, he would have no idea what an atomic bomb looked like.

"I do not believe you" Kaysan teased. "You don't even know what an atomic bomb looks like. Even Bashar didn't trust you and dismissed you before showing us the bomb."

Qasid bristled at the taunt. He never backed down from a challenge and to prove his point, he described Moesha's bomb in great detail, even down to the electronics and timers. His complete and accurate description left no doubt in Kaysan's mind that Qasid had seen the parts of an atomic bomb. Kaysan remained outwardly skeptical and continued to challenge Qasid's story.

"They fooled you . . . you pathetic dupe. That was not an atomic bomb. I know what an atomic bomb looks like, and what you described is nothing like an atom bomb. I saw the one Bashar had, and your description is all wrong. Moesha fooled you with a fake bomb. When did you see this . . . this device you think was an atomic bomb?"

Qasid hesitated. He didn't want to tell Kaysan anything, but his taunting had angered him and he wasn't going to let this traitor tell him he didn't know what he saw.

"In Aurum, about . . . about . . . nearly a month after you slinked off and hid yourself."

Qasid regained his composure, before continuing. "Your cousin Moesha in Aurum will do what Bashar could not do. His bomb will kill thousands of Americans. I know that you will tell the Americans about this, but it is too late for you or anyone else to do anything about it. The second bomb is already in place in America, awaiting an al-Qaeda command to detonate it. Moesha will not fail as Bashar did. It is Allah's will."

Kaysan wanted to know which city they intended to destroy.

Qasid spat, "I wouldn't tell a dog coward such as you even if I did know . . . but I do not. You will find out when the mushroom cloud rises over the American city."

Kaysan knew the interview was over and this was all the information he would get out of Qasid. He returned to Kabul and immediately set up a meeting with Ambassador Crosby, where he repeated everything he had tricked Qasid into saying, word for word. Miriam seemed disappointed.

"We hoped Qasid was lying, and the existence of a second bomb was a ruse," she said. "We wanted to know if Qasid actually saw an atomic bomb or perhaps he was simply lying to get better treatment for himself. Is he delusional?"

Kaysan chose his words carefully. "I don't think he's delusional, and I don't think he is lying. He was not present when Bashar showed us the bomb, yet his description of a second bomb is accurate. He knows the leader of the al-Mossel group in Aurum, who happens to be my cousin Moesha Hashim. In fact, after Bashar took the bomb to America, the el-Mossel cells in Terkite and Anar Darreh disbanded and reunited in Aurum. Qasid would have searched for other cells that he could join in Western Afghanistan. It is probable that my cousin took Qasid into his cell in Aurum."

Clearly the news stunned the Ambassador. She had expected the report of a second bomb would turn out to be a hoax or a delusion. Now it appeared al-Qaeda had their hands on a second bomb, and it might already be on American soil. But if so, where could it be?

"Did Qasid say anything about where in America they took the bomb?" Miriam asked.

"No . . . I don't think he knows. He said I would know when a mushroom cloud rises over an American city, and that many would die."

The Ambassador dismissed Kaysan and ordered the Marine sergeant to drive him to his uncle's house in Kabul, where he would be an honored guest. No place in Afghanistan was safe for Kaysan; however, his uncle was a State Representative and lived in a secure section of Kabul, on well-protected and gated grounds. The fatwa forced the Americans to assign two soldiers to protect him twenty-four-seven. This was a promise that Miriam intended to keep, even for years if necessary. The Americans would protect Kaysan, until they defeated the Taliban and fighting kites again flew over Afghan cities.

Miriam sent a cable about the probable existence of a second bomb hidden somewhere in America, to the new Homeland Security Secretary, Max Perez, in Washington D.C. Secretary Perez read the cable and immediately sent for Mr. Karl. They shook hands in Secretary Perez's office and after Mr. Karl took a seat, he watched as Max fingered the cable from Miriam, and then handed it to him.

Mr. Karl quickly read it and then looked up. The information, if true, was shocking.

"This cable implies a second bomb is in America," he said. "I find this hard to believe. There were no other bombs. Are you sure the cable authentic?"

Secretary Perez looked annoyed with the question.

"This intelligence came from Ambassador Crosby, after she sent Kaysan to meet with Qasid. She would not pass this information along unless she thought it credible." Secretary Perez studied Mr. Karl for a few seconds, and then continued.

"I believe you know Kaysan fairly well. Could Qasid have duped him into believing there is a second bomb?"

Mr. Karl pondered the question for a few seconds, and then his face softened. "I do not believe so. It is not easy to dupe Kaysan, especially by a dumb brute like Qasid, who is incapable of fabricating such a story. I think we must consider this information credible."

Max asked, "If there is a second bomb, where do you think they hid it?"

Mr. Karl thought for a moment before he replied. "When we debriefed the Justin boy in Willow Creek, he claimed he overheard one of the terrorists complain that Minot was a stupid choice for their bomb. The man identified as Bashar tried to soothe the terrorist, by saying another bomb would soon explode in "Sin City" and kill many more Americans. After we interviewed the boy, we discounted his information about a second bomb. We thought it was more posturing by Bashar. Now that we have convincing information about a second bomb, this overheard conversation has become the best clue as to which city they intend to destroy."

Max paused for a few seconds. "The city of sin . . . sin city . . . could have been a reference to Las Vegas."

Mr. Karl concurred. "For many reasons, Las Vegas is a logical target for the terrorists. Islamic fundamentalists believe Las Vegas, a city of over a million people, is corrupt: a modern Sodomon and a city of gamblers, prostitutes, and other purveyors of flesh. Las Vegas would be a prime target for a group of religious fanatics bent on bringing retribution to America."

Max agreed. However, first he had to resolve a delicate problem. How should he best act on this information? It was like carrying a flask of nitroglycerin in one's hands. One slip and it would explode. Announcing that a second atom bomb was somewhere in Las Vegas would panic that city. Only leaders at the highest government level should make such a decision. Before he told anyone, he called for a private meeting with President Simmons and his staff. He asked Mr. Karl to attend that meeting with him.

*   *   *

The following afternoon, Secretary Perez escorted Mr. Karl into the Oval Office. President Simmons sat behind the large cherry wood desk, the same desk Lincoln once sat behind. As they entered the room, the President interrupted a conversation he was having with Vice President Jim Cairn and greeted Max. Max introduced Mr. Karl and the President then invited his guests to take a seat with the members of his cabinet already seated on couches around the room. Max sat down with the Secretary of Defense Maryann Richards, FBI director Tommy Skylstad, and CIA director Anton Uzbek. Mr. Karl found a chair across from the couch and sat down. Several presidential staff members and Secret Service personnel stood at attention around the room. President Simmons then dismissed everyone but his cabinet members and guests. When the room had cleared, he then turned to Secretary Perez.

"So, Max, what do you have for us today?"

"Mr. President, I have disturbing, yet credible information. Al-Qaeda has a second atom bomb hidden in this country, we think perhaps in Las Vegas."

To give those in the room a few seconds to digest such alarming news, Max paused. He searched the faces of the cabinet members and Vice President. Everyone, except for Jim Cairn, looked shocked and tense. The Vice President sat quietly, wearing his usual poker face.

Max continued. "We believe two teams of Afghani EMM terrorists stole enough enriched uranium and plutonium to assemble two atom bombs. They took fissionable materials from two Russian depositories, one in Kazakhstan, and the other in Uzbekistan. We recently checked with the Russians, and they swore that they had only lost material for one bomb. They claimed terrorists stole it from their depository near the city of Astana in Kazakhstan. They also claimed they had caught a second team in Uzbekistan and confiscated the bomb materials. However, we now have information that another EMM cell, one operating out of a town along the southwestern Afghan border, built a second bomb from fissionable material they stole from a depository in Uzbekistan. The EMM partially assembled the bomb, shipped it to Vera Cruz, Mexico, and smuggled it across the U.S. border to Las Vegas, where they are awaiting instructions from al-Qaeda to explode it."

Vice President Carin looked skeptical. "How do you know the bomb is in Las Vegas?"

Max nodded to Mr. Karl, signaling that he should answer the question.

"This knowledge is based on information from Keith Justin, the boy who disarmed the Minot bomb," Mr. Karl answered.

President Simmons sat expressionless for a few seconds, and then looked over at Mr. Karl. "Please tell us how the Justin boy knew Las Vegas would be the target for a second bomb."

"Mr. President," Mr. Karl replied, "Keith Justin overheard the terrorists talking as they assembled the Minot bomb in his barn. Keith is a bright boy, and a national hero. I interviewed him in Willow Creek shortly after the Minot incident. He claimed he overheard one of the terrorists in English complain about the plan to destroy Minot. "It is a small, insignificant town, while that sinful city escapes Allah's just punishment," he protested. The leader of the group responded that the man shouldn't worry, because in time, the EMM would wipe that sinful city off the map. We believe the "sinful city" is an obvious reference to Las Vegas."

President Simmons searched the faces of those around the room, and then tuned his attention to Vice President Cairn. "Jim, what do have you to say about all this?"

Jim Cairn served on the Home Security Intelligence Committee, and in that capacity, worked closely with Secretary Perez. Al-Qaeda had been bragging about other bombs for months, but ever since Kaysan's testimony that there was no other bomb, everyone in the administration relaxed. He admitted that this was not the first time he had heard about the possibility of a second bomb.

"Mr. President, I don't have hard evidence there is a second bomb. Nevertheless our Intel indicates terrorists may indeed have a second bomb. Personally, I trust Secretary Perez's assessment. The Russians swore the terrorists only stole enough material for one bomb, and they claimed this incident was an isolated breach in their security procedures. In my experience, the more insistent the Russians are with their denials, the more likely it is that they are lying. Their record-keeping of nuclear materials is so poor that they would be unable to confirm exactly how much material went missing from any one of their depositories. In fact, last year the Germans intercepted plutonium on a train headed to the port of Lubeck and traced it back to a depository in Russia. The Chechen terrorists who stole it are now in a German prison and the plutonium is in NATO hands. I think the story of a second bomb has teeth."

President Simmons frowned.

"Jim, do you agree that this second bomb could be in Las Vegas?"
"Yes. If there is a second bomb, Las Vegas is the most logical place to look for it. Max's assessment is correct," Jim said, without emotion.

"Mr. Karl, you interviewed Kaysan Hashim several times and accompanied him from Afghanistan to the United States," the President said, looking down at his notes, "and sat with him as he testified before the Congressional hearings about the Minot bomb. At that time, Mr. Hashim testified there was but one bomb. Now, the same person tells Ambassador Crosby of a second bomb. For weeks now, al-Qaeda has tried to convince us that they have other bombs, yet we concluded their threat was mere posturing. I understand that Mr. Hashim is now under CIA protective custody in Kabul. How convinced are you . . . personally, I mean . . . that his information is credible?"

Mr. Karl cleared his throat.

"Mr. President, I believe this intelligence is accurate. Since renouncing al-Qaeda, Kaysan Hashim has been a reliable informant and a friend to America. He knows Qasid Sachem, the terrorist recently captured in a raid on an EMM cell in Aurum. Qasid was a member of the el-Mossel cell that assembled and transported the Minot bomb. After his capture, Qasid began bragging that he knew of a second bomb. Ambassador Crosby asked Kaysan to pretend to be a fellow prisoner and interview Qasid. After Bashar al-Fulani, the leader of the EMM cell in the Afghan mountains, left for Canada with the Minot bomb, Qasid joined another el-Mossel cell in Aurum. This is the cell that we now suspect transported a second bomb to America. When Kaysan interviewed him in the Ghurian jail, he correctly described an atomic bomb he claimed to have seen in Aurum. I think we should take this report seriously."

"So then, for now, let's accept as fact that we have a second bomb in Las Vegas, awaiting detonation instructions from al-Qaeda," President Simmons offered. "What can do we do about it?"

No one offered an answer. Finally, Max spoke up.

"Mr. President, we don't have many options. We could try to evacuate Las Vegas, but there are one-and-a-half million people in that area and a large-scale evacuation would be impracticable and would cause a citywide panic. Moreover, if we are wrong about the bomb being in Las Vegas and are unable to find it, the false alarm would play right into the terrorist's hands. They want to create panic so that Americans will turn against their government. It has been weeks since the last al-Qaeda threat expired, yet they have issued no further threats."

FBI Director Tommy Skylstad spoke. "The absence of recent threats means nothing. Al-Qaeda has not given up pursuing their goals. They are waiting for the right opportunity to act. They are incredibly patient."

CIA Director Anton Uzbek spoke next.

"Mr. President, I think it best to keep this information restricted to those in this room. I agree with Tommy, al-Qaeda is patient. They are waiting for the right opportunity to detonate the bomb, at a time when they can gain the maximum result. Fortunately, this will give us time to find the Las Vegas el-Mossel cell and disarm the bomb. If we let them know that we are aware of a second bomb, it might panic them into either going deeper undercover or prematurely detonating it."

The President agreed with Anton's counsel. It would be impractical to evacuate a city the size of Las Vegas, especially based on a presumption. And if they revealed that they knew of a second bomb in Las Vegas, the el-Mossel cell might panic and detonate it."

"We shall keep this information close to our vests, until we can find the bomb and disarm it," the President ordered. "No one is to leak anything said in this room: not to your staff, not to your friends, not to your colleagues, not even to your family. No matter how trusted your friends or family are, this information must remain top secret.

"Max, I am placing you in charge. Find the bomb and disarm it. You have top level priority and access to all government services and intelligence for this assignment. We will provide you with whatever you need. Anton, you and your department will do everything possible to assist Max, and Tommy will select a team of special agents and place them under Max's supervision. I will expect daily updates from Max. I cannot stress this enough; give Max your full cooperation and expect it will take time for his team to ferret out the bomb. Max and Tommy, tell your staffs only that we are looking for a suspected al-Qaeda terrorist cell in Las Vegas. Say nothing to anyone about an atom bomb. Mr. Karl, you have a top level security clearance, but can you personally assure me of your discretion in this matter?"

"Yes, of course Mr. President," Mr. Karl promised.

The President looked around at the others in the room. "If the media catches even a hint about a second bomb, I will know the leak came from one of you in this room, and it will not go well for the informant. Are there any questions?" There were none.

The President shook Max's hand. "Good luck Max, your country is depending on you."

CHAPTER TWENTY-FOUR:
THE SEARCH

Max and Tommy met with their respective staffs and outlined the plan to search for the al-Qaeda cell presumed to be somewhere in the Las Vegas area. Since the most experienced field agents worked for the FBI, Tommy chose his top investigator, FBI agent Alan Rollins, to organize and manage the search team. Tommy used a cover story about an al-Qaeda cell planning to blow up a Las Vegas casino. He told Alan and the local police department that they were conducting a search to find and arrest an al-Qaeda cell located somewhere in Las Vegas and to confiscate bomb-making materials. He ordered Alan's team to carry scintillation detectors and hinted the terrorists may have radioactive materials to construct a "dirty" bomb. He did not tell anyone the main purpose of the search was to find an atomic bomb. His strategy was to find the cell, arrest the members, and then send in a search team trained to find and defuse bombs. Homeland Security and the FBI had a history of close partnership and worked together on many cases. However, Alan thought it most unusual for the FBI director and the Homeland Security Secretary to lead this investigation. Trained to follow directions and not to ask questions, he accepted the assignment and began to assemble his team.

Max didn't have much information that he could share with Alan's team. He could only say that a Muslim terrorist cell from Afghanistan, the EMM, had recently infiltrated the country and was hiding in a safe house somewhere in the Las Vegas area. FBI Intel had confirmed the cell had arrived in Vera Cruz and since the American & Mexican border provided an opportunity for illegal entry, Alan assumed the terrorists had crossed over the border north of Vera Cruz and were hiding somewhere in Las Vegas. He theorized the cell must have an American contact, a citizen who rented an apartment and provided forged documentations such as passports, visas, driver's licenses, and work permits.

After the 9-11 attack, the feds declared all explosives as federally controlled substances. Federal law now required private citizens to obtain a permit before buying explosives, even in small quantities. Terrorists preferred to use plastic explosives for their bombs. Permits for such materials required an extensive background check and an involved permit process. It would be much easier and faster for terrorists to smuggle explosives across the border rather than go though the permit process. The border patrol recently caught illegals smuggling drugs and other contraband transported in small aircraft, ultralights that could elude radar and fly across the border at a few hundred feet. The border patrol had recently intercepted an ultralight carrying 300 pounds of plastic explosives. Confiscating such contraband was unusual. Smugglers profited hundreds of thousands of dollars from illegal drug traffic, yet since explosives had little street value and were dangerous to handle, they rarely accepted such shipments.

Alan interrogated a Mexican national recently caught smuggling Semtex across the Arizona border. Imprisoned in a jail outside Phoenix, he couldn't provide useful information. He claimed his contact was a man from Nogales, a Mr. Goleta, who hired him and promised ten-thousand dollars to fly plastic explosives from San Luis Rio to a small town outside Yuma. A Mr. Orin Jarkin would pay him for the contraband, on delivery. The Mexican government imprisoned Mr. Goleta in Nogales and charged him with smuggling arms, yet when Alan visited the Nogales police, they wouldn't share information about Mr. Goleta, although they did allow him to interrogate their prisoner. Alan strongly suspected that Mr. Goleta and Mr. Jarkin were involved in the plot to destroy a Las Vegas casino, yet without Mexican police cooperation, he had no leads to follow. Instead, he decided to focus his search for Mr. Jarkin in Vegas. No such person turned up in the FBI files or as a resident of Yuma or Las Vegas or surrounding towns.

Alan flew his FBI team to Las Vegas and established headquarters in a rented house in Henderson, where they began searching city records for recent rentals and new landline telephone connections. He reasoned the al-Qaeda cell would need to keep close communication with their leadership in Afghanistan and Iran and make extensive use of the internet and cell phones. Although recent laws enacted by the Administration required hotels and motels to register any guest who stayed over three days, the law did not apply to apartment or house rentals. Utility companies provided the best information about new rentals. The gas and electric and telephone companies kept installation records of all new customers. Internet providers kept customer lists, and cell phone companies recorded new customer activations. Federal law had made disposable cell phones illegal, so the search began with new cell phone and landline customers. Las Vegas was one of the fastest growing metropolitan areas in the country and the utility activation lists for the past three months produced thousands of new customers. Alan and his team narrowed the list down by cross-matching recent broadband internet service accounts, landline installations, and electric power connections. Cross-referencing narrowed the list down to a few hundred potential locations; after interviewing each new subscriber, Alan's team had not yet turned up a single solid suspect.

On the sixteenth day of this tedious investigation, their persistence paid off. Having exhausted the search in Las Vegas proper, the FBI expanded the search to include bordering communities and towns. A two-member FBI team began knocking on the doors of recent telephone and internet subscribers. At a Henderson apartment belonging to Mr. Hamad Gustoes, the team hit pay dirt. Mr. Gustoes had rented this apartment two months earlier and installed telephone and cable service that included broadband internet. No one answered the agent's knock on the apartment door, so they parked across the street and began surveillance. Over the next two days, several men and women came and went from the apartment: people whose dress and appearance suggested a Middle East origin. These folks wouldn't normally raise suspicion, but this apartment seemed unusually active.

Each night, a local Afghani eatery delivered take-out meals to the apartment. Judging from the amount of food, the agents assumed four or five people lived in that residence. Other evidence of a fundamental Muslim connection also surfaced. Several women dressed in burkas came and went from the apartment, several times each day. An FBI agent tailed two bearded men from the apartment to a local mosque well known for encouraging jihad. The FBI got a wiretap warrant and monitored the apartment phone line, cell phones, and cable internet activity. Most of the conversations were in Arabic or Farsi, and the calls were placed to people in Iran, Denmark, Afghanistan, and Pakistan. The conversations and e-mails seemed innocuous, consisting of talk about the World Cup soccer games, mutual friends, and details about life in the United States. Alan suspected a hidden code had been imbedded in the messages, yet his cryptographers in Washington couldn't uncover the hidden messages.

A judge issued a search warrant and on a Friday evening, twelve FBI agents and three CIA officers burst into the apartment. They found three men in the front room watching television and a woman in the kitchen cooking dinner. Their search uncovered two kilos of hashish hidden in a clothes hamper: reason enough to arrest all four occupants. An unmade bed in a third bedroom suggested a fourth man possibly lived there. Nothing in the apartment suggested a terrorist plot, so the police could only file drug possession charges. One of the arrested men held an expired student visa. The other two men carried forged Egyptian passports. They released the woman. She had a valid green card, claimed the men hired her as a housekeeper, and she did not live in the apartment. The three suspects refused to cooperate with Alan's interrogation and the two Egyptians especially aroused his suspicion. Both men stood over six feet tall, were dressed in Arab attire, and had full black beards. One man closely resembled the only picture the CIA had of Passhia bin-Alaheim: a blurry yearbook picture taken when he was a professor at the University of Cairo. The man identified as Professor bin-Alaheim in the yearbook photo had a crescent-shaped scar on his forehead and the man in custody also had that same scar. He matched the general description on an FBI warrant for Passhia, the only surviving member of the Minot terrorists. However, the suspect's prints only partially matched the FBI and Interpol database files. All the same, the lack of a definitive fingerprint match did not dissuade Alan. His gut told him this man was indeed Passhia, the alleged leader of EMM operations in North America. Alan needed confirmation of this man's identity, so he called Mr. Karl.

"I want you to go to Minot and bring Keith Justin here to Las Vegas to help identify one of our terrorist suspects," he told Mr. Karl. "We arrested three alleged terrorists and I think one of them may be the infamous Passhia. They are not cooperating and Keith is the only person who can identify one of these men as Passhia, the sixth Minot terrorist."

Mr. Karl contacted Nora, who told him Keith was in California attending the University of California in Santa Cruz. Airline travel had resumed on a limited basis, so he promised Alan he would travel to California the next day and bring Keith to Las Vegas, to identify Passhia.

Alan reported the results of the apartment raid to Max, who then, so as not to arouse undue suspicion, went alone to the apartment with a Geiger counter. He found no signs of radioactivity that would indicate enriched uranium or plutonium was ever in the apartment. Climbing onto the flat roof, he discovered a mast and antenna intended for long-distance communications. Following the cable down the side of the building, he noted where it entered the apartment and then called Alan's team back to the apartment for a more thorough search. They discovered a small room hidden behind a large wardrobe. In the room, they found three UHF transceivers, a CB home base transceiver, and an amateur radio station, complete with an illegal linear amplifier intended to boost the station's power to a kilowatt. The Call sign of the station had been issued to Mr. Orin Jarkin, the same man involved in the delivery of Semtex to Yuma. The FBI issued an "all points" bulletin for the arrest of the mysterious Mr. Jarkin.

Tearing out a back bedroom closet wall, they found two dozen weapons, ranging from several Uzis to various rifles, grenades, and handguns, with several boxes of ammunition. They also found twenty bricks of Semtex explosive, enough to build a moderate-sized bomb. A backpack hidden in a closet contained detonation caps and timing electronics. They recovered a dozen bulletproof vests and blueprints for the Federal Building in downtown Las Vegas. The CIA also confiscated three computers, two satellite telephones, and several cell phones from the apartment.

That same day al-Qaeda dropped the other shoe. Reuter's news service received a videotape from the top al-Qaeda leader, Said bin-Patina. Patina spoke from his headquarters in Yemen and threatened that if we didn't meet his list of demands, he would direct his EMM operatives in America to explode an atomic bomb in some unnamed city. Those demands included immediate withdrawal of all U.S. forces in Iraq and Afghanistan; the release of all prisoners of war held by the U.S.; abrogation of the U.S. & Israel defense pact; condemnation of Israel for destroying the Iranian nuclear enrichment plant in Zanjan; abrogation of the U.S. Defense Treaty with

Israel; and a payment of one hundred billion dollars, to al-Qaeda. Patina gave the U.S. government ten days to comply, or he would command one of his sleeper cells to detonate their bomb. If the demands were still not met, other atom bomb explosions would soon follow.

The Administration initially dismissed Patina's threat as nothing more than the usual terrorist posturing. The U.S. government routinely dismissed threats from al-Qaeda or EMM leaders as blustering or outright hoaxes. Over the years, the al-Qaeda organization grew weaker, while their EMM arm gained strength. Convinced that neither al-Qaeda nor the EMM had more atom bombs, Homeland Security and the FBI assumed the latest threat was just another in a long line of worn-out scare tactics from a defeated, ragtag band of terrorists desperately seeking attention.

However, President Simmons, Jim Cairn, Tommy Skylstad, Anton Uzbek, and Max Perez took the latest threats seriously. Aware of a second bomb, they alone knew this threat was much more than normal saber-rattling by al-Qaeda leaders. Anton Uzbek suggested Max should seek help from the Las Vegas police, a request that Secretary Max advised against. Involving the local police would certainly alert the media and raise suspicions. If the press connected the raid in Henderson with the recent al-Qaeda threat of an atomic bomb hidden somewhere in the U.S.A., a citywide panic could follow.

The FBI examined the contents of the computers confiscated from Mr. Gustoes' apartment. They found nothing on the hard drive that could be considered incriminating, only a series of innocent-looking digital pictures taken at Lake Mead. They showed the photographs to Mr. Karl, and one picture immediately caught his attention. It featured a yacht: a large Chris Craft moored at Sandy Point on Lake Mead. The name painted on the transom was *"el-Helmand"*. Mr. Karl immediately remembered el-Helmand as the name of a major river and province in Afghanistan. This was more than a coincidence. A search of registration records showed the boat belonged to a Mr. Orin Jarkan, a wealthy Las Vegas importer from Karachi, and a Pakistani national.

Max asked a computer expert to further examine the computer picture for hidden messages, and his hunch paid off. An examination of individual pixels on the picture found an embedded message containing a report from Moesha Hashim to al-Qaeda, in Yemen. In the report, he bragged about his successful mission to transport the bomb from Aurum to Las Vegas, where he met with the EMM leader in North America, Passhia bin-Alaheim, a former professor at Cairo University. The report embedded in the picture also detailed Moesha Hashim's transport of the bomb from Aurum to Las Vegas:

"One month after Bashar and his el-Mossel companions sailed for Canada, I and five of my EMM comrades left Aurum, with a partly assembled atom bomb, and drove to the Iranian port city of Bandar-e-Abbus. There we boarded an Iranian fishing trawler to Djibouti and then took a Lebanese registered freighter from Djibouti through the Suez Canal and into the Mediterranean, where we stopped at the port of Benghazi. We then sailed passed Gibraltar and across the Atlantic, to the port of Vera Cruz, Mexico. The atomic bomb traveled inside two 3-foot by 4-foot tarp-covered crates, stored in the ship's hold. The Mexican authorities in Vera Cruz examined my papers but didn't bother to inspect the crates; thus, we had no trouble offloading them onto a rented pickup truck and then driving to the U.S. border at Laredo, Texas. I presented the Laredo Customs officers with a copy of the manifest, claiming the crates contained a shipment of Persian rugs. A U.S. customs inspector climbed into the bed of the pick-up, threw off the canvas tarp covering the two crates, and ordered me to pry open the second of the two crates. I did as ordered, and the customs officer dug into the crate. Finding nothing but Persian Rugs as the manifest claimed, he lifted several layers of rugs by their edges, but neglected to take any of the rugs out of the crate. Finding nothing suspicious, he allowed me to nail the cover back on the crate. Had the inspector been more thorough, he would have discovered there was much more than rugs in these crates. We crossed into the United States and drove west to Las Vegas, where we met with Passhia."

Nothing in the decrypted picture pointed out where in Las Vegas Moesha intended to store the crates, or described the al-Qaeda cell location. Max was faced with hard evidence that somewhere in this city, an atomic bomb waited for terrorists to explode it. He decided to ask for help from the Las Vegas police. He knew involving the local police represented a calculated risk, but Las Vegas was too large an area to search without their assistance.

He told the police that they had credible Intel about a terrorist cell hiding in their city, but said nothing about a bomb.

Like flies annoying a horse, reporters buzzed around police headquarters 24/7 and monitored police scanners, ready to pounce on the latest scoop. The ever-vigilant media would jump on a bomb story like ticks on a dog, and the last thing Max wanted was to have some snoopy reporter nosing around and asking sensitive questions. And now that the threat was imminent, Max knew he was running out of time. He made his request for help to the Police Commissioner, who immediately agreed to assign two dozen investigators to the search.

That morning, Alan picked up Mr. Karl and Keith at the McCarran Airport and drove them to a nondescript motel on the outskirts of the strip. In the morning, he accompanied them to the downtown Las Vegas FBI headquarters and took Keith into the lineup room where they waited as six bearded men took their places in the lineup.

Keith wasted no time in identifying Passhia. "He's the second man from the left."

"Are you sure?" Alan asked.

"Yes, I am certain. The second man from the left with the scar on his forehead is the one Bashar called Passhia."

Alan escorted the handcuffed Passhia to the interrogation room and sat him down in a chair across the table from Max. Keith and Alan observed from behind the one-way mirror.

Max leaned across the table, and placed the yearbook picture in front of the suspect. "We know who you are. You are Passhia bin-Alaheim, the professor in this picture."

"You are mistaken. I am not that man," Passhia insisted. After his denial, he sat stone-faced and unresponsive to further questioning; his lips moved silently as if in prayer.

Max motioned to the mirror and mouthed, "Bring Keith in."

Keith and Alan joined Max at the table. Passhia glanced at the boy, but said nothing.

"Max leaned across the table. "This is Keith Justin, the boy who disarmed the bomb in Minot. He had identified you as the man with the terrorists on the Minot farm. We know that you smuggled another atom bomb into our country. Keith has identified you as one of the Minot terrorists, and we know you are the head of the EMM in North America and recently made a trip to Aurum, where this latest bomb originated."

Passhia showed no sign of emotion. However, Alan almost fell off his chair. Up to this point, he believed the terrorists planned to bomb a Las Vegas casino with Semtex. This was the first he had heard of an atom bomb. He tried to hide his shock.

"We want to know the bomb's location, and you are going to tell us where it is" Alan insisted.

Passhia looked at Keith and an arrogant smile crossed his face.

"So then, this is the brat from Minot."

Keith looked hard at Passhia.

"I remember you. You were in my barn with your terrorist friends. They called you Passhia. You stole our truck and drove away. Your friends thought you were a coward."

Passhia's arrogant smile faded, and he looked away from Keith.

"Tell us about the bomb," Max repeated.

The evil smirk returned on Passhia's face. "I will tell you infidels nothing."

"Where are Moesha and his companions," Alan demanded.

Passhia looked at his hands and remained silent.

"You are a coward, no better than a dog," Keith said. "You condemned your friends to die and escaped in our truck."

Passhia glared at Keith. Hatred contorted his face. The child had hurled the ultimate insult by calling him a dog. There was no worse insult than calling a Muslim man a dog or a pig.

Passhia spit at Keith and tried to reach across the table. "You are nothing but a little spoiled brat."

"Alan, please take Keith outside," Max said. When Keith had left the room, Max initiated plan B.

"Enough of this nonsense, we do not have time for your games," Max said as he hit a button on the table. Seconds later, a nurse and doctor entered the room.

They rolled up Passhia's left shirtsleeve and injected him with a hypodermic syringe.

It only took a few seconds for the sodium pentothal to take effect.

Max demanded an answer to his question. "Where is the bomb?"

Passhia mumbled something in Arabic.

"In English," Alan insisted.

Passhia's speech became slurred. "Go to hell you infidel bastard."

Alan slapped the picture of the *el-Helmand* yacht on the table in front of him. "Your friends are on this boat . . . do they have the bomb with them?"

Passhia said nothing but could not contain his surprise when he saw the photograph.

"Do you know Mr. Jarkin?"

"He is a friend," Passhia mumbled.

Alan repeated his question, "Where is the bomb?"
Passhia struggled to remain silent; even so, the Pentothal began to have an effect.

"It's with Moesha . . . on the boat," Passhia groggily whispered.

Alan pressed on. "On the boat, the one in this picture?"

Passhia nodded.

Max had heard enough. He left the room and gathered a swat team in the briefing room, only explaining that they were going to Lake Mead to arrest terrorists. Mr. Karl, Alan, Max, and a six-member CIA swat team drove out to Sandy Point, in three black SUV's.

Docked at the end of the nearest pier, a 40-foot yacht, the *el-Helmand,* prepared to cast off. The swat team ran out onto the dock and boarded the vessel. Orin Jarkin and his two companions were taken by surprise as the team crashed into the wheelhouse. Although the suspected terrorists were armed, no one resisted arrest.

Orin Jarkin, short and portly, with neatly trimmed gray beard, stepped away from the wheel. Wearing a captain's hat and dressed in a loud Hawaiian shirt, he didn't appear formidable: more like someone on holiday rather than a Middle-East terrorist bent on blowing himself and an entire city into dust.

Mr. Karl handcuffed Orin and demanded to know who else was on board. Orin smiled, one of those self-assured smug smiles that made Mr. Karl want to slap the man. Again, he repeated his question, and Orin hacked up spittle and aimed it at Mr. Karl, but the phlegm ended on his jacket rather than his face. Mr. Karl raised his arm as if to strike Orin, but Alan grabbed it and prevented him from doing so.

"That will solve nothing," he chided. Then he put his face three inches from Orin's.

"Where are Moesha and the others?"

"They have gone."

"Gone . . . gone where, and when did they go?"

"They left hours ago," Orin hissed.

"Where did they go?"

Orin looked out the window and did not answer.

"We have captured your friend, Passhia, and he told us about your boat and the bomb," Alan said. "Your plan is falling apart."

For an instant, Mr. Jarkin looked startled, and then the arrogant smile returned.

"Where is the bomb?"

"What bomb?" Orin spat out.

"Where were you going with this boat?"

His smile faded, "Out to fish."

"The pictures," Mr. Karl reminded Alan.

Sounding annoyed, Alan asked, "What about them?"

"One of the pictures is of Hoover Dam. That is where the boat was heading. Not only do they want to destroy Las Vegas, but they also want to take out Hoover Dam. Should they breach the dam, imagine the downriver property damage, the loss of life, and the destruction of a major power generation plant. It would be a disaster of biblical proportions."

"Enough of this," Max said, facing Alan. "The bomb is somewhere on this boat."

Max turned on his handheld Geiger counter and climbed down the narrow stairs leading below deck, followed by Mr. Karl and Alan. At the bottom of the stairs, the Geiger counter alarm sounded. Although plutonium is extremely radioactive, a thin layer of lead will safely stop most of the high-energy emissions; yet, the Geiger counter meter signaled a nearby source of radioactive material. Led by increasing meter readings and the device's frantic beeping, Max slowly walked toward the stern, finally stopping in front of the last stateroom door. Alan took the safety off his gun, smashed the locked door open, and cautiously entered the stateroom, with Mr. Karl and Max close behind. The stateroom beds had been pushed to one side, to make room for a three-by-four-foot crate. Max pried the cover off the crate and dug through a layer of packing material. A black sphere the size of a soccer ball, held in place by webbing tied to a PVC birdcage, emerged from under the material.

A closed laptop computer rested on one of the beds, and a cable connected it to a small black box inside the crate. Several wires led from the black box to lumps of Semtex attached around the sphere. Alan cautiously opened the computer and when he did so, the laptop screen sprang to life. Tropical fish swam across the screen and a box in the center of the display depicted a digital clock counting down toward zero. The clock read three hours, twenty-three minutes, and five seconds. When the clock reached zero, Hoover Dam, Las Vegas, and much of the surrounding area would be history. Alan debated a way he could disarm the bomb, without accidentally triggering it. He was not a bomb expert but knew he could not simply shut off the computer or cut some wires, for any wrong action on his part could detonate the bomb. He picked up his transceiver and asked for the team member familiar with bomb disarmament to come down to the stateroom. Bill Peters was longtime FBI field agent and an expert on atomic weapons and bombs. So far, no one had said a word about an atomic bomb, yet when Bill peered inside the crate, he immediately recognized the device.

He let out a long low whistle. "It's a fully-armed atom bomb, set to go off in fewer than three and a half hours."

Alan said, "We know that. Can you disarm it?"

Bill examined the bomb's construction. He recognized the design came from a popular web site, one that anyone could download from the internet. It was a simple but effective design. Bill sighed and looked at Alan. "It's a 10-15 kiloton plutonium bomb. If it explodes it will take out the dam and much of Las Vegas."

Max added, "We understand that. Can you disarm it?"

Bill examined the various wire connections and carefully opened the lid on the black box. Inside, a battery and circuit boards with flashing red LED lights signaled a fully-armed bomb.

"I don't think I can. It is most likely booby-trapped and it would be dangerous to mess around with any part of it," he warned. "The bomb is wired in such a way that if I cut any wire out of sequence or tamper with the clock or the computer, it will probably automatically detonate. To disarm the bomb without triggering it, I have to talk with the person who armed this bomb."

Max turned to Alan. "Find the maniac who armed this bomb and bring him here."

Alan stared at Max as if he was insane.

"That's impossible. We know who this guy is, but not where he is. He armed the bomb and then drove away as fast as possible. It may take hours or even days to find him."

Bill ignored Alan's objection and turned his attention to the clock display running on the laptop computer. He clicked on the clock display and the screen maximized the Windows clock menu. The clock was counting down from an initial setting of seven hours. Three hours, twenty-one minutes, and eighteen seconds remained.

"Why not just change the clock to count down from a larger number?" Alan suggested.

"I'm afraid if I change any of the settings, the program may reset the clock to zero, in which case the bomb will explode."

"Well then, just cut the main wire leading from the detonator printed circuit board to the battery."

Bill pointed to the PC board. "See these relays and the small 9 volt battery soldered to the PC board? The relays are engaged. If I cut or disconnect any wire in the wrong sequence, the bomb will detonate."
Mr. Karl, who until now had stayed out of the way, stepped forward to have a closer look at the bomb.

"Then turn the damn computer off," he advised.

"That will detonate the bomb for certain," Bill warned. "I have to talk with the person who wired this bomb. Without his help, anything I do is likely to detonate it."

The clock read three hours, nineteen minutes, five seconds.

Max turned to Alan. "The clock is counting down as we argue. Find the damn terrorist who armed this bomb."

Alan looked defeated. "You expect me to find him and bring him here within three hours? We don't have the slightest idea where he is. He drove away from here with his friends as fast as his van would take him. There is no way to find him and bring him here in fewer than three hours. It's not going to happen."

Bill stood and faced Alan.

"Well then, that being the case, we only have two options. I can make an educated guess about which wires to cut and in what sequence, or I can try to alter the computer clock. However, either action will probably detonate the bomb, blowing us, the dam, and most of Las Vegas to kingdom come. The third choice, which I think you should reconsider, is to find the maniac who armed this bomb and force him to tell me how to disarm it before the computer counts down to zero."

The first two choices were unacceptable. Alan knew Bill was right. Messing with the device in any way would detonate it. They would have to find Moesha and his companions, bring them here and then force him to help disarm the bomb. How could he do this in less than three hours?

Max pondered the problem.

"The computer countdown clock has been running for the past three-and-a-half hours, and by now, the terrorists will be no more than 250 miles from Las Vegas," he reasoned. "They activated the bomb and are trying to get as far away as their van can take them before it detonates and takes most of Southern Nevada with it. Have the highway patrol set up roadblocks within 250 miles of Vegas. If they can capture the terrorists, a helicopter could bring them here within minutes. Pray that we can do this before the bomb goes off."

Alan contacted the State Highway Patrol on his transceiver. With only a three-hour head start, he assumed the terrorist van would be no more than 250 miles from Las Vegas, yet in which direction? They could have taken either the Interstate 15 heading north toward Salt Lake City, or west to Los Angeles, or driven south on U.S. 93 to Kingman and then continued east on Interstate 40. Mr. Karl pointed out the terrorists could also be heading north toward Reno, on U.S. 95.

Alan ordered the highway patrol to form roadblocks on each of those highways: one-hundred, two-hundred and three-hundred miles from Las Vegas. They had entered the country from Mexico, so he presumed they might try to cross back into Mexico near Las Cruxes. He directed the highway patrol to concentrate on Interstate 40, west of Albuquerque. His hunch paid off. The gray van, carrying four men, tried to run the state police roadblock near Gallup, New Mexico. In the shoot-out that followed, the police killed two of the four gunmen and captured two others. The FBI identified one of the captured men as Moesha Hashim and the other as Salaam Al-Mansur. Both men were on the FBI's list of most wanted terrorists. They loaded the struggling Moesha and Salaam into a waiting helicopter and flew them across Arizona to Lake Mead. Alan and Max were waiting at dockside, when the helicopter landed fifty minutes later.

The bomb clock now read under 45 minutes.

Handcuffed, Moesha struggled in the arms of the two FBI agents, who dragged him on board the *el-Helmand.* Max and Alan followed, dragging Salaam with them. Moesha cursed and swore at the FBI agents as they forced him below deck and pushed him and Salaam into the aft stateroom. Both terrorists fell to the floor in front of the crate. Alan helped Moesha to his feet. He stared at the computer as the clock continued its countdown to zero. Salaam remained on the floor, until Mr. Karl helped him to his feet. Max spoke to the visibly shaken terrorists.

"We need your help to defuse this bomb," Alan began. "In exactly 40 minutes, the bomb will vaporize us and destroy much of Las Vegas, killing thousands, perhaps tens of thousands of innocent people—and for what? Hate, vengeance, notoriety? It is all so insane."

Moesha said nothing in response, and then spat into Max's face.

Max wiped the spittle from his cheek and tried again. "Are you prepared to die? Unless you help us disarm the bomb, we will all die . . . he looked at the clock . . . in just 39 minutes."

A wicked smile grew across Moesha's face, as Max's words sunk in. "Yes, I am prepared to die, if such is Allah's will."

Bill confronted Salaam. "Are you also willing to die? Is this Allah's will? If you do not help me disarm the bomb, you will surely die."

"I don't know how to disarm it," the terrorist said, visibly shaken. Alan knew this was a lie. While the terrorists were on the helicopter, he used his laptop to search the FBI files for information on both captives. Salaam had graduated from the University of Paris, with a degree in Computer Science and Electrical Engineering, and worked two years in French Nuclear Power plants. He would be the one who had wired the bomb and programmed the computer.

Max picked up a copy of the Qur'an and held it in front of Salaam's face. Salaam stared at him, and then his gaze focused on the book.

Max opened the Qur'an to a marked page and asked him to read the passage in Arabic out loud. The passage rebuked believers to not harm innocent women and children, even when fighting a Jihad.

After Salaam read the passage, Max challenged both men.

"Do you not believe the Prophet's own words in your holy book?" The self-righteous smile faded from Moesha's face, but he remained impassive. Salaam's composure melted and he began to shake. Max realized he had hit a nerve with Salaam, so he pressed on.

"Do you not realize that Allah will never forgive you for what you are doing? He will condemn you and your followers to the fires of Hell for all eternity."

Salaam's voice was barely a whisper. "No, Allah will reward us in heaven," he insisted.

"He will not. Don't you believe what we read in your holy book? Allah will not reward you for such an evil act . . . . an act that he condemns through his messenger Muhammad. No, Allah will send you to Hell forever for this terrible sin."

Salaam looked away from Max and stared at the crate. He looked confused and perplexed. Max's words were having an impact, but only on Salaam. Moesha only stood impassively and smirked.

Max continued to speak directly to Salaam. "There will be no virgins waiting for you in heaven. Soon you and your friend will burn in Hell." He lit a match and held it under Salaam's extended hand as Alan forced his hand to remain over the lit match. Salaam tried to withdraw his hand, but Alan held it over the match.

Max continued, "I understand the pain of Hell is horrible, and it will never, ever end." Salaam winced in pain as he looked again at the computer screen.

"Fewer than thirty-five minutes to Hell," Max taunted.

Moesha looked at Max. "You Christians do not understand the Qur'an. We are fighting a holy war, a Jihad commanded by Allah. The Qur'an justifies our mission."

"Oh, quite the contrary," Max argued. "I do understand your holy book. I spent two years in Saudi Arabia studying Arabic and the Qur'an. Our Imam taught us all about Muhammad's commandments, and how the Prophet urged believers against killing innocents and condemned suicide. I understand the Prophets words, they are clear. Allah does not tolerate killing innocent women and children. He has clearly forbidden what you are about to do. Such action will not please Allah. You will not have a reward in heaven. Allah will condemn you to Hell for this senseless act."

Since he was a child, the thought of Hell had terrified Salaam. The match continued to burn his hand and the pain in his palm grew intensive. Would Allah send him to Hell for this act? No, Passhia had assured him that Allah would reward him. Today, he would be in heaven, would he not? Thoroughly confused, Salaam's forehead furrowed as the pain in his palm grew intolerable.

"Stop", he finally screamed. Max blew out the match. "Show me the words," Salaam asked. Max opened the book to the marked page, and held the holy book so Salaam could read the passage. His finger slowly traced the Prophet's admonition in Arabic from right to left and his hand began to shake.

Tears streamed down Salaam's face. After some time, he spoke. "You are correct, that is what Allah has commanded."

"Then help us while there is still time," Max pleaded. "Allah forgives those who repent."

"Don't listen to those blasphemers, they are liars." Moesha hissed. We have seventy virgins waiting for us in heaven."

Max smiled and said sarcastically, "With all the fundamental Islamic suicides over the past years, I'm afraid heaven long ago ran out of Moslem virgins."

The clock read 33 minutes.

Salaam knelt down beside the bomb and gently fingered the various wires leading from the printed circuit board to the computer, batteries, and detonator caps.

"Salaam, get away from the bomb," Moesha hissed.

"Cut the blue wire first," Salaam ordered Bill.

"Wait, he could be lying," Mr. Karl warned. "Perhaps it is the red wire you should cut first. It is always the red wire."

Bill looked at Alan who nodded. It was no time to second-guess the instructions of the frightened terrorist. Bill shrugged his shoulders and cut the blue wire. The instant he severed the wire, the computer started beeping and the clock quickened its countdown. Thirty minutes, twenty-five, and then twenty. The clock counted down even faster and the beeps increased their cadence. Nineteen, sixteen, thirteen . . .

"Now, cut the yellow wire . . . quickly," Salaam said.
Bill cut the yellow wire, but the clock continued its interminable countdown. Twelve, ten, nine, eight . . . The beeps merged into a constant scream. Seven, six, five . . .

"Now cut the red wire leading from the battery to the printed circuit board," Salaam ordered.

With a shaking hand, Bill cut the red wire. The clock continued to count down. Max's eyes grew wide when he realized the clock had not stopped and continued to wind down to zero.

Four, three, two, one, and then the clock read 00.00.00. The beeping stopped.

Moesha closed his eyes and his lips continued to move in silent prayer. Everyone held their breath. Seconds went by, before Max looked at Bill and realized that they were both still alive.

The bomb had not exploded.

CHAPTER TWENTY-FIVE:
THE FATWAH

Friendless and abandoned by his comrades, Qasid Sachem sat alone and brooded in his dark, dank Afghanistan prison cell. He had suffered for four, long years in this Ghurian hellhole; part of a life sentence handed down by a U.S. military tribunal. Over the past year, his anguish and determination to escape intensified, until it filled his every waking moment. In his mind, his trial had been a sham. His conviction, based on the testimony of Kaysan Hashim, a former friend and paid informant of the Americans, was fabricated. The court had failed to prove the allegation that he had killed two UN soldiers in a Kandahar gun battle. His court-appointed lawyer, a shave-tail second lieutenant with a newly earned law degree, presented a superficial and inept defense. The Kandahar witnesses testifying against him lied, and so did the Kandahar officers who arrested him. The tribunal sentenced him to life, meaning that he would most likely die in this stinking prison, a punishment worse than death. His captors expected he would never again see the outside world, but he would prove them wrong.

Qasid was a brute and a lout, but not dim-witted. While in prison, he attended English classes and learned to read American newspapers. He read about the power outage in America and the failed al-Qaeda attack in Minot. He fumed over Bashar's botched mission and seethed over the newspaper reports that a boy had thwarted the plot to destroy an American city. A brat called Keith Dexter had done this. He read that in Las Vegas, the same boy had identified Passhia bin-Alaheim, and by doing so, helped the FBI to find and disarm the second atom bomb. It was humiliating that a mere child had ruined both carefully orchestrated plots. Al-Qaeda declared a *fatwa* against the Dexter boy, and Qasid appointed himself to carry out their judgment. But first, he would have to escape from Ghurian.

Qasid devised an escape plan, yet one that depended on an outsider's help. Unfortunately, he had no friends, either inside or outside the prison. Kaysan had been his only visitor in all these years, and that lying traitor would never agree to help him. None of his so called friends or relatives in Kandahar and Farah had even so much as sent him a letter. He was dead to these people. If he could get a message to his companions in the Arum EMM cell, someone from that cell would help him. Perhaps Sabur Hussein, the EMM member who did not go with Bashar to America, would help him. After Bashar left for America, he fled to Aurum and was now an important leader in al-Qaeda. Sabur would help him escape. Or possibly, Safid Tondi, a friend of Kaysan's cousin, Moesha, from Terkite, would help. Yet without visitors, there was no way to smuggle a note to either Sabur or Safid. Isolated and friendless, Qasid pondered some means to contact them. If only someone would come to visit him, though he knew there were no prospects for a visitor.

Perhaps he could get a message out through another prisoner, but he had isolated himself and made no friends while in Ghurian, at least no one close enough to ask for such a favor. His reputation as an unpleasant, sullen, and ill-tempered fanatic encouraged the other prisoners to shun him. Those in Ghurian, guards as well as prisoners, avoided Qasid. Fellow prisoner, Nursal Furdusi, was an exception. He alone ignored the admonitions of other prisoners and occasionally shared a meal with Qasid in the dining hall. He knew that Nursal often received visitors, and perhaps he could persuade him to ask one of his visitors to smuggle a message out to his cousin Moesha. But first, he would have to form a bond with Nursal. For the next several weeks, this became his primary goal.

One evening, Qasid sat alone at a table in the dining hall. He searched the hall for his dining companion, but Nursal wasn't at any of the tables. Minutes later, Nursal walked into the hall, and after filling his tray, searched for an empty seat. Qasid stood, motioned to Nursal, and pointed to his empty table. Nursal recognized Qasid and sat down with him.

"I am late for dinner," he explained. "I had visitors."

Qasid's interest perked at this news. "Who were your visitors?"

"My cousin from Farah," Nursal said.

That is perfect, Qasid thought. Nursal has a friend in Farah who visits him.

Over the next few weeks, Qasid worked hard at bonding with Nursal. They exercised together in the compound yard, prayed together in the prison mosque, and ate together during evening meals. Bit by bit, Nursal began to share his life story with Qasid and Qasid shared his own story with Nursal. His new friend had served four of his five year sentence in Ghurian prison. Caught attending an al-Qaeda meeting in Mazar-e-Sharif, the military court convicted him of subversive activities and sentenced him to serve five years in prison. Five years for attending a meeting! Over the intervening years, Nursal had grown increasingly embittered toward his captors. On the fourth anniversary of his imprisonment, he filled a jar with 365 pinto beans and placed it on a shelf in his cell. Each bean represented one day remaining in Ghurian, and each evening before prayer, he would remove a single bean from the jar and throw it out the window of his cell. Once, when Qasid visited him in his cell, Nursal took the jar from the shelf and handed it to Qasid.

"When this jar is empty," he beamed, "I'll return to Farah and join with my al-Qaeda compatriots to pursue the jihad against America."

Qasid examined the jar and noted that it was only half-full. He almost leaped for joy, for his new friend would soon be free. He couldn't have found a more cooperative and loyal companion than Nursal, and for six months, he groomed his friendship and counted the days when Nursal would be set free. When the beans in Nursal's jar dwindled to only a hand full, Qasid made his move.

"Nursal . . . I have a plan to escape this hellhole, but I need your help," Qasid pleaded. "I have a friend in Terkite, Safid Tondi, who will help me carry out my escape plan. However, Safid has never visited me here in Ghurian, and I do not know why this is. Perhaps he is afraid to do so. If you could send a message to him in Terkite and ask him to pay me a visit, I'm sure he would do it. Allah will reward you if you can do this for me . . . of that you can be assured."

Nursal looked perplexed. "Qasid, I don't know. My release from prison is conditional, and for two years, I will be on strict probation. The police will watch me and know of my every move. If the Americans or Afghan police see me associating with any questionable characters or suspected al-Qaeda members, they will send me back to prison for another five years. I cannot risk what you ask of me. I will die in this place if they sentence me to another five years. I cannot do this, not even for a trusted friend such as you."

"Safid is not al-Qaeda, he is EMM," Qasid pleaded. "I don't think the Americans are aware of his terrorist affiliations. All I want you to do is to deliver a message to him. You don't even have to take it to him; just see that he gets this poem."

Nursal remained hesitant. "I have never heard of the EMM. The prison guards will thoroughly search me before I am released. Should they find a message on me, they will certainly throw me back in prison."

Qasid placed his hand on Nursal's shoulder.

"Do not worry my friend. A poem I will write, using certain verses from the Qur'an, will disguise my message. A cipher well-known to EMM members will allow Safid to decode my message from the Qur'an. In this way, all you need to do is see to it that he receives the poem and let him know that it is from me. He will know that my poem hides a message. The EMM often used this means of hiding communications. It is a risk free plan." Nursal considered the proposal for a few moments, and then reluctantly agreed. Qasid breathed a sign of relief. His plan now stood a chance of success.

As promised, when Nursal processed out of jail, he carried Qasid's poem with him, sequestered in a copy of the Qur'an. As expected, when the guards searched him they found the poem in the book, but it seemed innocuous so they returned it to him. Qasid knew Safid would recognize the coded prose and decipher it. The message detailed Qsaid's escape plan and Safid's expected part in it. As soon as Nursal arrived in Kandahar, he mailed the poem to Safid in Terkite and named Qasid as the author.

Weeks later, Safid visited Qasid in Ghurian prison. In hushed tones, they discussed the escape plan. Safid was to make several more visits and each time, bring along books, many books, each with pages 100-300 treated with a liquid explosive.

On the first day of Ramadan, while most of the prisoners were at prayer and the guards at dinner, Qasid carefully cut the treated pages from a dozen books, crumpled them and stuffed them inside a jar placed next to his cell door. Using his mattress for protection, he lit the fuse and cowered in the far corner of his cell. The resulting explosion blew the cell door off its hinges and flung it across the hallway, where it crashed against a cell across the hall. Smoke filled the hall and the only guard on duty rushed to the scene of the explosion. Qasid grabbed the guard and slit his throat with a knife he had fashioned from a bone. Knowing the explosion would alert other guards, he worked quickly, dressing himself in the guard's uniform and rolling the naked body under his cot. He took the guard's keys, unlocked the cell block door, and hid in a dark alcove in the main hall. A minute later, six guards came rushing in from the dining hall. He waited until they had passed, made his way down the hall to the exercise yard, and climbed to the top of the outer wall, where he found a pair of wire cutters heaved there by Safid. A car with its motor running waited below. He cut a hole in the barbed wire, climbed down to the street and got into Safid's car. They sped off into the night and drove to Farah. Qasid hid for several days in a secret room in the home of Safid's friend, Ahmid. As expected, the Afghanistan police searched all the towns between Ghurian, and Farah, including Ahmid's home. They even searched Safid's home in Terkite, yet found nothing.

Qasid hid out in Farah for a month. When he was sure the Afghanistan police had tired of searching for him, he traveled to the EMM cell in Anar Darrah and hid in the basement of an EMM member. Two days later, the homeowner told him to travel alone to Safid's home, in Terkite. Qasid left on foot the next night and under a full moon, walked the ten kilometers to Safid's house in Terkite, arriving just after midnight.

Safid greeted Qasid and ushered him into a dimly lit room in the back of his mud-brick house. A dozen bearded men sipped steaming cups of sweet tea and sat cross-legged on the dirt floor around a low round table. They suspiciously eyed Qasid as he entered the room. Safid introduced him and urged him to take a seat. A man dressed in a black robe and afghan hat was the first to speak.

"What is your business with us?"

Qasid turned toward the speaker, whose full black beard streaked with gray and dignified mannerism labeled him as someone of importance. The man did not introduce himself, so Qasid decided to call him Graybeard.

"I have come on a mission of retribution. Allah has commanded me to fulfill a fatwa." Qasid examined the face of each man around the room, but not one person showed any sign of reaction to his statement. He continued . . .

"My plan is carry out the execution decree for Keith Justin, the brat who is behind our failed bomb plans in America."

Those around the table continued to stare at him except for Graybeard, who gazed into his cup of tea.

Finally Graybeard put down the cup, looked at Qasid and squinted.

"And exactly how do you propose to do this?"

Qasid met the speaker's steel gaze. "With Allah's help, I will travel to Canada, cross over the border into the United States near Vancouver, and then find my way to California. Justin is studying at the University of California in Santa Cruz. There I will find him and kill him."

"And what to you wish of us?" Graybeard asked.

"Money and papers for my mission."

Safid smiled and nodded at Grey Beard, who then motioned for Qasid to continue.

"I need travel money, a passport, a Canadian visa, and a work permit. I also will need you to contact your EMM friends in Vancouver and the San Francisco Bay Area, and ask for their help in my mission."

Graybeard looked around the room, and took note of the facial expressions of other cell members, and then turned back to Qasid.

"And who are you that Allah should have selected you for this task?"

Qasid looked down at the floor and whispered, "I don't question Allah's ways. He has spoken to me."

"How do you know that it is Allah and not your own ego that is speaking to you?"

"While I sat in the stinking American prison in Ghurian for three years, all I thought about was escape and revenge. No one ever came to visit me in that hellhole. So I prayed. I prayed for a visitor, but no one came. I read the newspapers about the failed al-Qaeda missions to explode bombs in America, and knew that those who thwarted Allah's plan must be punished. I prayed that Allah would release me from prison, and if he did so, I would carry out the fatwa. And then Allah answered my prayers. I met another prisoner about to be released and convinced him to contact Safid. Allah told me what he wanted me to do and with his help and that of Safid, I escaped from Ghurian. Now here I am, ready to do Allah's bidding."

Graybeard stood and with a nod to Safid said, "It is agreed then. We will see that you have enough money to complete your mission. Safid will help you get the necessary documents. We will make sure that when you arrive in Vancouver, the local EMM will be there to meet you and then transport you to the border."

With a wave of his hand he dismissed Qasid and Safid. As they left the room, Grey Beard called after them in Arabic, "May Allah go with you."

Safid drove Qasid to Kandahar, where in the back alleys, he bought a fake passport and ID card. Safid then drove him to the Kandahar Airport, where Qasid bought a ticket to London and a second ticket from London to Vancouver.

Two days later, the Canadian Pacific airliner from London landed at the Vancouver airport. Security personnel ushered Qasid into customs, where a sleepy-eyed immigration officer inspected his fake passport and visa. Satisfied with the documents, he stamped them and then asked what his business was in Canada. Qasid replied that a mosque was under construction in Coquitlam and the Imam there hired him to work on it. The inspector asked for his work permit and finding all documents in apparent order, admitted Qasid into the country.

He recovered his backpack from customs and stepped outside into the hustle and bustle of airport traffic. He marveled at the endless line of cars waiting to unload passengers and luggage and the uniformed skycaps that ran to assist people and carry their bags into the terminal. He waited at a bus stop, until a bus marked "City Center" pulled alongside and stopped. Qasid stepped on board and found a window seat. He enjoyed the view of the city as the bus made its way downtown. The bus driver droned on, describing the features of the city, but the surrounding landscape not the tourist features interested Qasid.

To the north, the waters of English Bay and Burrard Inlet streaked by the incoming tide, joined with the deeper blue waters of the Pacific Ocean to the west. A line of snowcapped mountains stretched across the northern horizon, their shimmering images reflecting off the tranquil inlet which extended to the foot of the city, where gentle waves lapped against the docks and seawall. A large luxury liner hugged the wharf next to a passenger terminal. The unusual sail architecture reminded him of the Sydney Opera House in Australia. Various boats plied the busy harbor, leaving ribbons of white foam in their wake as they cut through the steel blue waters. V-shaped waves formed by their passing moved across the bay as a seaplane skimmed the water, bouncing off those waves as it struggled to rise into the cloudless sky. The city rested on several gently sloping hills carpeted by a diverse assembly of skyscrapers and buildings lacking any common architecture. The afternoon air was hot and muggy and as the bus crept through the noisy traffic, noxious fumes drifted into the bus and forced Qasid to close his window. At the downtown bus terminal, he found a phone booth and dialed the number in Coquitlam, given him by Safid. A man answered and told him to wait near the Bus Terminal taxi loading zone. Twenty minutes later, a Mercedes pulled up to the curb. The driver threw open the passenger door and motioned for Qasid to climb inside. They rode in silence to Amit's home in Coquitlam, a bedroom community east of the city. Sasha, Amit's widow, met them at the door and after introducing herself, ushered Qasid into the den, where a bespectacled, gaunt man with a salt-and-pepper beard and wearing an Afghan hat sat behind a large oak desk.

The man put his pen down and looked long and hard at Qasid, who stood stiffly at attention and returned the man's unnerving stare. They silently studied each other for the better part of a minute, until the man motioned to the empty chair in front of his desk. Qasid slid silently into the chair.

"I am Muzzammil Adhami, the leader of al-Qaeda in Western Canada. You can address me as "Mo". And you are . . ."

"Qasid Sachem"

"So before me sits the infamous assassin, Qasid Sachem," Muzzammil began. A haughty smirk spread across Mo's face. "I am told you have come here to fulfill the fatwa against the American boy who caused our failure in Minot and helped send Passhia bin-Alakeim to a Nevada jail."

Qasid nodded. "Yes, that is true. It is Allah's will that I kill Keith Justin."

Mo mocked him. "Allah's will? How is it that Allah would select a poor Pashtun like you to do his will?"

"Allah works in wondrous ways . . . ways that I cannot possibly explain," Qasid replied.

Mo pondered Qasid's words and then mumbled, "Then so be it. We will help you carry out the fatwa."

Mo reached into his desk drawer, took out a snub nose revolver, slipped six .45 caliber bullets into the chamber, and then handed the revolver to Qasid.

"This is the weapon you will use to kill the boy. It is untraceable. Allah be with you." With a wave of his hand, Muzzammil dismissed him.

The next day, Sasha drove Qasid east of Vancouver to the border town of Langley, and without so much as a good-bye, let him out on a street corner. At the southern edge of town, an empty guard station and a swing gate marked the border. Qasid ducked under the barrier and walked unchallenged to the border town of Lynden. From there, he hitchhiked to Bellingham and caught a bus to Seattle, where he found a cheap motel for the night. At sunrise, he walked to the train station and bought a ticket on the Amtrak Coast Daylight, departing that morning for Oakland, California. He boarded a sparsely-filled day coach and selected a seat near the back. He moved the back of the seat in front of him forward, creating a small private compartment. He settled into his seat as the train lurched forward and left the Seattle depot on time. He took a copy of the Qur'an out of his backpack and began to read. The train had nearly reached Centralia, when a small boy sat down on the bench seat across from him.

"My name is Adam, what's yours?"

Annoyed, Qasid looked up from the Qur'an. The boy looked to be about ten, with light brown skin and a short crop of black curly hair. Qasid said brusquely, "My name is George . . . now go away."

"That's not your real name, you don't look like a 'George' to me," the boy insisted.

Qasid continued reading and tried to ignore the boy.

The boy persisted. "What are you reading?"

"It is the Qur'an," Qasid answered, with even greater annoyance.

"What is it about?"

"It is a holy book, written by the greatest prophet, Muhammad".

"Who was he?"

"I told you, he was a prophet. Now go away."

The boy got up and went back to his seat at the front of the coach.

After a one-hour stop in Portland, the Amtrak Coast Daylight sped down the glistening tracks, east of the Cascade spine, and as the sun began to set, crossed over the Oregon-California border. Qasid put his Qur'an in the backpack and watched as the snow-covered Mt. Shasta, shining with a pink glow, grew in size until it dominated the entire eastern horizon. Enjoying the lovely scenery, he became aware that he was no longer alone. The boy had returned.

"What's a prophet?"

Qasid did not look away from the window. "Are you here again? What about 'go away' do you not understand?"

"What's a prophet?"

"A prophet is someone who speaks for Allah."

"Who is Allah?"

"You would call him 'God'."

"So then, Muhammad spoke for God . . . in that book you read?"

"Yes, but we do not call him God. We call him Allah."

"Why do you call him Allah?"

"That is his name."

"Is Allah all-powerful and knowing, just like God?"

Qasid couldn't believe that he allowed this impudent whelp to draw him into a discussion.

"Allah **is** God. I am telling you for the last time, GO."

But the boy didn't go. "Tell me about your God, Allah."

"There is only one God, Allah. Allah is God."

"Is Muhammad as great as Allah?"

Qasid had had enough of this little pest. He reached across the space between the two seats and slapped the boy across the face. Not a hard slap, but enough to redden the boy's cheek.

"Enough of these questions. Now, go as I told you to do."

Tears welled in the boy's eyes as he ran back to his seat. Seconds later, a large, muscular black man stood in the aisle alongside Qasid's seat and glared at him.

"Why did you slap my son?"

Qasid surveyed the man towering over him and judged this was not a man to be trifled with.

"The boy was annoying me and would not go away when I told him to do so."

The conductor had been collecting tickets at the front of the coach but now hurried down the aisle.

"Is there a problem here?"

"This man hit my son," the man replied.

The conductor confronted Qasid. "Did you hit the child?"

"He was annoying me," Qasid said defensively.

"Let me see your ticket."

Qasid dug his ticket out of the backpack and handed it to the conductor.

"I see you have a ticket to Martinez and bordered in Seattle. Let me see your passport."

Qasid's mind reeled. He opened his backpack and pretended to search for his papers.

The train slowed as it approached the town of Dunsmuir. Qasid dug through his backpack and vowed that he wasn't going to show this arrogant conductor any papers. He had been lucky at Vancouver customs and knew that his fake passport wouldn't pass scrutiny with the American police. The train lurched as it pulled into the depot, causing both the man and conductor to grab for handholds. Qasid took advantage of their momentary inattention, grabbed his backpack, and sprinted through the door separating his coach from the next one in line and ran toward the back. The conductor gave chase but the departing passengers gathering their belongings from the overhead bins got in his way.

Qasid ran through two more coaches and pushing passengers aside, found the door on the last coach open and jumped off the train. He ran across several sets of tracks and then sprinted in front of a northbound freight train. The long freight train prevented the conductor from chasing him any further, but Qasid realized he had his train ticket and would alert the local police. Running out to the highway, he stuck his thumb out for a ride but scores of cars and trucks ignored his plea and none even slowed down. After several minutes, a U-Hall truck pulled over and the driver motioned for Qasid to climb in.

The mustachioed driver looked at Qasid and explained, "I don't usually pick up hitchhikers, but I needed someone to talk with on this long drive. Where are you headed?"

"Martinez," Qasid replied.

"Well, you're in luck. I'm going to San Jose, and I can drop you off in Martinez."

Qasid couldn't believe his good fortune. This fellow would take him all the way to his destination. Allah was certainly watching over him.

"My name is Pete, Pete Langley. And you are . . ."

Qasid used the alias on his fake passport. "Hussein Faroke," he replied.

"Well Hussein, sit back and relax. We have a five-hour drive ahead of us."

Pete tried several times to chat with Qasid, but the man's one word responses did not constitute conversation, so after few miles he gave up trying and for the next few hours, they rode in silence. Pete let him off at a restaurant along Highway 680 near Martinez, and Qasid called the safe house number. Minutes later, a red Subaru arrived and the driver motioned for Qasid to climb in. The Martinez safe house, a sprawling ranch style residence built on top of a golden hill, offered a view of the Carquinez Straight and the oil offloading docks and cranes that hugged the southern shore. Two large tankers moored in the bay waited their turn to offload their cargo of oil. Huge storage tanks covered the surrounding hills and smoke poured from dozens of refinery smokestacks in the valley. A woman dressed in a black burka ushered Qasid into the den, where a man dressed in a pinstripe suit and blue tie worked on a stack of papers. He invited Qasid to sit down.

"My name is Rashad," the man began, without looking up from the papers spread on his desk. "We expected you on this morning's Coast Daylight, but you were not on board."

"It is a long story, but I had to get off the train in Dunsmuir and hitchhike here."

Rashad glanced at Qasid and then said, "Let me see your papers."

Qasid handed Rashad his passport, visa, and a letter of introduction in Arabic, from Sabur Hussein.

Rashad examined the documents, and then took off his glasses and stared at Qasid. "This letter claims you have been selected to fulfill the fatwa against the boy, Keith Justin, but who is Sabur Hussein? I've never heard of him."

"Sabur is an al-Qaeda cell leader in western Afghanistan. He helped me escape from prison and has supported me in this mission."

The man returned to signing papers on his desk, while he talked. "A mission intended to kill the Justin boy?"

"Yes. Al-Qaeda selected me to carry out this fatwa," Qasid said dryly.

"Who sent you here to see me?"

"Muzzammil Adhami in Vancouver told me to come here."

The name Muzzammil struck a chord with Rashad. He looked up from his papers and peered over his spectacles at Qasid. "So . . . Mo sent you here. What does he expect me to do for you?"

"I need someone to drive me to Santa Cruz and help me find and execute Keith Justin."

Rashid thought for a moment and then offered, "I will drive you to Santa Cruz."

On Thursday afternoon, Qasid and Rashad drove through San Jose, crossed over the Santa Cruz Mountains to Santa Cruz, and then traveled north on the Coast Highway, to the UCSC campus. They stopped at the Student Union building and asked for a copy of Keith's class schedule, his dorm room address, and cell phone number. They went to the dorm and watched from across the street as Keith got off the bus and entered the building. They returned to Santa Cruz, checked into a motel, and together went over the details for Keith's execution. Qasid showed Rashad a newspaper picture of Keith, and together they decided the best time to carry out their plan would be next Monday afternoon, after Keith's Chemistry lab finished at the Science Building. They would wait for Keith outside the Science Building, but first they needed to visit the site and confirm their plan.

Friday afternoon, they drove through the campus and found the Science building. Rashid let Qasid off across the street from the building and parked his car down the street. Qasid sat alone in a campus bus shelter, watching students pour out of the Science building. Several students crossed the street and gathered around the shelter to wait for the campus bus. He spotted Keith chatting with a group of students until the bus arrived at 4:05 p.m., and Keith and the other students got on the bus. Qasid and Rashid returned to the motel, where Qasid wrote a rambling four page letter he intended to mail to the San Jose Mercury, after shooting Keith. In the letter, he explained his twisted reasoning for killing the boy hero, and justified the murder by his conviction that he was fulfilling a fatwa and doing Allah's will. Then they waited in their motel room for Monday afternoon to arrive.

CHAPTER TWENTY-SIX:
THE CYPRUS TREE

Keith Justin was thrilled with the university environment. Within days of his September arrival on campus, he signed up for classes and began to make new friends. He liked everything about the university: the students, teachers, and especially the permissive attitude prevalent on the campus. Despite the foggy, damp weather, his daily dress code consisted of flip-flops, a 49er T-shirt, and cutoffs. He and his roommate-mentor, Ron Passavente, became best friends. Ron belonged to the UCSC water polo team and convinced Keith, who had been on a swimming team in high school, to join the team. Keith kept in touch with his parents and his grandparents, Jim and Dee, who often picked him up at school on Friday afternoon to spend the weekends with them. Jim and Dee were not the only adults who looked after Keith.

Mr. Karl also took an active role watching out for Keith's welfare. After Keith identified Passhia as one of the Minot terrorists, Mr. Karl became increasingly concerned for the young man's safety. The American press had published Keith's part in disarming the first bomb, and his key role in identifying the lead terrorist in North America. The EMM might try to take revenge on the boy, and there were rumors about a fatwa. After the second bomb was defused, Mr. Karl drove Keith from Las Vegas back to Santa Cruz and alerted the local FBI in San Jose about his concerns. With no children of his own, Mr. Karl wished he had a son like Keith and vowed to keep tabs on the young man with weekly phone calls.

UCSC Dean Dr. Markley was another of Keith's sponsors. He kept his promise to Keith's dad and took the boy under his wing. Keith had an invitation, more like an edict, to attend dinner at Dr. Markley's home every Monday night. This was Dr. Markley's way to keep track of Keith and fulfill his promise to Keith's father. The Dean's daughter, Janet, a senior at Santa Cruz High School, immediately caught Keith's eye. She was intelligent, pretty, and best described as energetic and perky. She admired this young, handsome hero of national fame, and was not bashful about letting her family know of her interest in Keith. She invited him to escort her to the Fall Sadie Hawkins Dance, and soon afterwards, they began dating regularly.

Ano Nuevo, or New Year's Island, lies a few miles up the Coast Highway from UCSC. Ano Nuevo State Park is a sanctuary for sea lions, sea elephants, harbor seals, sea otters, and other marine wildlife. Occasionally, whales migrate past the island, and between the marine animals and the breathtaking beauty of Monterrey Bay, there was always something to hold Keith and Janet's attention. They became frequent visitors to the park and would sit for hours on a weathered bench placed under an old Cyprus tree and watch the panorama of wildlife. On weekends, or sometimes after school, Janet would drive to UCSC, pick Keith up, and then drive to the park and hike the path leading out to Cyprus Point. At lands end on the peninsula was an ancient Cyprus tree that held special meaning for Keith. Bent and twisted into curious shapes and forms by the relentless wind, the tree represented the strength and perseverance of his dad whose qualities he hoped to inherit. The constant barking of seals and sea lions and the crashing surf made conversation difficult, so they often just sat together, held hands and watched for whales or enjoyed the frolicking animals.

The week that Qasid arrived in Santa Cruz, the Water Polo Team had scheduled a match with Sacramento State on Saturday. That morning, Keith and Ron boarded the team bus. The Coach's rule was no cell phones on the bus or at the match, so Keith turned his off. They arrived in Sacramento before noon and went immediately to the Olympic pool on campus. UCSC lost the match, but the loss did not dampen their spirits. Their coach had planned a two-day overnight stay in Sacramento, including a Saturday night dinner with members of the State Legislature and a Sunday tour of the Capitol. The team returned to Santa Cruz Sunday afternoon.

After his weekend away, Keith was eager to see Janet. As the bus neared Santa Cruz, he turned his cell phone back on and called her, suggesting that he could skip his chemistry lab on Monday afternoon and spend some time together before the family dinner that evening. Janet readily agreed, and on Monday afternoon she picked Keith up at his dormitory and they headed north to Ano Nuevo. Janet showed the attendant her season pass and then they drove out to the Cyprus Point parking lot. A small sign pointed to a trail that traversed the narrow peninsula of towering cliffs: all that remained of a coastline that once extended further into the sea. In time, the ocean would reduce this peninsula to a pile of rocks, but for now, it stood like a fortress against the relentless, rapacious sea. The sandy path wound between weathered shrubs and bushes and patches of ice plants, each arrayed with purple, crimson, and pink flowers. Out at sea a small fishing boat plowed through the vast expanse of white-tipped blue-green water and closer in a string of brown pelicans flapped their way up the shoreline. A storm far out at sea sent massive waves crashing against the seaweed-covered boulders that lined the foot of the peninsula, sending curtains of windblown seawater high into the air. At land's end, a lone gnarled and twisted Cyprus Tree stood in defiance of the constant wind and greedy ocean that threatened to someday topple it into the sea. Fifty yards of frothy surf separated a large rock island from Cyprus Point and lands end. Once a part of the peninsula, the island had long ago succumbed to voracious waves and now lingered as an isolated refuge for dozens of barking sea lions, elephant seals, and harbor seals. Hundreds of screaming seagulls and other marine birds darted in and out of the guano-covered rocks and soared on the winds thrust skyward by lofty cliffs. Sea Otters played in the seaweed beds and floated on their backs, using rocks to crack open abalone shells. Avocets played tag with waves crashing on the small sand beach that bordered the south side of the peninsula. Between the sound of roaring waves and cacophony of screeching birds and barking sea lions and elephant seals, it was difficult to carry on a conversation. Nevertheless, as they held hands Keith told Janet all about his polo match in Sacramento.

*   *   *

After the Las Vegas bomb incident, Mr. Karl was appointed by the CIA to follow EMM activities in the States, and as such he would be immediately contacted about any recent EMM activity. Sunday afternoon Mr. Karl received a phone call in his Washington DC office from the FBI office in Redding, California.

They told him that after Qasid's confrontation with the train conductor in Dunsmuir, the local police filed a report with the Redding FBI that included a description of Qasid. They sent along Qasid's confiscated train ticket for analysis. By Saturday The FBI had lifted a fingerprint from the train ticket and identified the owner as Qasid Sachem, the EMM terrorist who recently escaped from the Ghurian prison in Afghanistan. Qasid was on the FBI's list of the 25 most wanted terrorists, and now he was in the United States and headed to Oakland.

Mr. Karl shuddered. Just a week ago Keith had called him and told about a man who had called from Afghanistan to warn him about a rumor of a fatwa against him. Now a known EMM terrorist was in California, and for what purpose? Santa Cruz was only a two hour drive from Oakland, and his instincts told him that Qasid had come to California kill Keith. Mr. Karl tried to call Keith, but his cell phone wasn't on. Mr. Karl fumed that it would be just like the EMM to send someone like Qasid to assassinate Keith Justin. After a call to alert the FBI office in San Jose, his next phone call went to Dan Justin in Willow Creek. Mr. Karl explained what he knew and his concern for Keith, and then tried to soothe Dan by assuring him the FBI was on the case. Dan didn't trust the FBI could protect his son. He tried to place a call to Keith's cell phone, but it was still off. Dan left a message that Keith should call him as soon as possible, and then called Dr. Markley, who said that due to the Water Polo match in Sacramento, they didn't expect to see Keith until Monday evening for dinner. His next call was to Nora's father in Santa Cruz. Jim told him that they hadn't heard from Keith since last weekend.

Then Dan sat Nora down and told her about Mr. Karl's disturbing call and that he had been unable to contact Keith.

"Dan, we have to go to Santa Cruz at once", she said without hesitation. "Don't expect the FBI to protect him."

Dan knew Nora's assessment was correct, so he made plans for the both of them to fly to California first thing Monday.

The Airlines had only recently started to resume full service throughout the country and last week Northwest Airlines began service from Bismarck to Denver. Dan called the airline, and made arrangements to fly through Denver to San Francisco and then to Monterey where he would rent a car take the short drive to Santa Cruz. They should arrive in Monterey by Monday afternoon. Nora called Jim and Dee with their travel plans.

*   *   *

Unaware of Keith's weekend polo match in Sacramento or his plans to cut class Monday afternoon, Qasid carried out his plan to execute Keith. At 3:45 p.m., Monday afternoon, Rashad dropped Qasid off at the bus shelter across the street from the Science Building and then parked a few hundred yards down the hill. As students sauntered across the street, Qasid took a seat in the shelter and fingered the gun hidden deep in his pocket. As on Friday, a group of students gathered around the shelter and chattered as they waited for the bus. However, Keith was not among them. Qasid waited until the bus came and went, but Keith did not appear. He walked across the street to the Science Building, climbed the granite steps, and wandered down the hall to the chemistry lab. The lab was empty and Keith was nowhere to be found. He left the building, walked down the street and climbed into the car with Rashad.

"What happened?" Rashad asked.
"The boy didn't show. Take me to his dorm. Perhaps he is there."

They drove to the dormitory and Qasid knocked on Keith's dorm room door. Ron Passavente answered.

"I was looking for Keith Justin. I am a friend of his," Qasid said.

Ron looked with suspicion at the tall, well-built man, with a full black beard and Afghan cap. He didn't look like someone Keith would have as a friend. "And who is asking?"
"My name is Hussein Faroke," again using his forged passport name. "I am an associate of Keith's father. I was passing through town and Mr. Justin asked me to look in on his son."

"Well, Keith is not here right now. He took the afternoon off from school," Ron explained.

"That is too bad. I wanted to take him to dinner. Can you tell me where I might find him?"

Although Ron knew that Keith had gone with Janet to Ano Nuevo, he wasn't about to share that information with a stranger, so he lied.

"I'm sorry, but I don't know where he is."

Do you know how I might contact him this afternoon?"

Ron gave him Keith's cell number, and Qasid went back to the car and borrowed Rashad's cell phone. He dialed the number Ron gave him and Keith answered he and Janet drove toward the park.

"Mr. Keith Justin?"

"Yes."

"My name is Hussein Faroke. I am a friend of your father's. He asked me to stop by and visit you to see how you are doing. I will only be in Santa Cruz for the day. I am calling from outside your dormitory on campus. Would it be possible to meet with you this afternoon? Perhaps we could meet in Santa Cruz for dinner."

"Well, I have other plans for dinner," Keith answered.

"That is most unfortunate. I will only be in Santa Cruz for the day, and your father insisted that I see how you are doing before I leave."

Keith's father had never mentioned knowing a Hussein Faroke, but the man was insistent.

"I want to keep my promise to your father, and he has a message for me to give to you. If we could meet for only a few minutes I would be most grateful."

Although wary, Keith relented. "Well, all right then. If you want to meet with me, I will be at Ano Nuevo Island State Park, with my girlfriend. The

Park is about 15 miles south of the campus, on Highway 1. We will be out on Cyprus Point. Ask the attendant for directions."

"I will be there shortly," Qasid said and hung up.

"There is an unexpected development," Qasid explained to Rashad. "He is at a park with his girlfriend. Perhaps this is for the best . . . there will be fewer witnesses in a park."
"Yes, but unfortunately we may have to kill the girlfriend as well," Rashad lamented.

"No matter, we will do what must be done. It is all part of Allah's plan."

*   *   *

Monday afternoon Dan and Nora arrived in Monterrey, rented a car, and drove to Jim and Dee's home in Santa Cruz. He tried calling Keith again, but there was no answer. Dan knew Keith would have finished classes by late Monday, so expecting to find him in his dormitory he and Nora left her parents home and drove to the UC campus. Ron Passavente answered Nora and Dan's knock on the door and told him that Keith and Janet had gone to Ano Nuevo Island. Ron also told them about the strange visitor who had been asking for Keith earlier that afternoon. Dan placed a call to Mr. Karl and told him what he had learned. The description that Ron gave of the stranger matched that of Qasid. A knife twisted in Dan's gut. Mr. Karl said he would have FBI agents go to Ano Nuevo, but Dan knew they would be too late. He tried to call Keith, but again Keith's cell phone was either off or outside of cell service. In a panic he and Nora got back in the car and drove as fast as the car would go toward Ano Nuevo Park. Nora whispered a prayer along the way.

*   *   *

Rashad and Qasid pulled their car up to the Ano Nuevo tollbooth.

"We are looking for a young couple," Rashad explained to the attendant. "They told us to meet them in the park."

The ranger eyed the two men sitting in the car. "The only people in the park right now are a young couple out on Cyprus Point. They often come here. You can probably find them sitting under the large Cyprus Tree out on the point. Understand that the park will close in 45 minutes. That will be $3.00, please."

Rashad paid the fee and then drove along the access road, leading to the Cyprus Point parking lot.

Minutes later, Dan and Nora also arrived at the gate.
"I'm looking for my son and his girlfriend. Are they in the park?"

"Yes, they are out on Cyprus Point," the attendant answered. Then he added, "Two men were here asking for them a few minutes ago."

"Were they foreigners?"

"Yes, the driver's heavily accented speech and their attire and beards made me uneasy."

Nora leaned across Dan and made eye contact with the attendant.

"These people are terrorists and they want to kill my son. Call the Ranger."

The gate attendant turned on his GMRS radio and alerted the park patrol officer making his final rounds before the Park closed at 6 p.m.

"Shawn, I just admitted two suspicious-looking fellows in a blue VW. They headed toward the back parking lot. There is another couple here at the gate claiming that they are the boy's parents and the men I just admitted to the park may be terrorists. Go to the point and check them out." The officer acknowledged the Ranger's concern, and then drove toward the Cyprus Point parking lot.

*   *   *

The two terrorists drove into the parking lot. It was empty except for Janet's car.

"Park over there, next to that car and the trail sign," Qasid ordered.

The two men parked, got out of the VW, and then began hiking single-file down the Cyprus Point trail.

Janet and Keith sat on the bench under the Cyprus Tree watching the seals play on the island, and talked.

"Keith, you seem lost in thought today. Is something wrong?"

Keith looked into Janet's eyes and told her this story.

"I believe that things do not just happen, like a series of random events. I believe there is a plan for each of us, a Divine purpose if you will, and our job is to follow that plan as best we can. Last week, I received a message from someone in Afghanistan, someone I do not know. He warned me that because of what I did in Minot and Las Vegas, al-Qaeda had issued a fatwa against me."

Janet looked shocked. "A fatwa? Isn't that a death warrant? Did you tell the police?"

Keith held her hand more tightly, turned to her and raised his voice above the noise.

"No, but I called my CIA friend, Mr. Karl in Washington D.C. But I want to tell you the story that explains why there is a fatwa against me." Janet listened attentively.

"When the big power outage first happened, our family faced a difficult decision. We sat around the kitchen table and talked about the insanity in Santa Cruz: the thefts, break-ins, and even murders. People were scared for their lives, and so were we. I'm sure you and your family were scared too. The last edition of the local newspaper claimed the police were "powerless", and the nation was slipping into anarchy. Mom said we were not powerless like the newspaper claimed, but were capable of making our own decisions. Dad had a plan, but it was mom who made the decision to leave Santa Cruz. Our family packed the trailer and drove to our friends' farm in Willow Creek, North Dakota. It turned out to be a harrowing three-week trip, but we made it. The folks in Willow Creek fared much better than our friends had in California. Midwest farmers come from strong stock: independent and able to survive without government help. Throughout the next several months, we lived with our friends, the Dexters. We thought we were safe there, but one day a group of terrorists invaded our farm and took our parents captive. Before the terrorists captured dad, he told me to go to the barn and hide. I hid my brother and sister and the other children who were playing in the barn, and then I hid. The terrorists discovered my brother and sister and the Dexter kids and took them into the house, but they didn't find me. I remained hidden in the barn loft and soon the terrorists came back. I listened as they talked in Arabic and English about an atomic bomb that would destroy Minot and the Air Force base. I watched from the loft as they assembled the bomb and placed it into a waiting van, and then went back into the house to prepare.

"I realized that I was the only person who could stop them from killing thousands of innocent people. Dad taught me that individuals must combat evil. I wasn't powerless, and when the men left, I climbed down and secretly disabled the bomb by cutting a few wires. Those poor bastards blew themselves up outside the Minot air base but because of my sabotage the nuclear bomb did not fully detonate. This saved countless lives and I was named a hero and given a scholarship. That is why I am here in Santa Cruz and it is why I met you."

Unaware of the two men approaching on the path, Keith put his arm around Janet and drew her closer. The two men began to shout and Keith turned around as two men trotted down the path toward them with guns drawn. Qasid pointed his gun at Keith shouted for Keith and Janet to get on the ground. Rashad, a few steps behind Qasid, repeated the command.

The cacophony created by the seals and crashing waves made it difficult for Keith to understand what the men were screaming; but he fully understood the language of the gun. He drew Janet even closer, instinctively shielding her from the approaching threat. Rashad rushed the bench and forced Keith to let go of Janet and kneel down on the ground. He bound Keith's hands behind his back with a chord. Qasid turned his attention to the young woman, who sat frozen in fear on the bench. He waved the gun at her and demanded she join her boyfriend on the ground. As she knelt beside Keith, Rashad bound her hands behind her and then pushed her face down into the sandy ground.

Qasid grabbed Keith by his hair and jerking his head backward looked into the boy's eyes and said, "Before I put a bullet in your infidel head, I want you to know why I am doing this. You are the 'so called' boy hero, who ruined our carefully designed plan to detonate an atomic bomb on American soil. For this you will die, and so will the girl. It is Allah's will"

"Allah does not demand the murder of innocents," Keith shouted.

Janet struggled to get to her feet, but Rashad forced her back to the ground. Sobbing, she pleaded for Keith's life. Rashad kicked her and told her to shut up.

Meanwhile, the park officer had parked his patrol car in the parking lot and hiked to the top of the sand dunes separating the Cyprus Point trail from the parking lot. He focused his binoculars on the four people on the point a hundred yards away. Two men were standing under the tree, while waving guns at a young man kneeling and a woman lying on the ground next to the bench. Drawing his gun, the ranger hurried down the trail. Rashad and Qasid were so focused on the two youngsters that neither terrorist noticed the patrol officer until he was only a few yards away. He shouted for them to drop their guns.

"Put your weapons down and face me," the patrol officer demanded.

The two men spun around and faced a 9mm Beretta pointed at them. Rashad immediately dropped his gun and stepped away from Qasid, but Qasid continued to point his gun at Keith's head and screamed, "Drop your weapon or I will shoot the boy." The officer hesitated, not sure what to do.

Sensing the officer's uncertainty, Rashad lunged at him. The officer side-stepped the onrushing man and shot him the head as he stumbled passed. Qasid watched as the bullet passed through his friend's head and lodged in the trunk of the Cyprus, sending shards of bark in every direction. Blood and bits of brain spurted from Rashad's head as he crumpled to the ground. Momentarily frozen in horror, Qasid didn't notice that Keith, still on his knees, had edged toward him. The distraction gave Keith the chance to thrust his body against Qasid's legs. The move threw him off balance. He fired a wild shot as he stumbled backwards, but the bullet fell harmlessly into sea. A second bullet from the officer caught Qasid in the shoulder. He staggered backwards and tripped over an exposed root. As he tried to regain his balance, he caught his foot on the root and disappeared headfirst over the cliff. The officer holstered his gun and called the other park ranger on his radio. Then he untied Keith and Janet and sat Janet down on the bench. Keith walked over to the cliff edge and searched the rocks below for Qasid's body. The terrorist lay in several inches of foam and bloody water. Wedged between two barnacle encrusted boulders, he was trying to stand up when a large wave crashed over the boulders, knocked him down and dragged him out to sea. Keith watched as the waves dashed Qasid's body again and again against the sharp rocks. Finally Qasid disappeared in the swirling foam to become food for the sharks and crabs.

"A fitting end for a devil," Keith muttered.

He turned away from the cliff and found Janet. She had gotten up from the bench and was standing next to the body of Rashad. She stared at the ever-widening pool of blood that stained the sand. The Park officer placed his jacket over her shivering body. Janet fell into Keith's arms and sobbed.

"They were going to kill both of us, weren't they?"

"Yes, they were." Keith pressed Janet hard into his body.

Seconds later and out of breath, Dan ran down the path to the Cyprus tree. Nora was several yards behind. Keith saw them coming along the path and released his grip on Janet.

"Dad!"

Dan hugged his son and Janet. "Are you two all right?"

"Yes Dad, we're okay. The terrorists tried to kill us. But what are you doing here?"

Dan looked at the body under the Cyprus tree. "The terrorists . . . I knew they were after you and mom and I flew out here."

Out of breadth, Nora ran up and grabbed Keith by the shoulders. "Keith, are you unhurt"

"Sure Mom, I'm just fine." Nora looked into Keith's eyes, looking for some sign of deception, but there was none. Her son was indeed fine.

Putting his arm around Janet again, Keith said, "Mom, Dad this is Janet." Janet began to cry uncontrollably, and Nora embraced her. "It will be ok," she tried to reassure her.

"Dad, you and Mom knew about the terrorists?"

Yes, we did. Mr. Karl called and warned me yesterday. Where's the other terrorist?"

"At the bottom of the cliff, feeding the crabs, I hope," Keith said.

By now Janet had composed herself. "You are Keith's parents. I'm so glad you are here."

"That we are, but we need to get away from this place," Dan said.

"Let's go to Janet's house," Keith suggested. "Dean Markley is expecting us."

Dan turned toward the park Ranger, who was putting his cell phone away. "We're going to take these young folks to Dr. Markley's house on the UC campus. Have the FBI meet us there when they show up. They will want statements."

The Ranger acknowledged their plan.

Dan, Nora, Keith and Janet walked together back on the path to the parking lot. Before Keith and Janet got into her car, Janet asked Nora, "It was all so horrible . . . to see two people killed like that, but they were actually going to shoot us." Nora commented, "Yes, that was their plan, but it was not God's plan. In the end, it was the terrorists who were powerless."

Dan proudly smiled at his brave son, climbed into the rented car with Nora and followed Keith and Janet out of the park. They would have quite the tale to tell Dr. Markley.

*   *   *